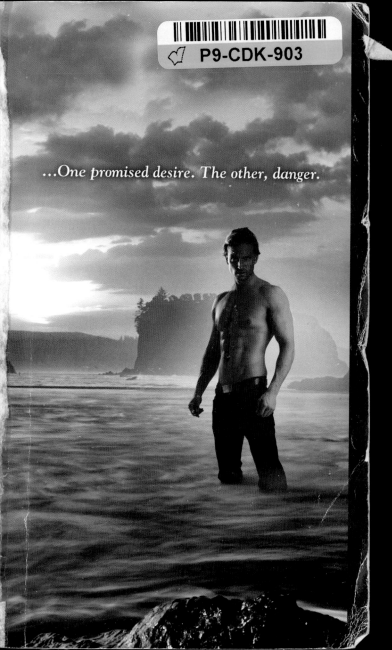

...One promised desire. The other, danger.

Praise for the Se...

WATER BOUND

"Awesome as always!" —*Romantic Times*

Praise for the Drake Sisters novels

HIDDEN CURRENTS

"A wrenching and turbulent story." —*Romantic Times*

TURBULENT SEA

"This book is hot!" —*Fresh Fiction*

SAFE HARBOR

"Don't even think of missing this one."
—*Romance Reviews Today*

DANGEROUS TIDES

"Rich with enchantment and spiced with danger. Pure magic!"
—*Romantic Times*

OCEANS OF FIRE

"A rousing romantic thriller and a true classic!"
—*Romantic Times*

THE TWILIGHT BEFORE CHRISTMAS

"Chilling, suspenseful, passionate and rewarding."
—*Library Journal*

MAGIC IN THE WIND

"A delightfully fresh and entertaining read. I want more!"
—*The Best Reviews*

continued...

DARK GUARDIAN

"A skillful blend of supernatural thrills and romance."
—*Publishers Weekly*

DARK LEGEND

"Vampire romance at its best!" —*Romantic Times*

DARK FIRE

"Fun and different . . . pick up a copy of this book."
—*All About Romance*

DARK CHALLENGE

"[An] exciting and multifaceted world." —*Romantic Times*

DARK MAGIC

"Feehan builds a complex society that makes for mesmerizing reading." —*Romantic Times*

DARK GOLD

"Wish I had written it!" —Amanda Ashley

DARK DESIRE

"Terrific." —*Romantic Times*

DARK PRINCE

"For lovers of vampire novels, this one is a keeper."
—*New-Age Bookshelf*

Anthologies

DARKEST AT DAWN
(includes Dark Hunger *and* Dark Secret*)*

SEA STORM
(includes Magic in the Wind *and* Oceans of Fire*)*

FEVER
(includes The Awakening *and* Wild Rain*)*

FANTASY
(with Emma Holly, Sabrina Jeffries, and Elda Minger)

LOVER BEWARE
(with Fiona Brand, Katherine Sutcliffe, and Eileen Wilks)

HOT BLOODED
(with Maggie Shayne, Emma Holly, and Angela Knight)

Spirit Bound

A SEA HAVEN NOVEL

CHRISTINE FEEHAN

J

JOVE BOOKS, NEW YORK

THE BERKLEY PUBLISHING GROUP
Published by the Penguin Group
Penguin Group (USA) Inc.
375 Hudson Street, New York, New York 10014, USA
Penguin Group (Canada), 90 Eglinton Avenue East, Suite 700, Toronto, Ontario M4P 2Y3, Canada
(a division of Pearson Penguin Canada Inc.)
Penguin Books Ltd., 80 Strand, London WC2R 0RL, England
Penguin Group Ireland, 25 St. Stephen's Green, Dublin 2, Ireland (a division of Penguin Books Ltd.)
Penguin Group (Australia), 250 Camberwell Road, Camberwell, Victoria 3124, Australia
(a division of Pearson Australia Group Pty. Ltd.)
Penguin Books India Pvt. Ltd., 11 Community Centre, Panchsheel Park, New Delhi—110 017, India
Penguin Group (NZ), 67 Apollo Drive, Rosedale, Auckland 0632, New Zealand
(a division of Pearson New Zealand Ltd.)
Penguin Books (South Africa) (Pty.) Ltd., 24 Sturdee Avenue, Rosebank, Johannesburg 2196,
South Africa

Penguin Books Ltd., Registered Offices: 80 Strand, London WC2R 0RL, England

This is a work of fiction. Names, characters, places, and incidents either are the product of the author's imagination or are used fictitiously, and any resemblance to actual persons, living or dead, business establishments, events, or locales is entirely coincidental. The publisher does not have control over and does not have any responsibility for author or third-party websites or their content.

SPIRIT BOUND

A Jove Book / published by arrangement with the author

PRINTING HISTORY
Jove mass-market edition / January 2012

Copyright © 2012 by Christine Feehan.
Cover handlettering by Ron Zinn.
Cover design by George Long.

ISBN: 978-0-515-14956-2

JOVE®
Jove Books are published by The Berkley Publishing Group,
a division of Penguin Group (USA) Inc.,
375 Hudson Street, New York, New York 10014.
JOVE® is a registered trademark of Penguin Group (USA) Inc.
The "J" design is a trademark of Penguin Group (USA) Inc.

PRINTED IN THE UNITED STATES OF AMERICA

10   9   8   7   6   5

For Judith Paul
and Thomas Durden, with love

Be sure to go to www.christinefeehan.com/members/ to sign up for my PRIVATE book announcement list and download the FREE eBook of *Dark Desserts,* a collection of yummy recipes sent by readers from all over the world. Join my community and get firsthand news, enter the book discussions, ask your questions and chat with me. Please feel free to e-mail me at Christine@christinefeehan.com. I would love to hear from you. Join me for a fun-filled time at my FAN convention. Visit www.fanconvention.net for more information. I hope to see you there!

ACKNOWLEDGMENTS

Of course this book couldn't have been written without the amazing help of the very talented award-winning artist Judith Paul of Images Kaleidoscopes, with whom I consulted over the making of kaleidoscopes, art conservatory and just about everything else having to do with being an artist who sees the world in colors. Special thanks to Brian Feehan, who spent hours doing the virtual run over rooftops, hand-to-hand combat and making traps for authenticity. Last but not least, Clint Wyant, a member of the sheriff's department, graciously spent time with me hammering out the details of law enforcement on the Northern California coast where the Sea Haven novels take place. I greatly appreciate his time when he's coming off those long shifts at four A.M.

1

STEFAN Prakenskii paced up and down the small cell. He knew exactly how many steps he could take before he leapt to catch the bars and do pull-ups—a dozen more before pacing to the end of the cell and dropping down for push-ups. There was no getting used to the smell of the prison, or the slime on the walls or the way the showers didn't work and the need for constant vigilance to stay alive, but he didn't mind any of that. He could tolerate anything; he had endured much worse.

He was a patient man, but once he had determined it was useless for him to remain in the cell, that his mission was a complete bust, he wanted out. It was a waste of time for him to stay, yet his handler hadn't agreed a month earlier to pull him out. Every day was increasingly dangerous and irritating, his mind becoming consumed with the only thing decent in the prison.

Swearing under his breath, Stefan took from the wall the latest photograph of the woman his cell mate obsessed over. She stood on a beach, the ocean waves rising behind her, a little turbulent and obviously windy, but there were no landmarks Stefan had a chance of identifying. She was undoubtedly beautiful with her long black hair blowing in the wind. Dressed in jeans and a tee she still managed to look elegant and sexy at the same time. If he were a man who was interested in relationships, no doubt he would understand his cell mate's fixation with her. And the idiot was totally obsessed with her. There were hundreds of photographs taken over a period of years of just this one woman pinned all over the walls.

It didn't seem to matter how intelligent a man was, or what he did for a living, in the end it seemed a woman often brought even the greatest of criminals tumbling down. And this particular woman was no exception. Stefan planned to use her to take down Jean-Claude La Roux's international empire if that was what it took.

He glanced down at the picture in his hand. She looked pensive—no, sad. What had put that look on her face? Surely a woman like her was not pining away for a man like Jean-Claude. A small band of inviting skin peeked out between her tee and her jeans temptingly. His thumb slid over that little strip as if he might feel just how warm and soft she truly was.

No doubt Jean-Claude was a man of untold wealth. Stefan supposed a woman might find his good looks attractive, if you liked oozing charm. His charm covered a multitude of sins, but then women might find that edge of danger exciting as well. Women could be just as easily swayed by the wrong things as men could be by beauty.

"What the hell are you doing with that?" Glaring at Stefan, trying to intimidate someone impossible to intimidate, Jean-Claude La Roux snatched the small photograph from the hands of his cell mate. "You have no idea who I am."

Deliberately Stefan showed his teeth and then spit on the floor of the cell. "That refrain is getting old, Rolex." He infused total contempt into his tone, calling the man the hated name he'd given him.

A man like Jean-Claude, the head of a vast crime empire, would detest a common criminal taunting him. It was an affront the man couldn't accept. In the two months Stefan had been undercover, trying to collect information, he'd had to defend his life on several occasions—a tribute to La Roux's authority even there in the prison. Jean-Claude hated Stefan, and one word from him had sent several prisoners trying to curry favor by attempting to get rid of Stefan, the thorn in his side.

There was no doubt that La Roux was every bit as powerful in prison as he was out of it. On the surface, sentencing him for his international crimes in France seemed good. The French prison system wasn't considered a place to coddle prisoners, but even with mold on the walls and water-stained slime trailing from the ceiling, Jean-Claude managed to appear wealthy and powerful. Every other prisoner gave him a wide berth until Stefan had come along. He goaded La Roux at every opportunity, and not one of the men paid to teach Stefan a lesson, or kill him, had succeeded.

There was no doubt in Stefan's mind that given an hour alone with Jean-Claude, if he was free to interrogate him in his own way, he would have all the information the government needed, but here, in this French prison, with guards watching day and night and the government all too aware of their prisoner, he didn't have a chance to extract what he needed from the man. That left only one possibility. Jean-Claude La Roux had to escape. He sighed. He'd told his handler that same thing many times over the last two months.

Stefan gestured toward the photograph-covered walls. "You have a lot of pictures, Rolex, but you sure don't have any letters. I think your woman is on that beach with another man laughing her ass off."

Jean-Claude replaced the photograph, his hand smoothing over the glossy paper. Stefan noticed, with some satisfaction, that the crime lord's fingers trembled when he touched the woman's face.

"You do not see a man in any of these photographs, do you?" Jean-Claude looked him over with obvious contempt.

Stefan knew he wasn't much to look at. He was tall, with wide, ax-handle shoulders, a thick muscular chest and large arms with bulging muscles. He didn't look suave or wealthy, or charming. He looked a brute, not very smart, with longish hair and lots of scruff. Scars webbed his skin and his knuckles were callused and shiny. He had a square jaw and dark blue-green eyes that looked straight into other men's souls and found them guilty. Stefan exuded raw power through sheer physical strength, and men like Jean-Claude automatically dismissed them as muscle and brawn—never looking beneath that surface to see if there was any intelligence behind the mask of a brute.

In his mind he used his real name, Stefan Prakenskii, as often as possible because, truthfully, he used aliases so often, he was afraid of forgetting who he was. And maybe he had already, long ago, lost his identity. What was he? Who was he? And who really gave a damn anyway? There wasn't a beautiful woman standing on a beach looking sad, pining away for him—and there never would be. He was successful at his job because he refused to let women, like the one Jean-Claude obsessed over, into his realm of consciousness.

He glanced again at the pictures covering the stained wall. There were hundreds of them. Jean-Claude had the woman under surveillance for a long time. She had changed little over the years the man had spent in prison, but he was right, there was no man ever photographed with her. Stefan cursed under his breath and turned away from the pictures.

The woman would get under anyone's skin if you stared at her long enough. Really, what else was there to do in a tiny prison cell but notice her lips and eyes and all that long glossy hair? Jean-Claude was feeding his own addiction, growing it into a monster, and Stefan had uncovered that weakness immediately and used it against the man, making him ripe for an escape. He didn't see other men with her in the photographs, but who could stand thinking about another man touching all that soft skin?

"I will say this for you, Rolex, she's beautiful. Where the hell did you ever meet a woman like that?" It was time to change tactics.

For the first time, Stefan allowed a little admiration to creep into his voice. Just as he suspected Jean-Claude couldn't resist the need to talk about his woman or respond to the first sign that a man such as Stefan who only seemed to admire obvious strength, might respect the crime lord at least for his ability to attract a beautiful woman.

"She was an art student, studying in Paris," Jean-Claude said. "She stood outside the Louvre—all that long hair flying around her face—and she paused to scrape it back away from her face and for just a moment . . ." He trailed off.

Stefan didn't need him to say it. The crime lord had probably lost his breath just as Stefan had the first time he'd looked at her photograph. She could easily have been a model on the cover of a magazine—yet more. There was something undefined, a quality he couldn't put his finger on, something innocent and sensual at the same time— mysterious, remote, just out of reach. Something terribly elusive and yet made a man want to reach out and grab her, to hold her for himself alone.

Oh, yeah, the woman definitely had an impact on a man, especially one locked in a cell without a companion. Stefan had endless patience when he was on the job, but seriously, this was a bust. Jean-Claude would make a beeline for the woman and for the microchip he'd stolen from the Russian government—a microchip worth a fortune on the black market. That chip contained information that would set their defense system back fifty years if it got out.

"She any good at painting?" Stefan asked.

Jean-Claude nodded. "She's good at everything she does."

Stefan remained silent, waiting for more. He knew it would come. Jean-Claude wouldn't have said anything at all if he didn't want to talk.

"She's already made a name for herself in the art world.

Her kaleidoscopes have won international awards. Her paintings are sold for a fortune, and she's a conservator of old artwork for private collectors. They fly the paintings to her under
heavy guard."

Jean-Claude sounded proud of her. Conservators were
rare, responsible for restoring the health of paintings hundreds of years old. It was difficult work and a somewhat
small community. He doubted if there were many award-
winning kaleidoscope artists. The information would be very
helpful in uncovering her identity. Stefan had already sent
several pictures back to his people in order to start the investigation into just who the mystery woman actually was.

"I have to hand it to you, having a woman like that willing to wait for you."

Jean-Claude didn't say anything, but stared down at the
quiet, pensive face. Stefan knew the words would eat at him,
the idea that maybe she wasn't waiting for him. La Roux had
a better cell than most inmates. He wasn't like the majority,
suicidal and depressed with the conditions, which told Stefan guards were smuggling him items and doing their best
to curry his favor right along with the prisoners. It hadn't
taken long for word to get around that if a guard displeased
Jean-Claude, one of his men retaliated against the guard's
family.

Stefan had been in this disgusting place long enough.
There was nothing more to be gotten from the crime lord.
He had told his government to break the man out of prison
and either snatch him as he came out or let him lead them to
the microchip. Either way, it was better than rotting in the
small confines of the cell staring at a woman whose name
he didn't even know. Obsessing over her right along with
Jean-Claude. He was leaving tonight before he lost his mind
staring at a woman who would never look at him twice.

"I hate saying anything nice to you, Rolex, but she's got
the face of an angel. I can't imagine that any woman lives
up to that." He needed to find a way to keep the man talk-

ing. After two months, he still didn't even know her name; Jean-Claude was that tight-lipped.

Jean-Claude glanced at him, and then at the picture. He smiled for the first time since Stefan had been shoved into his cell. "I'm sure you can't. She speaks seven languages. Seven." A snide lip curl told Stefan Jean-Claude was certain he could never learn more than one language.

Stefan spoke French fluently, with a perfect accent, and his undercover persona—John Bastille—certainly didn't appear as if he were an educated man, other than in criminal pursuits. If truth was told, Stefan could match dream woman language for language, which meant she was educated and all the more alluring. He was a bit surprised that Jean-Claude liked intelligent women.

"She's the type that would argue," Stefan pointed out, staying in character. His type of muscle man wouldn't want a lowly woman arguing with him. It said something that Jean-Claude wanted a smart woman.

"She definitely speaks her mind," Jean-Claude agreed, a small half smile creeping into his eyes as if remembering a moment he found particularly amusing. "You wouldn't understand."

Stefan pushed down the 101 crude things his undercover persona would have said, knowing it would end the conversation immediately. Jean-Claude hadn't said more than three or four sentences in the two months they'd shared a cell. Instead he looked down at the floor as if in sad reflection.

"I had a woman once. One worthwhile—not a prostitute. I should have been a little nicer to her, then maybe she would have stuck around." He flashed a quick, envious grin at Jean-Claude. "She didn't look like that one. What's her name?"

Never once in all the months had Jean-Claude referred to the woman by her name, or said where she was. He was very closemouthed when it came to the angel on the wall. It bothered Stefan that he secretly thought of her like that. *Angel.* Mysterious. Elusive. So out of reach of the ordinary man. Out of reach of a man who lived completely in the shadows. A man without a real identity.

"Judith." Jean-Claude's voice was clipped and warned Stefan not to push any further on the woman's identity.

Triumph surged through Stefan. Jean-Claude was bored in the cell. And he wanted to talk about his woman. He *needed* to talk about her. Stefan wanted him to crave her, to take the opportunity to escape when it was presented to him—not by Stefan, of course, but by one of the guards. It wouldn't be that difficult to arrange. Having Jean-Claude La Roux owe a favor would be like hitting the lottery. At the same time, Jean-Claude didn't give anything away for free. What was he after?

"Pretty name. She looks exotic, but that name is American, isn't it?" Actually the name was of Hebrew origin, but Stefan doubted very much if the crime lord was aware of that fact or even cared. It was a stab in the dark, a calculated feeler.

Jean-Claude eyed him warily. "What the hell difference does it make?"

Stefan allowed a surge of anger to show, more triumphant than ever. He'd struck a nerve. The mystery woman could very well be from the United States, not Japan as he'd first thought. "Not a bit. Just makin' conversation. The hell with it." He turned his back on the crime lord—a calculated risk. Showing indifference was the only way Jean-Claude might keep talking. If he thought Stefan was too interested, the man wouldn't say a word.

Turning away from La Roux only had him staring at another wall of photos. He was surrounded by the mysterious woman. She definitely looked of Japanese descent, but not entirely—she appeared tall and her skin tone lighter. It was possible she had an American parent. The coastline in the picture could be in the United States rather than Europe. He hadn't considered that possibility before.

One of the pictures he loved the most was of Judith— he had her name now—walking barefoot in the sand. The wind was blowing hard and her long silky-looking hair streamed behind her. He could see small footprints in the wet sand. For some strange reason, that photograph got to him. She seemed so alone. So sad. Waiting for someone. Jean-Claude? His stomach knotted at the thought.

"You married to her?" He didn't look at Jean-Claude when he asked, preferring to listen to the tone of the voice, rather than the answer.

"Engaged," Jean-Claude replied after a long pause.

"She know it?" he asked slyly. Stefan hadn't seen a ring on her finger in any of the photographs, and he'd looked for one.

Jean-Claude shrugged. "It doesn't much matter what she thinks. She's my fiancée and when the time comes, she'll be with me one way or another." He picked up one of his many books and held it out to Stefan. "You ever hear of this crap?"

Stefan pushed down the little twinge of pleasure in knowing the woman wasn't quite as taken with Jean-Claude as the man was with her. He took the book, one he'd looked at a couple of times, shocked at the subject matter. He feigned ignorance. "*Aura*? What is that supposed to be? I never heard of it."

"Can you believe this crap? Do you see colors around people's bodies? New Age bullshit, is what it is." There was such anger, such bitterness in Jean-Claude, a suppressed rage that made Stefan worry a little for the first time about Judith.

"Your woman believes this stuff?" Stefan asked, keeping vague puzzlement in his voice.

"Damn right she does. Takes it very seriously. I've read all about it, but I've never met a single person who believes in it or can see colors surrounding people other than her."

"So she's a little bit crazy." Stefan flashed a lecherous grin. "Don't you think her body sort of makes up for all that? Keep her mouth busy and you don't have a problem." His stomach knotted tighter. His gut actually hurt.

Jean-Claude shot him a furious look. He snatched the
book out of Stefan's hand and threw it against the wall of
the cell. "I don't know why I would expect someone like
you to understand."

Stefan didn't want to understand. He wanted out of this
stinking cell, away from the man whose soul was rotten.
There was no mercy in his world. No soft skin. No dark
eyes a man could get lost in. He wasn't even real, no more
than a dark shadow sliding in and out of places others
called home and leaving behind death and chaos. He didn't
know what a home was and he no longer cared. He had lost
his humanity long ago in places like this, surrounded by
corrupt men who traded in human flesh and wreaked havoc
on the world for money.

He'd been in the business too long when he started to
fixate on a woman just because she was the only thing that
remotely resembled innocence in a stinking prison cell.

"You know, Bastille," Jean-Claude began.

Stefan went on alert. For the first time Jean-Claude
sounded different. They were getting to the business of why
the crime lord had deigned to speak to him about his
woman. Jean-Claude had been steadfastly silent and it just
wasn't in him to have a friendly conversation, no matter
how much he might want to talk to someone about Judith
and the photographs. He'd given to get something.

Stefan turned around, leaned one hip lazily against the
cot and raised an eyebrow.

"Why didn't you kill me? You knew I ordered the beatings and the hits."

Stefan kept his expression carefully blank. He shrugged.
"No money in it. I want out of here. I came to do a job, and
once it's done I'll get out."

Jean-Claude's eyebrow shot up. "A job?" he echoed.

"Relax, Rolex, you aren't the mark." Stefan allowed a
small smile to creep into his eyes. "I won't say it didn't cross
my mind a time or two, but there's no percentage in it."

"But you would kill me if someone paid you to do it."

"We're not exactly friends." This time amusement reached his voice.

"I underestimated you," Jean-Claude admitted.

Stefan noted with satisfaction that the crime lord realized just how close he had been to death. All those nights with Stefan lurking like a lethal viper just feet from him. "Everyone does." Again, Stefan showed no malice.

Jean-Claude studied the scarred face. "I could use a man like you."

"I'm not sticking around. I'll be out of here by tomorrow." Stefan spoke with supreme confidence.

"How?"

Stefan shrugged again and stayed mysteriously silent.

"You have a way to escape?"

Oh yeah, there was interest in La Roux's voice. He wanted out. Once out, he'd have the money to buy a new identity and face. Stefan did it all the time.

Stefan turned away from the man and sank down onto his cot, silently declaring the conversation was over. When they went to dinner, a man would be found dead in his cell. As the prison locked down, John Bastille would be absent and Jean-Claude La Roux would know there was a way out. When he was approached by a guard to help him escape in a couple of weeks, he would jump at the chance.

The prisoner, already dead in his cell, was a Russian traitor, one in for arms' dealing, but he was guilty of so much more than that. He worked for Jean-Claude and was responsible for giving the crime lord the location of one of their top engineers, Theodotus Solovyov, who had designed their current defense system. The attack on Solovyov had left Stefan's brother, Gavriil, with a permanent injury, placing his life in danger.

Gavriil, undoubtedly one of the government's top agents, had been appointed bodyguard to Solovyov. He had managed, in spite of superior forces and being outgunned, in spite of being stabbed seven times, to keep Solovyov from being kidnapped and to drive off the kidnappers, but the microchip Solovyov had sewn into his coat had been taken. Only Solovyov and his wife had known the microchip had been placed there. Solovyov had been sold out by his own wife, and Gavriil's mission had been considered a failure.

A man like Gavriil Prakenskii was not forgiven failures, nor was he retired gracefully. He was simply retired. Gavriil managed to escape from the hospital and had disappeared. He would never be safe again, not bearing the Prakenskii name. The only Prakenskii truly safe was their youngest brother Ilya, who had been groomed to be an Interpol agent. He had worked for the secret assassination squad for a short time, and his services had been required on and off, but he hadn't been given the life of living in the shadows the way his older brothers had.

Stefan had helped Gavriil escape, carrying him through the darkened streets to a waiting car where he smuggled him out of Russia. It had been a very narrow escape, and without a doctor, Gavriil would have died, but he was gone now, using another identity, and Stefan doubted if he'd be lucky enough to ever see his brother again. Once he'd learned from Gavriil that only Theodotus Solovyov and his wife, Elena, had known about the microchip sewn into the coat, they both had known Elena had to have been the one to sell out their country.

As soon as Gavriil was out of danger, Stefan followed the money trail, found not only Elena's guilt, but the tie back to Jean-Claude La Roux. Elena died after providing the name of her lover. Her lover had given up the rest of the hit squad before he had died. One by one Stefan had hunted every participant who had destroyed his brother's career and put his life in jeopardy, killing them all except for the one in the French prison. That last detail had been attended to earlier in the evening.

Stefan lay down on his cot, ignoring Jean-Claude's puzzled look. The man wanted more information and was probably regretting that he'd set the tone for their rocky relationship. There was immense satisfaction in knowing Jean-Claude was going to regret a lot of things—ending Gavriil's career not the least of those regrets.

FOUR days later, Stefan took his time in the hot shower, grateful for a decent room, clean bathroom and comfortable bed. He wrapped a towel around his hips and stepped out onto the cool tiles. Setting his gun down on the sink, he dried his hair, staring at the fogged image in the mirror. John Bastille was no more, and Stefan Prakenskii was back. He wasn't any better looking than Bastille had been, even cleaned up. His body was in shape, every muscle loose and ready, his waist tapered, hips narrow and his core strength absolutely solid. He was like a machine, trained for any possibility. He knew a thousand ways to kill someone. He could seduce any woman out of her clothes, her sensibilities and her secrets—and had done so more times than he could count. He could hit a target a mile away in a high wind without a problem. He could deliver a needle as he brushed past his target without them feeling anything more than an annoying insect bite. He had no idea how to be anything else.

Picking up his gun, he went into the small room, his home for the night. He had the door primed—he wasn't a trusting man and never would be. The windows looked out over the river, his last resort should he be attacked and there was no other way out. He had set an escape route over the roof and one through the hotel as well. He had four exit strategies and his room was an arsenal. Still, he never felt safe.

There was a restless feeling in him that hadn't been there before. Maybe it was time to get out. He'd lost too much humanity. His senses were going numb, or maybe they had been gone all along and he hadn't noticed—or cared.

In spite of his determination not to look, he found himself standing in front of the dresser where the photograph he'd lifted from the wall, his favorite of Judith on the beach, lay right where he'd put it. He'd tossed it there, trying to tell himself he would turn it over to his handler in order to better help with finding her identity. A little mistake like that could blow everything. Blow the entire two months of living in a dirty cell with a monster. What was he thinking? He didn't make mistakes.

He picked up the photograph and stared down at that pensive face. His thumb slid over the band of soft skin revealed between her jeans and tee, as he had done in the cell. What was it about her that got to him? She was a mistake, and yet, knowing it, he'd taken the photograph anyway. It wasn't her striking looks—and he did think she was beautiful; he was inexplicably drawn to something inside her that had shone through in this picture.

He forced himself to toss the photograph back onto the dresser. He would never see her, never know what happened to her, but if he was making mistakes, regretting who he was, then it was time to employ his exit strategy. Every man in his business had one because in the end, they all knew too much about the secret project that had developed them in the first place.

He dressed carefully, slipping into his weapons as easily as the suit that had a casual elegance when his wide shoulders filled it out. His face was subtly different, his eye color a striking blue, a few of the scars gone. He'd trimmed his dark blond hair into a much neater style and shaved all facial hair. His watch was in place, an equally elegant piece without being too showy. He looked like a wealthy businessman, but the kind who had fought his way to the top. He stood there for a long moment, his fingers running over the woman's face. Cursing his own stupidity, he tapped the photograph once in a kind of frustration.

"You're going to get yourself killed over a woman," he said aloud.

As if on cue, his pager buzzed. Puzzled, he opened his computer and signed in. At once text spread across the screen. The woman had been identified with the clues he'd given them. Judith Henderson—an artist on the rise. She'd made quite a name for herself as an expert conservator restoring damaged paintings. Private collectors sought her out and entrusted paintings worth millions to her care. In addition to her restoration work, she was an acclaimed artist in her own right, both as the creator of international award-winning kaleidoscopes and as a painter whose original works commanded hefty sums. She lived in a small village on the Northern California coast called Sea Haven.

Everything in him stilled. Sea Haven. How often would that little village touch his family? His youngest brother, Ilya, had settled there. Another younger brother, Lev, had disappeared there, declared dead, going down with a yacht in the ocean. He didn't believe Lev could be killed so easily. Was this a trap of some kind—a trap for him? Or maybe for Lev? Was it possible he was being used to try to find his brother? A man like Lev, with all his abilities, didn't die easily. He didn't panic, not in the worst of circumstances.

Petr Ivanov, a man with no human feelings whatsoever, had been sent to find and eliminate Lev, should he still be alive. He had reported back that Lev had indeed died in the yacht accident. The body had never been found, but the investigation had been thorough. If Ivanov hadn't really been convinced of Lev's death, he wouldn't have risked his reputation on his report. Everyone had supposedly stopped looking for his brother. Did that mean they really believed Lev was dead? Or were they setting up Stefan to lead them to his brother?

He didn't react to the news scrolling across his screen. Like Lev, he was not a man to give in to panic. He waited in silence. In stillness. A new message appeared on the computer screen, and his heart jumped before it settled.

He was to go to Sea Haven and establish a relationship

with Judith Henderson. Files would follow detailing the mission. He felt himself go very still. Originally, he was to interrogate Jean-Claude when they broke him out of prison. He would easily acquire the needed information from La Roux and his handlers knew he would. Traveling to Sea Haven, as much as he wanted to go find out about his brother, would be stepping into a mine field.

He waited another heartbeat and sent back his reply. *I do not understand. I am to interrogate Jean-Claude.*

The anonymous orders continued to scroll across the screen. The plan had been changed. If anything went wrong when La Roux escaped from prison, they wanted to make certain they could acquire him should he go to Sea Haven. Stefan needed to get there well ahead of him and establish his cover with Judith Henderson. If necessary, should the crime lord show up, he would interrogate both Jean-Claude and the woman once he had both of them in his custody.

Stefan's gut reacted, lurching sickeningly. He actually tasted bile in his mouth. Extracting information from La Roux was one thing, but the woman too? He opened his eyes to look at the text a second time, willing the orders to magically change. He must be damn tired to have such a physical reaction to the order.

He closed his eyes briefly, shaking his head. This mission was definitely something other than what he was being told. It made no sense to think agents would break Jean-Claude from prison and then lose him. He was being sent to Sea Haven, not because they thought they'd lose the crime lord, but because he was bait to lure his brother, Lev, out into the open. They hadn't accepted Petr Ivanov's report on his brother's death after all. The orders served a twofold purpose. Revealing Lev's whereabouts, and if by some miracle La Roux slipped away from the other agents, he would be in place to extract the information they needed and then kill him.

Swallowing his absolute repugnance of the orders, he

typed in his agreement. Moments later, he received a down-loaded file containing everything they had on Judith Henderson. He signed off and poured himself a cup of coffee, sank down into a chair, rubbing his temples. He'd been getting blinding headaches lately, another sign he was crashing. This assignment had gone south fast. He couldn't afford to be crashing, not if they were sending him to Sea Haven.

A part of him wanted to go, and that sent a frisson of concern through him. He didn't want to lead Petr Ivanov to Lev, and if Lev was in Sea Haven, he would find Stefan, no matter how solid the cover was. He swore in three languages and took a sip of his coffee. Judith. Damn the woman. She'd gotten under his skin in that prison cell. He hadn't known it was possible for anyone to do that, let alone a woman he'd never met.

He opened the file, reading about her life. Japanese mother. American father. Both deceased in a car accident. She got her height from her father. Those long, beautiful legs. He forced his mind back to data, committing her life to memory. She had one brother, older, who had raised her after the death of her parents.

Paul Henderson, now deceased, executed, with a single gunshot to the forehead, but not before he'd been tortured. He had gone to Paris and left with his sister. They both disappeared and Paul resurfaced in Greece. He was killed there. Judith turned up *after* Jean-Claude was imprisoned and took her brother's body home to the States. What did that mean?

Had Jean-Claude been looking for Judith? He turned the thought over and over in his mind. It fit. It was possible she'd run from the man with her brother's help. She was intelligent, and men like La Roux couldn't afford intelligent women. They figured things out. Once she realized La Roux was dirty, Judith may not have been able to live with it. On the other hand, she may have taken something valuable from him.

The thought didn't sit well with Stefan, but either

scenario could explain both the death of her brother and
Jean-Claude's continued interest in her. As did the fact that
she'd dropped out of sight until Jean-Claude had been imprisoned. Judith's resurfacing suggested she truly didn't
know just how dangerous La Roux really was, or just how
far and expertly he could wield his considerable power
from his prison cell.

Stefan continued to scroll through the downloaded dos-
sier. The file included several images of Judith's paintings,
both the ones she'd painted before she left Paris, and the
ones she'd painted after. The moment his gaze touched the
first painting he felt a hard one-two punch to his gut. Her
drive and passion literally robbed his lungs of air. He
couldn't take his eyes from the series, studying each painting carefully. They were intriguing and beautiful, deep,
three-dimensional colors, amazing lines, all passion and
fire. Her drive and passion.

"There you are," he whispered. "I see you."

She poured herself into the painting, holding nothing
back, breathing life into her work so that every seascape,
every tree, cloud or bush had movement and sang or sobbed.
Color was a musical instrument in her hand, wielded by an
expert, her courage astounding. She understood colors and
their meaning. She drew her strokes like caresses, both
bold and shy, sensual and innocent. She was a seductress
with her colors, a dream within reach, yet unattainable.

Stefan ran both hands through his hair. She was out there
for the entire world to see. She had bared her soul in these
paintings. God, she was breathtaking. He felt his body stir,
a shock beyond imagining. He was always in command of
himself, physically and mentally. He'd been trained since he
was a child. His body came to life at his command and
performed when and where he needed it to. What the hell
was this woman doing to him with her paintings and her
photographs?

There was more of the real woman in the paintings than

in the mysterious photograph he'd stolen from the crime lord. She'd hidden herself, drawn inward, held herself aloof from the world, but here, in every bold stroke he could see her fire and passion.

Stefan forced himself to move on. Her time with Jean-Claude was well documented. The rumors about La Roux had begun to surface and there were a few pictures of a younger Judith smiling up at Jean-Claude, wearing happiness like a second skin in all the surveillance photos. His reaction to seeing the crime lord with her was primeval, visceral, even animalistic. He wanted to kill the man with his bare hands. He flexed his fingers and slowed his breathing, pushing all emotion from his mind.

Stefan studied Jean-Claude's expression. The arm around Judith's narrow waist was possessive, as was his expression, but there was something more. If a man like La Roux was capable of love, it was there. Whatever it was, maybe obsession—and Stefan was beginning to understand the word—the look on Jean-Claude's face as he stared down at the laughing Judith, said it all. He would pay any price to keep her. For certain, if the man eluded the other agents, he would be going to Sea Haven to collect whatever he thought of as his—and that included Judith.

Stefan read the file carefully, committing it to memory before examining the few photographs of Judith's work after her escape from La Roux. Each painting was good, no doubt about it, but her later work was far different from her originals. She was very restrained, showing the absolute beauty of the piece she worked on. Flawless color schemes, bold, courageous strokes, but for him, the painting themselves were flat. They were still beautiful, but she—Judith, the essence of the woman—wasn't there anymore. All her passion and fire was restrained, gone, replaced by a mask that was good, brilliant even, but not real.

"Too late to cover up now. I see you," he whispered again. "I'm coming for you."

He pressed his fingers hard just over his eyes where a headache was beginning. Damn it all. He didn't want another life. He didn't dream about another life. He played the cards dealt to him like the automaton he'd taught himself to become. He didn't feel. He didn't even want to feel. He no longer thought about his parents and how, in the darkness of his homeland, guns had been put to his mother's and father's heads and the triggers pulled. There was no safety inside four walls. There would be no safety for him anywhere—ever. And anyone with him would be at risk. Anyone he loved would be taken from him. Better not to ever take the chance, so never feel.

He repeated the mantra softly aloud. His steps whispered on the carpet before he even knew his own intention. He crossed to the dresser and picked up the photograph of Judith Henderson again, drawn by some force greater than he could resist. A woman who spoke seven languages. Intelligent. Beautiful. An artist. He didn't even know what that would be like, to have the freedom to paint, to pour your heart and soul onto a canvas.

He knew languages. He was intelligent. And he knew paintings. Everything about them. It was all necessary to his business of shedding one skin and acquiring another. His temples throbbed and he sank back into his chair, the photograph in his hand. What was it about her? That lost, lonely look? The wind in her hair? The sun shining on the water? His imagination, so long repressed, leapt forward in spite of his desire to suppress it. She was waiting for someone to come and unlock that passion and fire. She was waiting for the right man to give it to.

What the hell was he thinking?

2

D ARK purples swirling with black lines moved across the high cobalt ceiling, weeping crystalline tears. With so much sorrow filling the room, floor to ceiling, simple stone and wood could barely contain the intensity of emotion. Sorrow lived and breathed.

Rage moved in the walls, breathing in and out, so that the slashes of red and orange undulated, bulging outward and then pressing back, great gulps of air to control the force of anger, the need for retribution, for vengeance. Rage lived and breathed alongside sorrow there in the spacious confines of the large, dark studio.

A breeze drifted in from the open French doors leading to the patio and backyard where great grasses obscured all view of the studio from outside, teasing at the flames flickering at the tip of each of the dark candles illuminating the paintings. The dancing light caught glints of jagged glass embedded in the dark, angry paintings. Bold, red Japanese characters wept out a single name—Paul Henderson.

Judith Henderson leaned forward in the high-backed chair and swept a great bold stroke of black to draw in all light and consume it. There could be no forgiveness. Never. She could not forgive the torture of her brother, his senseless death. Tears ran down her face and she brushed them away with her forearm, added another weeping stroke to intersect with a fierce, bold promise of vengeance.

"Someday, my brother," she promised aloud to the seething room. "I'll find the right instrument to strike back and I won't hesitate—not this time. I'll wield it with deadly force and I *will* avenge your torture and murder." Her soul was already black with her own guilt. What was one more deadly sin among so many?

She touched the edge of the canvas almost reverently. Paul had stretched this one, as he had so many of her earliest paintings and she reworked it, over and over in oil, trying desperately to rid herself of the dark rage permeating her soul. Sometimes she could leave this studio as it should be, dark and locked away from the world, but other times, like now, she was driven to come here, obsessed with her need to let out the dark, obscene rage, the guilt and tremendous sorrow that was stamped into her very bones.

This studio, and the art hidden away inside it, held all her darker emotions—feelings she didn't dare allow out into the universe. Anger. Fury. Defiance and guilt. She poured those things into her paintings and the individual cells for the kaleidoscope. Sometimes she shook when she painted, strokes bold and angry, sweeping across the canvas as she allowed herself the freedom of true expression. In this room she used only big, broad brushes, nothing like the finer brushes used in her restoration and painting for the public.

Every dark thought, every dark need, strong enough to wake her in the middle of the night and leave her sweating on the sheets, was carefully left in this room, just as carefully and deliberately as she cared for her paints and brushes. This was a room of depression and madness. Dark. Ugly. One of heavy sorrow, guilt, shame and absolute, utter despair.

Judith sent another bold stroke sideways from corner to

corner, the brush sweeping along its side, giving the edgy quality she needed for the rage in her to express itself. She gave the same attention, if not more, to these paintings. This studio was the only place she dared allow life to the darker emotions seething like a volcano deep inside her.

In the center of the room was her worst and best master-piece, a large kaleidoscope she kept covered, just as she did the paintings. She didn't want anyone accidentally stumbling into this place of dark power. The kaleidoscope was particularly dangerous, each cell compiling a year's worth of murderous fury, five of them, for each of the years that had passed following her brother's murder. She had a separate studio for working on kaleidoscopes, but it was far different from this one. She sent another stroke screaming across the canvas, this one a deep, almost midnight purple.

The breeze slid again into the room, sending the flames flickering again and the overpowering scent of the dense oils creeping into the very walls, giving the black anger held prisoner there a distinct odor. She took the edge of her brush and splashed a thin line across that promise of vengeance as an exclamation point. A jagged piece of glass ripped a cut through the skin on the outside of her hand, not for the first time, dripping her blood into the painting. Her sweat and tears often ended up inside these paintings, mixing deep into the sections of glass so that when she painted over the shards, pieces of herself were just as deeply embedded.

Judith cursed her "gift" for the thousandth time. She could bind any element to her, she shared emotion, and she could amplify and use that emotion for destructive pur-poses. Here, in this room, it was safe enough to allow herself the luxury of tears, of anger, of hatred, of the very real need for revenge, but she could never risk taking those things outside these four walls.

The breeze blew insistently, carrying with it a melodic note. Soft, incessant—one that penetrated the layers of her concentration.

"Judith."

Her name sounded like the whisper of wind shifting the scent of darkness.

"The telephone is ringing. Where are you? You home?"

Judith blinked several times, looked down at the great fat drops of blood dripping onto the floor now. It took a moment to focus, to remember where she was and what she was doing. She'd lost herself completely this time, pouring her hatred and guilt onto the canvas. She recognized the voice of Airiana Rydell, one of her beloved sisters. It wasn't that hard to imagine her padding barefoot through the house, bare feet sinking into the thick, creamy carpet, platinum hair swinging as she searched for Judith.

A hint of urgency crept into the melodic voice. "Judith? Are you all right? Answer me."

Judith made her way to the edge of the French doors and inhaled sharply to try to clear her head. She was consumed by her painting, still in a deep fog, struggling to get out and make sense of where she was and what she needed to do. It took a few moments to push back the dark, swirling waters of rage and sorrow threatening to eat her from the inside out and find the way back to sanity.

"Be out in a minute, Airiana." She struggled to keep her voice even as she wrapped a clean cloth around her hand to soak up the drops of blood. "Take a message for me, will you?"

Very carefully she cleaned her brushes, taking her time, knowing Airiana would cover for her on the phone. Airiana would know she was fighting her way back. She came into this room only when the darkness threatened to completely consume her and she had to find a way to dissipate some of it. She feared if she didn't, sooner or later, her emotions would escape and she would harm someone accidentally.

"Breathe in. Breathe out. Find beauty in the world around you." She allowed the familiar mantra to take her back to the world she lived in.

She had sisters. Five of them. Each one of them had shared an equally traumatic experience. They had met in Monterey, California, a beautiful coastal town where an amazing woman had brought together a group of victims of violence—of murder—for counseling. Each of the women felt responsible and each was at the very end of their ability to cope with shame and guilt. Until Monterey. Until they met one another and formed their lasting sisterhood.

They trusted few people. Believed in even fewer. But together they were strong. Together they could live their lives in peace. Find happiness again. Maybe not in the way others would have thought was right, but it was their way and Judith embraced her life in the small village of Sea Haven where she worked.

They called each other family and that's what they were—sisters. Many people in the world had family of the heart, kin by choice rather than by blood, and hers had come along in her darkest hour and saved her life. Five years ago they'd made the decision to buy a farm together just outside of the village of Sea Haven, on the Northern California coast. The community was small and close, the villagers interdependent on one another for success, which made them all very friendly and tolerant of one another.

"You okay, Judith?" Airiana called again, this time insistent.

It was a common question they all asked one another.

"Be right out," she said again, dodging the question. It was never good to outright lie. Bad karma, and in any case, Airiana was fairly good at seeing through lies.

Airiana was the most difficult of all her sisters to mislead. Like Judith, she could read auras, the electromagnetic field of pure energy surrounding human beings. She saw the energy in colors surrounding people, allowing glimpses into their emotions as well as character. Judith rarely trusted her gift, while Airiana relied on hers. All of her sisters knew that if Judith was in this particular studio, it wasn't a good day.

Judith carefully put all her brushes and paints away and draped the canvas she was working on. No one could ever see this painting. No one could ever peer into the swirling dark kaleidoscope. These pieces were far too powerful on the senses, created from a forbidding, despairing place she rarely allowed herself to go, but sometimes had no choice.

With great deliberation, she locked the French doors and drew the thick, heavy drapes, preventing light, preventing any view whatsoever of this studio.

She blew out the many candles, plunging the room into darkness, and took a deep breath of the soothing lavender as she struggled to find peace again. After hours of allowing her darker emotions free reign, it took time to bury them again, to cover them up and find tranquility. She needed to maintain complete and absolute serenity at all times when she was in the company of others.

Judith took another deep breath of the lavender, the scent now slightly faded, and stepped into the hallway of her home. The soothing color of ivory washed over her. She looked at everything as a canvas, including—or especially—her home. Because each of the sisters had their own designated five acres on the farm and were able to design their own home, she had started with an amazing blank canvas.

The lower story was all about her work, the three studios, a playroom, a bathroom and a bedroom just in case she'd worked too long into the night and just crashed without bothering to go upstairs. Her living space was all about glass and views of the gardens surrounding the house. Open space and welcoming. She loved her home and the hard-earned peace she found there.

She met Airiana in the hallway and gave her a quick hug.

"I was worried," Airiana admitted, her deep blue eyes searching Judith's face for hidden shadows. "You only go into that studio when you're really upset, Judith. You haven't been there for a few weeks."

That wasn't strictly true. In the last few days leading up to the anniversary of Paul's murder Judith hadn't been able to sleep and she'd spent several nights in the studio surrounded by her anger and sorrow.

"I know it's distressing to you," Judith said gently. Just the sight of Airiana restored her inner balance. She wasn't alone, dealing with the mass of emotions she was forced to suppress. She had her sisters. They loved her in spite of her reckless past and they would stand by her.

"What happened to your hand?" Airiana demanded. "Should I call Lexi?"

Their youngest sister worked with healing herbs, among other things. Judith forced a smile, holding up her hand. "A scratch. Nothing more. I'm dying for a cup of tea. Did you put the kettle on?"

"Before I came downstairs," Airiana said, her gaze flicking once more to Judith's hand before she sighed and let it go.

"Good. Should be near boiling by now."

Together they went up the stairs leading to the main living quarters. Judith loved looking at Airiana, always calm in the face of any crisis. She was quite a bit shorter than Judith, slim, with an almost boyish figure, small breasts, a narrow waist and slim legs. Her hair was natural platinum, streaked with silver and gold, amazing in the sun. Her eyes were enormous, a deep blue, fringed with golden lashes. Small specks of gold dusted her nose.

Airiana was one of the smartest people Judith knew, and that included Damon Wilder, Sarah Drake's husband, who worked on defense systems for the United States. No one would ever guess looking at the little pixie who was Airiana. She looked more like a dancer than a think tank. Airiana simply made people feel good with her presence and on days like this one, Judith welcomed her company.

"You always pick the perfect day to come and see me," Judith said, meaning it. "I suppose you already chose the

tea and put it in the teapot as well." Airiana always seemed
to know when Judith—or anyone—needed cheering up.

Airiana laughed. "Of course. You know I'm not shy about
making myself at home. When you have a husband and a
dozen kids running around, I'll still just let myself in and be
the favorite, wonderful auntie. And we're having black tea. I
needed a boost."

Judith shook her head, smiling wider and keeping her
eyes bright and sunny when deep inside, she wept continu-
ously. She was trapped by her own gifts, terrified to ever
take such a chance again, to feel for a man, to trust. She
wouldn't be the one having children, when she'd always so
desperately wanted a family.

The hardest aspect to control wasn't her facial expression; it was holding a happy aura in place. Thankfully, she
was truly overjoyed to see Airiana, so the blossoming color
was there, spreading across the deep sorrow, shame and
guilt she hid from the world. She tended to guard her energy
around Airiana, which resulted in a muddy gray surrounding her and always raised Airiana's eyebrow, but other than
asking her if she was okay or needed anything, Airiana held
to their code of not prying.

The upper story was spacious, the living room large,
opening into the dining room and kitchen area, so anyone
visiting would feel welcome in any room. Banks of windows provided amazing sunlight and gorgeous views of the
surrounding gardens below.

"There is nothing in the world like a good cup of tea at
the right moment," Judith pointed out. "Thanks for putting
on the kettle." She stretched. "I spend far too much time
sitting on my butt. I think it's growing significantly."

Airiana turned her finger in a little circle. Judith oblig-
ingly spun around. Airiana widened her eyes. "You are so
right. Middle-aged spread is setting in." She burst out laughing again and ran for her life with Judith hot on her heels.

"The thing about long legs, you short little shrimp, is that I can outrun you."

"Not with a large ass, you can't," Airiana called over her shoulder as she sprinted through the spacious rooms. The accusation that anything on willowy Judith could be large was so absurd, she laughed so hard she couldn't see where she was going and crashed into an armchair. Tumbling over the side of it, she landed on the floor and blinked up at Judith. "Yikes. I guess your butt isn't quite as big as either of us thought."

"I am *not* even close to being middle-aged, smart-ass."

"True, but you're still always going to be older than me," Airiana pointed out smugly.

The front screen pulled open and a woman stuck her head in the door. Tall and blond, she was the picture of athleticism, her hair pulled back into a ponytail and her body in a tight, stretchy shirt and running shorts. As she stood on the porch above the stairs, she tapped her foot and wiped at the sheen of sweat on her face.

"Blythe." Judith waved as she greeted the oldest of her sisters and the acknowledged leader of their sisterhood. "You went running again this afternoon? You ran this morning."

"What in the world are you two doing?" Blythe Daniels ignored the inquiry and stepped inside to sink down onto an ottoman and remove her running shoes.

"Well," Airiana said from the floor, "basically we're discussing Judith's butt and how big it's grown while she sat and painted today."

"Really?" Blythe frowned at them both, looking very concerned. "I don't have my glasses to examine you up close and personal, Judith, but there isn't much there. In fact, your butt might be considered flat."

"I have a very cute ass," Judith protested.

"You were the one just saying it was ballooning," Airiana reminded her. "I was trying to be supportive and helpful."

Judith flung a decorative pillow at her head. Airiana sent a push of air to counter it, stopping the pillow abruptly so that it fell to the floor.

"Show-off," Judith accused. "I'll make the tea. Blythe, do you need a glass of water?"

"Thanks, love one."

"You shouldn't run twice in one day, Blythe, especially not today. Doesn't Levi teach our self-defense class tonight, or do I have my days mixed up?" Airiana asked. Once again her blue eyes inspected her oldest sister with some concern.

Judith paused in the open sweeping wide arch leading to the kitchen to hear Blythe's answer. All of them had personal demons they fought, and Blythe was no exception. She was just so *good*—the only word Judith could think of—it was distressing to all of them when she went through these periods of insomnia. She got up early and ran and often ran late in the evenings. It was rare for her to include an afternoon.

"No, Levi's definitely going to throw us all over the gym tonight," Blythe said, wiping at her face with the hem of her shirt. "I think last week every bone in my body ached. He's worse than Lissa and her martial arts training."

"Don't forget her Pilates. And her weight training. And her Zumba classes," Airiana added and threw herself onto her back on the floor, groaning. "I'm exhausted just thinking about it. Lissa can think of a million ways to do us all in."

Judith forced a laugh. It was becoming easier to feel the emotion she was trying to portray to her sisters. "Not like Levi."

Levi Hammond was married to Rikki, another sister, and Levi believed in preparing them all for any situation. They practiced self-defense moves over and over, and he was a very exacting teacher. Lately he'd been adding weapons training. Lissa, of course, already a third-degree black belt, was particularly fast at catching on, while Judith felt very out of her element. She could do martial arts katas, all those beautiful graceful forms, flowing across the room, every movement exact and elegant, but she just couldn't seem to get some of the more practical self-defense moves down.

Lissa was always unfailingly patient with her. Levi, less so. He was determined to ensure Judith could handle herself in any situation. She knew he was right, but that didn't make her any better at self-defense. She busied herself pouring the boiling water into the teapot and slipped a cozy over it to allow it to steep.

Blythe drank a full glass of water by the time the tea was ready, ignoring the other two laughing at her. The three women curled up close on thick, comfortable chairs, tucking legs up.

"I have to say," Judith confessed, "I was totally wrong about Levi. He's crazy about Rikki and has been good for her. I've actually grown very fond of him."

"I didn't expect to like him so much either," Airiana admitted.

Blythe shrugged her shoulders and looked at them over her teacup.

"Oh no, you don't," Judith shook her head. "You don't get to be silent on the subject of Levi. He's with our beloved Rikki and I thought you said they were good for each other.

"I think they are," Blythe said. "He pushes her just a little to stretch her comfort zone, but he accepts her and seems to love her for who she is. They seem a perfect match."

"There's a *but* in there," Airiana pointed out.

"No one really knows anyone," Blythe said. "You have to take people at face value. What they say, how they act, but if they lie, if they don't show all sides of themselves, you never know who you're truly dealing with."

Judith ducked her head, pretending to take a sip of tea. Blythe always told the truth and this time she hit so close to the mark, Judith felt it like an arrow through her heart. There was a sudden silence and when she looked up, she realized both of her sisters were looking at her in alarm.

"What is it, honey?" Blythe said. "I didn't mean to stir up old ghosts. Perhaps mine were just a little too close today. I haven't been able to sleep and I guess I'm feeling a little melancholy."

Judith took a deep breath and pulled back from that yawning precipice of despair and sorrow, knowing if she went over the edge, she'd take Blythe and Airiana with her. "I'm sorry," she whispered. "I was thinking of Paul today and it's just so close. The idea that Levi could hurt Rikki when we stood for him, when we've accepted him into our family—that's just so horrible." She hadn't been sleeping lately. Was it possible she was affecting Blythe? It wasn't out of the realm of possibility.

"But it happens," Blythe said.

Airiana put a comforting hand on Blythe's shoulder. "Yes it does, Blythe. Sometimes, especially when we're quite young, we trust the wrong people."

Judith nudged Airiana with her bare foot in an effort to lighten the mood. "Some of us are still quite young."

Airiana gave her a mock scowl. "I am not the baby of this family, Lexi is."

"You're close," Judith teased. "Not quite grown yet. Didn't you get carded going into an R-rated movie last week?"

Blythe burst out laughing as Airiana winced. "You can't deny it, Airiana, and you're never going to live that one down—at least not for a very long time."

Airiana joined the laughter as she shook her head at the absurdity. "Clearly the woman needed glasses."

"Who called earlier?" Judith asked as the laughter subsided.

"I almost forgot," Airiana said. "Inez called. She said she needed you to call back as soon as possible. Someone's inquiring about buying the gallery and she's hoping you can take the time to show them around."

"That would be so nice for her and Frank to get out from

under that payment," Blythe said. "She really struggled to keep things going for Frank while he was in jail. His health is so fragile right now that they can't keep both the store and the gallery. You've been so good to them, Judith."

Judith indicated Airiana with her teacup. "I've been working at the gallery more than in my own shop. If Airiana wasn't helping out, I wouldn't have been able to help them." She grinned at her sisters. "I might just get out of working out tonight."

"Oh, no you don't," Blythe protested. "If I'm going, you have to go too."

"Levi doesn't even let Rikki off the hook," Airiana pointed out. "You're going to go, Judith. Call Inez back, but don't you dare try to make an appointment to see them this evening. We promised Levi we'd learn self-defense."

"But I'm hopeless," Judith wailed.

"Only because you won't hit anyone," Airiana said. "Personally, I enjoy hitting the man. Try it, honey, you might like it. Just pretend he's someone you don't like."

Judith's heart jumped. She forced her mind away from that possibility. Airiana had no idea just how dangerous that would be. Judith could tap into every element, draw power from all energy, ignite the room with Lissa's fire, flood it with Rikki's water, bury it with Lexi's earth or use Airiana's air to blow a house down. She couldn't afford—not ever again—to lose control of her emotions. She didn't even dare acknowledge a darker emotion, for fear of what would happen.

She was *afraid* to hit someone, especially someone she loved. She ducked her head to hide her expression, hanging on to her smile a little grimly. "Levi thinks I'm a pansy ass."

Airiana nudged her with her toe. "Isn't that better than having a big ass?"

"Or no ass at all?" Blythe asked.

Judith gave them both a mock scowl. "You're both obsessed with my butt." She studied Blythe's face. "But you didn't come here to discuss any of this, did you? What's wrong, Blythe?"

Blythe sighed and put down her teacup. "You know Elle and Jackson are in Europe. He's taken a leave of absence for six months and they're touring right now. But they'll be coming back. The seventh daughter has always lived in the Drake house in Sea Haven. They're definitely coming back. Joley Drake married Ilya Prakenskii. We can pretend that Levi is a Hammond all we want, but Ilya's going to know. And Jonas is going to tell Jackson."

Judith bit her lip. Levi Hammond would not be welcomed to Sea Haven by Jackson, Elle's husband. Levi had been there when Stavros was holding Elle Drake captive. He'd been deep undercover trying to stop a major human trafficking ring and he couldn't risk blowing his cover to save Elle. But, none of that would matter to Jackson. Elle had been raped and tortured for months by Stavros, and as far as Jackson was concerned there was no goal important enough to justify turning a blind eye to her suffering.

"You're afraid they'll make his life hell," Airiana ventured.

"Or worse. Rikki is too fragile for that." Blythe rubbed her temples in agitation. "If they force Levi to leave, Rikki will go with him, and she won't do well out of this environment. It took her so long to adjust."

"The Drakes can't force us out of Sea Haven," Judith said. "But if they can't get over who and what Levi was, and they make his life here impossible, I'm willing to relocate."

Blythe looked up at her. "Really think about it, Judith. We all should before making a personal decision. You have your business and studios here."

Judith nodded. "I love Rikki. She's my sister and she's autistic. She needs us. She needs the ocean and she needs Levi. If they go, I'll go with them. It doesn't matter to me where I work. I love this place, but our family is what matters most, not where we are."

Airiana let out her breath. "I've been worried too. I didn't realize anyone else was."

"Have you spoken to the others? To Lexi?" Judith asked.

Lexi spent most of her time on their large farm. She grew the vegetables they sold to markets and at the farmer's markets in the surrounding towns.

"Everyone but her," Blythe admitted. "Lissa said she'll relocate as well. It will be hard for Lexi. She's put so much into this place."

"Do you really think it will come to that?" Airiana asked. "Jonas did fairly well when he found out and he's married to Hannah, Elle's sister."

"That doesn't mean Jackson is going to have the same reaction," Blythe pointed out. "I'm their first cousin, a family member, and believe me when I say, they can close ranks just as we can. If Jackson can't come to terms with Levi, Sea Haven's going to become a difficult place for us to live. Rikki is very sensitive and she'll feel it." She shrugged her shoulders. "I'm just trying to anticipate that it might happen."

"All of us have been worried," Judith said. "I think Levi worries, but probably not in the same way. He wouldn't care one way or the other if he's accepted, and I suppose Rikki wouldn't either if she could stay out of the village."

"A child would feel it," Airiana ventured. "A child always knows when they're being ostracized."

"I doubt if Rikki would consider having a baby," Blythe said. "But at least we're all in agreement. I'll approach Lexi on the subject as well, just to be safe."

"It might be difficult to sell the farm," Judith pointed out. "Times are hard right now, although the farm is making money."

"Which will make it easier," Blythe said. "Showing a profit is going to be beneficial. But we can cross that bridge when we come to it."

"Have you looked at other places where we might all relocate together?" Airiana asked. "This works for us all. Can we find something similar somewhere else?"

"We'll find the right piece of property if we need to," Blythe said with conviction.

"Are you going to talk to Rikki and Levi about this?" Judith asked.

Blythe shook her head. "Not Rikki. I thought I'd talk to Levi tonight, but not until I see Lexi. I thought I'd break it to her after I leave here. I just wanted to make certain the two of you were on board."

Judith looked around her house. She'd designed it from top to bottom, just as they all had. They built the houses together, each doing quite a bit of the carpentry. She'd planted her gardens just the way she wanted. She had a Japanese garden with a waterfall cascading down rocks into a quiet pool of koi, surrounded by every shade of green available. Each night, from her bedroom window she looked down to her night garden of white flowers, lifting their faces to the overhead stars. She loved the peace created, a midnight sky with white above and below just spoke to her soul. And there were all the gardens where riots of color reigned, so many blossoms vying for space and attention, a wild melody of color. It had taken every day of the five years she'd lived there to get her gardens the exact way she wanted them.

It would be wrenching to leave—but family came first. Rikki's needs were priority. As awful as leaving would be, Judith wouldn't look back. She had learned the hard way that people mattered most, not where she lived or the job she did. "You know what Levi is going to say, Blythe," she said gently. "He'll say the hell with all of them."

"I know," Blythe agreed. "But in the end, like us, he'll do what's best for Rikki."

Airiana cleared her throat, fiddled with the handle on the teacup and then forced her eyes to meet Blythe's. "Couldn't you talk to Elle? You are her cousin."

Blythe shook her head. "I'm not on the best of terms with the Drakes, Airiana. You all know that. We get along, mostly because they're never impolite and neither am I. We were all raised to never be rude."

"Blythe," Judith said gently, "they all love you. No one blames you for your mother's death but yourself."

Blythe blinked back tears. "Maybe that's true, but I can't ask anything of them and I doubt it would matter if I did. They'd just say they aren't forcing us out, which technically would be the truth. They would politely freeze us out."

Airiana hugged her. "I'm sorry I brought it up. I know this is a difficult time for you and it was inconsiderate and selfish of me to even suggest it. I really am sorry, Blythe."

"No worries, Airiana. I think it's just that time of the year." Her eyes met Judith's. "For you too. How are you doing?"

Judith shrugged. There was nothing else to do but smile and say "fine." Whatever that meant. Her brother was dead and there was no bringing him back. Paul had been murdered, plain and simple, because of her. Because of her stupidity. Her carelessness. Her actions. Blythe blamed herself for her mother's death, but she wasn't the direct cause, no matter what she thought, whereas Judith knew she absolutely was.

"I guess I'd better call Inez back and set up the meeting with the potential buyer for the art gallery. I hope this one's for real. Inez can't afford to keep funding both businesses."

"There was a rumor going around for a while that Jackson bought part ownership in the grocery store," Airiana said. "Do you think that's true?"

"If it is, then Inez is in worse financial shape than I thought she was," Blythe replied. "She loves that store and it's always made money for her. If she had to do that, it means she poured way too much into keeping Frank's gallery alive."

Both women looked at Judith. As manager of the gallery, she knew better than anyone else just how much the place was making. She shrugged, unwilling to talk about Inez's business even to her sisters. She glanced out her window to the garden below, needing to see the riot of color, great splashes of it, to soothe her wounded spirit. The wind blew across the flowers, setting up waves of color in every shade.

Even as she watched, a shadow slid across the flowers, dampening the effect for just a moment. She glanced upward, toward the sky, expecting to see a seagull or vulture flying overhead, but there was only blue sky. She felt, rather than saw, Airiana stand behind her.

"What is it?" Blythe asked.

"I don't know," Airiana said. "But that shadow passed directly over this house, and that's worrisome."

The three women exchanged a long look. Sea Haven was a place of power, there was no doubt about that. The location had energy of its own and it attracted people with psychic energy as well.

"You're the air element," Blythe said. "All of us know it, so don't look at me all wide-eyed. What does that shadow mean?"

"I have no idea," Airiana admitted, "but I don't like it. I think trouble may be coming our way."

"Ilya? Joley and Ilya are doing a huge benefit concert, but she is pregnant. Maybe she needs to come home and rest," Blythe guessed.

"I doubt if Ilya would throw his own brother out of Sea Haven, not even for Joley. Nor would she ask him to do something like that."

"I don't think Ilya really knew any of his brothers," Blythe pointed out. "He's closer to Jonas and the Drakes than he is to his family. He wasn't raised with them, nor did he have any contact with them."

"Great," Airiana said, "I don't know about either of you, but just this once I'd like to say damn it. Just damn it. This is our home and I hate the thought of leaving. I will, if we have to, but I really hate doing it."

Judith forced a smile. "We'll be all right. Right now we don't know how the Drakes are going to react to Levi's presence. We know we're all willing to relocate if we have to—well, all but Lexi." She glanced at her sister. "Blythe, you'll be talking to her today, right?"

Blythe nodded. "I don't feel we can just pretend leaving isn't a real possibility. Finding another place like this—with the ocean for Rikki, enough land for Lexi to farm, enough for us all to live together—that's going to take time. And we'd have to sell this place."

"Lexi will be upset," Airiana said.

"She's put her heart and soul into this land," Judith acknowledged. "It will be harder for her than for any of us."

"Maybe we can just not say anything until we know one way or the other," Airiana said. "All we're really doing is speculating."

"We promised each other we'd always tell the truth no matter how difficult. This is a joint decision we have to make together. When we're all on board, then we'll talk to Rikki," Blythe said. "Rikki has to see us all together and know we're more than willing to move with her and Levi."

There was a small silence. No one wanted to leave after they'd spent five years working to build their dream homes. Lexi had worked hard to get the farm producing enough to make money. It hadn't been easy, but they'd all pitched in with every job, making the dream they all shared come true.

Judith stood up, gathered the empty teacups and took them to the sink. "Shadows can be just shadows," she called over her shoulder. "We could just be paranoid."

"That's true," Blythe admitted, getting to her feet as well. She did a slow stretch. "I guess I'll go talk to Lexi and see you tonight at the gym."

Judith swung around with a small grimace. "Honestly, I detest self-defense class. I feel like the teacher's duncey student."

Airiana flung her arm around Judith's waist. "Honey,

you are the teacher's dunce student. Fortunately we all love you, so it doesn't matter if you can kick butt or not."

"I totally can kick butt. I've got all the moves." Judith huffed her disapproval, glaring down at Airiana's smirking face. "I just prefer not to hit people. I'm more evolved and civilized than the rest of you."

"Well, you did flip Blythe onto her back last night," Airiana conceded. "But then you burst into tears and that sort of ruined the whole effect."

"Levi was so exasperated," Blythe said and burst out laughing at the memory. "Did you see his face? I thought he might run out of there."

Judith couldn't help but laugh as well, although remembering the moment when she'd thrown her sister to the mat made her a little nauseous. The sound of Blythe's body hitting the mat, the air rushing from her lungs had been sickening. Judith couldn't explain to Levi—or her sisters—that she wanted to learn, she just didn't want to hurt anyone in the process. She believed she could defend her sisters fiercely if she had to, but to deliberately hit one of them or throw them down so hard it knocked the breath from them was abhorrent to her. And what if she lost her temper? What disaster would she bring down on everyone then?

"He definitely doesn't like any of us to cry," Airiana agreed. "And have you ever seen him when Rikki is upset? He's crazy about her."

Blythe sighed. "I have to admit that he is. I watch him all the time. I still drop by in the early morning hours for coffee and Rikki's always waiting outside for me. Levi brings the coffee out and seems happy enough to see me, but he rarely takes his eyes off of Rikki. I'm happy for her."

Judith nodded, knowing Blythe was right. Levi Hammond was so in love with Rikki, her autism didn't seem to be in any way a deterrent. "Does it make you think maybe there's someone out there for the rest of us? He's so different, and I can't imagine either one with anyone else. They were made for each other. Maybe there really is a Mr. Right."

Her voice lacked conviction and she knew it. There would never be a Mr. Right for her. She couldn't trust herself, or her talent, to not ever put those she loved in peril again. She was attracted to the wrong kind of man. In the past few years, she hadn't even dared look at a man with any degree of interest. She didn't dare go down that path ever again. Worse, she felt as if her own body had died. She hadn't been the least attracted, physically or emotionally, to any man she'd met in the past five years.

Blythe shook her head. "I'm past the age where some knight in shining armor is going to ride in on a white steed and sweep me off my feet."

Airiana did a few little dance steps across the thick, creamy carpet. "I think Levi is going to be starved for male company, poor man."

Judith forced another laugh, but that shadow passing over her house hadn't kept going, it had slipped inside her and a deep dread blossomed and grew.

3

SHE came toward him, walking with unhurried steps, unaware of his presence. Stefan stood in the shadows, just inside the alcove by the gallery door, his back to the building, where he could see anything coming at him. Judith Henderson was far more breathtaking in person than in her photographs. She was still a good distance away, so he had plenty of time to absorb her. Tall, long legs, her suit as elegant as they came. A pencil skirt hugged the curve of her hips lovingly. Her short, flared matching jacket was severe black, but the bright red silk shirt beneath it clung like a second skin and looked as sexy as hell.

Women didn't affect his pulse, or his body, yet deep inside where no one could see, the earth shook so hard something cracked wide open, deep, a fissure he couldn't repair. Emotions long buried, thought dead, rose with the force of a volcano, shaking him. He felt stripped of his armor, vulnerable, broken open and entirely exposed. His hand slid inside his jacket to the familiar feeling of the butt of his Glock. The moment he touched the weapon, he knew he was in trouble.

Judith Henderson threatened him on an elemental level. The danger was almost tangible, yet he was at a loss as to why. She had that same faraway, lost look on her face that was in the photograph he carried with him, next to his skin in the inside pocket of his shirt where he kept the small tablet that would end his life should he fall into the wrong hands. This woman was the type who brought men to their knees. Even the strongest man bared his soul, handed his heart into keeping and was lost for all time just from a smile from those angel lips. He could hold his breath just waiting for her to smile—at him—for him. Just him.

He willed her to look up. To see him. He braced himself for the impact, knowing it was coming. Judith took two more unhurried steps in her high heels with that splash of tantalizing red streaking through the unrelenting black. His heart would have kicked into high gear if he'd allowed it, just at the anticipation of her gaze meeting his, but he was far too disciplined for that. He didn't take his eyes from her, absorbing her into his being. God, she was beautiful.

Her eyes flicked to the shadows and away again. Deliberately he shifted his weight. Her gaze jumped back to the alcove—to him. Her eyes widened, met his. His body reacted, blood rushing hotly through every vein, through his heart, spreading like a firestorm to settle in his groin. The shock of it, of that unrelenting, fierce ache, shook him. He was never out of control, his body completely disciplined, yet he was full and hard and throbbing with need, just with her eyes meeting his.

This time, there was no controlling his wayward heart. Thunder roared in his ears, filling his head with warning, with need. Her gaze was more of a punch, hitting him low and wicked hard. She drove the breath from his lungs and sanity from his mind.

If he opened his mouth, he doubted if sound would emerge. All of his training, all of his discipline was gone in one moment. Power surrounded the woman in her perfect suit on her perfect body. Innocence radiated from her. Brightness shone through all that soft skin. Yet there was unconscious seduction in every movement of her body, the way her lips were made for fantasy nights, those eyes, dark and mysterious like the woman herself.

He could read that power she wore like a cloak just as easily as he could read the aura surrounding her. She hid her powerful energy, hid every dark shadow inside her, presented a different face to the world than what was deep inside of her. But he saw her—all of her—and he wanted what he saw. What man wouldn't? This was a woman a man would never get out of his mind. He saw instantly why Jean-Claude La Roux was so obsessed. She crawled inside a man before he ever had a chance to run. Just with one smoldering look. That innocent seduction.

Through it all, there was something else. Something much deeper that he reacted to. Elemental. Elusive. She was far more than that bright innocent seductress every other man would see and want. She was filled with sorrow. Lost. He wasn't a hero. He wasn't the man who stepped forward and saved the innocent. He was lost himself. Shadows had invaded a long time ago and stolen his life. But he would give anything he had left to be the man who found a way to save Judith Henderson. He wanted to be that man and it made no sense. She was a complete stranger, but that tiny piece of humanity left in him reached for this woman.

"Mr. Vincent?"

Her voice was as seductive as the rest of her. Velvet soft. Stroking over his skin like the touch of fingers. She was already inside of him. He could feel her there where he could never get her out.

"Miss Henderson?" His accent was perfect. He was already firmly anchored in his role as Thomas Vincent, an American businessman recognized in the art world with enough credentials to impress anyone. Like any good cover, he'd worked on it for some time, in case he ever needed an

American businessman. The art was easy enough, he had studied hard and with his ability to retain what he read, it was simple enough to pull out his extensive education and add it to the role he immersed himself in.

Judith took another step toward him, her gaze moving over his body. Even in his elegant, perfectly fitting suit, he knew he wasn't much to look at. He had the physique of a bodybuilder, impossible to hide. His tapered waist and narrow hips only exaggerated the bulk of his chest, arms and shoulders. His eyes were penetrating and deep blue-green, almost an aqua, his natural color. He normally wore tinted contacts, but it had been necessary to give a little of himself to this woman. What there was left of him—and it wasn't much.

"Yes, I'm Judith Henderson. I hope I haven't kept you waiting long. I was held up at the studio and didn't have a number to reach you. I'm so sorry."

A man would forgive this woman anything, especially when she looked at him with such obvious sincerity. Her eyes were enough to drown a man. He slowed his breathing and took control of his rapidly beating heart. He sent her a smile—a real one. Her head jerked up and she blinked rapidly, a sign that his crooked smile had an effect on her.

He found he didn't want to play her, not the way he did other marks, but every move was smooth and practiced, traits drilled into him since childhood. He hadn't been the most handsome man in their school; he'd been too rough and edgy to be called that, but he had undeniable charm and a hard, muscular body a woman couldn't help noticing. Sometimes, the scars on his face and body were a deterrent, but more often, women found them intriguing.

"No problem. Sea Haven is beautiful. I spent the time wandering around. You'd said you might be a few minutes late and it gave me the opportunity to look at the gallery location. Sea Haven certainly appears to be everything the advertisement said."

"If you're looking for a place to raise a family," Judith said, "this is the perfect place."

He flashed another smile. "No family. I just decided I wanted out of the rat race. At my age, peace begins to look good."

"You're from New York?" She moved up to the gallery door, taking out a set of keys.

There was no wasted effort. Every movement was graceful. He stepped close enough to inhale her fragrance. Exotic. Citrus. All woman. Stefan had been in the company of beautiful women more times than he could count over the years, but she was the first one to capture his interest—not the interest of the undercover agent, but of the man. It was a complication unwelcome but not entirely a shock. He knew from his reaction to her photograph that this assignment was going to give him trouble. He just hadn't realized until this moment how much.

"Yes. I was a silent partner in a gallery there, but decided I had enough of taxis and parties. I read about this town some years ago and filed it away. The town sounded so charming and unique, an artist's paradise."

"An article?" she prompted with a small smile over her shoulder as she pushed the door to the gallery open and stepped aside to gesture him inside.

Gallantly, and because he was always uncomfortable with anyone directly behind him, Stefan stepped back to hold the door for her. "Yes, on a supermodel who grew up here. The writer had obviously fallen a little bit in love with the town as well. There were beautiful pictures of the countryside, and the ocean with the sun shining on the surface."

She flicked on the lights as she turned to face him. Her skin looked inviting, soft and so warm he curled his fingers into a fist and held it tight against his thigh to keep from being tempted into touching her inappropriately. The woman needed to be outlawed.

"That would be Hannah Drake. Her family has been

here for over a hundred years. I'm not certain, after New York, our sleepy little town would have all that much to offer you. There's not really a night life here, Mr. Vincent. Everything closes up rather early."

He kept his wolfish smile to himself. Sweet little Judith had her suspicions. Now why would an innocent woman be in the least skeptical about a buyer wanting to live in her quaint, charming town? She looked the epitome of coopera- tion, every graceful movement soothing. Her steps were unhurried as she moved through the spacious, beautiful gal- lery toward what clearly was an office. One would never think they were in a chess match with such a beautiful, soothing woman gracing the gallery.

He indicated the deserted street. "Doesn't look like a night life, but I noticed a crowd moving around in the store two doors down."

"Every third Friday evening of the month we hold an artist's walk. The various shops participate. We have wine tastings and it's a good draw for a crowd. Usually I open the gallery for the event, but I actually hosted the event in my own shop this evening, which is why I was a little late. Fortunately my sister locked up for me. Ordinarily it's very quiet here at night."

"Just what I'm looking for," he assured her, just as charm- ing right back. He could match her play for play. He was the pro. As smooth as she was, she was still an amateur. He found himself looking forward to the exchange.

She sent him another look from over her shoulder, her silky black hair cascading like a waterfall, adding to the already painful ache in his groin. She looked like an exotic flower, exquisite and rare. And damn it all, it wasn't safe for a woman like her to be showing strange men around an empty gallery at night. She was temptation personified. As much as he didn't want to explore the possibility of her being an agent for another country, the thought still crossed his mind. She was just too seductive without even trying.

Her walk. Her dark eyes looking at him over her shoulder through all that smooth, silky hair. She was made for fantasy. For long nights.

Her manner didn't appear affected—in fact, just the opposite. She seemed naturally sensual—something all good agents were trained to be. He'd been uncharacteristic by not calling too much attention to her, not asking for more background, more checks. He cursed himself for falling into the inevitable trap some women seemed to bait so easily. His initial reaction to her—that terrible need to be the one to change that look in her eyes, to be the man she relied on—made no sense. He was a cynical man. He'd seen it all. He didn't believe in love and he sure didn't believe he would be pulled into a trap by a woman. He'd thought himself immune, but he recognized danger when he saw it.

"The gallery was closed for a time and lost a bit of ground, but since reopening, it's recovering nicely, at a very steady rate." She flipped on the lights in the office.

The room was spacious, but private, with a door leading to a bathroom and another that led outside. The entire front of the gallery was tinted glass to protect paintings from the sun while allowing a sweeping view of the ocean across the street.

"Frank actually owns this building outright. The price includes the building and surrounding lot as well as the gallery name and inventory. If you're really interested, he owns the block beside the building as well and I believe he'd consider selling that also."

For the first time, he actually wished he was an American businessman and could settle there in the little village by the sea, this woman at his side. He wouldn't mind owning his own art gallery. He frowned and pressed his fingers to his temple, the beginnings of a headache slipping up on him unnoticed. What was he thinking? Men like him didn't settle down. They hunted, and then they were hunted.

"Are you all right?"

His gaze found and captured hers. He gave her another lopsided smile. Charming her. He caught the rise and fall of her breasts beneath that slim jacket at her sudden intake of breath. "Long flight and then a good four-hour drive. The scenery was beautiful though."

"Did you fly into San Francisco, or Oakland?"

The question should have been conversational, but there was something in the way her eyes tried to move from his but couldn't. His heart accelerated. As a game of chess, he wasn't certain who actually was ahead in moves. She didn't seem to have to do much of anything—that sensual caress in her voice endangered his sanity as nothing else could. She *had* to be innocent, no one could be that good. He'd come across some of the best agents in the business and none had ever waged such a brutal, vicious attack on his body and his self-control.

"San Francisco." Deliberately he glanced away from her, a shy businessman a little outclassed by a beautiful woman. "I was looking at a gallery there as well, but I could tell I would be trading one big city for another. A different way of life, perhaps, but still not what I'm looking for. Sea Haven appeals to me."

He stepped close to her, crowding her a little on the pretense of looking into the safe she had crouched down to open. The thought of her head level with his aching groin made his cock jerk and thicken that much more. He took a breath to get his body back under control, reminding himself that wayward part of him belonged to him, not her. He took care not to accidentally brush up against her. He had to be that sharp businessman, a little shy with women, charming, but not pushy.

Judith was attracted to him and that made her wary. The fact that she physically responded to a stranger obviously bothered her on the same elemental level it bothered him. She removed several books with unsteady hands, but she hid it well. He filed that away, more pleased than he should have been at the evidence that she was having as much trouble as he was. He had no business thinking of her as anything but a mark.

His job was to find the best way to seduce her into trusting him. For the first time that he could ever remember, he didn't much like his assignment and hadn't from the beginning. He'd convinced himself it was because he sensed a trap for his brother—that he was being used to bring Lev out into the open so he could be terminated. Now, he knew his reticence was more than that—it was also about this particular woman.

"I love living here," Judith admitted, as she slowly straightened, the books in her hands.

Stefan knew he was giving her the idea that something tragic and personal had happened to him to make him want peace—to make him decide to turn his back on city life. She was looking at him with just a little bit of compassion. She didn't want to be interested, but she couldn't quite help herself. He made the observation with intense satisfaction. Thomas Vincent had to make his pursuit of Judith low-key or she would run.

"I think I would as well." He was a little shocked to realize he spoke the truth. Settling down had *never* been something he considered, or even imagined, yet the conviction in his voice was real. "Do you get many strangers in town?"

"The locals all know one another. We're a fairly close bunch—our livelihood depends on one another. But this is a tourist town. Many people vacation here. It's beautiful and all the artists settling here have attracted visitors as well."

That wasn't necessarily a good thing. Petr Ivanov could very well blend in to the many vacationers and tourists, making it more difficult for Stefan to ferret him out. Ivanov was good at blending and even better at disguises.

Stefan let his gaze slide away from Judith's again. He drew his finger around his collar as if it had become just a little too tight. "I have a confession to make." He hesitated

just a moment and then sent her a quick, apologetic grin—
a wolf in sheep's clothing. "I saw one of your early paintings at a friend's house. He's a collector out of New York.
It was titled *Moon Rising,* and I was awed when I saw it. I
tried to buy it from him but he wouldn't budge. I offered a
quarter of a million dollars, and he still wouldn't sell."

It was easy enough to sound honest, because he was telling the absolute truth. As part of his cover as an American,
over the years, he had cultivated high-profile friends. Ste-
ven Cabot was the owner of a prestigious international law
firm. He also was a collector of art—both paintings and
sculptures. It was pure coincidence that when Thomas Vincent had mentioned he was interested in artist Judith Henderson, Cabot had become extremely excited. He raved
over a painting he'd acquired some years earlier and took
Thomas in to see it.

Stefan's reaction had been that same physical one he'd
had the first time he'd viewed her paintings in her file. Gut-
wrenching and totally ensnared. He saw far more than the
moonlit sky spilling down on a field of white flowers. The
piece was breathtaking. Marvelous. Ingenious. The painting was filled with passion, sensual and innocent—just like
the woman standing before him. It wouldn't have mattered
so much if Steve hadn't stood staring entranced up at it.

For the first time in his life, Stefan Prakenskii experienced black jealousy. The emotion shook him, descending
like a dark cloud when he was someone who refused to acknowledge feelings. For one terrible moment, Steve Cabot's
life had hung in the balance. Judith's painting was all about
life and living, not about death, and he respected that, forcing himself to turn on his heel and walk away from dark
temptation. He had known then he needed to retire, to disappear, before he no longer knew the difference between right
and wrong.

Contrary to the beliefs of his superiors, he had a code he
lived by and he was too close to crossing that thin, blurring

line. For good or bad, this was his last mission and he'd taken it for two reasons. He was going to know once and for all if his brother was alive—and he meant to keep him that way. And he'd wanted to meet her—Judith—in person.

"That's insane. He didn't pay anything near that for it."

She looked both pleased and a little horrified. He liked her all the more for her reaction.

"He obviously loves it as much as I do," Stefan said. "In any case, knowing that your work is sold through this gallery was a major part of my decision to consider buying. I felt it was important to disclose that." He ducked his head a little, but refused to look away.

Her gaze moved over his face, dwelled for a moment on his mouth and then jumped back up to his eyes. A slow smile tugged at her lips. Her mouth truly fascinated him, giving him enough fantasies to last forever. She had beautiful teeth, small and delicate to go with her exotic features. Her eyelashes were long and sweeping, two thick crescents that drew attention to her large dark eyes. He made a conscious decision not to just drown there, and pulled back from the edge of disaster. He couldn't fall out of character for a pair of enormous bedroom eyes.

"I'm very flattered, Mr. Vincent."

"Call me Tom. All my friends do."

"And I'm Judith." She placed the books on the desk and indicated the chair. "Why don't you take a look at these while I do a few things out on the floor? Of course you'll want your bookkeeper and lawyer to go through them, but it's my opinion that the gallery is a sound investment. If I had the money, I would have tried to buy it."

He frowned at her. She sold her kaleidoscopes all over the world as well as her paintings. She had her own shop and worked as a manager of the gallery.

She laughed softly. "I own a farm with my sisters. We pour most of our money into that venture. It's beginning to pay off, but the first few years were tough."

"Really?" Interest crept into his voice. "A working farm?"

Judith laughed again. "Is it so farfetched?"

"Your sisters?" He knew damn well she didn't have any sisters—any family at all. "All women running a working farm?"

"Don't sound so skeptical. We're actually turning a profit."

He leaned one hip against the desk and, while amusement gleamed in his eyes, his expression turned almost eager. "You actually drive a tractor? You know how?"

"All of us do." She flashed her dark eyes at him and for the first time, he thought her smile and accompanying laughter was truly genuine. "I don't, however, wear a business suit while running heavy equipment."

"I've always wanted to drive a tractor," he confided with a boyish grin. "I never had the opportunity." He shook his head and shoved his hand through his hair, carefully messing it up so that he looked a little less sleek and a little more charming.

"While you're here, I'll have to take you out to the farm so you can have your chance," Judith said, and then looked a little shocked at her invitation.

He knew she regretted the impulsive offer as soon as it left her mouth. He waited a heartbeat. Two. "I didn't mean to put you on the spot, Judith," he said gently. "You don't even know me. As gracious as the offer is, and I really do appreciate it, I wouldn't expect you to take me to your farm." He gave her his best, open smile and looked as innocent as a caged wolf could manage when it wanted its way.

She fell into his trap quite neatly. "You're not putting me on the spot at all. I think it would be fun, as long as you don't go wild and wreck the corn beds."

"I'm in then." Surprisingly, the idea did sound kind of fun. Spending time with Judith was clearly dangerous, but suddenly the idea of riding on a tractor was actually appealing to him. He'd never thought about having the experience of it, but if he was going to disappear, maybe farming would interest him. If not, he'd still sit next to Judith on a tractor and enjoy watching her face as she tried to teach him to drive the thing.

"I'll be here for a couple of weeks. I thought it was important to spend time here and really get a feel for the place."

"I'm not working at the shop tomorrow and the weather should be nice." Her chin was up, her spine straight.

She was determined to see it through and as quickly as possible before she changed her mind. He kept his smile to himself and sank down into the chair at the desk in front of the open books. It was time to get to "work" and allow her off the hook before she became too wary. She was already on the verge of flight.

"What time? Sounds fun." He didn't actually know what fun was, but spending time in her company and sparring with her was definitely intriguing. He had time to establish his presence in Sea Haven before Jean-Claude was broken out of prison and picked up. Hopefully, there would be nothing to do but to leave. In the meantime, he would study the people and get a feel for the town. He would look for Petr Ivanov as well, and if he found him, Ivanov would have to disappear. Stefan couldn't leave him behind to find Lev, if his brother was still alive.

"Let's do eleven or twelve. That will give me time to get some work in at home."

He made certain not give into the temptation to look up, studiously studying the book. "Sounds good to me. If you write down the address, I can find it. I'll bring lunch, otherwise, you'll think you have to provide one for me."

"Why would you think that?"

He did allow his gaze to jump to hers, amusement showing through. "You're that kind of a woman."

Her eyebrow went up. "What kind of a woman would that be?"

"The hospitable kind, of course. And I'm not going to take any more advantage of your kindness than I already am just by agreeing to the tractor ride."

"Oh, no you don't. Thomas, you're not just getting a ride, you're going to drive it."

The teasing note in her voice disarmed him. He'd never really engaged in teasing with a woman and he pushed down the warmth spreading through his body. He had to remind himself he wasn't Thomas Vincent, that he was seriously playing this woman. None of it was real, no matter how real it felt to him. He sat up straighter. Or how real he wanted it to be.

Cursing under his breath, he forced himself to keep from looking at her again. He had more discipline than this. How in the world could he allow a woman to rock his world? She was just like everyone else in his world: a target. Disposable, a tool to be used and thrown away. He had no other way of life and he didn't know how to change or even if it was possible.

"Are you thinking of chickening out?"

He closed his eyes briefly. Her voice, velvet soft, bedroom husky, slipped under his skin and found its way inside of him, no matter how much he tried to punch up his armor. He couldn't stop the stealing glance. She was sitting on the edge of a counter, her long, slender legs crossed, that modest skirt suddenly not quite as modest. Again, he had the feeling she had no idea how sexy she looked sitting there, or the fantasies she might put in a man's head.

Her hair fell like a silky waterfall, cascading over one shoulder, covering one breast, a rain of blue-black, straight and shiny. He had the sudden urge to bunch it into one fist and jerk her to him, his mouth taking hers, over and over, long kisses until she was so drugged on him, that she begged him to strip off her clothes and take her right there on the counter.

Judith sucked in her breath sharply and pressed a hand to her heart. Her gaze met his. Immediately that one-two punch to his gut came. She slid off the counter and pulled the edges of her jacket together protectively. "Who are you?" she whispered. "What are you? Because you're no ordinary businessman from New York."

Her hand crept toward the phone. She actually took a step back, and then, as he stood, suddenly bolted around the counter. Her hand swept up the receiver. He was there at the same time, cursing his wayward mind, astonished that she was so psychically gifted that she either read his thoughts or felt them and knew she was in trouble. His hand closed over hers very gently, but his strength easily prevented her from picking up the phone.

The moment his skin touched hers, electricity arced and snapped over him. He felt the impact through his body, a sheer physical reaction, blood rushing hot, spreading like a wildfire out of control. She was far more dangerous to him than he'd ever realized. His entire being focused on her, shaking the very foundation of what he believed about himself. He took a breath and kept to Thomas Vincent's reaction, pushing down the lethal reaction a man like Stefan Prakenskii had when he felt threat on the most elemental level.

"Just hear me out. If you still want to call the police or have me leave, I'll go," he said, keeping his voice pitched low, velvet soft.

Stefan knew Judith didn't really have much choice in the matter. He had her hand pinned, but she wasn't thinking about that. He could tell. He didn't make the mistake of smiling. He didn't feel much like smiling and doubted if bashful American businessman Thomas Vincent would either. He'd just been caught with his pants down by a beautiful woman.

"I don't tell people . . ." He broke off and shook his head, letting go of her hand and shaking his head. "You're going to think I'm insane. Look, let's just call it a night and I'll look at the books some other time." He ran his finger around the inside of his collar again and rubbed the bridge of his nose looking, for all the world, like a very uncomfortable man.

"Just tell me." Judith's dark gaze slid away from his, giving him a glimpse into her insecurities.

Her psychic abilities were strong. He could feel the sheer potency of her energy surrounding his. When his energy rubbed hers, the boost was so powerful he expected to see sparks, an explosion, something tangible. Yet Judith didn't feel in control of her power and that gave him an advantage. If she was uncertain of herself, that left the door open for inexplicable things to happen—like Thomas Vincent accidentally sending his fantasy straight into her mind.

He shrugged. "Fine. I have certain abilities and I think Sea Haven has an energy that amplifies . . ." He trailed off uncomfortably again.

The moment Thomas's hand had settled so gently over hers with such hidden strength, preventing her from calling the sheriff, Judith's entire body felt the surge of heat rushing between them. The fire was hotter than anything she'd ever experienced, a flash of need that grew and spread and left her aching and restless.

Shocked, ashamed and certain she'd humiliated herself for life, she swallowed hard studying Thomas Vincent's averted face. His awkwardness was endearing and completely at odds with his large, muscular appearance—as was his speed and his gentleness. She had done her research on him the moment Inez had asked her to meet with the man. She distrusted outsiders on principle and since Levi had married her sister Rikki, even more so. Her entire family was fully aware Levi Hammond wasn't his real name, but none of them cared. He was theirs now, and they'd protect him just as they did each other.

She'd searched the Internet for Thomas Vincent and his name came up repeatedly in an instant. He was much more than he had said so casually. He was a man who had a reputation for brilliant deals, swooping in on failing businesses, turning them around and then selling them for quite a profit. He was reportedly worth millions. He was the only son of a railroad worker. His mother had died in childbirth and he'd been raised by his father. The father had never remarried and had died several months earlier of cancer. It was easy to see why he was such a powerful figure in the business world, but a little shy with women.

There were several photographs of Thomas Vincent with his father, and the two had looked very close. Her heart had gone out to him. It was no wonder he was contemplating a life-changing move. And God help her, she was attracted to him. That was the biggest red flag of all. She would never again risk falling for someone and put those around her in danger. She didn't make good choices. But never once in the last five years had she thought this could happen to her—this amazing invigorating, exhilarating response to a man.

She wanted to help him out of his dilemma even though he'd scared her to death. She had been flirting. Not overtly, but she'd definitely let a little leg show, hoping to draw his attention. She'd had very erotic fantasies about him throwing her down on the counter—something completely out of character for her—and she'd somehow connected with his mind.

Her wild fantasies about him had gotten out of hand and he'd picked them up and thought himself responsible. Clearly he had psychic ability and, by her reaction, there was no doubt that she'd given away the fact that she was adept as well. She should have been surprised, but the truth was, Sea Haven did have energy, power, whatever one wanted to call it. And those with psychic abilities were attracted to the small epicenter of it.

"If you're trying to say you have psychic abilities," she said, "I do as well."

He looked infinitely relieved, sinking back down into the chair by the computer. "Most people think I'm crazy. I never admit I even believe in psychic gifts."

She stayed behind the counter where she felt a little safer—or where she could keep him safe. She hadn't realized until that moment how sex-starved she'd been. She didn't date. Didn't trust anyone enough to get that close to her—close enough to share intimacy. Judith couldn't do one-night stands. She was all or nothing, and for a very long time, it had been nothing. Of course, it had to remain that way, but . . .

He pushed his fingers through his hair, messing it up further. She hadn't realized it was as long as it was, or as thick. He had beautiful hair. Judith couldn't help her fascination with the thick wavy strands, her fingers itching to touch. Why did he have to be so attractive?

"I'm sorry about . . ." He trailed off, looking as if he was blushing a little. "About, you know. I don't normally get erotic images of women in my head, but you're very sexy and it's been a long time for me." Each word of his confession was delivered painfully.

She couldn't let him take the blame. As humiliating as it was, he had the courage to confess what he thought was his sin, she couldn't do less.

Judith moistened her lips. "Actually, Tom, I think you're off the hook this time. I'm standing behind the counter here because I'm not sure you're entirely safe. I seem to have a few wayward thoughts of my own. I'm totally sorry."

He lifted his head, his eyes meeting hers. "You don't have to take the blame, Judith."

"I'm being honest. Believe me, if it wasn't the truth, I would never say it."

A slow smile pulled at Stefan's mouth even as his body

went so rock hard he was afraid he would burst. A strange roaring began in his head. The thunder of his heart was loud enough to wake the dead. He didn't want to think too much about the real reason such elation swept through him. Doing a job meant getting it done, not necessarily being happy in the doing of it. He didn't have emotions swaying him one way or the other—or making him vulnerable.

He shouldn't give a damn that Judith Henderson thought she was having the exact same erotic fantasy about him as he was about her. He shouldn't care that she was attracted to him other than to make his job easier. He shouldn't be in danger of drowning in her amazing eyes. He was in her presence an hour and he was fucking up big time.

"Are you still willing to take me for a tractor ride on your farm tomorrow?" He had to give her the out. Thomas Vincent was a decent man, and in keeping with his reticence with women, Stefan had no choice. If it was left to him, the counter wouldn't save her. Nothing would save her—or him.

"Of course. I can't very well condemn you when I was being just as bad. We'll just agree to behave ourselves." She offered him a faint, hopeful smile.

Oh yeah. She believed the Thomas Vincent act, or else she'd be much more alarmed. He could read the wariness in her eyes, but the fact that he was keeping his distance and so careful to take the blame for a healthy male's thoughts was a good sign. She was a little bit flattered as well. He averted his eyes, not for Thomas, but because she was so damned beautiful, so bright and innocent, he was choking on his own deception. Not once in his life had he felt shame for misleading another person, but Judith, with her willingness to confess an embarrassing moment to a complete stranger, with that profound sorrow weighing her down that she kept so carefully hidden from the rest of the world, made him feel unworthy.

"I think that's a good idea," Stefan agreed. "If you don't mind, I'll keep my mind on the books for a little while."

Resolutely, Thomas Vincent turned his attention to the books lying open on the desk while Stefan Prakenskii centered his attention on his surroundings and the woman.

The front of the gallery was all tinted glass, allowing a magnificent view of the turbulent ocean, while still protecting the paintings and sculpture from the sun. It would be difficult, but not impossible to see inside during the day. With the lights on at night, it would be easy. The office was protected and there were obvious exits, four of them. It led into the back workroom, which provided even more cover as well as another exit.

He winced a little as Judith moved in front of the bank of windows, the lights exposing her exact position to anyone watching. He had to push down the desire to call her to him on some pretext, just to get her out from in front of those windows. She wasn't in danger—yet—but she would be if Ivanov was close by. The man had no regard for life. He was a pure sociopath, and he loved his job. He lived for the killing of others. Stefan had long ago come to the conclusion that the man killed for enjoyment, not for duty. He wouldn't see Judith's brightness or her innocence and if he did, it wouldn't matter. It might only add to his pleasure of taking her life.

Stefan sighed. Before setting up a meeting with Frank Warner, he had slipped into Sea Haven a couple of weeks earlier and spent time there setting up for his mission. He had already walked through the village numerous times, familiarizing himself with every street and alley, every conceivable hiding place and escape route. He'd driven the highway again and again, investigating the side roads that led away from the sea until he knew he could run them in the dark at high speeds. He'd set up several escape routes and already secured a storage facility where he kept money and passports in various names.

Petr Ivanov would come, if he hadn't already. Stefan knew he'd been set up. One didn't use his talents to babysit an old girlfriend on the unlikely chance that a prisoner the secret branch of the government was breaking out of a prison would elude the very agents helping him escape. That made no sense. His being in Sea Haven wasn't about Judith Henderson or Jean-Claude La Roux—it was about finding Lev Prakenskii and eliminating him. And his handler would know Ivanov would have to kill him too. They couldn't leave Stefan alive.

He rubbed his temples. Why had they decided to retire a couple of their best operatives? Was there a purge going on for a reason? Had some reporter uncovered the truth about the "orphanages" that had really been schools to train agents and assassins. In the new government, with the alliances that had been formed, it might not be in the best interests of the country to have those schools discovered.

"Headache?" Judith asked sympathetically. "I've got aspirin in the medicine cabinet."

She'd been watching him just as closely as he'd been observing her.

"I think I'll call it a night if you don't mind. Too much traveling and not enough sleep." It would give him another excuse to see her again after the tractor ride.

"Of course I don't mind." Judith was as agreeable as he knew she'd be. He was a master manipulator, trained in the best schools, every lesson a life or death one. He had survived and someone like Judith had no chance against him. He tasted bitterness in his mouth and kept his eyes averted as she locked up the safe.

4

THE moment Stefan stepped outside the gallery into the coolness of the night, he knew he was in the biggest trouble of his life. Maybe in for the biggest fight *for* his life. It wasn't the sniper who had him in the crosshairs, or the itch on the back of his neck that told him the assassin was definitely in the small village of Sea Haven. He was an operative, trained practically from birth to use people, surroundings, anything and everything as tools—yet instinctively, without thought, he put himself between Judith Henderson and a sniper's bullet, instead of using her body to shield his.

Everything in him froze. What the hell had he just done? What was wrong with him? His actions didn't make sense. He stood, completely exposed, his body blanketing hers, the scent of her enveloping him. The wind tugged at her hair and strands blew back at him to slide temptingly over his skin. He was astounded at his actions, shocked, horrified even, but his feet wouldn't move. One shift and he would be on the far side, placing her body between his and the water tower where he was certain Petr Ivanov lay up there with a rifle and scope. Petr was there—Stefan felt him. Felt the slick wash of menace that always alerted him, one of many psychic gifts. Still, he didn't move. Where the hell was his ingrained sense of self-preservation? Years of survival training? All his expertise?

Warning bells went off like miniature explosions in his mind. His left palm itched so badly he rubbed it along his thigh. He remained where he was, as if his feet had grown roots. His heart pounded and he tasted passion in his mouth, a fruit he'd never known but recognized instantly. Judith. She filled up all the emptiness in him. Somehow in the small space of time he'd spent with her, she'd poured herself into him and brought him something he never imagined: hope. She represented life. Living.

He was aware of people moving up the walkway to their right, from the direction of the tower. He might be able to use the small crowd as a shield, work his way around to get behind Ivanov. If he could, he would track Ivanov back to his lair and kill him. The disposal of his body would be easy enough and that would give him time to find his brother without fear of exposing him to an exterminator.

Right now, the most imperative thing in his world was to protect Judith. He kept his body between the sniper and Judith. His mind demanded to know what the hell he was doing, but his body remained firmly in place.

He doubted if Ivanov would take the shot even if he had it. It was too soon. The assassin wanted Lev. His brother had disappeared here, presumed dead, and Petr Ivanov wasn't buying it. His plan was to kill both Prakenskii brothers, not just Stefan. So he wouldn't shoot, but just in case, Stefan's sense of self-preservation should have forced him to move. It was impossible to though, and the terrible itch on the back of his neck grew.

Damn the woman. What in the hell was taking so long? "Do you need help?" he offered politely, staying in the role of Thomas Vincent.

"The lock seems to be stuck."

Judith glanced over her shoulder at him, and his heart nearly stopped. There was something incredibly alluring about her face with that fall of silky hair across it. Her gaze drifted over him and for a moment time seemed to stand still. He wasn't the only one tasting passion in his mouth, it was there, in her eyes. He had caught glimpses of fire in her earlier paintings and he hadn't been wrong. No matter how cool and controlled she acted, the fire was there seething beneath the surface, ready for the right man to bring out.

He pulled back from his thoughts very sharply. What right man? He was nobody's right man. He lived in another world, far from this one, and he had no right thinking a woman like Judith Henderson could be his. Not even in his imagination—yet he didn't move, not an inch.

"Let me try." He didn't wait for her to step aside, but reached around her with both arms, trapping her between the door and his body, careful to keep her hidden from Ivanov's scope while he took the key from her hand.

His fingers brushed hers. A jolt blazed through his body, the force of it shaking him. She was more frightening than any enemy he'd ever stalked and killed. She moved him when nothing ever had. A captive in the circle of his arms, she went very still, but he felt every breath she took. Heat rushed through his veins and settled like a fireball in his groin. He had used sex as an effective weapon, a perfect tool, extracting information, controlling his body, allowing an erection when needed, sustaining it for as long as it took, but he couldn't remember a time when his body responded to a woman in the way it was doing now, almost as if it had a mind of its own.

The strange and very unique phenomenon was both shocking and exhilarating. He'd never been on a roller coaster, but he felt almost as if he was on one now—thrown this way and that, off balance, all over the place, nearly incapable of breathing. His lungs felt starved for air. He was aware of everything about her, strands of her hair, the length of her lashes, her parted lips, the rise and fall of her breasts even as he pushed the key into the dead bolt and wiggled repeatedly to get the lock to fall into place.

"I have to tell you, Judith," he confessed, half Stefan and half Thomas, "it's getting harder and harder to breathe."

He expected her to push him away. Anything to save herself—or him. Maybe she didn't realize the danger she was in and it had nothing whatsoever to do with a sniper's bullet.

"I noticed that. My lungs are burning too."

He groaned. Her honesty was going to kill him. He wasn't an honest man. He didn't even know now if he was deliberately manipulating her, which he was entirely capable of. He had no idea who he was anymore. Judith seemed so out of his league, everything that he was not and could never be. She was genuine. Soft. Compassionate. He could see it so easily in her.

He was all hard edges and shadows. He had no idea of the kind of world she lived in. His was violent and ugly. There was no laughter and no honesty. The lock clicked with a hard thud and he had no reason to keep her caged. But he didn't move his body away from hers as he handed the key back.

"I'm not good with women." That was a blatant lie. He manipulated women without trying. Thomas Vincent might not be good with women, but Stefan used sex as a weapon, seducing a woman into giving him anything he wanted. *Everything* he wanted. He had been trained and had complete control of his body—until Judith.

He certainly shouldn't be having trouble controlling a massive—and painful—hard-on just because he was inhaling her unique scent deep into his lungs. Or touching all that silky hair.

"I'm not all that good with men either," she confided.

His gaze captured hers and held her there. In the intimacy of the night, Stefan felt as if the world had turned upside down. There was more power in Sea Haven than he realized—or more power in this woman. He had come prepared for warfare, but not for this slow seduction of every one of his senses. He didn't feel. He wasn't permitted to feel and yet, with his body a breath from Judith's, he was more alive than he'd ever been.

He pushed the key into her hand and checked the door before slowly, almost reluctantly straightening. He couldn't quite move away from her, and never once did he take his gaze from hers. Stefan placed one hand carefully above and to the side of her head, leaning that inch or two closer until her breasts were a heartbeat from his chest.

"Never in my life, has this ever happened to me." She couldn't fail to hear the honesty in his voice. It was the stark truth. "I don't even know what the hell is happening." That was definitely Stefan Prakenskii and he winced. It was an accusation. A snarl. A demand for the truth—worse, stepping out of his role as bashful Thomas.

Was she an agent, just so damned good that he had no chance against her? Had she duped Jean-Claude just as easily? He'd witnessed Jean-Claude's obsession with her firsthand and yet he still found himself caught in the snare.

She reached up, hand trembling, her fingers nearly brushing his face before she stopped herself. "I don't know what's happening, Thomas. Whatever it is, it can't happen. I wouldn't do that to you."

Her statement was as honest as his. She thought herself the one in the shadows. She was hiding behind that sweet demeanor, holding the real Judith still, frozen, a prisoner behind a wall she refused to take down. *She was afraid of herself, of who she really was.* He saw her, where he knew others would never conceive of the smoldering fire buried deep. The fire and something else—lethal power that reached out for the matching dangerous power in him.

She was afraid—for him. She was afraid of herself. And

that told him so much more than anything she might have admitted aloud. She held great power and was unused to wielding it. So what was it? What could she fear?

"We'll be okay, Judith," he assured, the compulsion to be that man for her, the one man she could tell the truth to without fear. He needed to be the man to free her from that clawing fear she held so tight inside of her. He'd never had the need to protect anyone or save anyone. What was it about her that got to him?

She shook and ducked her head, but not before he caught the sudden terror in her eyes. She looked away only a moment and then she was back, but he had already seen the real Judith.

Her shoulders straightened, her chin went up, and her eyes met his courageously. "I'm not a good woman, Thomas. Whatever this thing is between us, you have to know it can't go anywhere. It *won't* go anywhere. You seem like a decent man. I'll work with you if you really are interested in purchasing the gallery, and I'm willing to show you around, but you have to know that's all it can ever be."

He was fiercely attracted to her physically. Drawn to her psychic power—whatever that was—but now something else crept in and made being in her company all the more dangerous. And all the more necessary. Admiration. Respect. And he was drowning in the need to be a better man. The kind of hero who rode on white horses and rescued beautiful women with sorrow-filled eyes.

Sadly, Stefan Prakenskii was no such man. He was the kind of man who deceived women, targeted them, used them as tools of his trade and cast them aside without much thought. He didn't even reside in the same world a woman like Judith lived in. She might think she wasn't a good woman, but she'd shown her vulnerability to him and a man like Stefan leapt at that opening. Took it and used it.

He didn't worry that Petr Ivanov would show undue interest in Judith, because he would believe Stefan was cementing his cover story by using a woman. Women were such easy targets, so vulnerable to a man preying on them—a man such as Stefan. He could read his quarry, every expression, the body language, and he was practiced and smooth at knowing exactly the right thing to say. Ivanov would expect him to use a local woman to insert himself into village life.

"I understand. I don't know what it is between us, Judith," he said, his left palm itching until he couldn't help but run it down his thigh before he made a fool of himself and cupped her breasts right through all that tempting red silk. Even with her declaration—or maybe because of it—he had an urgent desire to lean that scant few inches that separated them to taste her mouth.

"I don't expect anything to happen, but I won't believe that you're not a good woman. I have a sixth sense about these things." That might be something Thomas Vincent would say. Stefan Prakenskii would have taken what he wanted—and he wanted Judith. The wanting was turning into something very dangerous.

Abruptly he dropped his arm and stepped back. He refused to be ensnared. Whatever small part that was left of his humanity was not going to be stripped from him. He forced himself back into the role of bashful Thomas, knowing that man was far safer for both of them.

Judith Henderson was forcing him to evaluate his life, to reassess what he wanted. He'd been all over the world and on some level, without realizing, he'd been searching for something to give meaning to life. He was a machine residing in the shadows and now, looking at her, he realized there was a glimmer of hope still left in him. His trainers hadn't quite stamped out every bit of him. There was that tiny spark left. A glowing ember, no more, but it was there, hidden from sight, but still valiantly smoldering.

"I'll walk you to your car." It was necessary to establish that Thomas Vincent was a man who would walk a woman to a car, or to her front door, looking out for her safety. That would allow Stefan to give her some protection against Ivanov, and, if he were honest with himself, spend a little more time in her company.

"It isn't necessary, although it's kind of you. Sea Haven isn't exactly a high crime area."

"I'll walk you to your car," he affirmed, uncaring if he sounded like Stefan instead of Thomas. She wasn't walking down the street with a bullet just seconds from striking her. "Where is it?"

"I'm parked just down the street a few stores down to the left."

Of course she'd parked there. The tower where Ivanov was holed up was in that same direction. Stefan sent up a silent prayer to a God he had no faith or trust in, that he was judging the situation accurately and Ivanov wouldn't pull the trigger and kill him right then. He walked beside Judith, his eyes, out of habit, moving restlessly over the rooftops and delving into the all the little courtyards tucked into the sides of the buildings, leading to more intriguing shops.

He was careful to keep his hands free as he moved along the street. Every few seconds his eyes tracked backed to the tower and the surrounding rooftops. It was a habit and if Ivanov was watching him closely through the nightscope, he would expect that behavior.

A wooden bench sat just back from the buildings in a small courtyard leading to more shops. A homeless man sat hunched against the building, ignoring the bench. He simply watched the ocean as it sprayed white foam high into the air, crashing against the cliffs.

The small crowd of wine tasters seemed to be congregated around the door of a shop several businesses down, all talking at once and laughing, drowning out any real chance of catching sounds that would help him locate Ivanov's exact position. There was no doubt in his mind now; his body's radar confirmed to him that he was being tracked with a weapon. The enemy was out there and watching him.

He turned his head toward Judith, bending slightly down, smiling, listening to her even as he noted every possible cover between where they were and her car. Self-preservation was automatic to him, so ingrained in him, he would always know every license plate in his general vicinity, buildings and landscape, the natural flow of his surroundings. He was a chameleon, blending in, a snake shedding one skin and growing another easily—a shadow with no substance.

They were approaching the homeless man. The man had one hand inside his jacket where he easily could be concealing a weapon. Stefan allowed his gaze to sweep the man, noting every detail. He had seen him around the village every day for the last two weeks as he'd scouted the place, and had spoken to him many times. The street people often were aware of any stranger in town and cultivating a good relationship often proved useful. Impersonating one of the homeless was an easy enough cover as well. Ivanov might certainly use such a cover, which was why Stefan had acquainted himself with every homeless person in the small village.

He kept to the far side of the street, something he ordinarily would never have done. Each step was a single heartbeat. He was on high alert now. If he was wrong about Ivanov being in the tower, or on a rooftop, impersonating the homeless would get him close to his target. His knife was up his sleeve and he could make the throw before Ivanov could get off a shot. The homeless man smelled the same and looked the same, but a pro would be able to pull that off.

"Just a moment, Thomas." Judith touched his arm as they approached the small courtyard.

Her touch was barely there, but he felt warmth penetrating at that gentle brush of her fingers, distracting his full concentration—and he couldn't have that. He'd never experienced such a thing before. No matter what was going on around him, no matter who he was with, his life was all about the hunt and surviving.

Stefan didn't know whether to drag her into the next alley, slam her up against the wall and kiss her until she was every bit as senseless as he seemed to be, or to be done with it, grab her head in his hands and wrench hard enough to break her neck. Instinctively he dropped back a pace behind, just enough to put him into position. His stomach knotted. The vise was back, squeezing his heart until his chest ached. That thought brought him up short. Just how deep had he fallen into her spell to be so damned desperate? Every survival instinct screamed at him to get out while he still could.

"This will only take a minute," Judith continued, oblivious that her life hung by a mere thread.

Inwardly he cursed his inability to overcome who and what he was—even with an innocent. And he was becoming convinced she was innocent. He had radar for the enemy, man or woman, and it had never once let him down. She wasn't as she portrayed herself to the world, there was too much emotion bottled up in her, held back away from the world. He saw it there, smoldering deep below the surface. Damn it all, she had him twisted up inside, a conflicted mess that a few hours earlier he would never have believed could happen.

She bent low to speak to the man on the ground. "Are you warm enough, Bill?"

He nodded. "Blythe brought me socks and new boots." He pointed to his feet sticking out from under his blanket. "Been nice lately." His gaze shifted to Stefan, then darted away again. "Saw the devil today. He stood across the street, just there." He indicated the railing separating the street from the bluffs. "Devil had death in his eyes."

Judith frowned. "I don't know what that means."

"Like this one." Bill indicated Stefan. "Death in his eyes."

Judith looked up at Stefan a little helplessly and shook her head as if apologizing for the accusation. That little observation told Stefan more than he'd learned in two weeks about the old man. He was most likely gifted, probably was the reason he'd been attracted to Sea Haven and at one time, he'd been a soldier of sorts, probably serving in the Vietnam War.

"Bill, do you want me to take you to the clinic?"

Stefan knew she thought the old man was ill, but Bill had no doubt seen Petr Ivanov with his dead eyes and recognized a sociopath. The exterminator could easily be identified as the devil carrying death with him. He didn't want to think too closely about what this man had seen in his own eyes.

Bill shook his head, shrinking back as if the idea of a clinic was far worse than facing the devil, and maybe for him it was.

"Have you eaten today?"

Bill nodded. "Still got credits at the store and coffee-house."

Judith smiled at him. "Have a nice evening, Bill."

"You too, Miss Judith," the old man mumbled.

It was obvious to Stefan that Bill felt genuine affection for Judith. It had taken a concentrated effort over time to get the old man to even speak with him briefly, exchanging only pleasantries. The occasional hot coffee and pastry hadn't been enough to loosen his tongue.

"I'm sorry for what he said about you," Judith said. "He gets confused sometimes. He's been on the street for years. Everyone contributes, even the high school students. They put money on a tab for him at the local stores. He won't take much in the way of help, though. He has several places

he sleeps and won't go to a shelter, not like we have anything like a shelter around here." She sighed. "There isn't a
lot of help for the mentally ill."

"He doesn't want help," Stefan replied honestly. "He's
free. He lives the way he wants to live."

She fell silent for a moment, walking a few steps before
she looked at him again. "Do you think so? He's been
around for as long as I've been here, and Inez says for
twenty years before that. He actually went to school here
and then left for a while. When he came back . . ." She
shrugged.

"He has the right to choose. He fought for that right and
he's entitled to do what he wants. If he chooses to sit in the
sun for two days without moving, he feels that's his right."

Judith swept her hair over her shoulder, her eyes meeting
his. Once again he experienced that strange, unsettling reaction in the pit of his stomach.

"I never thought of it that way. I always think he's sad
and I feel bad, wishing I could find a way to make his life
better."

Stefan couldn't help himself, his hand slipped to the
small of her back in a gesture that would be natural to anyone but him. His left hand. The one with the itching palm.
The moment he touched her, the itch subsided. But the fact
remained he had no business tying up one of his weapons.
He didn't touch people and they didn't touch him. The ir-
rational compulsion irritated him. He didn't do things that
could get him killed.

He clenched his teeth but didn't deny himself the contact
with her. This was a nightmare. She'd sounded so forlorn.
Lost. In need. What the hell was he thinking? If anyone
was in need, it would be him. He'd lost his soul a long time
ago, shed everything human and yet here he was, thinking
he was going to be that man. The one to take that note out
of her voice and remove the sorrow from her eyes. The man

who would provide a shield for her so that she was never afraid to express any emotion she felt.

He wanted to be the man who gave her freedom—the man she turned to in the middle of the night. The one who had the right to touch her, to hold her, to keep her safe. He would kiss that look off her face and make love to her until she couldn't move, only look at him with her glorious eyes and be genuinely happy, not pretending, or finding moments, just little pockets of happiness. He would be that man for her.

He swore under his breath as they continued down the street. She hadn't moved away from him, nor had she given him a look of censure. Just where the hell was her sense of self-preservation?

"You're not doing a very good job of saving us," he accused.

Those dark eyes drifted over him and then her long lashes swept down. "I know," she admitted in a low tone. "I'm pretending. Just this once."

His heart leapt. She didn't have to explain what she meant. He was pretending too. He swept his hand down that waterfall of silk. It was a long way down, all the way to the curve of her buttocks. Blood pounded and roared in his ears. Heat rushed through his veins. He had an almost overpowering urge to bunch that hair in his fist and drag her head around so he could taste the passion in her mouth. He *felt* the fire in her rising to meet the firestorm blazing through his body.

Never in his life, until Judith, had he had a natural physical reaction to a woman. He had thought it impossible. It was both exhilarating and terrifying to be so out of control. For once in his life, he felt like a man instead of a machine. Judith had given him that. He would always have these moments with her if he could allow himself to embrace the feeling.

They were only a few steps away from the crowd. Already a couple of people were turning toward them, noticing Judith and waving a cheery hello. He had seconds to savor the fact that he'd found the answers to questions he'd always thrust into the back of his mind. He'd traveled around the world hunting and often stood outside the homes of people, looking at the lights, listening to the low murmur of voices, watching a woman bend her head toward a child and wondered what it would be like to feel that depth of emotion, if only for a moment, for another human being. With all the silky hair burning like fire through the center of his palm, he'd found what he was looking for.

As they came up to the edge of the crowd, he dropped his hand, giving himself enough room to use any of the many weapons concealed on his person. He was Thomas Vincent and these were the people who would be his neighbors if he bought the gallery—if he settled in Sea Haven and found a woman to spend the rest of his life with.

"Judith! We missed you, honey." A tall blonde greeted Judith with a kiss. Her gaze rested on Thomas, but more with polite interest than anything else.

"Thomas, this is my sister, Blythe Daniels," Judith introduced him. Her fingers brushed his arm, as if bringing him closer.

Blythe noticed that very small intimacy, even there in the dark, and that told Stefan she was someone to take great care around. He flashed a smile and took her hand when she held it out. There was the smallest current of energy, enough that his warning radar went off. There was more to Blythe than met the eye.

"Thomas is considering buying the gallery," Judith offered.

"Of course. It's beautiful. I've always loved that building and the view is spectacular," Blythe said.

"I have to agree." Stefan flashed another shy smile toward the blonde.

Stefan slipped into his role easily, more familiar with the chameleon than with Stefan Prakenskii who really didn't exist. Thomas Vincent might be interested in Judith Henderson, but he wasn't threatened by that interest. Thomas would be attracted to any number of women. He might be uncomfortable because he was a little shy where women were concerned, but he didn't mind contemplating a pleasant future.

Stefan Prakenskii knew he would go up in flames with Judith, burn alive and crave more—*need* more. His entire body and mind responded to her, killing his sense of self-preservation and destroying years and years of discipline and training. For him, there would only be this one woman. She was a virtual stranger, yet he knew her almost intimately already. He'd spent a lifetime traveling the world and not once had this incredible, impossible phenomenon happened to him, and he knew with utter certainty it wouldn't again.

"The building is worth a fortune," Thomas agreed readily. He turned, allowing his eyes to sweep the rooftops on a pretext of looking back at the property. "This is quite a town."

Behind Blythe, another older woman laughed as she held out her hand. "I think we're too small to qualify as a town. We refer to ourselves as a village. I'm Inez Nelson. It's a pleasure to meet you. The gallery is a very important part of Sea Haven."

For her small size, she had a firm handshake and penetrating eyes. She definitely was assessing him carefully.

"Thomas Vincent," he introduced himself.

"Don't let her sway you, Thomas," Judith warned. "She's Frank Warner's fiancée, so she has a vested interest."

"Did your wife come with you?" Inez asked blatantly fishing.

Blythe and Judith laughed aloud, clearly used to Inez interrogating people and taking no offense. Thomas wouldn't

either. He was a charming man. He widened his smile to a
boyish grin and shook his head.

"No wife, ma'am. It's just me."

Inez's eyes immediately lit up. "Oh, how nice. This is
the perfect place to raise a family."

"He'd need a wife for that, Inez," Blythe pointed out.

Inez smirked. "Exactly. I believe neither of you is married."

"That's it." Blythe took the wineglass from her hand.
"You're cut off. Thomas, please ignore her. Her tongue is
out of control tonight."

Inez looked unrepentant. "No more so than every night.
How else are we going to entice this handsome man to give
our little community a chance?"

"She should be the one showing you the books," Judith
said.

"I wouldn't mind hearing what she's offering." Stefan
entered into the game. "Do either of these two come with
the gallery? I could use a wife and children and so far, I've
failed miserably in that department."

"I might be able to arrange it," Inez agreed. Her voice
turned mock innocent. "Judith, would you care for a glass
of wine or two?"

Judith laughed. "You're incorrigible, Inez. On that note,
I'm going home."

She caught Stefan's arm and tugged. He saw the movement, knew she was going to reach for him and could have
avoided her touch as he normally would do, but he let her
fingers settle over his wrist. It felt a little as if she'd trapped
his heart in her hand.

"I'll be taking him to safety as well, so get moving onto
your next stop and quit trying to sell Frank's gallery using
foul means," Judith teased.

Stefan's mouth went dry at her touch. He took her fingers and tucked them into the crook of his arm, pretending
he was Thomas, when it was Stefan drawing her close be-

neath his shoulder, indulging his terrible need to be with this woman. The fire between them refused to go out, no matter how hard either of them pretended it wasn't burning hot and bright.

Worse, there was a chance that if it was simple physical attraction, they could have a fiery affair and be done with it, but somehow, the attraction went deeper, bone deep. Even that wasn't a good enough explanation for what seemed to be happening. As he walked with her, he realized it was that her spirit moved against his—maybe even absorbed his. However it had happened, this woman was forever written on his body, claiming him.

She turned her head and her gaze collided with his. A vise squeezed his heart hard at that look of longing he saw in her eyes. He wasn't alone feeling the strength and intensity of the pull.

"It's because we both have gifts," Judith whispered. "I've heard that can happen. The gifts complement each other or something."

She was courageous, he had to hand her that. There was no pretense. Judith might not show herself to the world, but she was honest with him when it mattered and he admired that. She could have remained silent.

He did the worst possible thing. He tied up his other hand by sliding it over the top of hers. He couldn't resist feeling her soft skin, couldn't resist the connection. For the first time in his life he wanted someone of his own to hold on to. Someone to *see* him. Someone to make him real and not the insubstantial shadow he knew he was. Not someone—Judith.

"You make it hard to breathe," she admitted, turning her head away from him to look at the ocean crashing along the cliffs.

"I thought you were doing that to me," Stefan said and moved his body more protectively in place to keep Ivanov from seeing her face too clearly if the scope was trained on her? That, too, was strictly the truth, not Thomas, but Stefan, his lungs burning for air.

Touching her was a miracle. Her skin seemed to melt into his. Ivanov would read nothing more into his gestures than a cementing of his cover, but Stefan didn't want the exterminator to get a good visual of her face. For the first time in his life, he felt genuinely protective of a woman.

"Has this ever happened to you before?" Stefan asked. Everything inside him stilled, waited for the answer. He knew Jean-Claude. He'd spent a couple of months locked up with that man and knew his obsession with Judith. He didn't want her to have responded to the man with the driving intensity he felt between them.

She shook her head. "Never. I don't have relationships. Once. But not like this. I was very young and . . . stupid. This is too fast, too encompassing and I don't trust it. You shouldn't either. We're going to be adults about this." Her eyes met his again. "Right?"

If Ivanov hadn't been watching them, he would have taken matters into his own hands and Thomas Vincent and his cover could be damned. She would have been up against the side of the nearest building, away from prying eyes, his mouth taking hers, his body hard and hot and unashamed with true desire. The real damn thing. Was that adult enough for her?

She inhaled sharply at the flare of heat in his eyes. He knew she could see that smoldering fire he couldn't hide from her.

"Right?" she whispered again.

He wanted to reassure her, but she'd been courageous enough to be honest with him and he could do no less. "I'll try for you, Judith, but in all honesty, I've never had this feeling for any woman."

She might believe it of Thomas, but not of Stefan. There was no Stefan. He wasn't real, that man who seduced women out of their secrets and left their lives in ruins. No

matter that the women were spies, or working for criminals, there was nothing easier for him, and yet now, he had
no idea what to do with her.

He wanted to run away with her and never look back at
his past, shed the assassin and become her hero, the man
who would fill her nights and days with nothing but happiness. Who the hell was he kidding? He didn't know what
happiness was until he'd walked down a dark street with a
woman who was virtually a stranger.

"I can be that man," he said aloud. The words slipped
out before he could stop them.

For a moment her eyes went liquid. "I know you can,"
she whispered. "But I can't be that woman, Thomas. I want
to be, but I can't."

He heard the regret, the pain, in her soft murmur and his
heart did a hard somersault. She was killing him as surely
as Ivanov's bullet would. *Thomas.* He detested Thomas.
His biggest rival. The man would destroy any chance at all
he had with the one woman who counted in his world.

"We'll see," he said, uncaring that she heard him. It was
a warning and he meant it.

Walking along the wooden sidewalk with the wind blowing a fine mist across his face, and Judith's hand tucked into
the crook of his arm, he had the strangest feeling of peace.
He allowed himself to indulge in fantasy for that last few
feet before reaching her car.

"This is mine," she announced, putting her hand on the
hood of her Mini Cooper. She sounded as regretful as he
felt.

Stefan stepped in front of her, effectively preventing her
from walking around to the driver's side. "I'm coming out
to your farm tomorrow to drive the tractor and I'm bringing
lunch."

She took a breath and pushed at the hair blowing over
her shoulder into her face. "You know that could get us into
trouble, don't you?"

He nodded slowly. "I'll keep you safe."

She took a breath and nodded. "All right then. I'm counting on you."

His first step toward being that man and he already knew he was going to blow it. If the street hadn't been filled with her friends and Ivanov hadn't been lying in wait up in a tower, he would be kissing her senseless.

Stefan forced himself out of her way, almost afraid to let her go, fearing she would slip away. Truthfully, he was even more afraid of himself—that the shadow man would come to his senses and simply disappear into thin air, leaving only Thomas behind.

He went with Judith into the street, and opened the car door for her. She stood for a moment just looking at him and he realized she was every bit as afraid for their moment to end as he was.

"Thank you for a strange but rather wonderful evening, Thomas," Judith said and slipped into the car.

"You're very welcome," he said as he closed her door and patted it before giving her a friendly wave and walking back to the wooden sidewalk, taking danger with him.

5

Stefan stood on the edge of the sidewalk watching until Judith's car was safely down the street, lights disappearing as she rounded a corner before he turned back toward the gallery. He let his gaze sweep the rooftops without lifting his head. In the darkness, it would be impossible to spot Petr Ivanov. The exterminator didn't make mistakes. He also wasn't much of a long distant assassin. He liked up-close work, rather than a rifle.

Keeping his steps unhurried and measured, shoulders straight, Stefan strolled down the main street, checking out the various storefronts of the shops he passed, as if he were simply acquiring knowledge of Sea Haven's community. The ocean rolled and sprayed across from him, the windows of the stores reflecting the shimmering moon as it emerged from behind a veil of clouds. His years of experience gave him the discipline needed to take his time, to maintain an even pace.

If Stefan didn't believe his brother was dead, then neither did Petr. Ivanov had written the report on Lev's death in an effort to make everyone believe the hunt for Lev was over. The exterminator had lost the trail here in Sea Haven. Stefan was certain now he was nothing more than bait for the assassin to finish the job.

The water tower was a little over three stories high, which gave Ivanov a good view of the street, the stores and rooftops on two streets. The double row of stores, one facing the main street and ocean and the other facing the next street over, was nearly all in plain view of anyone lying up on the floor of the water tower with a sniper's rifle. There were only a few places hidden from his sight and Stefan's body itched to get to one of them quickly, but he forced himself to keep to his casual saunter. He strolled, carefully studying each building as Ivanov would expect him to do.

Between the water tower, where Judith had parked her car and Stefan's ultimate goal, there were three stores and his gallery. *His.* That brought him up short. He had to be solidly in character to think that. He pushed the stray thought aside and continued with his hunt.

The one smaller building, a wine shop, had a flat roof, but the others were sloped, or steeply pitched, as were most of the buildings on the main street. They were close together, providing another route through the town. Deliberately he slowed his steps, not wanting to reach his goal until the small crowd of people had completely enclosed themselves in the wine shop. Music and laughter poured into the street, the people unknowing of the two dangerous men hunting each other on their quiet streets.

The narrow alley leading back to the second row of shops was just past the gallery, just ahead. Once inside that space the gallery would shield him from view and Ivanov would have to shift position to keep him in sight. The mouse would become the hunter of the cat. Stefan just needed a couple more minutes—a few more steps.

He let out his breath slowly, evenly. No hurrying. Just strolling through town, getting acquainted with the layout. Three more unhurried steps and he turned into the small courtyard beside the gallery, leading to the shops behind the main street, the one blindside the assassin had. He sprinted behind the gallery, knowing Ivanov wouldn't panic for a few minutes, assuming he was exploring and would reappear soon. The back porches were small and stone steps led through gardens of flowers and green plants.

Immediately he sprinted through the brush and flowers, racing around the gallery between the two rows of buildings, staying in the shelter of the back porches' overhang, coming up behind the corner structure. The tower was in his sight now and he crouched low, going completely motionless— waiting with all the patience of a great jungle cat.

Thomas Vincent was gone, and in his place, Stefan Prakenskii became what he was: a hunter. And he *was* hunting, totally in his element. He completely shed his brilliant-but-bashful businessman persona and moved quickly to turn the tables on the assassin. He felt his lungs expand and something stealthy and feral unwound in the coil of knots in his belly.

The minutes ticked by, one slow second at a time. The sky darkened again as the clouds moved swiftly, obliterating the light from the moon. Even with the expanse of ocean surface, the darkness went from gray to inky. The wind built to a howl and then subsided, gusting off the sea in a fit of temper.

Stefan's gaze continually swept the rooftops, looking for all the places a sniper could hide with a full view of the main street of town, but always came back to the tower. There were several water towers in town, many had been converted to be used for other purposes, but the one on the main street gave the best view of the streets and buildings. There were only a few blind spots and Stefan crouched in one of them. He was absolutely positive that Ivanov was in that tower.

Minutes ticked by. This was definitely a waiting game and few were better at it than Stefan. His breath slowed, his heart, his body calm and coiled, just waiting. Killing Ivanov could cause a few problems down the road, but it would keep Lev safe, and possibly Ilya—at least until the brothers had time to regroup and get the message out to the others to expect a possible purge. Banded together, the Prakenskii brothers would make a terrifying enemy and anyone coming after them would know it.

The sky grew darker still as another gust of wind scattered roiling black clouds over the few remaining stars. Something moved against that dark sky. A figure slid down the ladder from the top of the tower to the second story, a rapid descent, and stepped quickly into the shadow of the circular tank where Stefan lost sight of him for just a moment. In that split second, Stefan realized Ivanov's instincts had kicked in and he knew the tables had turned—that Stefan was aware of his presence and was now hunting him.

At once he was up, leaping onto the fence surrounding the back of the building and running along it, careful to keep from tripping on the posts sticking up. The two-by-four was a slim runway in the dark. The wind sent another ferocious gust, dropping swirling leaves from the trees over his head and shoulders and he jumped to the slanted roof of the building connected to the fence. The structure was large with multileveled roofs. He landed on the lower one and nearly slipped on the slick buildup of green moss from the constant fog and mist coming off the ocean. Evidently the sun failed to reach this section of roof, making footing difficult.

On the roof above him, Stefan heard the quick running of footsteps. The pitch on the higher roof was steeper, but Ivanov crossed it like a cat, with great long strides, well ahead of him, already leaping to the roof of the long, narrow, two-story gift shop. Stefan caught a glimpse of the assassin as he streaked over that surface.

Stefan raced across the moss-covered roof and launched himself onto the next building. The roof had a good pitch, and he couldn't follow Ivanov's exact line from the angle he'd started and gain ground, so he was forced to run along the more sloped edge, requiring balance, although if his quarry thought that would slow him down, he was wrong. He streaked across the lower end of the roof in pursuit of Ivanov and launched himself over the small alleyway where the homeless man had wrapped himself in a blanket in preparation for a cold night.

Stefan landed lightly onto the roof of the wine shop, trying to be as silent as a cat, although he doubted if, with the noise emanating from the shop from the small crowd, anyone would hear the chase. The last thing he wanted were witnesses such as Old Bill. Thomas Vincent would not be chasing killers over rooftops. He took four running steps and felt fire slicing along his cheek while an angry bee buzzed in his ear. He dropped flat and rolled toward the edge of the roof, grateful Ivanov's expertise was not in long-distance killing—or shooting on the run. The assassin could shoot, but he wasn't known for his skill on the run while all the Prakenskii brothers had that gift.

Stefan slipped over the edge as the second shot kicked up a tile next to his shoulder. Fragments rained down on his face. Holding the weight of his body by his fingertips, he counted to ten and pulled himself back up. Ivanov would fear he would drop to the ground and follow his escape route from there. Clearly the exterminator had prepared for every possible scenario. They'd all been taught to do that so many years ago, back in the schools they'd attended, the ones shaping them into monsters.

Stefan would have to be careful. Ivanov had made this run before, setting up his escape over the rooftops. He had probably practiced this exact route in the dead of night repeatedly—and he was armed with a silencer, which wasn't unexpected. But the shots were. Ivanov wanted to get away, not draw more attention to himself. He wouldn't want to give up on the idea of killing Lev, if that was why he'd come. Ivanov was nothing if not tenacious.

The wine shop was a compact square and it was filled to capacity even with such a small group, the sounds bursting through windows and doors. It was difficult to hear the whisper of steps running over the roof with the noise coming from the crowded building. With great stealth, Stefan pulled himself up so that just his eyes were looking out over the roof. Ivanov appeared to have abandoned the rooftop, but just to be on the safe side, Stefan remained cautious as he pulled himself up. When no shot came, he was up and running, keeping low as he did so, building momentum to jump to the next rooftop.

Stefan raced up the side of the art gallery roof, angling to cover as much ground as possible and yet position himself directly behind Ivanov, fighting the wind every step of the way. The exterminator had already managed to make it down the other side and was making the leap to a smaller gallery that sold hand carved furniture. The building was single story with a normal roof, but it was set well back from the street. That gave Stefan the chance to make up a little time as he was already on the lower side of the roof and he gained a few steps, leaping onto that roof as Ivanov jumped to the next long building, a woodworking gallery.

Rather than run straight, Ivanov angled back toward the street again, toward the front of the building, and then disappeared down the other side of the roof. That action warned Stefan that the killer had a plan. He didn't slow his pace, but heightened his awareness as he ran, puzzling over the route, trying to get ahead of the assassin in his mind to figure out what he had in store.

Below him was the main street of the town. Across the pavement the ocean pounded at the cliffs, dark water throwing spray high into the air. The wind slammed into him as he raced over another gallery, this one two stories with multilevel roof lines so that he had only brief glimpses of Ivanov who had managed to gain the roof of the bar.

Instant awareness hit him. A neon sign had been flashing two nights earlier when Stefan had checked the streets so carefully. The beckoning light pulsed red and blue in the night sky, but it was now unlit, leaving the overhung balcony roof dark and silent. He changed his angle as he jumped the distance between the two buildings, landing on the sloped roof rather than that tempting flat upper deck.

Ivanov was two buildings ahead, running up the third-story roof of the Sea Haven Hotel. Stefan had to keep him in sight at all times. If the exterminator was allowed to lengthen that distance between them, the odds of his getting away went way up. Stefan was totally exposed to the increasing strength of the wind as he ran across the next building, a larger store that sold clothes and an assortment of high-end gifts. The building was quite large and by the time he'd crossed the roof, Ivanov had disappeared on the other side of the hotel's roof.

Cursing, Stefan raced up the very steep angle, the tiles slippery. Ivanov paused for a moment, glancing over his shoulder even as his feet angled three steps to the left. Stefan would have thrown his knife, but the angle was all wrong and in a flash, Ivanov went over the ridge to the other side of the hotel, disappearing from sight. Stefan put on a burst of speed, marking the exact spot Ivanov had used to go over the ridge of the hotel. He needed to follow that exact route, otherwise he could be in trouble. Why had Ivanov taken the time to move to his left when a straight line would have been faster?

Something grabbed at Stefan's ankle, biting deep, sweeping his leg out from under him. He went down hard and rolled immediately, knife in one hand, the other up to defend himself, his radar screaming a warning at him. A dark shadow launched itself at him, knife stabbing down. He caught Ivanov's wrist with one hand and drove toward the man's side with his own knife.

He heard Ivanov grunt as the blade penetrated through clothing to pierce the skin. Ivanov kicked him hard in the ribs and Stefan slipped backward on the steep slope. The exterminator took another swipe at him as Stefan tried to save himself from falling off the roof. The attack with the knife came in a figure eight, catching his forearm twice, nicking his jaw and slicing shallow cuts through skin as he fended the blade off with his arm. He lunged at Ivanov a second time, his own blade slicing across the assassin's stomach, driving him back and away. Stefan continued to slide backward even as he dug in his heels to slow his steady descent to the edge.

Jamming the blade of the knife hard into a tile, he gripped the handle and rolled over, getting his feet under him, all the while trying to keep Ivanov in sight. The tile splintered, the bottom half falling away to hit loudly on the gutter and fall farther to the ground below. Stefan whipped his head around, looking for the next attack from Ivanov, but just that fast, the exterminator was gone, running back up the hotel roof, timing his footsteps to avoid the trip wire he'd laid out probably days earlier for just such an opportunity as this.

Stefan gave chase, clearing the trip wire this time. He made it to the top where the roof peaked and stopped to look over the other side, cautious now that he had given Ivanov a few seconds to formulate another ambush. The roof of the next building was empty. His quarry had disappeared. He went still, listening. The waves slammed into the bluffs, crashing over rocks and sending white spray high into the air. The sound of music and laughter poured out of the bar, but there were no footsteps running over the rooftops. Another vicious cut of the wind whipped through his clothes. He ignored it all, his mind fully on his prey.

Stefan proceeded much more cautiously. Ivanov could be waiting anywhere just ahead to ambush him. He eased down the descending slope leading toward the next building, examining that rooftop, quartering every section with extreme care. He crouched down and touched two small spots on the tile, lifting his fingers to his nose. Blood. He was leaking a few drops, but this was definitely Petr Ivanov's blood. He let out his breath slowly. Chasing a wounded Ivanov was much like pursuing a wounded Grizzly, but he had no real choice. If Lev was to be safeguarded, Ivanov had to die.

The spots were in a diagonal pattern, leading across the roof, not straight to the next one. Ivanov could not possibly have made it over the peak before Stefan had done so on the hotel's roof without Stefan catching sight of him. That meant one thing . . .

Stefan examined the layout of the hotel roof. Toward the front of the building, a jutted outcropping overhung a small balcony, which several other rooms on the third floor had. If Ivanov had slipped into one of the rooms and back out on the other side, he could be anywhere, even coming up behind him. The urge to pursue was great, but self-preservation lent him caution.

He hunkered down again, studying the three windows. If he had been the one considering that he might be chased across the rooftops, he would rent the corner room, leave the window open and slide in, close it and go out through the downstairs and mix with the people, or go back out the window in the front and access the roof to come in behind any pursuer.

Swearing under his breath, Stefan crept back toward the peak of the roof, avoiding that beckoning balcony and the front of the building. He searched the street below. The wine shop was still filled to capacity but the street itself was empty and dark. Two kids made out behind the restrooms across the street, and Old Bill the homeless man moved restlessly in his small alcove between buildings, but otherwise no one moved.

Keeping low, he inched his way down the steep roof to peer onto the building between the hotel and bar. A flitting shadow moved, so small, at first Stefan thought it might be a cat, but he took a chance, suddenly running down the side to leap onto the building. The shadow stretched as it crossed to the bar, racing around to the front where the broken sign helped to hide the fleeing assassin.

Stefan jumped, flinging his body down onto the flat deck just above the bar, driving Ivanov to the floor. He hit hard, the distance a little too long, the angle steep, forcing the air from his lungs. He heard an ominous crack and Ivanov's breath rushed out in a hiss of pain even as Ivanov gripped his knife hand.

They rolled over and over, crashing into the broken sign, the metal and glass cutting into Stefan's back and shoulder, both men fighting to keep blades from piercing their bodies. They fought silently, fiercely, a ferocious life-or-death battle between two highly skilled warriors. Breaking apart, they both scrambled to their feet and circled each other in that same silence.

Stefan was a man of few words. He didn't need to bolster his courage with a lot of threats. His enemy's breath was slow and measured, but accompanied by a hiss of pain with each inhale, indicting a bone had fractured or actually broken. Ivanov was a deadly enemy, fast and skilled. One misstep and he was dead. The assassin didn't get angry, he simply killed. Three times his blade slashed across Stefan's wrist and forearm. The exterminator was marked up as well.

The sound of laughter spilled out of the wine shop, suddenly much louder. Ivanov rushed him, slapping his blade aside, forcing Stefan to catch the man's wrist. At the last moment he realized the assassin's intention, but it was too late. The momentum carried them both over the low railing so that they fell to the sidewalk below. Stefan landed under Ivanov, holding grimly to his wrist to prevent him from whipping the blade across his throat.

For a moment, Stefan couldn't move, almost paralyzed, desperate for air, his lungs burning, his body barely registering pain as it dispersed along every nerve ending. Ivanov slammed so hard into him, the force drove his body back into the sidewalk a second time, so that the world faded a little around the edges. He held firm on the wrist of his attacker, even as he attacked with his own knife, whipping past Ivanov's guard to streak the tip of the blade under his chin, carrying through with the sweep to slash his upraised arm.

Ivanov threw the blood from his weeping arm at Stefan's face, trying to hit his eyes and temporarily blind him, at the same time twisting his wrist in order to slide the blade against Stefan's skin. Stefan had no choice but to let go. Ivanov leapt back, whirled around and rushed away.

The door to the wine shop opened and people spilled into the street, calling to one another and laughing as they said their good-byes. Stefan rolled over, suppressed a groan and got to his feet. He slipped back into the shadows as quickly as his body would allow. Ivanov was hurt. At least one bone was broken and like Stefan, he'd suffered numerous cuts. Hopefully he'd hide in another of his holes licking his wounds and regrouping, allowing Stefan enough time to do his job, find his brother and hunt the assassin down.

"I'M so happy, Blythe."

Judith couldn't contain the sheer joy spilling out of her through every pore. She *felt*. Every single cell in her body was alive again, truly alive. She didn't understand how or why, but here in the privacy of her home, she could let herself be absolutely, utterly happy. She laughed aloud and threw herself onto her bed, sprawling, arms and legs out like a child making an angel in the snow.

"The house is glowing," Blythe observed. It was impossible not to feel Judith's happiness. Blythe laughed softly and sank down onto the end of the bed. "Literally glowing, Judith. I'd say tone it down, but I haven't *ever* seen you like this and it feels good."

"It's him. Thomas." Judith hugged a pillow to her stomach, her left hand smoothing over the cool Egyptian cotton.

"There's just something about him that reaches for something in me. He's so . . ." She trailed off and rolled over, looking at Blythe. "I don't even know how to explain him."

"You have stars in your eyes." Blythe pushed back the fall of Judith's hair and studied her face. "What happened between the two of you?"

Blythe couldn't help but be happy along with Judith, swept up in her joy. She wanted to be practical and caution Judith to go slow, to remember that Thomas was only thinking of buying the gallery and could be gone in a few days, but the happiness pulsating throughout the house was too contagious.

"Nothing." Judith sat up, unable to be still. "Everything. I wanted him. Not just wanted him, Blythe. I wanted to be inside his skin with him. I felt like Sleeping Beauty. He came along and woke me up and I don't even know how. I feel alive for the first time in years. I can't remember being happy, Blythe, not like this."

Blythe took a deep breath. Someone had to be reasonable. Practical. "Sweetie, you can't just blindly jump off a cliff. You know that, right?"

She might know it, but that was the biggest part of the problem. "I might be afraid—no, terrified—and yet . . . honestly *exhilarated*. It feels as if I've woken up after a long sleep." Her eyes met Blythe's. "I forgot how good it feels to be aroused by a man. To know he thinks I'm desirable and beautiful."

It had been so long. She'd been afraid she was permanently damaged as a woman, so scarred by her past that her mind and body refused to acknowledge men. So broken that no one could fix her. Yet, miraculously, she'd been attracted to Thomas Vincent. The real deal. A fierce, driving passion that had come out of nowhere and was so overpowering it had driven all sense out of her head so that elation was alive in her. There was no containing the intensity of the emotion, no reining it in. She could breathe all she wanted and no way was it going to help. She didn't want to rein it in. She wanted to feel . . . *everything.*

"Most men find you desirable and beautiful. You don't notice them, Judith," Blythe pointed out. "This isn't like you. It's . . ." She trailed off.

"Intense." Judith finished her sentence for her. She touched her lips realizing she'd said the word aloud. She laughed softly. "I feel like dancing."

"A little scary don't you think?" Blythe's voice was gentle.

"I know, Blythe, I do, but right at this moment, I'm willing to jump right off that cliff with my eyes closed. Tomorrow I'll wake up and be Judith again, all contained and frozen, but tonight, just for tonight, I want to believe I can live again."

Blythe frowned. "Frozen? Is that how you've felt? That you aren't really living? Judith, I thought you were happy here with us."

"I am. I have been. It isn't the same, Blythe. I worked so hard to contain my feelings. Do you really think someone is so perfectly pleasant at all times? I smile when deep inside I want to scream. I get frustrated and angry just like anyone else, but those emotions aren't safe for me to feel around other people. So I push them down and smile until I'm perfect and pleasant and safe."

Judith leapt up and paced across her floor, unable to stay still. She wanted to. She felt a little crazy with her heady happiness and she knew Blythe was growing afraid for her. She couldn't care about that right now. There was no tamping down strong emotions and any intense emotion would affect everyone around her. Living in such close proximity to those she loved was a good idea, until her body woke up, until she stopped feeling dead inside. She could contain anger and sorrow, but the sheer joy and trepidation, the way she felt so *alive* being with Thomas Vincent—that was impossible. Joy spilled out and, God help her, she needed to feel real emotion again, even if it was in the safety of her home and for one single night.

She couldn't stop smiling even with Blythe witnessing her out-of-control behavior.

"Just tonight. Just for now. Inside my house where no one else can be affected, Blythe. I called you because you seem to absorb my feelings rather than react to them. I *have* to allow myself this one night of complete happiness." There was a plea in her voice, but she couldn't help it. She wanted to know she was wholly a woman and she had to share this incredible moment with someone she loved. "Please be happy for me."

It was amazing to feel fully alive again, a vibrant, desirable woman. Of course she wouldn't do anything about it, but the sheer relief of knowing she *could* was as stimulating as the best champagne.

Blythe moistened her lips. "It's impossible not to be happy for you, Judith. I've never seen you like this. I just want you to make certain you know all the hidden dangers. You have to see him at the gallery. It's not like you can totally avoid him."

Judith took a breath and made her confession in a rush. "I invited him here tomorrow. To ride the tractor with me and have lunch. I told him I'd show him around the farm."

She felt so guilty. Well guilt was there, but maybe not uppermost. She could close her eyes and hold the image of Tom—*Thomas*, he would always be a Thomas to her—looking as if he might blush and stammer any moment. He was so amazing. He looked tougher than nails and had a reputation as a brilliant businessman, yet with her he'd been almost shy.

She had almost felt sorry for him until that moment when her eyes had met his and there was nothing at all shy about the way he was looking at her. He looked as if it was all he could do to keep from throwing her down on the counter as she'd been imagining. He looked capable of being rough and hot and so needy he could barely wait to get her clothes off.

She knew she looked reserved and cool, but her needs had nothing to do with *reservation* or *cool*. Deep inside was a well of passion—of fire—and somehow, Thomas Vincent had managed to find it. She wanted to weep with joy—with fear. She destroyed people, those closest to her, her family, people she loved. And when she loved, she loved with every fiber of her being.

"You did what?" Blythe asked, shock showing on her face. "*Invited* him here?"

Judith took a deep breath, pressing a hand to her churning stomach. Blythe wasn't any more stunned at her behavior than she was. The farm was sacred—their sanctuary. All of them had secrets, and now, more than ever, they had to be careful.

"What about Levi?" Blythe asked, her voice more gentle than accusing. "Have you considered that we need to protect him from outsiders? And Lexi? She's very uncomfortable with strangers around."

"I don't plan on taking him anywhere near their homes," Judith defended. Where was the remorse and guilt she should be feeling? She hugged herself as she crossed to the window and looked down at the carpet of small white star flowers swaying gently in the breeze. Above her, the stars scattered across the sky, the two pinpoints of white creating the effect of being in the middle of a beautiful galaxy.

"Have you thought this through? Is spending time with him outside of the gallery a good idea?"

"No, of course not. I don't care though, Blythe." She turned back to look at her chosen sister, willing her to understand. "I want to feel this. I want to be swept off my feet. I want to ache for him and cry for him and feel all twisted up inside. I *need* this."

Blythe studied her for a long time, and then slowly nodded. "I think you're right, Judith. It's been a long time coming and you deserve to be genuinely happy. I just want you to be careful with your heart. Don't just give it away without thought. You're an all-or-nothing person. Let's at least do a little investigation."

"I did. As soon as Inez gave me his name, I looked him up on the Internet and he truly seems to be a decent guy. He's got a good reputation in the business world. A few charity events had his picture. There were a couple of articles written about him. No hidden wife. No criminal history, no ugly divorces. He's just a nice man who works far too much."

"And wants to come to Sea Haven and buy a failing art gallery."

Judith shrugged. "We came here to start a different way of life."

"We have pasts, Judith," Blythe pointed out. "We aren't the best examples. I'm just playing the devil's advocate because you're really jumping off the cliff and you aren't even looking for a safety net."

"Maybe I don't want one. Just this once I want to let myself feel something."

"You know you're a spirit element, Judith. Nothing can change that," Blythe stated the problem. "Is he reacting to you? Or you to him? Is what you're feeling genuine?"

"I'm away from him and I'm still feeling it," Judith said with a small shrug. "It feels genuine. I'm so happy and I actually feel beautiful and so *alive*."

"And you don't mind if I call Jonas and ask him to do a little checking up on Thomas Vincent?" Blythe asked.

Judith's gaze jumped to hers. "You're testing me, to see if I'm certain of him. I am, Blythe. I've steered clear of the bad-boy gene pool and I'm absolutely certain he's the genuine deal. His aura is difficult for me to read, but that isn't entirely unusual. Gifted people often have mixed auras."

"Gifted?" Blythe prompted, one eyebrow shooting up.

Judith found herself blushing for no reason. She'd felt his

spirit rising to meet hers. To be physically and intellectually attracted to someone was difficult enough, but to have her spirit reaching to embrace his, *rushing* to absorb and be absorbed—frankly it had never happened to her before, and she felt like a giddy teen with a crush on a rock star.

She nodded. "He's definitely gifted in some way."

Blythe shook her head. "That doesn't worry you even a little bit?"

"I refuse to be worried." She threw herself onto the bed beside Blythe and caught her hands. "Be happy with me. Let me have this. More than likely tomorrow I'll realize it was all me and he really was feeling my emotions amplified a million times over."

"And if that isn't the case?"

"I'll cross that bridge when I come to it."

"I'm calling Jonas."

Judith shrugged. "I'm fine with that. He isn't going to find anything."

"And you'll have to tell Levi and Rikki," Blythe cautioned.

"Levi can make himself scarce," Judith said. "It's only for a couple of hours. I won't take Thomas anywhere near their house or Lexi's."

Blythe raised her eyebrow. "You don't really understand Levi, do you, Judith? He isn't the kind of man to make himself scarce. He's going to worry about Rikki and you as well. He'll be around and he'll be watching, probably with a rifle on your Thomas the entire time."

Judith sighed. "Life certainly can get complicated fast. I just want to spend a little time with him, maybe feel like this a time or two more, even if it isn't really reciprocated." Her dark eyes met Blythe's. "Wouldn't you want to feel this way again? You had it once."

There was a small silence. Blythe turned away from her, pacing across the floor on long legs, her shoulders and back stiff. Shame washed over Judith. She followed her oldest sister across the room and laid a comforting hand on her shoulder.

"I'm sorry, Blythe. I didn't mean that the way it came out. I wasn't trying to attack you. I just meant that feeling again, waking up as a woman is amazing, and I know you felt this way at least once. This is my time. Maybe my only time."

She studied Blythe's averted face and made her confession in a little rush. "I was such an innocent when I met Jean-Claude, so silly, mistaking his lifestyle and strength for the real thing. I was so impressed with him and I thought the sun rose and set with him. I didn't pay attention to what he really was, just with what I thought he was, building a fantasy man in my head that didn't exist. I didn't even understand what love was back then."

Blythe turned her head and Judith could see her face was streaked with tears. "It's okay, Judith. I always fall apart around this time of year. It really has nothing to do with you."

"I'm just so embarrassed that I let a man like Jean-Claude into my life when I should have known better. All the warning signs were there, they were, Blythe. I didn't want to see them. I heard whispers and I ignored them. I saw the look on some people's faces and alarms would go off in my head, but I didn't stop. I just kept on with my ridiculous fantasy. And when it all came crumbling down, that precious princess in her golden tower dream, I couldn't even handle it myself."

Judith sank back down onto the bed and gripped the intricate footboard. "I made such a mess out of so many people's lives and got my brother murdered in the process. That should have been me, not him. I guess I don't deserve to feel this way, do I?"

"Judith!" Blythe swung around. "Don't you ever say that again. Do you think Rikki doesn't deserve happiness with Levi?"

"She was innocent. She didn't start the fires that killed her parents and her fiancé."

"And you aren't any more responsible for your brother's death, or even what happened to any of the others involved."

Judith gripped the footboard tighter. "Really? Do you really believe that, Blythe? It was my emotions swinging so far out of control that provoked all those people."

"You had no idea you were a spirit element. You'd never even heard the term before, let alone known what it was or how it worked. You didn't know anything about psychic gifts or how to contain or use them properly. Of course your emotions were intense. Your brother was tortured and murdered in front of you. Did you think you'd be gentle Judith, smiling sweetly at the men who had committed such an atrocity? That isn't even reasonable."

"I guess none of us are very reasonable when it comes to our own lives. I say that very same thing to you, Blythe, yet you still take responsibility for your stepfather and mother's deaths." Judith flashed a wan smile. "But of course, for you, that's different."

Blythe sent an answering smile back. "Of course. Every time I think we've all come so far, this time of year rolls around and throws you—and me—right back into a depression, wallowing in guilt and sorrow."

"And then I have to meet Thomas Vincent. Poor innocent man, walks into the big mess of our lives. I guess we're all just holding it together by a thread. Inviting a stranger into our lives even for an afternoon probably isn't very fair. I didn't think it through." She bit down on her lower lip. "Maybe I should I call him."

Blythe shook her head. "I think we can accommodate Mr. Vincent. Lexi won't mind. She's been saying she wanted to take a day off to read up on the temperatures needed in the greenhouse for some exotic plant she wants to grow."

Judith couldn't help but laugh. "That's our Lexi. She

doesn't have enough plants or enough forest to play in, she has to bring the jungle to Sea Haven."

"I love her so much," Blythe said. "I ache for her sometimes."

Judith nodded. "Me too. I think we all do. She's thriving here though."

"She hides from the world," Blythe pointed out.

Judith laid a comforting hand on Blythe's shoulder. "We're all hiding from the world, Blythe," she said gently. "Those gates make us feel safe here and none of us wants to venture too far out of our comfort zone."

Blythe frowned. "You're so right, Judith. No wonder I had such a reaction to you bringing a man here, I wanted our safe little world to remain intact. That's the same reason we were all upset when Rikki found Levi."

It was Judith's turn to frown. "Not exactly. We all tend to protect Rikki."

"We protect ourselves as well as each other. Bring him. We all need to be shaken up a little. It isn't good for any of us to hide away. Maybe at first we needed a sanctuary, but it isn't living—not really."

"I'll call Lexi right now," Judith said.

"She'll be very understanding," Blythe assured.

"So will Rikki."

Blythe nodded. "That's true, but Levi, not so much. We think Jonas is bad, but Levi has a protective streak a mile wide and it's extended from a wide circle around Rikki to the rest of us. He'll be watching out for you, Judith."

"I'm not certain Levi's way of watching for us is something we want to look too closely at," Judith admitted.

They exchanged a small smile of understanding.

6

HIGHWAY 1 was beautiful, the ocean lapping at the cliffs on one side, the other with forests spreading up the mountains and ribbons of silvery water cascading over rocks through the variety of trees. Stefan had never really appreciated the beauty of his surroundings as he did in this particular place. He loved the color, vivid greens in various shades and splashes of bright flowers vying for space on the rising mountains. In spite of the bruising across his chest and the thin knife wounds on his arms, he felt surprisingly good. Ivanov wouldn't be in any shape to follow him and he could have this one day with Judith to himself.

He shook his head at the absolute absurdity of what he was doing. Spending time with Judith Henderson was far more dangerous than chasing Petr Ivanov in the dark of the night but the need was too strong to resist. He'd never for one moment dreamt of meeting a woman like her. Falling in love was a fairy tale. He hadn't believed in such things, and certainly didn't believe he was capable of falling under a woman's spell. He was not a man who put aside who and what he was to indulge himself. For him, this peculiar behavior was just one more sign that he'd been in the business too long.

In the end, all the recriminations in the world didn't matter. He'd lain awake most of the night and thought about her, all the while rubbing his left palm along his thigh. Strangely, his palm had itched most of the night and this morning there was a strange burning. He knew, without a shadow of a doubt, that the weird problem with his palm had something to do with Judith. Part of him hoped that when he saw Judith again, the terrible longing in him would subside and he would realize the momentary madness was over.

The moment he turned onto the road leading to the farm, a shadow passed over his car. Out of the corner of his eye he caught sight of a bird in flight, performing a lazy circle above him, glittering eyes watching his every movement. His heart jumped and then settled to a normal rhythm. The bird watching him didn't mean Lev was alive. He knew his brother had many gifts, and one of those gifts allowed him to use the animals as spies.

The farm was a perfect place to hide. Judith had five sisters. Men like Lev looked for a woman who stayed below the radar—women such as those residing on the large farm. He would have to ask Judith about each of the women and make a guess as to which one his brother might choose to shelter him while he laid low and built a new cover for himself, one that permitted him to remain dead to his past life.

Was his brother close by? Was it possible he lived near Judith, that she actually knew him? He didn't dare question her about a man, she'd close down. Lev would have made it understood that someone was hunting him and a woman like Judith would protect him. A slow exhale of anger shocked him.

He slowed his car and looked around, contemplating his reaction to his logical conclusions. Why would it make him angry that Lev would use one of these women—one of Judith's sisters? Survival was paramount and any means used was considered justified. But was it? He had no real answers, or maybe he did, but he didn't want to look too closely at what he was doing.

His gut knotted as several birds settled in the trees lining the drive as he went through the open, very ornate gate that guarded the farm. The moment his body actually came parallel to the metalwork of the gate, he felt the shift in energy and power around him. The energy field was tremendous, the power coming in waves and spreading throughout the acreage. He could actually feel his body responding, the pull was that strong. His own talents leapt toward that energy, met and absorbed it until his body vibrated with the need for action.

Without a doubt, the people on this farm were elements— strong elements. He hadn't been wrong about Judith. It was no wonder he had reacted so strongly to her. Intellectually she would be compatible, someone who would keep up with his fast processing, his body certainly craved hers, but now he understood the full extent of the danger both of them were in. Whatever her element was, his psychic talents responded with tremendous power.

Stefan let his breath out more slowly and studied the birds. The shiny eyes were definitely watching him, adding to his conviction that his brother was somewhere in the vicinity. He had six brothers, and all of them were psychically gifted. Lev held dominion over animals. If he was here, where were the dogs? He would add to his security, using more normal animal means. That, again, would only be logical, so did that mean he was off base about the birds? He took another slow, careful look. There were several species, not one, and all were looking at him, giving him a slightly eerie feeling.

"So you're here, then, Lev," he murmured aloud.

Judith had really thrown him. Instead of being elated at being so close to finding his brother, Stefan had genuine misgivings. He didn't want Lev using Judith. *As I am doing,* he reminded himself. Thomas Vincent was visiting her, not Stefan Prakenskii, no matter how much he wished it were so.

With the pad of his thumb, he touched the small scratch along his jaw Ivanov had given him the night before, a short, thin line that still burned. He was crazy for coming to this place. He shouldn't have hope spreading through him like the warmth of the sun. There shouldn't be this need building, or anticipation.

He wanted to blame it on Sea Haven. The sun shone on the water so that it sparkled like diamonds. The wind teased the leaves on the trees and birds played in the thermals, creating a lazy, inviting atmosphere. Storms came in fast and furious, giving free rein to a wild abandoned passion that couldn't be matched. And there was an incredible woman who made him feel alive.

Swearing, he put his foot down firmly on the gas pedal. He should turn around, but he wasn't going to. He was going to see her again and if there was a God, he'd better be helping both of them, because Stefan Prakenskii was about to fuck up his life very, very badly.

JUDITH'S house was much larger than he expected. Gardens surrounded the two-story structure, brilliantly colored plants that appealed to the hidden artist him. He'd locked that part of himself away a long time ago, using it only as a tool of his trade, but for some reason, Judith had brought it crashing to the front, demanding release. His world needed to be a dull, emotionless place, yet all around him, colors were vivid and he couldn't possibly deny the rush of heat infusing his veins as he parked and stepped out of the car.

His gaze swept her home, taking it all in, the fire equipment everywhere, hoses and sprinklers, as if she was obsessed with fire prevention. Was that part of her need to hide the intensity of the passion in her? There was a security system, and, although he wasn't close enough, it appeared to be state-of-the-art. Was that because she feared a visit from Jean-Claude?

She was on the front porch, just standing there looking at him, her dark eyes serious and a little afraid, but shining with the same anticipation he couldn't stop in himself. Her long hair was down, straight as a ruler, falling below her waist. She wore slim jeans and a thin pink tee. He could tell she was in her comfortable clothes, the ones she wore around her family. This was similar to the outfit she wore in the picture he carried of her.

That same expanse of smooth, inviting skin peaked out at him. A thin gold chain glittered against her flat belly, the links gleaming and polished, drawing his attention to the skin that looked softer than any rose petals. His mouth went dry. She was completely motionless, just waiting, like some pagan goddess, an offering. Her small, tucked in waist served to emphasize the fullness of her high, curving breasts, molded by the tee. But it was her exotic eyes that drew him in completely. She watched him from under long, feathery lashes, her dark eyes tempting him with a mixture of innocence and sensuality.

In spite of his determination, his heart rate accelerated and his body tightened. The impact of her watchful stare sank deep into his bones. A brand. Her brand. She left it on him so easily. He felt—*home*, whatever the hell that meant. *Judith*. Her name moved through his mind. The tenderness he felt shocked him. He hadn't known there was such a thing in his makeup. He was in trouble—such trouble— and judging by that deer-caught-in-the-headlights look on her face, so was she.

She took a breath before starting down the stairs. He noted she was just as shaken as he was by the strange, compelling pull between them. He was damned glad he wasn't the only one mired in quicksand. Her gaze never left his as she moved so gracefully down the steps, reminding him of a princess descending a throne.

"You came."

Her voice wrapped him up in silk and satin. He studied her face. The need grew in her just as sharply as it did in him. She fought it, but she didn't try to hide it from him.

"I couldn't stay away."

The stark raw truth stood between them. He felt the wind on his face like the promise of a kiss, like the touch of her fingers, the caress of her hair.

Judith stepped closer to him, her dark gaze drifting over his face, touching on the fresh scratch. Her fingertip brushed over that small wound so gently he felt his heart move.

"What happened?"

He didn't want to lie to her. "Better if you don't ask."

He couldn't help himself, he caught her wrist and tugged her a little closer, until he could feel the beckoning warmth of her body, unwilling—or unable—to let go of her. "I brought lunch."

A small smile tugged at her mouth, lit the dark sobriety of her eyes. "Did you make it yourself?"

He almost denied the truth to give her a Thomas Vincent answer, but the truth slipped out. "Yes. I'm a good cook."

Her eyebrow went up, and a small dimple appeared in her right cheek. He couldn't help brushing his thumb across that little dent. Her breath caught in her throat.

"So it's real."

He didn't have to ask what she meant; he knew. He nodded his head, holding on to her gaze, unwilling to let this moment between them slip away. "I didn't think it was possible for me after all this time." That too was a Stefan Prakenskii truth.

His heart clenched unexpectedly. Never in a million years had he thought it possible to feel the way he was. The euphoria should have gone away. The need inside him should have dissipated, not grown—and it was still growing. Being with her was like being caught in a dream world, a wild, impossible fantasy.

"What are we going to do, Thomas? Because this can't happen."

The little hitch in her voice, that innocent trust in him, the belief in her eyes that he was a good man, shook him as nothing else could have. She looked at him as if he could find a way to save them. There it was again, the need to be her white knight. His armor was tarnished a long time ago and he acknowledged to himself that he had no idea what he was going to do about their situation, but he wouldn't walk away from her.

His fingers curled around the nape of her neck and he pulled her another step closer. Thomas Vincent was long gone and Stefan Prakenskii was not about to give up this woman, not here, not now.

"I'm going to kiss you."

She blinked rapidly. Those long feathery lashes knotted his gut and tightened his groin. His physical reaction to her remained terrifying and exhilarating, even stronger than the night before. This woman had a hold on him that was unbreakable. He was already lost, craving the genuine emotions she brought out in him. She opened floodgates. His needs poured out of him around her.

"Do you think that's a good idea?" Her voice was no more than a soft whisper, a caress that teased his cock into aching thickness.

"No." He knew better. He knew he'd be damned for all time. "But I'm going to kiss you anyway."

"It might be awful," she pointed out with a brief flare of optimism.

He had to smile. "Perhaps. We can only hope."

There was a small moment of hesitation. Her teeth sank into her lower lip, betraying her nerves. She nodded slowly, knowing just as he did, that it was a *very* bad idea. "Okay then."

He stared into her eyes for a long time. Forever would never be long enough for him to live there. Right there in her eyes. He saw inside of her, into something so beautiful it made his heart ache. She didn't move, didn't pull away, just absorbed him in the same way he needed to absorb her.

He was in no hurry. Craving rose like the sun, hot and bright and shocking. He wanted to savor this moment. Her acceptance of him. He felt her trembling—or maybe that was him. The great Stefan Prekenskii, seducer of women, trembling, needing.

Her tongue touched her bottom lip, her breasts rose and fell beneath that thin tee. Inexorably, he drew her another step closer to the heat of his body. She blinked, but didn't look away. Her scent enveloped him. The faint aroma, fresh and elusive, was a fragrance he expected he might encounter on an island paradise. Her hair fell over his arm, soft and unbelievably silky. Every detail burned into his mind, the individual strands that brushed his face as he bent slowly toward her. The flutter of those feathery lashes, her lips parting, the swift inhale.

His mouth settled on hers, the softest of touches. A slight brush only, just to savor that first feel of how soft her lips were—to test the strong magnetic pull between them. He should have known better—should have known it would never end there. He should have heeded all the warning signs—and there had been many. In one moment of honest clarity, he had known but it didn't matter. He wanted this and, once he'd touched her, there was no way to stop. Both of them were falling and it was too late to save them now that they'd made that first slight contact.

He pulled her across that breath of air separating them, tight, so that her body was imprinted on his, all that soft skin, the lush curves, his free hand sliding inevitably to that expanse of tempting bare skin. His fingertips bit into her waist, slid over her belly and caressed her hip as his mouth took hers.

The world around them burst into a fiery blaze. The heat soared until he could hear the roaring and crackling of flames. He'd inadvertently struck a match and lit a stick of dynamite. Her body melted against his while his heart roared in his ears and he lost himself completely in the beauty and wonder of her mouth. She tasted a little like an expensive champagne, going straight to his head and hitting him hard. She made him weak and he knew without a shadow of a doubt that she belonged in his arms.

He couldn't stop kissing her, over and over until they both were out of breath and their bodies were on fire. He found that small golden chain and he tugged and rolled the gold between his fingers the way he needed to do to her nipples. He ached to touch her, to memorize her, to devour her inch by slow inch. He tried not to be rough, but his mouth had a mind of its own, each kiss feeding his hunger beyond endurance.

His hand left her nape, fist bunching her hair, pulling her head back, taking what was his. *His.* Men like him didn't have homes. They didn't own anything they couldn't walk away from in an instant. All the money he had acquired over the years by fair or foul means stayed in bank accounts no one knew about, never to be spent on the luxury of a home—or a woman.

Yet, this woman belonged to him—was made for him. He didn't know anything about her and yet he knew everything. He kissed his way to her chin and back up to the heat of her mouth. He couldn't resist her mouth and evidently she didn't have any more of a sense of self-preservation than he did because she opened to him instantly, feeding on his hunger, returning it tenfold.

Every cell in his body responded to her. *Knew.* He knew without a single doubt that she was born to be his. Kissing her only got better. His fist tightened, holding her still. A warning signal in the back of his mind brought him close enough to the surface to remind him Thomas Vincent would never kiss her with such confidence. He wouldn't grow rough and demanding. He would never be so aggressive. Stefan ruthlessly pushed the warning away and took her mouth, exploring, teasing, demanding. *Sliding willingly into a deep abyss.*

Lust rose like a volcano, winding itself through pure passion as his fingers stroked caresses over her bare midriff, absorbing all that soft skin. Heat rushed through his veins, setting up a terrible addiction he knew he would never be rid of. She tasted too good. Matched fire with fire. She needed the way he did. Her hands fisted in his hair and she gave herself to him, holding nothing back, feeding his need more, driving him past control.

Truth was the only thing that could have stopped him from taking what he knew belonged to him right there at the bottom of the steps of her home. She was a spirit element. The truth was there all along—he'd even suspected it, and right now they were in terrible trouble because her spirit enflamed his beyond all measure. Her desire and his together burned hot and wild, a firestorm out of control. Her element amplified every psychic gift he had and added to the heat and need rushing through him like a fireball.

He forced himself to pull back, not wanting to blow his chance with her—if he hadn't already. If he had this woman—and what the hell was he thinking—it would be forever. Everything with her was a first. That first kiss, first touch, first attempt at finding a discipline that wasn't ingrained or trained into him.

He rested his forehead against hers, drawing in a lungful of air. "I could spend a lifetime doing that with you." He rubbed the nape of her neck with strong fingers. "Are you okay?"

Her gaze clung to his—filled with desire, filled with sorrow. She touched her lips, swollen from his kisses, with trembling fingers. "I didn't know I could feel like that."

"Neither did I," he answered honestly. He drew another deep breath. "You're a spirit element, aren't you?"

Her gaze searched his. "You know about spirit elements?"

He nodded slowly, throwing caution to the wind. Maybe Thomas would know, maybe he wouldn't, but today was Stefan's day and Thomas could, quite frankly, go to hell.

"Then you see why this can never happen."

Everything he was, every merciless cell in his body rejected her assessment. There was no going back, both of them had crossed the line starting with that first brush of his mouth over hers. She had to know it, she just wasn't accepting it. His life was changed forever. He was a marked man, would be hunted the rest of his life, yet he would not turn his back on this. He didn't know how he would manage to keep them both alive on the run, but he wasn't going to leave her behind. Not now. Not after having a taste of humanity, of civilization, of finally realizing just how powerful human touch was.

He knew terror when he saw it. Over so many years in his job he'd come to know fear intimately. He could smell fear. See it. Almost taste it. He'd seen that look in the eyes of his prey, and he detested seeing such stark fear in her.

"I don't see at all, Judith."

He bent his head to the temptation of her trembling lips, needing to stop her fear any way that he could. She didn't resist or step back. If anything, she stepped closer, opening her mouth to his, her arms sliding around his neck, holding him close. There was nothing gentle about his kiss. He demanded her response, needed to know she was feeling the same heat, the same terrible hunger that refused to be sated by one or two or even a thousand kisses.

The way her hair fell over his arm, her body moving restlessly against his, the feel of her lips, and the hot, sweet taste of her made him a believer. She felt perfect just where she was. She might deny there could be a future, and if he had a brain in his head, he'd believe her, but she'd changed everything and she'd have to face the consequences, just as he did.

Again, it was Stefan who lifted his head and breathed deeply to get control back. And that told him something else about Judith. Her spirit had already woven itself through his, and once let loose, it soared with the freedom, unwilling to be kept locked down so tight, under complete restricted control.

Intense training had ingrained in Stefan to use any tool to accomplish his mission. His mission had just become keeping this woman for himself and to make certain both of them stayed alive. If he was being truthful with himself, it was all about taking that look out of her eyes and replacing the fear and sadness with happiness—with him. The dawning knowledge that everything had shifted had him quickly reformulating plans. The emotions of a spirit element could be complex and difficult to control.

Stefan held her close against him, knowing she was confused by her own behavior. Her spirit element drove her, just as his gifts reached so quickly and confidently for her. He was at complete ease with every psychic talent he possessed, but Judith still fought hers, kept it under such tight control, that she was making herself sick. He was going to change all that. He just wasn't certain how he was going to do it yet.

His mouth brushed her ear, nuzzling the fall of black silk aside. "Are you going to show me your home?"

She pressed her lips together and shook her head. "Maybe later. I don't trust myself right now." She lifted her chin, her gaze finding his. "I know you don't understand. I'm saying one thing and doing another, but you're so . . ." She trailed off.

Sinfully tempting.

He heard her thought clearly in his mind. His left palm itched and he pressed it hard into her side, against her soft skin, against the temptation of that very sexy gold chain.

"Then you owe me a tractor ride."

Her eyes cleared, smiling at him. "I do, don't I?"

"I thought about it last night," he admitted, his hand slipping from the nape of her neck to slide down her arm, taking possession of her hand. "I could really be making a mistake. If I make a complete fool of myself and drive the thing into a tree, are you going to laugh at me?"

"Not only will I laugh," she admitted, "I will take a picture and send it to all of my sisters. They'll do a bit of laughing as well."

His heart jumped. The memory was dim, but her threat conjured up one of his few childhood memories, the laughter of his brothers filling their small apartment. For one wonderful moment he could almost smell his mother's perfume. Instantly the soles of his feet burned and throbbed with pain driving the remembrance to the back of his mind, replacing it with a little boy sobbing for his mother and brothers while a grim-faced man with cold eyes slammed a board over and over into the soles of his feet and ordered him to stop, to never mention them or think of them again—that they were dead to him. He shoved the memory away hard, slamming that door in his mind.

Judith made a single sound of alarm, her dark eyes leaping to meet his. She should have stepped away from him. His hands automatically went to her neck, fingers settling around her throat with so much deceptive gentleness. Anyone knowing personal information about his childhood was a risk to him. The training ingrained in him was strong and his first reaction was self-preservation. They stood in silence, her eyes on his. She didn't fight him. She didn't even move while her pulse beat hard beneath the threat of his fingers. She waited under the strength of his hands, her dark eyes trusting. Sympathetic even.

"Damn it, Judith. Don't you have any sense of self-preservation? Even a little bit?"

"What happened to you?" Judith pressed a hand to her

heart, at the same time shifting her weight as if her feet suddenly hurt. "Tell me, Thomas. Your feet—you're in pain."

He had to be much more careful with her. She felt what others were feeling, just as her emotions could affect everyone she came into contact with—especially him.

He shook his head. "It was a long time ago. I don't know why I thought of that."

"Your mother's laughter? Brothers?"

"Long gone."

"You were adopted then? And then you lost that mother as well to an illness?"

The compassion in her tugged at him. It was a legitimate conclusion. His family dead and a little boy adopted out. He never stepped out of character, never stopped protecting Stefan Prakenskii, yet he'd opened Pandora's box the minute he was in her company. He forced himself to shrug while he shored up his defenses.

"What happened when you were a boy? This happened in Russia? Your mother is Russian? Were you in an orphanage and someone abused the children?"

That he could answer fairly honestly. "Something like that. It was a long time ago, Judith, and if you don't mind, I prefer not to think about it."

He stroked caresses over her very vulnerable neck and cursed himself for being such a monster. She was bright and shiny and thought herself dark and too dangerous to allow her emotions free rein, but she didn't really know what a true monster was.

Judith went up on her toes and pressed a kiss to his mouth. "Let's go drive the tractor."

His fingers tangled with hers, held on. The shocks just kept coming. Men like him thought in terms of weapons. One never tied up any weapon and his hands were lethal. This was the second time he'd done the impossible and worse, he didn't care. He *wanted* the contact with her.

He let her tug, taking him with her. She rocked him,

rocked everything he had ever believed, turning things completely around. She moved like the wind, a fluid, graceful
breath of air at his side, making him feel like a king. He felt
her burst of happiness spread over and into him, amplifying
his own mood and he allowed it, letting down his armor just
enough to absorb her spirit deeper into him.

"I noticed a lot of fire equipment. Do you have to worry
about forest fires?"

The farm was surrounded by acres of forest, a vast variety of tall trees, very healthy-looking, almost guardians circling the large farm, protecting it from outsiders. The flutter
of wings was constant with the birds perching in the higher
branches and then taking flight to circle above the farm,
only to land again.

"Not really, but we like to be prepared for anything. We
bought this farm together, my sisters and I, and we hope to
stay here."

There was a tiny catch in her voice. He glanced at her as
they walked along a small winding path through her enormous flower garden. Her expression was a little sad again
and he felt her spirit take a dive, dread filling her and conse-
quently him. There was trouble here, more than he'd brought
with him.

"Why wouldn't you stay?"

She swept her hair back over her shoulder in that feminine way women had. The gesture suddenly seemed sexy,
a call to pure temptation. He found himself looking at her
neck, her profile, those long lashes and sensual mouth.

Judith broke into a smile. "Stop it. This time it's you,
not me."

He grinned at her, amazed at the genuine emotions rushing through him along with the heat. "Sorry. You're damned
beautiful, Judith. I'm really trying to be good now."

"Try harder," she admonished. "You're supposed to be
helping me."

"Believe me, honey, I am helping. If I had my way . . ."

He let the sentence travel off, watching the slow blush rise beneath her skin, giving her an alluring glow. "Distract me. Tell me why you think you might move from this little paradise you and your sisters have put together, because if I lived here, nothing would move me out."

Several crows called out loud, the distinctive *caw-caw* almost a reprimand. Tiny hummingbirds moved from flower to flower, small wings fanning the air so fast he could hear their sound as they buzzed around his head, dangerously close to his face. His shoulder brushed hers and he drew her a little closer, under the shelter of his shoulder. She was tall, but he was taller and it was natural enough to want to protect her from the darting birds.

She was silent for a long time as they wound their way through the flowers and shrubbery leading to the outer gardens. He noted that the various species of flowers were planted in thick rows of color, making up spectacular rainbows and rippling fields of vivid, brilliant color. The shorter stalks gave way to larger bushes, fields of rhododendrons of every hue. They grew tall and wide, providing a shield around her inner gardens. Great trumpet trees of pink, white, red and gold provided another layer protecting the house. Butterflies were everywhere right along with the hummingbirds, vying for the sweet sticky nectar of the beckoning flowers.

He tightened his hand around hers, stopping her in the midst of the towering fountains of bursting color. "You don't have to tell me, but I can feel how upset you are. Maybe I can help."

Shoulders stiff, she stood in front of him, shaking her head, a small unreal smile on her face as she refused to look up at him. "We just met, Thomas. It's not like I know you well enough to dump my problems on you."

"You know me well enough. I see you, Judith, even the parts of you that you hide from the rest of the world, that you hide from your family. I recognize that you're a spirit element." He took a breath, stopped her on the path through the jungle of trumpet trees. "Was it a man who hurt you? You guard yourself so carefully, Judith. You let me hold you, I know you'd let me have sex with you, but you'd never let me make love to you. You don't want love. Was it another man?"

She blinked rapidly and his heart stood still. Tears were close, clogging her throat and burning behind her eyes. He felt them as surely as if he were about to weep. Her ghosts were very close, standing between them, holding him off, forcing him back away from her, silent wraiths making it impossible for him to have her.

Stefan was not afraid of ghosts, he had too many in his past to ever worry about the unseen apparitions that tried to haunt him, but they'd taken a tight grip on Judith and were refusing to relinquish their hold. She was going to be difficult, make it as hard for him as possible to be with her.

He wanted all of her. He was risking everything for her. His life. His peace of mind. That tiny piece of humanity he'd hidden from his trainers. There was nothing more than a slice, but it was there, real and the only part of Stefan Prakenskii left. He was handing that over to her keeping. He was going to put his real emotions on the line for her and he would not accept less from her. She was going to give him her soul in exchange for his. And damn it all, for once in his life, he was going to be that fucking white knight whether she thought she wanted it or not.

She stood there looking so tragic and so meltingly beautiful, it was impossible to resist her. He pulled her into his arms with the hummingbirds darting around the brightly colored trumpets and his mouth against her ear so that when he whispered, his lips brushed that perfect little tempting shell.

"Don't cry or I'll have no choice but to be your hero and save you from yourself." His teeth bit down gently on her earlobe, tugging.

He hoped the hummingbirds weren't part of Lev's

security system because he was going to kiss her again and hope she saved them both from things getting too far out of hand. He could only imagine what his brother's sense of humor might be, sending those little sharp beaks into his skin. He walked Judith backward, pushing her deeper into the cover of the large trumpet trees, his mouth descending on hers as he did so.

He felt the shift under his feet, the heightening of his senses until each one was acute as her spirit flowed free. Power flared around them, bursting through him, adding to the heat rushing through his body. Electrical sparks sizzled over his skin. He felt the boost in his own psychic talents and knew they were fast fusing spirits together. His left palm burned in the center and he broke the kiss and caught her left hand, lifting her palm.

Judith looked bemused and a little afraid. "What are you doing?"

"I don't know," he said honestly and pushed air between them, his left palm to hers.

She cried out and yanked her hand away, holding it close to her, her expression shocked.

"Let me see."

His fingers settled very gently around her wrist, shackling her to him, already taking possession of her hand. He gave a relentless tug when she resisted, knowing he had gone so far off the Thomas Vincent script he was going to have do some fast shoring up soon. Stefan was in complete command at all times while Thomas would be careful not to push Judith too hard.

He turned her hand over and saw the brand there in the middle of her palm, two circles interwoven together. The circles appeared raw at first, as if they were a fresh brand, but beneath the brush of his thumb, the mark faded. He pushed healing air at her. He had seen that mark only one time before, when he was a child, on his mother's hand when his father had looked up across the room and smiled mysteriously at her.

"What happened? It was just air." She looked up at him, her gaze steady on his. "Wasn't it?"

"What are you so afraid of, Judith?" he asked again, a soft demand this time.

She took back her palm, rubbing it up and down her denim-clad thigh, a small frown on her face. When he reached to rub at the little line between her eyes she pulled back. "I told you from the start that I wasn't a good woman, Thomas. I was very truthful with you. I don't want to hurt you."

"So your fear is that you'll somehow hurt me?"

She swallowed and shifted her gaze from his. "Yes."

Her voice had dropped so low it was merely a thread of sound. He felt sadness beating at him until he ached inside and knew it was her—not him—generating the emotion.

He ignored her silent rejection of him and stepped close, invading her space, his hands framing her face. "I'm a grown-up, Judith. I don't need your protection, nor do I want it. I take care of my own. Let's just see where this takes us and know I've been properly warned."

Her dark eyes searched his. "There are forces that just . . ." She trailed off, took a breath and tried again. "You could be *physically* hurt, Thomas, not just emotionally, as if that wouldn't be bad enough. I can't let that happen."

He leaned into her and kissed her sultry mouth. She was worried about him. *Worried.* That knowledge sent a spiral of happiness blossoming through him. He didn't have anyone who worried about him. "It won't happen, Judith. Let's just go ride the tractor and forget about anything else right now. We're on your farm, the birds are singing and the weather is perfect. We have right now and the rest of the world is far away from us."

"Are you certain?"

"Absolutely. And you promised me." He kissed her again and then turned back toward their path.

Judith hesitated, rubbing her hand along her thigh again as if it itched. His own palm burned more than itched. She stepped up beside him and tangled her fingers with his. They walked through the winding, meandering path out into the next circle of the garden, a scattering of artfully placed maple trees and weeping willows, with a natural bubbling creek banked on both sides by varieties of fern incorporated into the extensive gardens.

The moment they were out of the shield of trumpet trees, and into the open Stefan's warning system kick into high gear. They weren't alone. Someone was stalking them in this little paradise Judith had created and that was okay with him. Stefan Prakenskii could handle snakes in the garden.

7

"WHO else lives here, Judith?" Stefan asked, his tone casual, displaying a mild, conversational interest only.

"The farm is one hundred thirty acres, and each of us has five acres so that we have our own private home. There are six houses here." There was the slightest hesitation he doubted anyone else would have noticed. "My sister Rikki is married." Her voice picked up speed. "We do have a central meeting place where we hold barbecues and work out. There's a fairly good gym now. Lissa is really into good health, mind and body, all that sort of thing."

So she hadn't wanted to admit that Rikki was married. Would Lev go that far to cover his tracks? It had been done before, but the results had been disastrous for both parties. Surely he wouldn't repeat such a terrible mistake. Although if his life depended on it . . . Stefan swore to himself. Of course Lev would take advantage of any woman to stay alive. What other choice would he have?

He took a calculated risk. "Maybe you should tell me what subjects are off-limits, Judith, so I don't make any mistakes here. I can't help being interested in your home and family, but if you're uncomfortable disclosing anything personal, I'll try to understand." That was definitely a Stefan Prakenskii maneuver, pushing her into a corner, something Thomas Vincent would never consider doing.

Judith sent him a small apologetic smile. "I guess you can tell I don't go out much. I've forgotten how to converse normally."

She was very, very good at sparring. He was proud of her for her comeback. It didn't suit his purposes so he wasn't going to let her get away with it, but as a sidestep, it was good.

"Then we'll practice. This is where you tell me how you came to buy this amazing piece of property." Start out small, nothing very threatening.

He felt the small flare of power instantly subdued. She was suppressing emotions again. It was a vital clue and one he would hold on to until he had enough to piece together enough information to tell him what was threatening Judith. Whatever she was afraid of was somehow tied up in the purchasing of the farm.

"I met some amazing women at a time in my life when I needed direction and maybe a safe place to rebuild my life—you know, take it in a positive direction. We built a strong bond of first friendship, and then sisterhood. Very quickly we realized we were stronger together. If we pooled our resources, we could build a better life together than apart. Blythe, my oldest sister, you met last night, had family here. She'd seen this little farm for sale and we snapped it up."

"It must have cost a fortune to buy a working farm."

"It was very run-down. We worked together to build it back up. The bare bones were there, and that was our first priority: to get the farm itself on its feet. We lived together in the big community building. It has a kitchen and a couple of bathrooms, so we had shelter while we planted and worked the land."

There was enthusiasm in her voice. He matched it and felt the expected kick of power, taking them both to the next level of passion for the subject—and she was passionate about the farm and her sisters. She kept herself restrained with a tight leash, but it slipped around him, little by little. He could handle her power, even aid her to control it. At the moment, it was in his best interests to allow her spirit a little freedom so she'd continue talking.

"Were you all raised on farms?"

"No. Why would you think that?" She quirked an eyebrow at him.

The sound of birds fluttering from branch to branch was loud in the small silence. A crow cawed. Another answered. His gaze shifted to the birds and then away. He pulled out his dark glasses and pushed them onto his nose. Lev was out there somewhere watching, and now, he was fairly certain he was correct. No one else had the kind of affinity for animals like his younger brother. The birds were definitely spying on him.

"Look around you, Judith." Stefan gestured toward the lush, prospering plants. "This farm is incredible. Someone has to know what they're doing. I can take over a business and turn it around, but I have to know what I'm doing."

Her shoulders relaxed a little more. "Lexi, my youngest sister, spent most of her life on a farm. She runs things. We just do whatever she tells us and it works."

It probably helped the prosperity that one or more of her sisters was an element: air, fire, water or earth. His heart jumped at the find. Maybe all four elements were represented. With Judith's powerful spirit, they would have no trouble using each of the elements to their advantage. The amazing gardens and rows and rows of vegetables, the groves of trees, made sense to him now.

If he was right, this might be the single most dominant conclave of elements alive. They would be impossibly powerful together, especially with Judith's spirit weaving through each of the talents. One was bound to the earth: Lexi. She would make things grow and prosper.

"I can't believe the job you've done here."

She gestured toward a small open trail wagon. "We can use this to get to the main part of the farm. Lexi was using the tractor on a new field recently. She said we could play around with it there without hurting any of her plants."

"Do you hurt her plants when you drive the tractor?"

She gave a little disdainful sniff. "Ha! You wish. She was referring to your lack of skill, not mine."

Genuine laughter felt amazing. This woman had given him more firsts than he'd considered possible. Teasing was a foreign concept to him and yet he found he enjoyed it immensely. "I'm warning you, Miss Henderson, I'm a very quick learner."

"We'll see."

He found himself weighing the advantages of pretending to be a little inept against showing off. He let her take the driver's seat, slipping into the doorless vehicle beside her. "So Lexi is a genuine farmer and you paint."

"Don't forget my kaleidoscopes," Judith said. "I love my kaleidoscopes."

"You're the artist. Tell me about Rikki, you said she was married. What does she do?"

"She's a sea urchin diver. She loves the sea."

He noted the pride in her voice. She had a soft spot for Lexi, but Rikki was very special to her. Her eyes lit up and she exuded warmth and happiness. He let his spirit absorb hers a little more, to feel that joy in her when she talked about her sisters.

"That's a strange profession." An affinity for the sea. For water. Stefan looked around the farm at the lush plants, and then up at the sky. A water element would be able to control rainfall, giving their farm much needed water to prosper.

"You mean for a woman?"

He grinned at the little bite in her tone. He nudged her with his shoulder. "Judith, you are a secret feminist, aren't you? No, actually I meant a sea urchin diver is something I haven't ever considered being. Tell me the truth. Had you ever considered it?"

She burst out laughing. "No, of course not. Rikki's autistic. She needs the sea like the rest of us need air. The pressure of the water, the solitary way of life, all appeal to her. You should see her though, Thomas, when she's on her boat or in the water, she's just incredible."

"Autistic."

Stefan tried to imagine what that would be like. What kind of fucking worm would stoop so low as to use an autistic woman to hide behind? Damn his brother. Rikki had to have been out in the ocean when the yacht Lev was working on had gone down. She must have picked him up and being trained in the art of survival, Lev had adapted quickly, persuading the poor unsuspecting woman that he loved her. Stefan was furious with his brother for marrying her.

"Is her husband autistic as well?"

A shadow passed over them and he glanced up to see a flock of birds wheeling overhead.

"Why would you ask that?"

"I don't know much about autism," he admitted. "I just thought maybe two people who have a similar difference might find each other."

"Thank you for not saying disability. Rikki is different, but she's whole, complete, and she's wonderful. Fortunately, her husband thinks so as well. He isn't autistic, but he's very protective of her. He helps her stretch her comfort zone a little, so that's good. Levi dives as well. They're a good match."

Levi. Stefan almost said the name aloud in disgust. *Lev, you're such a hound. I just might have to beat you within an inch of your life.* He found himself furious that his own brother would commit such an atrocity. There had to be a code didn't there?

"Do all of your sisters get along with her new husband?"

The wagon bumped over rough road. "I didn't say he was new."

He shrugged as casual as ever, but she was sharp, there was no question about it. He had to be careful of her probes. "I presumed from your earlier remarks that only you and your sisters bought the farm. You didn't mention him working it or building with you."

Faint color stole into her cheeks. She pushed at the long fall of hair, a gesture betraying nerves. She didn't like talking about good old Levi. *Bastard.*

"I guess I didn't."

Which told him nothing and yet everything. She wasn't going to tell him when Levi had come into her life. And that meant Lev had drilled it into all of them that his life was in danger and they believed him. Ivanov had come sniffing around this farm; he wouldn't miss Rikki being a sea urchin diver. Somehow she'd put the exterminator off the scent long enough that he'd filed a report and set Stefan up as bait to ferret out his brother.

"And Blythe?"

"She's a spinner. She owns a yarn shop in Sea Haven. She makes the most beautiful quilts as well as sweaters and all sorts of amazing things. Her yarn is sought after all over the world."

Once again enthusiasm and love poured into her voice. He was a man for detail, and Blythe was respected by Judith. It would be Blythe's approval that counted the most with Judith.

All around him were rows and rows of vegetables. He caught a glimpse of a house in the distance, but she didn't volunteer any information about it, so he ignored the structure as well. The road curved around and a lovely little meadow lay in front of them. He could see a large irrigation pond several yards away from the meadow. One side had been sectioned off and a shiny John Deere tractor sat invitingly out in the open.

"The attachment is a plow," Judith said helpfully. "Lexi's cultivating this area."

"How does it work?"

She stopped the trail wagon right there on the dirt road and hopped out. "The plow breaks up large lumps of earth much faster than we could ever do by hand." She glanced up at him. "I don't know how much you want to know and I don't want you to be bored."

He slid out of the wagon and walked around to get to her side. Leaning in close he caught a fistful of that inviting silky black fall of hair and tugged gently until she took the inevitable step into him. His mouth descended on hers and he had the distinct feeling of coming home. Her body melted into his, her soft breasts pressing into his chest, her arms sliding around him, holding him tightly, clinging as if to a safe anchor.

He wasn't safe—and neither was she. The moment his mouth settled over hers, the earth moved. Heat flared. The world changed. He was highly skilled at sex, and exceptionally practiced at the art of seduction, a cold, calculated seduction with him in complete control at all times. His brain always functioned and he completely controlled his body. That was all gone the moment her lips moved against his.

He hadn't ever taken pleasure in kissing. Not like this. Not this shocking loss of self, merging with her until he didn't want to live anywhere but in her. He didn't trust instant attraction, yet this was so much more. This was need. This swept emotions he'd forgotten he had into the forefront like a tidal wave.

He tasted innocence in her, tasted home. And that was crazy because he hadn't had a home since he was boy and

probably didn't know what the word even meant. *Judith.*
He was coming home. To her. To this farm. To this little village pulsing with so much power. Did the combination have
enough power to save a man like him? A man meant for the
shadows? His emotions welled up, real and strong, the intensity shaking him. He lost himself there in her mouth, in the
feel of her body moving restlessly against his.

She was reluctant to say they could ever have a relationship, yet her body melted into his the moment they touched.
She gave herself to him without reservation. He wasn't stupid enough to push his advantage any further and God help
him, he didn't want to. He wanted to do this right. He wanted
all of her, not just sex with her. The attraction was all-
encompassing and he'd been with nothing all of his life not
to recognize the real thing when it dropped into his lap.

The photo of her inside his pocket burned through the
thin layer of material against his skin, nearly as hot as her
kisses. He wanted her with every fiber of his being. He
came up for air and took another dive, going under fast.
Something stung the back of his neck hard and he jerked
back, nearly flinging both of them to the ground, afraid of
a bullet, before he heard the angry buzz of a bee.

Lev, you bastard. Back the hell off.

Stefan pressed his hand to the back of his neck. Already
there was swelling. "A bee just stung me."

For just one moment Judith looked carefully around
them, frowning, as if perhaps she'd felt that small surge of
energy. She was spirit and it would make sense that she
might feel power in the air as Lev directed the attack.

"Oh, no. Let me see." Judith turned her attention fully to
him, her expression anxious.

The sting was almost worth it to see that look in her
eyes, but he was furious with Lev and rather satisfied that
she might be as well.

*Who the hell do you think you are? I know that's you,
Lev.*

Then leave Judith alone. I know exactly what you're doing and you can forget it. Find yourself another woman to use.

Stefan closed his eyes, relief flooding him. He had been certain Lev was alive, but there was that small doubt he couldn't quite avoid. The sound of his brother's voice, no matter the harsh greeting, sent a surge of happiness through him.

"Are you allergic?" Judith asked. "Because this is already swelling. I need to take you back to the house and put something on it."

"I don't actually know whether I'm allergic or not," Stefan hedged. He was fairly certain he wasn't, but if it meant getting inside of her house, well . . . he wasn't in the least opposed.

Judith caught his hand and tugged him back toward the trail wagon. "We should go right away, just in case. Bee stings can be serious."

He slipped into the vehicle and raised his hand into the air over the top of the roof as she settled quickly into the driver's seat. He answered his brother with a worldwide, easily understood, finger gesture.

I've got you in my crosshairs.

Self-righteous, low-down bastard. Stefan repeated the finger gesture as Judith whipped the wagon around and sent it barreling over the rough ground, back toward her house.

Lev had *married* his cover, an autistic woman at that. Who the hell did he think he was judging Stefan when he'd committed an unpardonable sin? At least Stefan had a legitimate reason to be undercover in the first place. He'd come to find his idiotic younger brother and make certain he was safe. Now, he might have to take Lev down a peg or two, teach him a long needed lesson about right and wrong.

"You're upset," Judith observed, glancing at the muscles tightening in his jaw. "I'm so sorry this happened, Thomas."

"No worries, Judith," he assured her, all the while touching the back of his neck to shamelessly remind her of his injury. "I don't as a rule have problems with insects."

"You said you've never been stung."

He grinned at her. "Exactly. They leave me alone. That one was unusual, maybe a little vicious and jealous because I was kissing the lady of the realm."

The corners of her mouth went up and her dimple appeared. "I'm sure that's what caused the bee to sting you."

"If I were a bee, I might have gotten jealous. You do taste sweet." He pretended to frown, thinking it over. "Sweet with a taste of fire."

She blushed, the color creeping into her cheeks. "You're impossible. And if we're going to the hospital, I swear, I'm eating that lunch you brought."

"And I'm coming back for the tractor challenge. I refuse to allow a bee to keep me from proving to you that I can keep from driving the thing into a tree." He hesitated. Frowned. Made a show of rubbing the bridge of his nose. Glanced at her.

"What?" Judith asked. "Just tell me."

"You're going to think I'm paranoid." It was time to push just a little bit.

"I don't know why you would think that, unless you tell me you really did think the bee went after you specifically on purpose because you were kissing me."

He did think that, but he wasn't admitting it. "I was in the service, in combat a few times, Judith, and more than that, I have certain gifts. I wouldn't tell anyone else, but you seem to have abilities as well, we established that the other night . . ."

"And?" she prompted, just like he knew she would.

"Someone was watching us out there in that field. I could feel them." He hesitated again, deliberately appearing to choose his words carefully. "This is going to sound even crazier to you and at the risk of making you think I'm a lunatic, whoever was watching us was armed."

Stefan sent her another quick glance and looked away quickly, portraying Thomas Vincent perfectly. A man who had been in combat, with psychic gifts who knew the truth but was afraid of being ridiculed by a woman he was very attracted to.

He cursed himself for manipulating her. How was he any better than Lev? He was taking advantage of his training to extract information from her, playing on her sense of fairness, on her honesty. A woman like Judith would detest making him feel like a fool, especially when she knew it was the truth. Someone *had* been watching them, a sniper's rifle in his hands.

Judith's gaze shifted from his. "I'm sorry about that, Thomas." Her voice was quiet. Guilty.

"You *knew*?"

She moistened her lips. He decided there was no satisfaction in manipulating Judith. It made him feel every bit as low as he thought his brother was.

"I suspected it might happen," she admitted. "I'm really sorry if it made you uncomfortable. This farm is our sanctuary." She gave a small sigh. "It really isn't a big secret, we just don't talk about our lives to outsiders. My sisters and I met when we were all in a special victim's group counseling." Her gaze jumped to his and then shifted away. "Each of us is—was—a victim of violence in some way. A couple of my sisters are still at risk. We're very careful who we let on the farm—and very protective. I'm really sorry, Thomas."

"I'm sorry, Judith. I didn't mean to make you uncomfortable. You didn't have to tell me that. I appreciate that you did."

It was a lie and yet it wasn't. Damn the entire mess. She was being honest with him, honest to the point of revealing things about her sisters she felt guilty about telling him. He *had* meant to probe, deliberately pushing her into a corner until she had no choice other than to lie, leaving her guest thinking she believed him paranoid, or confessing the truth.

Of course Lev was out there with a rifle, watching someone coming onto the property, but his intentions weren't to protect the women. They were to protect himself. Damn Lev too.

Judith drove back to the shed and parked the trail wagon. "Let me take another look at your neck."

"It's a little swollen," Stefan admitted. "And it stings like hell, but I don't feel like I can't breathe. Isn't that what you're afraid of?"

Judith moved in close again, just behind him. Instincts and years of training honed into his very bones had him turning, catching her wrist as she lifted it to examine the sting site. He forced a smile, his thumb sliding over her skin to prevent bruising. She blinked up at him confused.

"Automatic reflexes are the devil," he said with a disarming boyish grin.

"Don't be a baby, let me see."

He half turned, retaining possession of her hand, forcing her to touch his neck with the other one. The position was a little awkward, but she didn't protest. Her fingers were gentle on his neck. The sensual brush of her touch went straight through his body. His groin tightened, flooding with hot blood in response to the warm breath against the back of his neck as she leaned in closer to inspect the swelling.

"I think the stinger is still in there, Thomas," she said, worry in her voice.

"What does that mean?"

He couldn't think straight and maybe the bee had gotten inside his head because he could hear a loud buzzing growing into thunder. It took a minute to realize it was his pulse pounding so loud. She had a way of throwing him without him even knowing it was happening until it was far too late to guard against her spell.

"It means I'll have to get it out."

"Can't we just leave it in?"

She slipped her arm around his waist, fitting neatly under his shoulder. A slight wind stirred the trumpet trees, drawing his attention to the darting army of hummingbirds. He was going to have to go through that gauntlet to get into Judith's house. Who knew what else his deviant brother would come up with to torture him in the hopes that he'd leave.

"No, we can't leave it in," Judith scolded. "And it really is swelling, Thomas. I need to put some allergy cream on it quickly. Come on."

Without even hesitating, Judith stepped onto the narrow lane woven through the thick stand of trumpet trees with those nasty little birds just waiting to do Lev's bidding. Two steps in and the birds flew at Stefan's head, tiny wings buzzing loudly, the sharp beaks going at his skin, veering away at the last minute. Some protective instinct long forgotten had him wrapping his arm around Judith's head, covering her face from the attack.

Judith let out a little shocked cry and picked up the pace with his, although she couldn't see much, her hands up defensively. He used his body to protect hers and his arms to shield her face, his anger growing into a slow burn.

Knock it off, Lev. If she gets one scratch on her I'm going to come after you and you seriously don't want that. He meant it too.

Stefan had come to save his brother's life, to warn him of an assassin stalking him, but now he wanted to punch him right in that smug mouth. Lev thought he had a good gig going here, deceiving these women—Judith's sisters— well, it just wasn't going to continue. And if his smartass playing around caused one of the birds to attack her, Lev was getting the beating of his life.

You could try, but I doubt you'll get more than the first punch in.

Clearly Lev had forgotten who was the older brother and in charge. Judith let out a second little sound of distress. He could feel her fear beating at him. Cold, black fury rose, smoldering just below the surface in direct proportion to her fear, always a bad sign.

You're scaring her, you bastard.

The birds abruptly backpedaled.

Why the hell didn't you just say so instead of posturing like a puffed up adder?

You're right, why on earth would I give you credit for having a brain? Stefan poured contempt into his voice. He was disgusted with his brother using these women. He took great care to push aside his disgust at himself for thinking to do the same thing.

The connection between them was slipping away over the distance. Stefan made certain to "feel" for a direction. Before he left, he was going to find out just which house belonged to Rikki, Lev's supposed wife, so he could pay his brother a little visit and toss him out on his ear.

"Are they gone?" Judith asked, her voice trembling.

Stefan's protective instincts kicked at him hard at that little catch in her voice. He removed his arm so she could see. They were almost out of enemy territory, approaching the last of the trumpet trees. "I believe we're safe," he assured.

"I've never seen them act that way before. Hummingbirds are aggressive, but they were actually attacking us."

"Maybe we were too close to a nest," Stefan suggested.

"I suppose that's as good an explanation as any." She sounded a little suspicious and took another careful look around with that little frown he found adorable, before giving him her attention again. "First the bee stings you and now the birds attack. I'm so sorry, Thomas. This was supposed to be a fun afternoon for you."

His arm tightened around her. "I'm an adventurous man, Judith."

She smiled up at him. "You're a good sport, I'll say that for you." She glanced at his neck, worry in her eyes. "Your neck really is swelling."

He could feel it. He'd been shot quite a few times, knifed,

tortured and other unpleasant things. It would be irony if he was done in by a small bee his brother had sent after him. Wouldn't Ivanov get a kick out of that? He did rather like the alarm in her voice for him. She was genuinely worried about him and since it was a brand-new, unfamiliar experience for anyone to actually gave a damn about him, he found he enjoyed it just a little too much. This woman could make him weak so easily.

She held his hand as they moved through the gardens together, the breeze sliding over them, tugging at tendrils of her hair and ruffling hers. He liked the way they moved together, the way silence settled over them both, easy and companionable. Stefan Prakenskii was never truly at ease with another human being. Thomas Vincent would have no difficulties being in the presence of others, as would any of his many personas, but not Stefan, and yet, it was Stefan walking beside Judith, holding her hand and feeling as if she'd handed him a miracle.

He couldn't turn his head easily with his neck swelling so much. The pain was nothing to him, a small, annoying sting he barely noticed, but it definitely got him Judith's attention. She rubbed her fingers over his arm continually, looking up at him with little anxious glances from under her long, feathery lashes, making him feel as if he'd been handed the world. It amazed him that one woman could actually change the way a man thought, his actions—more, his entire reason for existing.

She led him up the stairs to her house, a large, two-story structure. The house nestled in the center of the gardens, so looking out any of the many windows, they were surrounded by brilliant color.

"My studios are on the ground floor," Judith explained as she opened the front door.

Stefan stepped into her entryway and again, as he had at the gates to the farm, felt the subtle shift of energy around him. Judith's power lived and breathed in this house. The force rushed to surround him, building his joy at discovering Judith into almost euphoria. He was already fighting his physical attraction to her, a first for him, testing his years of discipline, but now, that raging hunger was amplified beyond measure.

He breathed deeply and moved inside. Her fragrance hit him hard, triggering such a need he simply turned, toed the door closed as he bunched her hair into his fist and walked her backward, his mouth coming down hard on hers. Her lips parted, accepting him, welcoming him, opening to his invasion, her arms sliding around his neck as he forced her back against the door.

There was nowhere else he wanted to be than right there, devouring her, tasting all that wonderful passion, a deep well, pouring flames into him, all his. He'd made his claim, branded her with his mark and given her his soul. He had to touch her skin, that bare expanse inviting his exploration. His hand caressed her, finding the intriguing gold chain. He tugged at it.

"You should be wearing this and nothing else, Judith," he murmured, trailing kisses over her face, down to her chin where he nipped gently with his teeth. "I swore I wouldn't push this. I want to do it right. I don't want a flash of heat for a night and then it's over. I want forever, Judith. Every damn night with you, every single day."

She clung to him, breathing as heavily as he was. "We can't have forever. You don't understand about me. You don't, Thomas, and I should never have allowed this."

"Then let's talk about it. Explain it to me. I know you're a spirit element. I have my own talents, Judith and of course they can get out of control, any talent can."

"*Exactly.*" She dropped her arms and stepped back.

He felt inexplicitly empty. *He* controlled his world, not a woman. Not his handler. No one else. And yet it was getting harder and harder to breathe, knowing she was a breath away from tossing him out.

He caged her in, both hands resting on the door beside her head. "We're going to talk about this, Judith. I'm not the kind of man to give up on something so important."

He took a breath knowing he was going to be absolutely honest with her in this moment. "I've *never,* not one time, wanted a woman in the same way I want you. Do I want to throw you down on the floor and show you a million ways I know to give you so much pleasure you'd never look at another man? Damn straight. But it's so much more and I've never felt the more before. Not one time. You don't throw the more away, not when it's a fucking miracle and will never happen in your lifetime again. So, no, I'm not leaving until we talk this out."

Her dark eyes searched his. She should have been afraid. He was an intimidating man with his bulk of muscle and his scars. She didn't appear afraid *of* him, only *for* him. Her hand slipped to his chest, fingers splayed wide. She drew in her breath, as if she felt that same burning in her lungs.

"Thomas, I'm trying so hard to save you."

He bent his head and kissed her again, a gentle, coaxing kiss bordering on tenderness. He had no idea where those gentler emotions came from, but she'd tapped into them and, although for him the rest of the world didn't really exist outside those shadows, she was real to him, and so were those emotions reserved for her alone.

"I need saving, Judith." He gave her the stark, raw truth. "But sending me away won't accomplish that. Fight for us. Give us a chance. That's all I'm asking."

"We barely know each other. How can I tell you things I've never told anyone else?"

"You know me. We both know. You're not like other people and neither am I. Maybe it's our gifts, but you know me, Judith. Your body recognized me. Your mind is fighting, but your heart and soul know as well. I'm the one. Give us a chance."

She sighed and slid her hand up to his wrist. "Let me

look at the bee sting." Before he could make demands, she shook her head. "I need time to think, Thomas. Please don't push me right now."

He stayed still, caging her between his body and the wall, wanting her shamelessly, his body's demands merciless. More than that, he wanted this moment to be right. He needed to handle this the right way and he didn't have any experience in matters of the heart. He operated outside such parameters.

"You're giving me all the firsts I should have had over the last thirty years."

"I don't know what that means."

"It means you can take a look at my neck and fuss over me."

A slow smile curved her mouth as he straightened and held out his hand to her. She threaded her fingers through his without hesitation.

"You're a good man, Thomas," Judith said with a small sigh as she led the way to her bathroom.

It was a feminine room. Spacious and filled with colorful things. The room was designed to be both restful and soothing, a place of the sea with splashes of color winding through shades of blue, gray and green. He sat on a low makeup bench, facing away from the mirror while she took tweezers and pushed his head down so she could shine the makeup lights directly on the sting site.

He heard a hitch in her breath and his world stilled to that moment. To Judith. To the sins she was determined to push him away with.

"A few years ago, when I was an art student in Paris, I met a man. He was wealthy and handsome and years above me in experience."

There was so much self-loathing in her voice he actually winced.

"I was dazzled by him, so dazzled by him that I . . ." Her

voice trailed off and he felt the burn as she caught the stinger with the tweezers and pulled, removing the tiny barb from his flesh. "I see auras. And his was muddy and complicated and violent. All the signs were there, but I didn't want to see them. I wanted to believe the things he said to me, not something no one else could see."

She dabbed some cream onto the sting. He waited until she put the tube down and caught her wrist gently and pulled her around to stand in front of him, wedged between his thighs. His hands settled on her waist.

"How old were you, Judith?"

She shook her head. "I was twenty-one. Very naive. A young twenty-one in terms of experience with men. I studied so much that I never really was around men, not that I'm giving myself an excuse. Somewhere, deep inside, I knew better. I just refused to heed the warning signs." She refused to look away from him, her hands resting on his shoulders. "One day I went to see him without calling first. I slipped in the back door to surprise him. The door to his study was barely opened and I heard voices. Screaming cut off. The smell of blood." She pressed one hand to her mouth.

He could see nightmares in her eyes. "He was torturing someone."

"Not Jean-Claude. He just stood there watching. His men. He was always surrounded by very scary men. He told me it was because of his money and his work, that people wanted him dead. I ran." She moistened her lips. "I slipped out before anyone saw me. I was so scared that I called my brother, Paul. He was older than me and had raised me after my parents had died in a car accident. Of course he came to help me, dropped everything and rushed over to France with money and a way to disappear."

8

STEFAN waited, needing Judith to trust him enough to confide in him. Her pain was all-consuming. Heartbreaking. He could feel it pressing down on him so heavily his chest hurt. The walls around him throbbed with pain—breathed in and out with it—although she either was used to the phenomenon or didn't notice. He expected the house to weep, and maybe it was. Judith was lost in that moment, as real as if it were happening all over again and he suspected, for her, it was. She probably had nightmarish recurrences night after night.

Judith's voice trembled, although he doubted she knew. She was looking directly into his eyes, but she was no longer with him, far away in another country over the sea reliving the horror.

"They caught up with us in Greece. Paul sent me on ahead of him but when he didn't join me, I went back. They were torturing him, trying to find out my location. I . . ." She trailed off again, took another big breath.

Stefan tightened his grip on her hands to give her courage. "Tell me."

"I—I lost it completely. My emotions were so intense. Fear. Rage. Sorrow. Guilt. I *loathed* myself and all of them. I wanted them dead. I wanted Jean-Claude dead. I lost complete control, and someone like me can't do that. It's dangerous."

He could feel those fierce emotions swirling around him, pulling at him, the house fighting to contain the force of energy coming off her in swamping waves. He felt battered, like great cliffs during a stormy, turbulent sea. Stefan adjusted his breathing and accepted the assault of emotions, absorbing the hammering intensity, grateful he'd learned to push emotions aside. He had no idea, given his ability to kill in so many ways, just what the continual pounding at him would have done, had he not been so disciplined. There was no doubt he felt that same rage, loathing, fury and terrible, endless sorrow swamping him.

"What happened?" His voice was a thin thread of sound directing her, barely infiltrating the memory she was locked so tightly in.

"They all turned on each other. It was a horrible bloodbath, the sound of guns so loud, reverberating off the walls. Men were screaming and shouting." She gulped air, her eyes wild now, her body shaking. Judith lifted her palms up and looked down at them, as if her hands and arms were covered in her brother's blood.

Her voice dropped to a whisper. "The police arrived."

Her eyes went nearly opaque, reflecting back at him the horror of that moment. He could see blood running down the walls to pool on the floor. Blood splattered over her face and clothes where she knelt beside her lifeless brother, his body torn, nearly unrecognizable as human.

"I was in shock, I think. I can't remember thinking anything at all. I just *felt*. So much anger. So much darkness. I *hated* Jean-Claude. I still hate him. But worse, the pain of losing Paul that way, it was so vivid and stark and raw, I couldn't contain it."

She obviously wasn't aware tears were running down her face as she blinked to clear her vision, to see him. She shook her head, confusion on her face. "I don't remember what I was doing. I try, but I can only hear the sound of the policemen yelling at one another. I tried CPR on my brother, but his chest and head were covered in blood and it kept splashing over my arms and hands. The sound was so awful." She clapped both palms over her ears, nearly hyperventilating.

Stefan rose, his movement quiet and very slow. She was locked deep into the memory of that moment and her emotions were, like then, out of control. The wind rushed through the house. Drapes went wild. He knew she didn't see, didn't see the fierce battering at him as she relived her brother's murder. Very gently he caught her wrists and tugged to bring her hands to his chest, stepping close to her. Her body was cold, hands like ice.

"The police have arrived, Judith."

She let out a small gasp, looking up at him with dazed eyes. "One of them came close to me, to try to help me, I guess." She frowned, looking as if she were more confused than ever. "There was so much blood. So much pain. I felt so much sorrow. I wanted to take his place, to be where he was. I was so sorry for what I'd done, so guilty that . . ."

He waited, needing to hold her, wanting to put a stop to this, but knowing it wouldn't matter. She would always have these moments etched into her memories for all time.

Judith swallowed several times, opened her mouth and closed it, gulped air and bunched his shirt in her fists as if she needed him to be her anchor. "The officer pulled out a gun and put it to his head. He shot himself, right there, before anyone knew what he intended. He was standing next to me, one moment reaching down to help me and the next his blood was everywhere and his body fell right on top of mine."

Stefan closed his eyes briefly, the sorrow so heavy in his

heart that he felt crushed. He knew it was her sorrow, her body crushed beneath the dead policeman. For a man who had lived most of his existence with emotions firmly locked away, he was getting a crash course in real life with a woman a man loved. The picture of lying in her brother's blood with the innocent policeman's body on top of hers, was all too real in his mind. For the first time in more years than he could remember, he wanted to weep for another human being.

Stefan pulled her rigid body into his arms, sweeping away her resistance with sheer strength. He held her tight, willing his body heat to seep into her, to warm her and bring her back from a place of death and despair. His hands slid into her mass of hair, bunching the silky strands in his fist, massaging her scalp with strong fingers.

"Come back to me, Judith. You're safe with me now. You can scream if you need to. Cry. But stay with me. There's no need to be afraid for me."

She shook her head, her fear beating at him.

"I can take anything you feel, the worst you have to offer, *il mio angelo caduto*. I'm not new at this. I've been there, right where you are. You aren't alone, not as long as I'm in the world with you."

Judith spoke seven languages, she couldn't fail to interpret his *my fallen angel* spoken in Italian with a perfect accent. She made a single sound of despair that broke his heart.

Stefan pulled her head back ruthlessly by the hair bunched tight in his fist, no longer asking. He wasn't that kind of man. His mouth found hers and took possession, driving his tongue deep, commanding her to acknowledge him. Acknowledge that she was safe with him, no matter the intensity of her emotions. He lived in the shadows. He understood battles. He wasn't new to the game and he would stand for her.

It took a few moments but she kissed him back, gripping him tight, holding him to her, while darkness and loathing beat at his body, while horror battered his heart and sorrow bruised his soul. Her body lost most of its stiffness, softening, melting into his in surrender.

Stefan kissed his way down the side of her face, following the tracks of her tears. "I'm here, Judith. I'm not running. Look around you. The house is still standing. I'm in one piece and I've got you safe. Do you really want to be alone?"

"I'm not the perfect woman everyone wants to think I am."

Her confession was muffled against his mouth and he kissed her again. "I'm not looking for perfection. I'm not a man who could live with that. I've committed a few sins myself, Judith. You're safe with me. You are. I'll tell you a million times if you need to hear me say it that often." He loosened his hold on her hair, allowing her to bury her face against him again.

"I can feel them both, above and below me, sandwiching me in. All the blood and brains and matter." She choked, began to cry again. "I hate him so much. Jean-Claude. I know I'm responsible. The counselor and my sisters say differently, but I was the one who ignored the warning signs. I saw what I wanted to see and my brother paid the price. I didn't control my emotions and the officer paid with his life."

She rubbed at her arms, her face buried against his chest, her ear over the steady beat of his heart. "There was so much blood, Thomas, and none of it was mine. It should have been me there, not my brother."

"Was Jean-Claude there?"

He felt the faint shake of her head and he pressed his lips against her ear, tenderness welling up like a fountain from some depth inside him he didn't know he had. He smoothed one hand down her back, pressing her closer to him.

"Of course not. He was safe in his little castle waiting for his men to drag me back to him. I went into hiding for two months." Her voice turned bitter. "I couldn't even retrieve my brother's remains and bring him home. Jean-Claude was arrested for running drugs, guns and human trafficking, but not murder. And he had my brother murdered. He's responsible."

She looked up at him. "I'm not absolving myself of my part in what happened, don't think that for a minute, but I've taken a look at the prison he's in, read all about it. France is supposed to be big and bad, but Jean-Claude has a cushy little cell and continues to run his operations right from there."

"How do you know that?"

She shrugged and stepped back. Stefan let her go, dropping his arms to his side, his mind racing.

"Have you visited him?"

She scowled at him, a fierce, black expression, loathing in her eyes. "*Never.* I will never give him the satisfaction of seeing me, knowing what he took from me just because he could."

Stefan chose his words very carefully. The intensity of emotions hammering at him had lessened just a little and he didn't want to trigger another assault. His body actually felt bruised and battered.

"Do you think he sent those men after you because he wanted you back? He was afraid of what you saw and that you might testify against him? Or did he give you something he wanted back?"

Her gaze jumped to his face.

"A wealthy man gives expensive presents. They often want them back in a fit of temper, especially if it is a family heirloom."

"I think he sent those men after me out of pure spite. He once told me that I could never leave him—that he wouldn't let me. I was young enough and stupid enough to be thrilled. I thought that meant he loved me and would fix anything that went wrong between us."

He reached out. Judith flinched away from him. He shook his head. "Don't." Hard authority edged his voice. He wasn't about to lose her, not now. "We've come this far, Judith, there's no point in retreating. Look at me."

He held out his arms to encompass the house. "I'm still standing. You relived the entire horrible event, experienced the same intense emotions and I'm handling it."

Judith sighed and walked away from him, over to the window to look out at her gardens below, breathing deeply, striving for control. Stefan followed her, doing a slow sweep of the countryside from the vantage of her large bank of windows. The bright flowers shimmered in the slight breeze and at once he felt a lessening of the intensity of Judith's emotions. Degree by slow degree, she was bringing her passionate nature back under control.

He didn't mind passion or fire. He could handle both. And he could handle her sorrow, her tears. She was his. It was that simple to him. She was his. Whatever she needed, he intended to provide. She shivered and he moved in close, rubbing her arms to warm her.

"This is happening too fast. I don't trust fast," she murmured, shaking her head.

"You don't trust," Stefan corrected gently. "Neither do I, but that doesn't negate the fact that we're already here. Let's eat lunch, Judith. Show me around your house. Let's just take a little breathing room."

"You think that's the worst of me?" She looked over her shoulder at him. "It isn't, Thomas. I wish it was the worst."

She was determined to drive him away, to expose her worst secrets. To her, he was Thomas Vincent, a good man. She had no idea that on her worst day, she couldn't hold a candle to the sins of Stefan Prakenskii.

He bent his head and placed his mouth against her ear. "Tell me then. Give me the worst, Judith."

"You're a good person, Thomas. Inside, where it counts, you're a good person. I don't understand why you think you could ever be with someone who can't control their emotions and others pay the price."

"You aren't less than me because your element gets away from you. Never think I haven't done far worse in my lifetime."

He turned her around to face him, automatically drawing her back away from the window. The habit was ingrained in him, like so many others he would never overcome even if his life changed completely. He was giving her Stefan's truth, not Thomas's. It was possible she would put his sentiment down to service in the military, misleading herself, but he would give her as much truth as he could, share himself with her, not his cover.

She studied his expression, his jaw, the coolness of his stare. "I want him dead. Jean-Claude. I want him to suffer and die." This time she didn't look away, her gaze steady, her chin up as if she was waiting for judgment.

"So you want justice." He shrugged. "That's hardly unusual, or something to be ashamed of, *mi angel caido.*" This time he changed to Spanish, wanting to drive home the point that he was also educated in languages, and that no matter how fallen she thought herself, she was his angel and always would be.

Judith continued to stare him straight in the eye as she shook her head slowly, deliberately. "Not justice. Justice was Jean-Claude going to jail for his crimes. I want revenge for the torture and murder of my brother. For the others that lost their lives that day. I'm well aware that my need for revenge makes me no better than he is, but I *will* find a way. My time will come. And I'm not going to let any innocent suffer because of my loss of humanity."

Stefan regarded her for a long time in absolute silence, so long that Judith wasn't certain he would respond. She'd told him the worst and refused to look away from him. He was a difficult man to read. His aquamarine eyes looked back into hers, but told her nothing at all. She heard the ticking of the

clock and her stomach did a slow flip. She realized she
didn't want him to think so badly of her when she knew she
deserved it.

"What kind of woman builds her life around revenge?"
she whispered, hating the silence between them, hating that
she couldn't read his inscrutable expression.

"I know I have five wonderful women in my life. The
farm. My painting and kaleidoscopes, both of which I love
and have achieved some success in my chosen career, but it
isn't enough, it won't ever be enough until Jean-Claude La
Roux has suffered the way he made my brother suffer."

The ticking of the clock grew louder. Her heart thudded
hard in her chest until she could hear every beat thundering in her ears. She hadn't realized until that moment how
he'd already changed her. Laughter was real. She felt at
ease in his company, she felt happy. She hadn't really been
happy since her brother's death and maybe she was a little angry and guilty that she could actually be happy. What
right did she have when Paul's last hours had been excruci-
ating agony?

She refused to lower her chin, or look away from Thomas.
He was so utterly still, his gaze never leaving hers. She had
confessed to save him—or to drive him away so she could
keep her anger and hatred bottled up tight, locked away in a
dark studio where no one would ever know her shameful
secret.

Silence stretched between them until she wanted to
scream with the terrible tension. Stefan stepped closer to
her, his strong fingers curling around the nape of her neck.
There was always such command in the way he touched her.
This time was subtly different. This time there was possession as if she belonged to him.

Her heart jumped. She tasted fear. He wasn't going to
reject her and once he claimed her, she was forever set on a
course. She wouldn't be able to walk away from Thomas

Vincent, not with the way her spirit responded to his. Now with the certain knowledge that he could handle her intense emotions and perhaps even help control them.

She shook her head and went to step back, away from him, away from the danger she instinctively knew she was in.

His hold on her tightened, keeping her still. "I understand you, Judith. The way you think and feel. I can handle every emotion you have and I can lessen the impact on anyone around us. I can shield others from the intensity. Who else can do that? You need me every bit as much as I need you. You need this man to suffer, I'm your man. You need to disappear and start over; we can do that as well. I've got you, *moi padshii angel*. Whatever happens, I've got you."

Russian this time. My fallen angel. She had fallen. Judith felt as if the very devil was standing in front of her, offering her the world, and the price was her soul. He wasn't handsome in the true sense of the word, not with all of his scars, but he was all male, sensual and compelling. He would never be a man who would allow her to walk all over him, nor could she manipulate him. There was far more to Thomas Vincent than she'd first thought.

"I don't know you at all." Her voice came out a shaky whisper.

"You know enough."

"You should be running from this house. It's called *self-preservation*, Thomas. I'm already damned. I've accepted that."

"That's bullshit, Judith. Revenge is a natural emotion when someone has gone through the trauma you have. You haven't come face-to-face with the man who had your brother killed yet. You haven't had the tool in your hands to do the things you want to do to him. There is no judgment or damnation for thinking about making someone suffer and die. That comes *after* you carry out your actual revenge. You may not go through with it when the time comes."

She didn't flinch. "I'll go through with it." There was steel in her tone this time.

She wasn't going to back down, not even to make him want her. She wouldn't lie to him, or drag him down with her. She'd lived in her own hell too long to allow anyone else to join her. The isolation and lie of her life was difficult enough without the weight of another terrible sin, dragging someone else down into the abyss with her.

"Until that time, Judith, don't be so hard on yourself. Everyone, at sometime in their life, thinks of revenge. I certainly have done so."

Looking into those cool, aquamarine eyes, she believed him. She found herself shivering. Thomas Vincent wasn't *just* the innocent businessman she thought him. Whatever he'd done during his time in the service hadn't been easy and he had a hard core of strength that went with his physical appearance.

She shook her head, confused. She wanted this man with everything in her. She had confessed to the counselor and to her sisters that she was the cause of her brother's vicious murder. She had *not* admitted her part in the death of the innocent policeman. She knew her sisters felt responsible for the violent deaths in their families, but the fact was, unlike the rest of them, she *was* responsible.

Not one other person knew until Thomas. He hadn't turned away from her and he hadn't been harmed when, once again, she'd lost control of her emotions. There was such amazing freedom in the knowledge that she could talk to him without hiding part of herself. She didn't have to lie to him. He knew the worst of her and he still stood there looking at her with that very dangerous and compelling hunger.

She was going to lose herself in this man. If she let him any closer, if she let him another inch into her life, he would become her world. There was no one else for her and she had stepped into the age-old lure of sexual attraction. She was sinking so fast now he had faced the worst in her and had stayed, she was afraid there was no way to save either of them. He might think he could really make a man suffer before he killed him, but in truth, whatever he'd done in service to his country had been a different situation altogether. She could never ask such a terrible thing of him and she doubted, if it came right down to it, that he would be able to do such a thing. It went against nature.

Stefan watched Judith carefully. He was adept at reading body language. He'd learned in a hard school and knew every nuance of the human expression. She was trying to find a way to gracefully retreat. She accepted that he thought he might understand her need for revenge, but he would never follow through. Interrogation techniques often were called torture by some. Certainly Judith would think so. That too, had been learned in a hard school. He knew all about interrogation and the consequences of not getting information required.

She wasn't expecting anything from him that he hadn't done throughout his lifetime, although, he was certain she would never actually go through with it. She might be able to kill Jean-Claude quick and clean, and only then, he was certain, if she wasn't thinking clearly. But Judith was incapable of torture. She might dream of it, even plan it, but she was totally without the killer instinct.

"You aren't going to run away from me, Judith," he said, meaning it. He'd emerged partially from the shadows and something incredible was in his sites. "I know you're scared, angel, but we can do this. Give it a little time. Show me around your house. Eat the lunch I fixed for us. We'll pick this up at another time."

His thumb brushed over her pulse, felt it jump and then began to beat more steadily. She blinked up at him before some of the tension drained out of her. Her tongue touched her lower lip, drawing his complete attention.

"You called me 'my fallen angel' in three different languages."

He flashed a small grin. "That's called showing off."

Which was true, but even more, he wanted to call her an endearment in his own language and it was better to throw her off by using several languages instead of just Russian. He found he detested lying to her. Even misleading seemed wrong. She'd put everything on the line for him, yet he couldn't reciprocate. If he admitted that he was Lev's brother, it would put her in a terrible position. One thing he knew for certain about Judith, she was extremely loyal and she would deny knowing Lev and protect him with every breath in her body, something his brother would count on.

Judith would be forced to lie to him and worse, she would suspect him of being a Russian agent sent to kill Lev. No doubt his brother had impressed on all of the women the need for secrecy. Damn the man. Lev's deception to cover himself left Stefan with no recourse other than to mislead Judith as well.

"You showed off beautifully," Judith said. "Italian, Russian and Spanish."

He nodded. "And I can speak French if you'd rather I use that instead."

"Why your 'fallen angel'?"

Stefan framed her face in his hands, leaned in and kissed her upturned mouth. His tongue ran along the seam of her lips, commanding she open to him. When she didn't respond immediately, his teeth caught her lower lip and tugged gently until she gave a small breathless gasp. He took possession, his mouth moving over hers, kissing her over and over, each kiss deeper and more demanding.

You are my fallen angel. Deliberately, he thrust the words into her mind, a connection that was as intimate as exchanging breath—as kissing her.

Her arms crept around his neck and she pressed her body against his, willing to give herself to him. He was as hard as a rock, aching, his body making urgent demands, but he wanted so much more from her and a part of him knew he needed to go slow. If this was to last a lifetime, she had to know he wasn't using her, nor was he taking a small part of her.

"I want it all, Judith," he said, drawing back, "not one night. Not just your body."

"I don't know if I'm even capable of giving more."

Because her voice was so unsteady, he took her hand and drew her toward the interior of the house, moving farther away from the windows. "We don't have to worry about what you can or can't do right now, Judith. Show me around your house."

"Are you certain you don't have to go to the hospital?"

There was a teasing, almost hopeful note in her voice.

"You just want to see if I faint or not if they give me a shot."

Her eyebrow shot up. "I can't imagine that."

He flashed a grin at her. "I can't either." And that was the stark truth. He'd stayed silent under all forms of torture and brought his body again and again to the brink of human endurance, never once faltering in his course to carry on. A needle was not felt. More than once he'd sewn up his own wounds.

"This is the main part of the house. I have a large master bedroom and bath. I'm a tub person, so I'm ashamed to say, it's enormous, deep and wonderful."

The room had a rounded bank of windows overlooking the gardens below. As in the rest of the house, the walls were creamy white, a backdrop for the bright splashes of colored quilts carefully folded in a corner of the room.

He nodded at the six thick quilts. A seventh was on her bed.

A blush stole into her cheeks. "They're beautiful and depending on my mood, I make up the bed accordingly."

"You have moods?"

"Absolutely." She was unrepentant. "*Very* moody."

He crossed the room, unable to prevent the image of her

writhing naked under him, pressed deep into the thick, soft carpet, all bare golden skin and silky black hair against that backdrop of cream. Well, okay then. He pressed his thumb into the center of his palm, small brushing caresses right where it itched the most. If he was going to suffer, she might as well accompany him.

Judith gasped, her hand going to her throat, her gaze jumping to his.

"I have moods too," he explained, allowing his gaze to drift over her body.

She pushed open the bathroom door to show off the spacious bathroom. He stepped in close to her, so close that she couldn't fail to feel the heat radiating from his body. He liked the look of the tub. If she was in it and he stood right beside it, all she would have to do was turn her head just a little and she'd be at the perfect height . . .

He groaned, his cock jumping, reacting to the thought of her hot mouth engulfing him, tongue stroking, mouth tight like a silken fist.

"You can't be in here either," she said and tugged at his arm to get him out of the doorway. Her breath was coming faster now, breasts rising and falling, the color sweeping up her neck into her face. "Do you think of anything other than sex?"

"Not around you. But I'm determined to behave."

"You're not behaving at all, you know." She closed the door firmly on her bedroom. "Is it safe to show you the guest bathroom?"

"Do you have a tub in there?"

"Yes, but not like one in the master bath." She paused, one hand on the door, looking up at him a little mischievously. "The shower is killer though." She opened the door slowly.

Oh yeah. His mind could see them in that large shower together, the two of them fogging up all that glass, hands soaping up her body, delving into all her secrets.

"This time it's you." His voice was a little hoarse.

"You aren't the only one with fantasies."

Not only did she look mischievous, and smug, but she looked absolutely adorable with her feathery eyelashes, tempting dimple and laughing eyes—and he didn't find women "adorable." He had never engaged in teasing before. He'd lived a lifetime in the shadows, years of seduction and intrigue, killing and disappearing, and only now did he feel he'd come alive and was experiencing so many firsts. He'd kissed many women, but kissing Judith felt like the first time. His body became aroused on demand, but with Judith, his body responded with a will of its own—another first for him. And now teasing. She made him laugh.

"You're deliberately tempting me," he accused, realizing it was true.

She flashed a smile at him. "Maybe a little," she conceded.

"You're going to give me trouble, aren't you?"

"Absolutely." She pushed open the guest room door revealing another spacious bedroom. "This bed is really comfortable."

He noted that large banks of windows seemed to be part of every room. She'd built the upper story with views in mind, not security. He could see great distances from every part of the house, but with open windows, even though the glass was tinted, a sniper could easily get a good shot. Inwardly he sighed. If he was to stay here on the farm, in this house—and what the hell was he thinking—he'd have to come up with a solution to the problem of those windows. How expensive was it to get bullet-proof glass in so many windows? He had money. Anyone in his position knew how to acquire and hide large amounts of money.

"Why aren't there dogs?"

She frowned at him as she closed the bedroom door. "Dogs? I don't understand."

"On a property of this size with so many of you being

survivors of violence, I would expect a few dogs to help guard the property."

"Oh, that. Yes, it makes sense. Lexi and Airiana really push for dogs and so does Rikki's husband."

Of course Lev would want dogs. "You don't want them?"

"Not until Rikki is comfortable with the idea. She has a difficult time with change. We've been talking about it for some time, sort of stepping around the idea, but now that she's married and her husband has weighed in on the issue, I think we're definitely going to have a few dogs. Airiana is very excited and I think Lexi will be relieved when we get them. She's alone a lot working and a dog would make a good companion."

"Is your security system new?" He indicated the panel of numbers just inside her hallway. "You aren't using it."

She made a face. "Levi wanted one installed in all our homes so we did it, but it's a nuisance." She led the way down the wide, sweeping staircase to the story below.

"Nuisance?" he prompted. "Judith, security isn't a nuisance. It's put in place to protect you. Each of your houses is a good distance from the others. Essentially, you're a woman alone living out here."

She rolled her eyes. "Now you sound like Levi. I like to go out onto my balcony in the middle of the night. Sometimes I sit in the garden or if I'm up late painting, sometimes all night, I leave the French doors open. My sisters come in all the time. I like an open-door policy. We're always in and out of each other's homes. If we had the security system on it would be going off continually."

"You have some serious issues, Judith. You need a little self-preservation drilled into you. All of you do."

"I'm *never* introducing you to Levi. He's got us all learning self-defense, weapons and even shooting guns. If the two of you ever got together we'd be an armed camp instead of a farm." She pushed open the door to an enormous room and stood back, a smile of pride on her face as she indicated for him to go in.

Judith's studio was huge and filled with light. The outside wall had been made of thick glass, the French doors wide and inviting one to the outside garden, which grew wild with brilliant, vivid colors. Tubes poured light down from the ceiling, illuminating the rows of beads, gemstones, glass, wire and charms. Genuine joy filled this room, and happiness was reflected in the chaotic colorful creativity spilling out of bins in every corner of the room.

The walls were white, the light fixtures, wide windows and large French doors drawing light into the room. Judith had hung pictures of her favorite mandalas—images repeated in patterns in the kaleidoscopes by the mirrors and objects in the cells. He studied those for a few moments, knowing this room and these images held one of the keys to Judith's character. She created beauty here, peace. This was where the artist poured her soul into her creations.

He looked around the room, noting every detail. This was where Judith really lived, not upstairs in her comfortable, beautiful home. Here, in this happy chaos her soul was at peace. He could almost hear her laughter, carefree and confident. This place represented Judith more than any other he'd seen in the house.

"That wall is set up for cutting the mirrors," Judith explained and pointed to the far wall where a large square table held some sort of rig he had never seen before. "I need perfect cuts and straight lines every time. This allows the placement of the mirror edge against the iron bar with this movable bar guiding the cutting blade."

"It looks a little dangerous."

She flashed a quick grin. "You should have seen me when I first got the thing."

The idea of anything hurting her, even while she was in the learning phase, bothered him on a level he didn't understand. Stefan hadn't realized he had any protective instincts left in him, and yet she seemed to be bringing all of them out.

He glanced at the second work table on the same wall. Blades, glue guns, cutters and specialty tapes lay in happy chaos. "At least you're well armed in here since you never set your alarm. I'd hate to be an intruder catching you in this room."

Judith laughed again and pointed to another wall. "That's my lampworking station where I twist and sculpt colored rods before they go into a cell."

Protective goggles lay beside the oxygen/propane torch and the tanks feeding it. Tall, clear vases held the bright, vivid colored glass rods she referred to.

"I use the small kiln to put cut pieces of glass I shape that I want in the mirror systems."

Another table contained boxes with packing material tucked under it for shipping. He could see that in the midst of what looked like chaos, she was really very organized. On one wall a row of long, narrow tables housed clear acrylic boxes containing an abundance of objects. Beneath the narrow tables were plastic drawers filled with cells, various parts, discs, lenses and eyepieces, all sorts of intriguing things she had collected as well as tubes and bases for various types of scopes.

Stefan was drawn to the splashes of bright color spilling out of the boxes on top of the table and sauntered over to look into the treasure trove of items. He turned to her with a raised eyebrow.

"Those are all the various bits and pieces I use in making kaleidoscopes," she explained.

She was happy in this room. He could feel a wealth of joy permeating the very walls, and the room itself as well as in the objects in the boxes. Although there were tens of thousands of items, each box contained only one color creating a rainbow effect, much like her gardens.

"Where do you find these things?"

"Everywhere. Aren't they glorious? All that color and texture and shapes? I look at something and immediately see the opportunities. Scopes can calm people, entertain them, make them laugh or cry. I make themed scopes and personal scopes." For the first time, Judith sounded just a little shy. "I'm making that one there as a special gift for Hannah Drake, well Harrington. She's due to have their first baby any time and I've promised Jonas I'll finish it soon."

She motioned with her hand and he followed her into the very center of the room where a chair on rollers reigned supreme in the middle of U-shaped tables forming her workspace. In truth, he would have followed her anywhere, but he found her both exciting and sexy here in this room.

9

STEFAN caught Judith's long hair in his fist, wrapping it around his thick wrist in one quick looping motion, stopping her abruptly. He was surrounded by her, by the essence of who she was, and there wasn't a single part of him that didn't respond to that feminine allure. Surrounded by the vivid, brilliant colors that seemed to physically express the light and joy in her only amplified the growing need in him. This woman was home.

She turned to him, stepped into the shelter of his body and lifted her mouth to his without hesitation. There was nothing at all gentle in his kiss. He devoured her, feeling their combined hunger rising like a tidal wave. His hands found bare skin beneath her thin tee, soft and warm and so inviting. She fit like a glove, but more importantly, there were no shadows around Judith for him to retreat into. She was like a glaring sun, a spotlight, bright and hot and so damned alluring there was no resisting her.

Her slender arms circled his neck, her soft breasts pressed tightly to his chest until he felt every breath she took, every beat of her heart. He kissed her until neither could breathe, until it wasn't enough and never would be. Her skin beckoned, smooth and heated and so soft he nearly groaned aloud at the simple pleasure of touching her.

Judith was everything he wanted, more, everything he needed to come back to life. It was impossible, totally impossible to resist her, here in this room where she lived and breathed and surrounded herself with such beauty. He knew the bright, vivid colors reflected who she really was and he needed bright. He needed beautiful. His dull world, filled with violence and death, craved what only Judith could bring to him. He craved her beyond anything he could have imagined, a drug in his system, an urgent need he could no longer ignore, even though he knew it would make his pursuit of her more difficult.

The heavy erection was a constant, painful demand impossible to disregard. His mouth turned from commanding to demanding. He kissed his way down her throat to the edge of her scooped tank. "I don't want you wearing anything but that gold chain," he whispered, kissing his way back up to her ear. His teeth nipped her earlobe. "Get rid of your clothes."

He wasn't the kind of man to ask. He couldn't change himself. This was Stefan Prakenskii with his woman, his other half, not a mark of Thomas Vincent's. Thomas would be polite, Stefan didn't know how to be, not when lust mixed so harshly with an unfamiliar welling emotion that was all-encompassing.

He stroked his palm up her silken skin, tracing her narrow rib cage, enticing her even as he made his demand. Once more he took possession of her mouth, sinking into the velvet depths, tasting wild honey and survival, kissing her again and again, feeding on her magic.

Stefan had learned at an early age to survive by controlling every aspect of his life, from his thoughts, especially his emotions and by handling any kind of pain. Kissing Judith was another form of survival. He had all but lost every vestige of humanity and here, in this room of absolute joy, he was surrounded by it. Her spirit merged with his until he couldn't tell where she began and he ended. Here, more than anywhere else in the house, her spirit was alive and strong, surrounding his, merging, and amplifying every one of his own emotions.

The walls of her kaleidoscope studio, the room itself, the very air, held the essence of Judith and there was no way to resist, not even with his gifts. Judith was a naturally sensual woman, her passion for life, for joy, for color was everywhere around him. She was wholly feminine and here, more than anywhere else, her sexual nature was just as easy to see as her compassionate side. She made him burn with need.

"Your clothes," he reiterated between his teeth, shaking with a desire that was more real than anything he'd ever known. "Take them off."

No amount of beating, no amount of caressing or stroking or any other form of inducement had caused him to lose control and yet now, with the one woman who counted, he could barely breathe with wanting her.

Judith tilted her head back so that her dark eyes could meet his. He could see the matching heat there, the need every bit as strong as his. Maybe she was a little less sure of what she was getting herself into than he was, but he read the hunger every bit as deep as his own. Very slowly she let her arms fall, hands catching the hem of her tee. His heart rose to his throat, threatening to choke him. She pulled the offending material over her head and tossed it onto the nearby table, shaking her hair out so that it fell around her like a living cape of black, shiny silk.

His breath refused to leave his lungs. The lacy cups of her bra slid from her body, leaving her full, high breasts as an offering. Her nipples were already hard, a dark entreaty, her breasts already flushed in anticipation, rising and falling with her labored breathing. God, she was beautiful, more beautiful than he'd imagined her to be.

He dragged her to him simply by curling his hand around the nape of her neck, his mouth once more descending on hers. There was no way to resist her. Judith, surrounded by the evidence of her brightness, was pure seduction to a man as lost as Stefan. He kissed her over and over, long drugging kisses, while his hands moved over her skin, cupped her breasts, thumbs teasing her nipples, feeling each stroke ricochet through both of them like a whip of a lightning.

Stefan kissed his way to her breast, drawing the soft flesh into the heat of his mouth while his hands dropped to the button of her jeans. His knuckles brushed her firm body as he tugged the front open. Hooking his fingers on the band riding low on her hips, as well as the silky thong, he pulled the material down, his mouth following the path to her belly button while she stepped out of them.

His hands gripped her hips while his body throbbed and demanded. "How experienced are you, Judith?" His voice had gone hoarse.

"What difference does that make?" Her voice was edgy, ready to retreat.

His eyes met hers steadily. "I don't want to hurt you and I don't think I'm going to be gentle, not the first time."

Heat blazed into her eyes. She moistened her lips. "I haven't been with anyone in over five years, and then only twice."

He groaned. It wasn't what he wanted to hear and yet he couldn't help but be pleased. Judith was his alone. Twice didn't count. She may as well have been a virgin. He rested his forehead against her soft belly and took a deep breath to regain a semblance of control. He'd never been without control—not until Judith. He'd never allowed his body a will and mind of its own—until Judith.

"I want you with every breath in my body, *moi padshii angel*, but this might not be a good idea right now." He knelt, arms around her waist looking up at her. "I don't know how much control I actually have and that's another damn first for me."

Stefan Prakenskii was baring his soul to his woman and Thomas Vincent could stay damned. If this was going to happen then it was going to be all Stefan and all truth here in this room of joy and beauty, here with this woman who he knew with certainty belonged to him.

"If we do this, you have to promise me you won't end it there. I want to know that you'll look me in the eye and know you wanted this as much as I do and we won't end our chances. Say it, Judith, while I still have the strength to stop." He had to know that she wouldn't try to walk away.

Her hand dropped into his hair, fingers curling through the thick strands. Her dark eyes met his, so mysterious, filled with desire for him—for Stefan. He'd given himself to her, that small piece of him that was left, that his instructors hadn't beat out of him. It seemed a little thing, but he'd never allowed another human being to even know Stefan Prakenskii existed. Prakenskii lived in the shadows, no more than a phantom some whispered about, but never really knew for certain of his existence. Even the dead could not positively identify him.

He held that small piece of humanity as close as possible, deep and hidden where no enemy could ever strip it from him. It was the one thing that made him vulnerable, the only thing he had left of his mother's love. His loyalty to his brothers was part of that, and it was very, very fragile.

Judith saw him. She might not know his name, but she saw him. They stared at each other, Judith stripped naked, bare and open to him, Stefan fully clothed but more naked and vulnerable than she could possibly imagine.

Judith moistened her lips. "I want you, Thomas, any way I can have you."

His body reacted almost before his mind comprehended that soft, whispered acceptance. His heavy erection grew thicker and much harder than it had ever been, a painful need mixing with the dark lust building so fast he could barely hang on to his control. He couldn't save her, not now, it was too damned late, not when she was looking at him with those eyes. Not with her body flushed and her breasts rising and falling with her ragged breathing. Not when she was every bit as needy as he was.

Her feminine scent enticed and tempted beyond his ability to resist. His hands, of their own accord, dropped to her thighs, jerking them apart to give him what he so desperately needed. He didn't—couldn't—wait. Without preamble, his mouth devoured her. He was brilliant at two things, killing and giving pleasure. With this woman his lovemaking was all real. His tongue made a single swipe through velvet folds and when he felt her answering shudder, he tasted the wild honey he'd been craving from her.

He knew it was far too late to turn back. She'd changed his life for all time. The way her hands fisted in his hair. The trembling of her body, her soft musical moans fed his addiction, and the exotic taste of her would forever set up a craving. Nothing mattered but having her. He had waited his entire life for a reason—something, just *one* thing to make sense of it all. She turned out to be a woman named Judith.

She cried out as he licked, a cat lapping at sweet, hot cream, her breathless cries only adding to the urgent need building like a tsunami inside of him. He couldn't stop the growling sounds of pleasure coming from his throat, the desperate hunger forever building into an insatiable lust. Her hot channel spasmed, providing more honey and he attacked like the starving man he was.

More angel, give me everything. I need you to give yourself to me.

He was asking for complete trust in him. The more she relaxed, the more she put herself into his hands, the better he could make it for her. His hand tightened on her hip, holding her still when her knees threatened to buckle, while he slid his finger deep into that hot, velvet tunnel. He groaned at how small and tight she was. He was a big man and she needed to be ready to take his size. Her inner muscles gripped his finger tightly and he lapped and sucked at the welcoming liquid spilling over. Nectar from the gods, sweet and flowing into his hungry mouth. He was the devil tempting the angel and nothing else mattered but that she succumbed to his deliberate seduction.

Judith cried out again, the sound strangled as she placed both hands on Stefan's shoulders to steady herself when her legs turned to gel and her body trembled violently with the gathering tension. She spread her legs wider, threw her head back, gasping, putting herself into his care, giving him the trust he'd demanded from her. Pleasure grew past anything she'd known and still he didn't stop, his wicked, sinful mouth driving her up until she thought she might come apart, just fragment into a million pieces, or lose herself in the sheer rapture of his mouth.

And then he used his fingers again while his mouth remained on her most sensitive button, suckling and flicking so that her breath came in gasping sobs. His exploring fingers stretched her, teased and stretched a little more. There was a tiny bite of pain, a burning that just floated into the exquisite pleasure and then dissipated as rapture built, coiling tighter and tighter inside of her.

"I can't take any more." Even to herself her voice was a husky, pleading moan.

Let go, angel, and just fly for me.

She had no choice, she really didn't. Not with flames building into a giant firestorm and her body bucking helplessly against his mouth and fingers. She felt every muscle in her body tighten, the coil so tight now it was frightening, and then she was flying apart, her soft cries filling the room.

Stefan held her hips to steady her, even as he stood, stripping away his jeans with one hand, turning her away from him, pressing her down with one hand on her back, forcing her over one of the tables. He left his shirt on. His body was covered in scars. Knife fights, bullet wounds, whip marks, years of enduring torture, it was all on the road map of his body. She might buy he'd gotten a few wounds in the service, but it would be impossible to explain them all and he didn't want to lie to her.

She was nearly sobbing, her body rocking back into his. "Easy, angel, we're going to go slow." He hoped he could.

His hand circled his cock, finding her slick entrance with the large, very sensitive head. Her channel was burning hot, surrounding that first inch, gripping tightly so that he had to still, throwing his head back, his body shuddering with pleasure. "Hold still, Judith," he entreated. "I don't want to hurt you."

Judith tried to stop writhing, stop the terrible restless need gripping her as she felt the hot head of his thick shaft lodge inside of her. Her breath caught in her lungs. Between her legs, she felt chiseled steel, hot as a brand, invading, stretching, *burning*. But more, it was the essence of the man lodged so deep inside of her she knew she would never get him out. The sensations poured over her so fast she couldn't catch her breath, couldn't possibly control the screams of her body, the demands. She had no experience with this kind of sex, yet everything in her responded. Even the small wisps of fear curling treacherously in her mind heightened her pleasure.

She felt a sob welling up and tears burned behind her eyes. She hadn't thought herself capable of this type of strong passion, the need so great, so incredible nothing else mattered but having him buried deep inside of her. She didn't care if it stretched and burned. She wanted him to take her so high that she lost herself in him. She was willing to give him everything she was as long as he gave her the same.

"Stay still, damn it," Stefan pleaded. He needed her to keep from moving so sensuously, her body sliding enticingly toward him as she tried to draw him deeper into her scalding feminine sheath.

She hissed something between her teeth that sounded as if she was trying, but the feeling of her soft, rounded buttocks and the long line of her spine with her hair spilling around her were every bit as sensual as her hips bucking.

He rocked forward, driving an inch deeper, pushing through those tight, strangling folds of silken fire, gasping with the flames racing over him. It was difficult not to slam himself deep into that inferno of paradise. He halted the moment he felt her tense, just staying where he was, surrounded by living velvet as tight as any fist.

"I'm all right," she panted. "Keep going."

"What's wrong?" He couldn't stop, not now. He closed his eyes and prayed to a God he wasn't certain existed.

"I want this," Judith insisted, her tone pleading, breathless, *needy*. "It burns a little when you're stretching me, but you feel amazing. Please don't stop."

He let his breath out and invaded deeper into that tight feminine channel. "You're so damn tight, angel." She was scorching him all the way down to his toes. He took a breath and eased in more.

"You're so damn big," Judith gasped and pushed back with a small cry, sheathing him another couple of inches.

He flexed his fingers. Blood thundered in his head, and a jackhammer pulsed between his legs, hard and demanding. With her squirming he could barely maintain sanity let alone control. He gripped her hips and as her body thrust toward him, he rammed home, burying himself deep, driving through those snug, nearly unyielding muscles. He bumped her cervix and she cried out again, taking several deep breaths.

"Please, Thomas, please . . ." She broke off pleading with a gasp as he began to move.

Stefan built the rhythm slowly, watching her reaction as closely as possible. She was burning him alive, feeding the flames with her passion, with her own need, a black magic woman, wrapping him up in sex and sin. His cock felt like steel, slamming into her over and over, disappearing into dark, hot depths. Deliberately he adjusted position, dragging over her most sensitive part so that she gave another cry.

Her long hair was everywhere, her breasts rocking with each hard stroke. The sight of her broke his last thread of control and he gave in to the wild need that had been building his entire life for this one woman. He drew in his breath sharply, his hold on her hips tight as he drove forward and yanked her back into him again and again.

He stretched them both out on a rack of torturous, pure carnal pleasure he hadn't known could exist, the tension building until her cries were music to him and his hard breathing matched the deep, pistoning thrusts of his hips. He couldn't stop, didn't want this to end, felt complete with her, with flames licking over his skin and his cock forging such heat they were welded together.

Lust rose into frenzied hunger and mingled with a far gentler emotion that took his heart and placed it solely in her hands. He slammed into her again and again, her pleas and the sound of their bodies coming together weaving the sensations into a deeper, darker coil. Judith gasped, a sobbing plea escaped, as wave after wave of shocking orgasms tore through her. Her muscles clamped down like a vise, dragging over him, a fierce, almost brutal assault that took him by surprise, ripping his own vicious release from him.

Stefan collapsed over the top of Judith, careful not to put too much of his weight on her while he fought for breath. He pressed his face against her back, inhaling her fragrance, feeling the silk of her hair against his face. *Are you all right?*

She reached one hand behind her and stroked his thigh. He could feel the pulse of her heart in the muscles surrounding him. *Absolutely. You?*

Never better.

She hesitated and he felt it like an arrow through her heart. *I'm a little frightened by how intense this is between us. I didn't expect sex to be so explosive. I can't control it.*

He waited a heartbeat. *Don't regret this, Judith. It's too good between us; don't pull away from me because it's scary. We can figure it out together.*

She was silent another moment. *I should have told you, I'm not on birth control. I haven't been with anyone and didn't expect to be.*

I should have protected you. I'm sorry, Judith. I wasn't thinking. He couldn't say it aloud, could barely manage to utter the lie telepathically. He would welcome his child growing inside of her. The damn truth was, he *wanted* his child in her. And that was another shocking first for him.

Judith went still. She turned her head to one side and looked back at him, her long, feathery lashes lowering over her dazed expression. *I'm a grown woman, Thomas. I can protect myself. I should have been the one thinking about it. And truthfully, there's a part of me that would welcome a baby.*

My baby, he corrected. *My baby.*

The intimacy of speaking to one another in mind only while their bodies were locked together heightened his pleasure. He wrapped both arms around her slender waist and pressed kisses down her spine. *I love this room.*

Me too. There was soft laughter in her mind.

Judith didn't try to move and he could feel every after-shock rocking her body.

This room will always be my favorite, although I'm quite willing to check out every single room in the house to see if any others are quite as exciting as this one. Slowly, reluctantly, Stefan allowed his body to leave hers. He kept one hand on the small of her back to keep her in place, not taking chances that she might see the scars on him as he dragged up his jeans. "How many tables are there in this room?" He wanted to ease back to give her time to come to terms with how quickly their relationship was moving forward.

Judith straightened with unhurried deliberation. Sweeping back her hair she faced him, his seed dampening her thighs, her body flushed, nipples erect, her gold chain glittering at him. She looked thoroughly made love to, her eyes just a little glazed, watching him with a mixture of vulnerability and shock. "The tables are for work," she managed.

"I'm willing to work," he teased, just to see more color stealing into all that soft skin.

She made a face at him as she reached for a soft cloth. "One of these days, you can make your own scope. I'll show you how."

Stefan's warning system went off loudly. Judith read people so easily. She saw things in them or she couldn't make a kaleidoscope suited to an individual and their needs. She would see into him just by the things he selected to put in his scope. He wasn't certain he knew what Thomas Vincent would choose for his cell, but whatever it was, those choices would be completely different than anything Stefan Prakenskii would make.

He kept the smile on his face even as he watched her closely. His suspicious nature couldn't help but come up with all kinds of reasons for her to probe into his character. They'd just made love, the best sex he'd ever had in his life and he'd made up his mind that this woman would be *his* woman—the only one he'd ever want or have for himself, yet his mind immediately went to conspiracy. That showed him more than anything how very fucked up his trainers had made him.

"That sounds like fun," he said, because she was waiting for a response.

Without looking away from him she smoothed away his seed with the cloth and it was the sexiest thing he'd ever witness. In spite of being sated minutes earlier his cock jerked hard. He nearly groaned aloud. Who was he trying to kid? He needed a lifetime to sate the craving she'd set up in his body. He nearly took the cloth away from her, hating to see the evidence of his possession wiped away. He forced himself to stay quiet, without protest as she dressed.

"I'm hungry all of a sudden," she announced with a small grin. "Do you feel like eating?"

"Sure, although we're down here, you may as well give me a quick rundown of the place. You can't really see anything of the downstairs from outside so I was surprised with so many windows. I expected these rooms to be more like a basement." He wanted to see the entire layout of the house. Windows made things difficult for security, but her gardens provided thick screens, at least during this time of year.

She flashed a pleased smile. "Painting requires a great deal of light. I'm a conservator of painting as well as an artist. Both require light, just as creating kaleidoscopes does. I like to be surrounded by color and all of the gardens are different. I mix the flowers with taller grasses and shrubs to help give myself the feeling of protection."

He didn't need to ask her why she felt in need of protection; she'd told him. He put his arm around her waist and leaned down to kiss her. If there was the smallest hesitation on her part, he ignored it. There was going to be a lot of kissing because, truthfully, he could kiss her forever and never be tired of it.

"Let's get you something to eat, Judith. You can open doors for me along the way and give me the big tour another time."

She wrapped her arms around his neck and held him to her. "I can't believe I haven't known you all my life. This feels brand-new, and yet as comfortable as an old shoe. It's a little scary how much it feels so right being with you."

Behind her back, Stefan lifted his hand to inspect his fist, scarred and calloused with training and fights. Part of him expected his flesh to be transparent. He hadn't been real since he was a boy and now, his blood flowed hot and his mind contemplated a life in this home with this woman, a daring dream. He didn't deserve a woman like Judith. There wasn't much good in him, but he'd fight to his last breath for her and he'd do whatever it took to make her happy.

"I know it has to feel like the devil showed up at your door and maybe he has. I just know this is right, Judith."

She pressed kisses along his jaw and then stepped back. "Come on, before we start something all over again."

"I'm willing."

She laughed. "Me too, but unfortunately, I had to ask Airiana to work in my store for me and she has something she's doing so if we're going to eat, we have to eat now and I'm truly starving. Besides"—she sent him another mischievous smirk—"I want to see just how good a cook you really are."

Stefan let her take his hand and lead him toward the door. He inhaled deeply and took in their combined scents. The room smelled like both of them now, sin and sex. He was the sin and she was the sex. Smiling to himself, he followed her out the door into the hall. Directly across from the kaleidoscope studio was another door. She pushed it open and stepped back.

"I have this smaller bedroom down here just in case I stay up all night, which is often, and I just crash down here."

"Another bedroom for us," he murmured appreciatively and was rewarded with her laughter.

The room next to the bedroom was another bathroom and shower, no tub this time, but the room itself was spacious. He was beginning to realize Judith liked everything as open as possible. She closed that door and moved on to the next door, which was quite a bit down the hallway, on the same side as the kaleidoscope studio.

"This is where I both paint and do my conservator's work."

Stefan stepped inside before she could close the door.

There was Judith in this room as well, he could feel her. This studio was very organized, a complete contrast to the happy chaos of the adjoining room. Once again, the double French doors led out to a garden and banks of windows invited sunlight, but the resemblance ended there. The ventilation was paramount here, due to the chemicals she used and she had several exhaust fans overhead as well as windows positioned to provide a cross breeze with the doors open. He could see the studio had been well thought out.

A small refrigerator stood in one corner and he raised an eyebrow in inquiry.

"I wrap my palette full of paint in plastic and freeze it to prevent drying out."

"I'm going to learn a lot from you." He studied the paintings she had in various stages of treatment and drying.

"Do you like to paint?" Judith's face lit up. She obviously loved what she did and anyone who cared that much, would want to share her love of creating.

"I play around with it, but I'm not that good. I find it soothing." He had never told another human being that either. He painted, and then destroyed the canvas immediately. A man living in the shadows couldn't afford to leave anything that personal behind.

He studied the exquisite silk kimono displayed on the wall opposite the French doors. The way the easel was set up, she clearly faced that beautiful garment.

"My mother's," she explained and there was love and reverence in her voice. "I like to keep her close to me. Out back, I have a Japanese garden and some of the plants I brought here with me, I actually dug them up from my mother's garden before I sold the house and planted them here. If I ever move, I'll take them with me. I have her tea set and a few other things. Part of my childhood was spent in Japan and then my father moved us here, to the States. She kept the house very Japanese. My father and brother loved it that way, and so did I."

He felt the sorrow in her rising. She hastily pushed it away. "Don't do that around me," he said sharply. "I have no problem with any emotion you're feeling, Judith. Be yourself with me. Feel everything from hate to love, happiness to sorrow. You're allowed."

She ducked her head and stepped out into the hall. "You know what can happen, Thomas."

He *detested* the name Thomas. "Not with me. I've seen what you can do, and if you're honest with yourself, you know I can handle it. You're afraid of yourself, but you'll never learn to control your talent unless you start using it."

"Maybe it's evil and not meant to be used."

Deliberately, he gave a derisive snort. "You're not afraid to admit you want revenge, Judith, so why be afraid of something so pure as the element of spirit?"

"That's *exactly* why I'm afraid of it. I can twist not only my own element, but my sisters' talents into something not meant to be. I don't want that for them. I guard how I feel so I'm not tempted."

His arm caged her in, hand on the wall beside her head, preventing her from moving. "You know better, Judith. I'm a violent man when necessary. I recognize violence when I see it. You may need revenge. You may even dream of revenge, but torturing a human being in your mind, and killing him there is far different than actually doing it. You would never, under any circumstances use your sisters to hurt another human being."

Judith blinked back tears, her eyes refusing to meet his. Stefan caught her chin in his fingers and forced her head. "You're ashamed of that. Ashamed you have the means of revenge and won't use it. You feel guilty."

She jerked away from him. "You see too much."

"Judith, there's no guilt in not wanting to twist those you love into something that would hurt another being, you already know that's too high of a price to pay—and there's always a price. There has to be a moral code, a line you

never cross, a personal code, even in something like revenge."

She took a breath. "You sound like you know what you're
talking about."

"More than you know, angel." He bent his head
and kissed her gently, a tender, comforting kiss when she
winced and shook her head. "You don't like being an angel,
even mine."

"I prefer it when you call me your fallen angel. At least I
know you aren't putting me on an impossibly high pedestal."

She was on that pedestal for all time no matter what
she did. Any sin she had would never compare to his blackened soul. He stepped back to allow her to escape. Judith
squared her shoulders and led the way toward the stairs.
They passed the last door on the bottom floor without her
touching it. Judith had been open about every part of her
house, obviously taking pride in it, yet she skipped a major portion of the downstairs without so much as glancing
at it, rather she'd taken great care to look away from it, instantly arousing his interest.

"Where does this door lead?" He managed to look innocent as he asked, but he didn't take his eyes off of her
noting her sudden withdrawal, the frozen look on her face
and guilt that crept into her eyes. His hand dropped to the
doorknob, but it was locked.

She shook her head, her eyes sliding away from his.
"Just another studio. I keep it locked and don't often go in
there." Color crept up her neck into her face.

She was flat-out lying to him, when she hadn't lied about
anything else and she wasn't very good at it. Nothing else
could have raised his suspicion more. What the hell was she
hiding? He tried not to let his mind make a leap back to
Jean-Claude, but the man was obsessed with her, had someone watching her, taking pictures for five straight years.
Was it possible she was holding something for him? Her
loathing of the man rang true, yet why would she lie?

He worked for his government and until he knew for absolute certain that he was on a list to be wiped out, he would make certain his country's secrets were protected at all times. He had to make sure that Judith was in no way guarding the microchip Jean-Claude had managed to keep hidden for the last five years. He had to get into that studio. A part of him acknowledged he didn't really believe she was still connected to Jean-Claude. He simply didn't like her keeping secrets from him.

He wanted her giving every part of herself to him, holding nothing back. He stayed still forcing her to look at him. She looked away quickly and then down at the floor. He gestured toward the stairs, with a small shrug. Judith took the lead and he deliberately brushed his fingertips over her denim-clad butt.

"You are one beautiful woman, Judith." If she needed the subject changed, he would oblige. He had no compunction about returning on his own and finding out the things he wanted to know. She didn't use her alarm system and he had been careful to commit the details of her home to the map in his mind. He would have no trouble finding his way around in the dark of the night where he mostly lived.

Instantly the tension drained out of her and she sent him a smoldering smile over her shoulder as she led him back into the kitchen.

"I like to have lunch on the balcony or in the garden when I'm not working at the store or gallery," Judith explained. "It's so beautiful outside, and the colors of the sky and forest along with the flowers always inspire me."

Stefan unpacked the food containers and handed them to her. "That sounds good to me."

He made certain that Judith forgot all about the uncomfortable moment standing in her hallway in front of the locked door. He got her laughing, kissed her thoroughly over and over and talked about creating kaleidoscopes, a subject he didn't have to feign interest in. The afternoon melted away and when she glanced at her watch, he took the cue and stood up to leave.

ATTENTION to detail, *meticulous* attention to detail was the secret formula that kept men like Stefan Prakenskii alive. He noted every detail of his surroundings at all times. License plates, make and models of cars, animals and tracks, whether shades were up or down, the slightest detail was significant and could save his life. He'd learned such things in a hard school, where one small screw-up earned beatings that left him crawling across the floor, or out in the freezing cold snow and ice until he could no longer feel his body.

Those years of training, of enduring, had taught him to accomplish his mission no matter the hardship, to go on even when his body and brain protested and there was only his will driving him. Judith Henderson had become his mission. He would not fail in his objective. He was staking his claim and no one—*no one*—would stop him. Stefan knew only one way to play the game and that was life or death. For him, Judith was life and everything else was death.

Stefan pulled his vehicle through the gates with the birds following him every step of the way. The double gate swung automatically closed behind him. He drove toward the highway, surrounded by the forest, until he'd rounded several bends and knew if anyone from the farm was watching, his car was long gone from sight and sound. He drove off the road, into the heavy forest and parked in the shelter of the trees. It took him only minutes to change clothes and shoes and then slide weapons and tools into place. He had two visits to make tonight. The first to Judith's locked studio and the second to his brother. In the meantime, he was going to sleep. He had learned to sleep anywhere at any time, even if for a couple of short minutes.

10

A single sound woke Stefan. His eyes snapped open, senses flaring out, one hand sliding to find the familiar butt of his Glock. Around him, the forest was dark. Overhead, clouds had formed, creating a series of rolling dark hills in the sky. Bats reigned supreme, darting here and there after the insects. Something heavy brushed along branches just once to his left. He had dismantled the interior light the moment he'd picked up the car from a lot, paying cash as always. He slipped outside the vehicle, not shutting the door completely, dropping low while he secured his silencer onto his weapon.

Stefan eased his way over the uneven ground, testing each step with the ball of his foot first for freshly dropped twigs and branches. The forest floor was deep in pine needles, leaves and other vegetation, his feet sinking inches into the tightly woven debris. Staying low, he moved to the right, circling, trying to keep downwind of anything in the thick stand of trees.

An owl hooted and another answered. The resonance

was off just a tiny bit. Stefan slid the gun back into his holster and palmed his knife.

I know you're out here somewhere hunting me.

His brother's voice filled his mind. Smart. He wasn't giving away his location. Stefan remained silent. He'd seen Lev one time since they had been separated as children. He didn't know what kind of man his brother had grown into. For his part, Stefan had to cling to one thing to keep himself humane: his loyalty to his absent brothers. He had no idea if they held to the same code that he did. Before meeting Judith, Stefan would have gone to hell and back for his brother, but now, he was angry that Lev had actually gone so far as to marry Judith's beloved sister to protect his cover. That was strictly taboo. Against their code. There had to be a line drawn somewhere.

Were you sent to find me? Kill me?

Stefan rarely lost his temper. Men like him didn't have tempers and if they did, they kept that damning emotion tightly under wraps. Reacting with anger—with any emotion—was usually a death sentence in his line of work. He felt a dam burst inside of him, hot magma welling up unexpectedly, his gut churning.

Ungrateful little mongrel. You're the one hunting me in these woods. I put everything on the line for you and this is the thanks I get. Come ahead, then, little brother.

Silence settled over the forest once again. Stefan didn't know whether Lev moved closer to him or was thinking things over. It occurred to him that his baby brother wasn't a kid anymore. He was every bit as lethal, with the same training under his belt, the years of hardship and pain that shaped them into dangerous killing machines.

The schools they'd trained in were run like military schools, using physical and mental challenges and hardships, eventually working in every kind of terrain possible. Weapons training was every bit as important as learning languages and being able to pass for a native of a country not one's own. Lev had been forced under water, thrown into choppy seas and lived in snow caves, just as Stefan had. The physical punishments had most likely been similar. The fact that he had survived meant his brother had the same mental toughness as Stefan. Those who didn't have absolute will and a hefty streak of resilient determination, didn't survive the training camps.

I knew you would come to my home, Stefan, and my wife is not like others. I couldn't allow that, even to see you.

That was definitely conciliatory. Could Stefan take Lev's word at face value? Deceit was weapon, just like everything else.

You don't marry your cover.

Again silence met his reprimand. Stefan moved cautiously forward. The breeze slipped through the trees, branches swayed gently and a few leaves fluttered. He froze as he realized the fluttering was a bird settling onto the branches above his head.

I married my wife because I love her. She's my world and I won't let anything—or anyone—take her away from me.

That brought Stefan up short. He hadn't considered, even for a moment, that Lev might have fallen in love with the woman. Stefan knew with absolute certainty that there was no other woman for him than Judith. He had been around the world, knew he was cynical and jaded. He certainly didn't believe in fairy tales, or love at first sight. And it hadn't been that, his feelings had grown over time without him even knowing. There had been something in her photographs that had attracted him to her, and then her paintings had revealed so much about her.

He had studied the file on her childhood, the way she was so gifted in art and color, the way she applied herself to her studies, in her own way, every bit as one-track as he had been. He embraced that small shadow of darkness in her. She hadn't quite learned to control her talent and therefore viewed the darker emotions as weaknesses instead of strengths, but she would learn once she got over her fear. And it was those darker emotions that would allow her to love him completely.

Physically, he was very drawn to her exotic appearance, her mouth and hair. He loved her Japanese heritage and the way she moved so gracefully. He was drawn to her passion and fire, matching those traits with his own.

It was just possible Lev was telling the truth. It made sense, especially if his wife was an element, as Stefan suspected. Like attracted like. Their psychic gifts would be magnets, continually pulling at one another.

A soft rustle had him rolling to his right, staying prone in the deep vegetation, his gaze sweeping the surrounding forest. Lev was close. He *felt* him close, a subtle wave of energy spreading out around him, encompassing the owl in the tree, probably using the owl's vision to spot Stefan. Although the ability to see through the bird's eyes would be a distinct advantage, the fact that Stefan knew his brother could do such a thing aided him. There was no way to use that kind of psychic gift without a shift in energy and Stefan was too adept not to feel it.

The wind moved again, and thunder rolled. Mist crept through the trees, eerie tails of streaming vapor coming off the roiling ocean. The sound of waves crashing against the cliffs was never ending, a part of the life on the coast, lending a certain rhythm to the earth sounds. Stefan strained to hear the smallest of sounds. The fog branched out like a great hand, reaching with fingers toward him. Out of the corner of his eye he caught a shadow coming at him and he leapt to meet it, knife in his palm.

The two hard bodies crashed together, went to the ground and rolled together. He had Lev's wrist in his fist, controlling his knife while Lev had his. Pine needles, twigs and leaves collected in clothing and hair as they rolled. The thick trunk of a tree smashed into Stefan's back hard. The two brothers came to an abrupt stop, staring into each other's eyes.

They remained locked in a life or death hold, neither relenting, neither giving an inch.

"I married her because I love her," Lev reiterated. "And I don't like you using Judith, even if you came here to find me. Judith is part of my family and under my protection. That makes her off-limits."

"You don't know what the hell you're talking about. Ivanov is in town."

"The hell you say." Lev didn't so much as blink, his grip as strong as ever.

"I chased him across the rooftops of Sea Haven, got cut up, managed to get in a few good swipes. He's hurt, but I rolled off the damn rooftop and he got away."

"I should have known he'd come back."

"I think he was planning on taking both of us out once I brought you out into the open. He arranged to have me sent here as bait."

Lev abruptly rolled off of him, sitting up, knife still in his hand. "Damn. Why would Sorbacov want you dead? He's the only one who could issue a contract. No one else would dare to go over his head."

"A reporter has been delving into the past and discovered records of the orphanages and the schools. He intercepted an excerpt of a document containing classified material on the training of children in military operations, spies and assassins. The excerpt was just detailed enough to keep the reporters in every other country digging deep. I think Sorbacov wants to purge the ranks, get rid of anyone who could be a threat to him. It was his father's operation and politically they're on shaky ground with this. If the program embarrasses the current government, the fortunes

and power the Sorbacov family has amassed will be gone
and with it all trace of them."

"Sorbacov massacred so many families, all because
they were his political enemies. The government allowed
his experiments because those of us who survived proved
to be tremendously valuable assets they needed at that
time." Lev rested his hand on his thigh, the blade still vis-
ible. "If the manner of our making is discovered, we cease
to be valuable and become liabilities."

"Exactly. It doesn't take a rocket scientist to figure out
that if Sorbacov would send me to Sea Haven on a foolish
task, I'm bait to see if you come out of your hiding place,"
Stefan said. "And if he kills you, he has no choice but to
kill me."

"Then we go hunting together."

Stefan sat up, shifting to make certain the tree wouldn't
block any sudden need to move quickly. He drew his legs
up, the knife sliding into the sheath strapped to his calf, but
his fist remained curled over the hilt. "I thought about that,
Lev . . ."

"*Levi*. You have to think of me as Levi. I'm Levi Hammond. I'm a diver with a wife I love and a home I'll fight to
the death for. I'm Levi Hammond."

"You're serious."

"You better believe it. Rikki gave me my life back. I feel
with her. I'm even beginning to extend those feelings just
a little bit to her family. I'm never going back, Stefan, and
I'll protect her and our home with every resource available
to me."

"Are all of the women living on this farm elements?
Every single one of them?"

Lev nodded slowly, as if a little hesitant to admit the
truth. "All but one. Blythe has power, but I haven't figured
out exactly what it is. The rest of them are all bound to elements. Rikki is a powerful water element. She saved my life
when the yacht I was working on went down. I hit my head

and still have problems remembering everything about my past. It comes to me slowly and in pieces. I'm not too proud of what I was, but she makes me feel worth something. I'm happy here, Stefan. I've found peace. I want to keep it that way. Ivanov has to go."

"Let me hunt him. You stay low. If anyone else is watching how things play out, you'll still be safe."

Lev shook his head. "You know I'd never let you do that. It's my fight too. And both of us know he's not above using the women to get to us. He'd kill any or all of them without a thought."

Stefan sighed. There was no real use in arguing with Lev. If he was married and had a home, he wouldn't expect someone else—even his brother—to bail him out of trouble. Lev wasn't that kind of man and secretly, Stefan was proud of that fact.

"You need dogs."

It was Lev's turn to sigh. He slipped his knife into the sheath inside his boot. "I haven't been with Rikki more than a few weeks. We were married very fast and, yes, I know what I'm doing. She pushes her comfort zone for me all the time, but I like to introduce things to her slowly. Airiana, one of her sisters, wants the dogs as well, so I'm trying to push the idea that Airiana gets a couple of shepherds or mastiffs and that Rikki and I do as well."

"Judith told me the youngest sister, Lexi, wants a dog."

Lev swore softly. "Judith shouldn't be telling you anything about her sisters."

"Fuck you, *Levi*, you're not the only one who can find someone. Judith didn't betray anyone's secrets," Stefan snapped. "Don't try to interfere."

"You're not going to use her, Stefan." Lev didn't back down for a moment. "If she's Rikki's family, she's mine. And that means she's off-limits to you. Go find another woman to cement your cover story. I've heard all about Thomas Vincent, the great businessman from New York.

I'll admit your cover is solid, even impressive, but you can't use Judith, not even to keep Ivanov off me."

"What makes you think I'm using her?"

"Of course you are. Tell me you didn't come here and target her to help with your cover. And I'll know if you're lying."

"Bullshit. You wouldn't know one way or the other. I can fool anyone, even you. Of course I came here under-cover, and as a rule, I would develop a relationship with a woman to help cement my cover, but Judith isn't that."

"What is she then?"

"Everything. Life. For me, she's what your Rikki is to you."

Shock registered on Lev's face. His blue gaze searched Stefan's face with slow, careful deliberation. "You're telling me you've fallen in love with Judith?"

Stefan winced. Put like that he didn't quite know how to answer his brother. He didn't know what love was. He only knew he *had* to be with her. His body, his mind, every single cell in his body knew she was meant for him. He was a man who used sex as a weapon and achieved release after release. It felt good, great even, but not like what it had been with Judith. His body had reacted of its own accord, mixing with his emotions until there was no one but Judith. Was that love?

"I don't know what to call it, Levi." Deliberately he used his brother's new identity. "I only know she's the person I'd stand in front of. For the first time in my life I want to stay somewhere. Be someone. Is that love?"

Lev smiled for the first time. "I'd say you're well on your way. I'd fight with everything in me to keep Rikki. She's fierce, Stefan, unafraid. She faces the world head-on. I'm so crazy about her, I can't see anything or anyone else."

Stefan felt his gut settle a little more. Lev couldn't fake that note in his voice. There were certain small things that gave someone away when they lied—or told the truth. The light in his eyes, the expression on his face and that awed, shocked note in the voice would be impossible to fake. His brother was very taken with his woman.

"Are you wrapped around her little finger?"

"Probably. Yeah. No question about it. I fell hard."

"I'm not leaving, Levi. I'm going to stay here and make Judith mine. And we're damn well getting dogs and set this place up for war."

Lev's eyebrow shot up. "War?"

"When we kill Ivanov, Sorbacov will send someone else after us."

"Ilya lives here," Lev informed his brother. "I doubt he would be in danger, although he went through the original school, but he was trained for other things. He worked for Interpol and retired legitimately from his job. We'll have to send word to the others. Have you seen any of them?"

"Only Gavriil. I helped him escape from the hospital. He went underground. He was hurt pretty bad, Lev."

"We can get word to him to come here if we can secure this place and come out into the open. With three of us here, it would be difficult for anyone to come against us."

"You know it sounds like a pipe dream," Stefan said with a soft sigh. "Men like us don't have homes or women of our own."

"I have a woman and a home and no one, including Sorbacov—*especially* Sorbacov—is going to take it away from me," Lev said.

"The one thing Sorbacov hasn't thought through, and it makes no sense, is the fact that none of us are going to want those documents to see the light of day," Stefan said. "We'd all become targets. No one would have a chance at a life. Our covers would be blown, our pictures in every country preventing us from moving around, we'd be hunted by everyone."

"He never meant for any of us to have a life," Lev pointed out. "We weren't human to him. We were tools he shaped into killing machines. None of us had a chance. Most of the kids I started with in those schools never made it all the way through training. He killed them when they couldn't perform to his satisfaction."

"Nevertheless, had he been thinking, he would have utilized his weapons and gone after the threat to all of us, which would ultimately have benefited him. Now he's got to hope his exterminators get to all of us before one of us gets to him."

"How did they get you to come here, Stefan?"

Stefan knew the question was bound to be asked and he hadn't yet made up his mind to trust his brother completely. Distrust was a way of life, a way to stay alive. Was he actually going to try to make a stand here, and if so, he'd have to be honest with both Judith and his brother. But there was still the matter of the microchip. He was loyal to his country. He might not want to live there—he spent very little time there and had no ties anymore—but he loved his country. If the information on that microchip was crucial to his country's defense system, then he had to make certain it was back in the hands of responsible people.

Lev swore under his breath and stood up. "I knew you were full of shit."

Stefan rose just as fast. "I don't have it as easy as you do, Levi. You're dead. They might suspect it's all a hoax, but they don't know for certain. I've been working on returning a very crucial piece of sensitive material for the last five years, following dead end after dead end. I'm this close." He measured with his fingers. "I'm still a patriot whether or not I've outlived my usefulness to our country. Gavriil asked me to make certain the microchip taken from Theodotus Solovyov is returned. I gave my word to him and even if I hadn't, I'd make certain Russia is safe."

"Is Judith involved in some way? How would tracking a microchip lead you to Sea Haven? That seems too big of a coincidence."

"What do you know about Judith's past?"

Lev's face closed down immediately. "The sisters rarely talk about one another. They guard their pasts carefully and I've never pried. I wouldn't want anyone asking questions about me and I give them that same respect. Here, we take one another as we are."

"I understand, Levi, but if you want to know why I'm here then you're going to have to accept that Judith's past is mixed up in this."

"You're telling me the truth? Judith Henderson is somehow a person of interest in the disappearance of sensitive materials our brother was guarding?"

"That's the truth," Stefan said and waited for his brother to make up his mind.

He could see why Lev wouldn't believe him. It was absurd to think that a woman like Judith could possibly be mixed up in international intrigue.

"Let me get this straight. Our brother, Gavriil, was assigned to guard Theodotus Solovyov and they were ambushed."

Stefan nodded. "Solovyov's wife betrayed them. She was having an affair and she sewed the microchip into her husband's coat. No one else knew. Gavriil was stabbed seven or eight times, but he kept firing, keeping them off Solovyov. The attackers left the briefcase and went for the coat. They knew exactly what to look for."

"I take it you tracked down the wife," Lev's voice was grim.

"Damn straight. Gavriil was taken to a hospital and knew orders would have been given to terminate him. I went out the window with him. I knew a doctor, a surgeon who owed me, who would take care of him if he lived long enough for me to get him to the doc. He's tough as nails, our older brother. And then I tracked down the wife and her lover and had a little talk with them. It wasn't difficult to get the information I needed. That led me to France—more precisely, Paris."

Lev closed his eyes briefly. "Judith was an art student in Paris a few years back. I remember Rikki telling me she'd been to France, studying."

"She met the wrong man. The trail led back to Jean-Claude La Roux, who at this moment is sitting in prison surrounded by photographs of Judith. The pictures span the last five years. He's had her watched all this time. I know, because I shared his cell, trying to get information out of him. He was picked up on a gun-running charge, but his crimes far exceed that. He's ruthless and vicious and even from prison, his network is still up and running."

"You think he has the microchip." Lev made it a statement.

"I tracked it to him. He had it in his possession right before the French arrested him. They got to him before I did. If he'd sold the information to the highest bidder, we would have known by now. Certainly some of the documents would have surfaced. And someone would have made a threat. There was very sensitive material on that microchip. Theodotus Solovyov was transporting the chip to a meeting. He is a brilliant man, and that chip contains the only copy of his latest work."

Lev rubbed his jaw. "Is it possible it also contains documents regarding the training schools we attended? The reporter who printed the excerpt, who was he?"

"It was a publication out of France, and the man is a respected journalist. We're certain he got his information from La Roux and since it was recent, La Roux must be planning a move on the microchip. He hasn't trusted anyone to retrieve it and act for him, so he has to be planning to retrieve it himself."

"He's getting out of prison?"

"We're helping him. The plan is to pick him up and inter-rogate him. That's how I knew someone very powerful had put out hits on us. I was with La Roux for two months. I know him better than anyone and I could have broken him quickly and extracted the information we need, but instead, I was sent here on the off chance that he escapes our men. Judith was his girlfriend. So essentially I'm supposed to babysit her."

Lev's face lost all expression, but Stefan ignored his brother's suspicions. He'd already told him the truth and he might as well finish what he'd started. "I knew they wouldn't send me on a simple babysitting job and of course, everyone knows the yacht you were working undercover on went down off this coast and that you're presumed dead. If I didn't believe it, I figured Ivanov didn't believe it either. I've been here a couple of weeks reconning, but Thomas Vincent of-ficially came into town yesterday. Ivanov was watching me."

"So you went after him."

"I knew he was using me to find you. I think killing you is a sanctioned hit, but when I reported back to my handler, he acted as if Ivanov had gone rogue and gave me the green light to kill him. If he really went rogue and they lost con-trol of him, they would have put the word out to everyone."

"And because they sent you here as bait, you're certain Ivanov is going to erase you as well," Lev mused. "How bad did you hurt him?"

Stefan shrugged. "He was hurt enough that he ran when he could have had the advantage. I think broken ribs, he was having trouble breathing and I cut him some, but he's a wounded bear now. And never forget, he was trained in the same school we were. He was in Siberia with me. He was a couple of years older and already he had a taste for killing. There was a blizzard, heavy ice and snow with howling winds. Kids were dropping all over the place, the cold killing them before we had a chance to construct any kind of shelter. Ivanov would bend over and watch them die. He liked to see the light go out of their eyes."

He had never spoken of that particular hell, the biting, vicious cold, the stinging ice that tore one's breath from the body and snatched lives from frostbitten, terrified children. He was certain Ivanov had covered the mouths and noses of several on the ground, killing them, rather than trying to save them as most of the others had done.

"He was brought into the school I was in briefly, when I was a teen," Lev admitted. "He was a bastard then. A kid died hard one night and everyone knew he'd killed him. He was removed a week later, but it was obvious he was protected by someone high up. Even the trainers avoided a confrontation with him."

"Don't underestimate him, Levi. I'm going to hunt him because he'll never stop, but when he's dead, if I'm right about this and it was Sorbacov who sent him, he'll send another because he'll always consider us a threat to him."

"I'll deal with whatever comes at us. The local sheriff, Jonas Harrington, knows everyone in town. He's a shrewd man with a few of his own gifts, so walk carefully around him. He knew me right away, but you take after our mother with your eyes and hair and I doubt he would recognize you. He met Ivanov and if I get word to him that the exterminator is back in town for some wet work, he'll find him fast."

"No local sheriff can handle a man like Ivanov and you know it, Levi."

"No, but he has connections we don't. Let him do the looking."

"It's risky," Stefan said. "Let him know up front that Ivanov is a straight-up killer. I'll keep hunting until I run him down. In the meantime, I can't tell Judith who I am or what I'm doing here until La Roux is in Russian custody and we return the microchip safely to Theodotus Solovyov."

"We might want to know what's on it, Stefan."

Stefan scowled at his younger brother. "That's treason."

"It's self-preservation," Lev protested. "If Solovyov had

requested the list of known agents out of those schools for a reason, wanting to use us as bodyguards, or for something else, Sorbacov would have provided him with the information. Theodotus Solovyov has the highest security classification possible and Sorbacov would have had no choice. We both know how politics are played out."

"And it all ends up in the hands of La Roux who figures he can blackmail Sorbacov. La Roux has connections enough in Russia to plan and carry out an attack against Solovyov, he would have no problems trying to blackmail Sorbacov," Stefan added. "Sorbacov tries to have him killed, probably thinks that he can take him out in the prison and has him arrested on a gun running charge, but La Roux has too much clout."

"So you think La Roux released an excerpt, some small thing he had managed to read before he was arrested to tell Sorbacov to back off."

Stefan nodded. "That's exactly what I think. That's why Sorbacov tried so hard to get to La Roux. He tried to get him moved to Russia, but France wouldn't let him go. He was afraid to kill La Roux outright because he didn't know where that microchip was or if it would come to light later. So he sent me in to see if I could buddy up to him and find out where it was or who might be holding it for La Roux."

"No way is Judith doing that." Lev shook his head. "I'm telling you, Stefan, I know this woman. I've only been here a few weeks, but these women are tight, they share a bond as strong as a blood bond. Judith would never be involved in gun running or selling secrets of countries."

"I agree. But Jean-Claude La Roux is very, very obsessed with her."

"It appears that you are as well," Lev said dryly, a hint of humor in his eyes.

Stefan turned cool aqua eyes on him. "Never think for one minute that what I feel has anything to do with what that bastard feels for her."

Lev's eyebrow shot up. "You really are serious about her."

"I told you I was. I'm going to hunt Ivanov, and you're going to secure this farm. If I can remove the threat to you, it will give us time to prepare for the next one."

"You know I can't let you do that, Stefan. We'll hunt him together."

"And your wife? What do you plan on telling her?"

"I tell Rikki the truth, always. I don't remember everything about my past, but when it comes back to me in bits and pieces, I tell her. That's the deal we have and, even over this, I won't lie to her. She's dealt with Ivanov before and she did fine."

Stefan hesitated. "I can't tell Judith I'm your brother until the business with the microchip is done, which means I have to walk a thin line of lying. When I'm with her, I give her whatever is real about me, but she knows me as Thomas Vincent, an American. I don't want to put you in the position of lying to your woman or to Judith, but I can't do anything until I know those defense plans can't possibly fall into the wrong hands."

He didn't know if he was asking or demanding, but he knew he was placing Lev in an untenable position. If Judith fully belonged to him, he wouldn't want to lie to her about his past or about the danger surrounding them. There had to be trust, a bond between a man and a woman that was sacred, or what was the use?

Lev shook his head. "I can't lie to Rikki. I can tell her that something from my past has come up and would she mind waiting a few days before I discussed it with her. I do want to tell her Ivanov is in town. He might confront her again and I want her prepared."

The protective note in his brother's voice convinced Stefan once and for all that Lev loved his wife and marrying her wasn't part of an elaborate cover. No one could be that good of an actor. The fact that Lev would risk asking her to wait to hear information pertinent to their lives spoke volumes. Stefan wished for that kind of open relationship with Judith. He'd never shared any aspect of his life with anyone since his parents had been murdered. His disclosures to Lev were the closest thing he'd managed to date. What would that feel like—to trust someone enough to place your life in their hands?

Stefan sighed. "You do what you have to do, Lev, but I have no choice until I know the microchip is secure. And don't go after Ivanov without me. You have no idea how dangerous he is. You may have had a brief encounter with him once, but I grew up in the same school with him. He didn't like anyone getting the better of him. Everyone learned very quickly to allow him to be number one in all things, or you didn't wake up in the morning. He killed at least five children I know of and the instructors knew it as well. They had cameras on us twenty-four hours a day."

"He definitely murdered the boy in our school. We all knew it. And it was no training exercise. The boy was in his bed."

"If one took him down in a combat situation, or stayed under water longer, learned faster, anything could set him off."

"Did you let him win?"

"My barracks consisted of a very tough bunch of kids. We set watch and constructed warning systems. Even then my talents were strong and I always knew if he was close by. I'll confess, I taunted him, tried to get him to come after me to give me an excuse to kill him, but he's cunning and he never took the bait."

"But he hates you."

"With every breath in his body. I have no doubt that he pulled strings to use me to draw you out. That would be his idea of revenge. Make me the instrument of my brother's death. He would make certain I knew you were dead before he killed me," Stefan said.

"Is it possible he really has gone rogue, that his need to kill you has finally eaten him up until he's made the break with Sorbacov?"

"He's always been Sorbacov's pet." Stefan rubbed the bridge of his nose thoughtfully. "Unfortunately, I think we have no choice but to proceed believing Sorbacov is purging the ranks and has sanctioned the hit."

"Sorbacov knows us. Wouldn't he send a team?"

Stefan shrugged. "Maybe he has and no one else has surfaced yet, but it's doubtful. He'd want to do this as quietly as possible without anyone knowing or raising an alarm. Ivanov is completely loyal to Sorbacov, not to Russia, not to anyone else in the government. I think Sorbacov is his only contact with reality. He wouldn't break it. No, Sorbacov sent him to kill us and doesn't want it to get out. Hell, every agent he has would turn against him if it came out."

"So by giving you the green light to hunt Ivanov," Lev mused, "Sorbacov is betting on his pet assassin to do his job before you do yours."

"That's my belief. I'm waiting word on La Roux's prison escape. They should be getting him out any day and once the microchip is safe, my duty to them is done and I'll tell Judith the truth and hope she understands."

"Stefan, I'm not your little brother anymore," Lev said. "Don't try to protect me."

Stefan let his gaze drift over Lev. He had grown into a strong man, very reminiscent of their father. He carried the natural muscle of the Prakenskii family and the same eyes Stefan remembered his father had. Lev had the inevitable scars of their profession and training, but to Stefan, he would forever be his younger brother, one he loved and yes, one he protected.

He stepped forward and for the first time allowed himself to be in a position of vulnerability. He caught Lev by the shoulders, providing a huge target to his younger brother if Lev was inclined to kill him. They both knew this was the moment of truth. Lev could get rid of the threat to his new family and no one would ever be the wiser, or he could step into the embrace and accept Stefan back into his life.

Lev hesitated for just a moment, searching Stefan's face, and then he gripped Stefan's shoulder, showing the same vulnerability. A small smile lit his eyes. "It's good to see you."

"Have you seen Ilya yet?" Stefan couldn't keep the eagerness out of his voice.

Ilya had been the youngest and probably didn't remember any of them. Their mother had tried to protect him, fighting to keep him when the men broke in and tore her youngest son from her arms. They'd all tried to protect the boy, but he'd been wrenched from them. Stefan always felt he'd let down his parents, not recovering his youngest brother.

Lev shook his head. "He was married a few weeks ago to one of Blythe's cousins, Joley Drake. Joley's a huge name in the music industry and apparently they didn't return from their honeymoon yet because she's doing a series of benefits for Japan and then more for the tornado victims here in the States."

"And he's friends with the sheriff?"

Lev nodded. "Close, I'm told."

Stefan pulled him close in a brief bear hug and then let him go. "Married life suits you."

"Rikki suits me," Lev corrected. "She saved me when I was drowning and I don't mean in the ocean, although that too."

Stefan understood what his brother was trying to express to him. Drowning in blood, in shadows, in the cold, was every bit as real as drowning in an ocean. He hadn't even known he was so far gone until Judith threw him a safety line.

"I have something else to do tonight before I leave, so do me a favor and call off your sentries," Stefan said. "I don't want one of your owls to slash up my face. Thomas Vincent would have a very difficult time explaining to Judith what happened to his eyes if your owl plucked them out."

"I don't have dogs yet," Lev pointed out. "I have to keep the women safe, especially now that Ivanov is back."

"Then show me to them and give me a pass," Stefan challenged, not willing to let it go. Lev may have accepted him as a brother, but he didn't extend that trust to the women.

Lev studied his expression for a long time before he nodded again. "I'm going to say this one time, Stefan, and I hope you understand. I would do anything to keep Rikki and her sisters safe. Anything at all, so don't betray my trust."

Yeah. His little brother had grown up.

11

JUDITH wasn't asleep. Stefan could see her pacing in the room he knew to be her bedroom, passing back and forth in front of the bank of windows overlooking her star flower garden. The light behind her cast her image easily through the uncovered window. Behind the gates of the farm, the women thought themselves safe from predators, but there he was, crouched low, once again in the shadows, a phantom come alive.

The surge of anger he'd experienced at his brother no longer surprised him. He realized Judith had not only brought his emotions boiling to the surface after so many long years of suppressing them, but surrounded by her gardens and so close to her home, every emotion would be amplified. Judith might try to contain her spirit, but the element was too strong and energy pulsed around her home and spread like warm honey throughout her enormous gardens. He had a wild urge to climb up to Judith's balcony and make certain she was too tired to do anything but sleep, with his body wrapped around hers.

The breeze coming off the ocean carried a hint of rain

with it, along with the first fingers of fog creeping inland. Soft gray clouds drifted across the sky, slowly obscuring the moon and stars, as if drawing a thick veil over the night. Under his feet the earth pulsed in anticipation. Stefan felt it, that strong burst of energy, of joy, as if the ground exploded with excitement, and then seemed to settle into a throbbing rhythm. He'd never felt such a sensation before and he sank his fingers into the rich soil to enhance his ability to understand what was happening.

The air around him moved subtly, the breeze shifting slightly, enough to bring the clouds into position over the vast fields of vegetables and sweeping gardens of flowers. The air pulsed with power as well, a unique flow of energy that told him that breeze had been directed. He watched Judith as she came onto the balcony and stood at the railing, looking out over the farm as if drawn there by an unseen hand.

She raised her face to the clouds overhead, but didn't move, obviously waiting for something. The wind tugged at her long hair and pressed her thin tank tight against her breasts, so that the material cupped the soft curves lovingly. Her flowing skirt moved gracefully around her long legs, lending her an utterly feminine mystique that took his breath away.

The rain began to fall over the flower garden softly, with a gentle, almost tender touch. It took a moment for him to hear the music in the drop, a clear pattern emerging, like a quiet symphony building slowly toward a crescendo. Judith wasn't directing the rain, one of the other women was, but she was definitely boosting the power of that element, her hands graceful, palms up as she faced the farm.

Stefan's breath caught in his throat. He was witnessing the combined power of elementals at work. The effect was shocking, mesmerizing and awe-inspiring all at once. He was used to psychic occurrences; every member of his family had natural talent. But this . . . this was a demonstration in the use of elements in everyday life for practical purposes.

Rikki, his brother's wife, was a water element, and Stefan was certain she was the one directing the rain over various parts of the farm. One of Judith's sisters no doubt was an air element and her light touch on the wind was masterful. The earth responded to another sister, earthworms churning, aerating the soil, working and thriving in the compost heap, welcoming the rain, answering the spirit binding the elements together from somewhere deep inside. The earth took the water deep beneath the soil, spreading it like veins running beneath the rich loam, carrying life-giving fluid to every plant. He felt the last element, fire, join the others, not with fire but as a bright flame driving their combined dream of a prosperous farm forward.

Water rained heavily in the forest, gently in the vegetable gardens and even more tenderly over the flowers, the chords of a weeping guitar. Through it all, the wind carried the sounds of a symphony, moving through the trees and gardens as the air element played the light notes of a flute. The drum of the fire element set the rhythm for all of them. The earth provided the melodic piano keys and Judith's spirit acted as the conductor.

Stefan's heart joined the rhythm. If he tried to tell anyone else about this unique phenomenon, no one would believe him. It was the most beautiful, invigorating thing he'd ever witnessed—no, *experienced*. He was right there, drawn in by Judith's powerful spirit. Stefan realized their combined dream wasn't just about using the elements to make their farm prosper, it was the way all five elements wove a tight bond together, sustaining one another, sharing courage and commitment.

Sitting quietly and absorbing the energy, he felt the very subtle notes of a male woven through the water element and knew his brother had somehow merged with his wife while she drew the water from the clouds. Another female presence was there as well, one he nearly missed. The sixth sister was powerful in her own right, although there was a subtle difference. She was no element, yet she seemed to be a part of each of them. Lev had said she was difficult to figure out, and Stefan could understand why. With her touch, the wind moaned like a violin and danced through the trees, tugging playfully at leaves and kissing the bright flowers.

Around him, nature itself responded to the surging power, bathing in the pounding rhythms, owls flying in the drops of rain, circling above the tree tops while on the ground, fox and deer emerged from the forest as if drawn to participate. It was only then that Stefan realized he was absorbing the powerful energy into his own body. Every emotion multiplied and enhanced. He could feel strength running through his muscles as power poured into him in the same way the rain poured over the farm. Fast. Slow. Easy. Hard. He absorbed all elements, feeling each of the energies mixing with his own psychic talents.

Stefan flexed each muscle carefully before easing his way across the field of flowers, careful to stay on the narrow path so there would be no signs of his passing. He couldn't afford to get too wet, not when he was going into Judith's house. He didn't want her to come across wet tracks on her cream-colored carpet. He moved around to the back of the house where the wild gardens of tall grasses and shrubs looked like a small jungle in the rain.

The entire lower floor was dark. It was more difficult to avoid the tall, bushy plants with leaves reaching out to capture prey. He slipped through them, taking care not to brush up against them. Leaving leaves or grass on her carpet would be every bit as bad as wet tracks. He bypassed the first and second studios, angling through the overgrown plants to reach the darkened French doors of the third studio.

Heavy drapes covered the doors, a big contrast to the other two much more inviting studios. Very carefully he put his palm an inch away from the outside of the glass, feeling the room. His warning system went crazy, every nerve, cell and muscle in his body shrinking back. His heart went crazy, accelerating, and his lungs burned for air. Even the hair on the back of his neck stood up. The power of the elements had amplified his natural radar, but even taking that into consideration, there was something extremely dangerous in that studio.

Stefan let his breath out slowly. What could she be hiding in this studio? The danger didn't feel like treachery, or conspiracy. He passed his hand slowly over the door, a slow inch-by-inch inspection, paying particular attention to the frame. There were no hidden trip wires he could detect, nothing that would alert her to a break-in. He laid his palm over the lock, at first not touching the door handle. No heat came off the metal. He very lightly wrapped his hand around the knob. The lock responded to him, welcoming his touch, sliding open for him without a push. The door didn't open.

He had never come across a lock that didn't open at his will. Never. Security systems were nearly as easy. But even with another light push, the door didn't open for him. Judith had double-locked this studio. She really didn't want to chance anyone getting inside. His suspicious nature kicked into high gear. What in the hell could she be hiding from the world? From him?

He ran his hand once more along the frame of the door. At the bottom of the double doors he felt the slightest of resistances and knew he'd found the second lock. She had a floor lock. Ordinarily, it would be impossible to get around the lock without cutting the glass or going in through a window. He glanced at the bank of windows used strictly for ventilation. No one could slip inside those narrow openings. There were dozens of windows, long and narrow,

opening to allow air through, but impossible for a child, let
alone a grown man, to slip through. She'd planned this studio meticulously, making certain no one could get inside
without her knowledge or consent.

He crouched low and laid his palm over that slight resistance. Patience mattered. Concentration and focus were es-
sential. He felt familiar warmth travel down his arm and
once again he flexed his fingers. His hand warmed, went
perfectly still, hovering over the spot a moment before
slowly descending to rest over the lower frame. Still the lock
remained stubborn. Judith's will was strong, at work here.
Stefan pushed the thought away and focused wholly on the
mechanics of the lock. It was a simple enough lock, but very
effective. A small slider turned the metal clasp, preventing
the door from movement. Once he "felt" the mechanism, he
could maneuver it open.

Once again, before he slid the French door open, he
checked for an alarm system that would alert Judith that
someone had invaded her secured studio. Using extreme
caution, he turned the handle and opened the door. The
heavy drapes, as black as midnight, blocked his view, but
he could feel the blast of rage, an explosive energy that
leapt toward him. Again, every cell in his body rebelled. He
slipped inside and shut the door behind him, his pen light
in his teeth, the only relief in the darkness of the room.

Stefan drew the drapes aside enough to allow him entrance. He found breathing difficult, the air so thick with
rage it was impossible to draw a full breath. He moved the
light around the room for a quick inspection to assure himself that he was alone, although his radar had already told
him of that. Nevertheless, he always double- and triple-
checked when it came to preparation and safety. Attention
to detail, no matter how small, was the one thing that kept
him alive over the years.

Every other room in Judith's house was painted white or
cream, a foil for the joyful colors she splashed through her

home and into the walls. Here, there was only unrelenting darkness. True, there was a mural running from floor to ceiling, great, thick tree trunks, broken and shattered limbs that twisted grotesquely, creating the illusion of a dark, forbidding forest.

This was what she no longer allowed into her paintings. She kept her emotions compartmentalized. This was a room housing all destructive emotions. She didn't realize one couldn't possibly live the way she was trying. Darker emotions often got one through the most difficult circumstances. There was a balance to life and Judith had tried to get away from that balance fearing the darker side of her mind.

Even here, in this studio of rage, he could see the artist in her. Above his head the ceiling was painted in deep purples and swirling darker, nearly bloodred black slashes. The effect was astonishing. The ceiling looked as if it was weeping dark tears. Looking at it, he felt sorrow creeping into his heart, an insidious tendril of emotion winding its way into his mind. He pulled his gaze away from the fascinating montage of color and inspected the walls.

The colors were more mottled on the walls, great ropes, twisted into vines of hatred and anger. Sorrow dripped through the black forest of rage. The blood drops were more vivid, the knife slashing through the paint in quick bursts of anger, while that deep purple wept over all of it. Candles were on the tables and shelves, many burned down to nothing, the wax pooled around the bottoms of the candles, becoming part of the macabre atmosphere. A creepy oily smell permeated the room adding to the morbid, almost gruesome feeling emanating from the walls.

He was surrounded by her once again, her darkest moments, her most intimate, chilling thoughts. As joyful and bright as her kaleidoscope studio was, as beautiful and soothing as her painting studio, this was the complete and utter opposite, although, he found there was still a kind of beauty in the unrelenting darkness, mostly because no mat-

ter what her emotion, the artist that was Judith always came
through.

"Oh, *moi padshii angel*, you're so lost," he murmured
aloud.

Stefan knew he was a phantom, belonging to the shadows, but at least he knew exactly who he was and how he
had gotten there. Judith didn't trust herself—didn't realize
that by creating this place, she only reinforced her own
belief that she was twisted. Five years of rage and sorrow
were held suspended in one space. No one could stay in this
room for any length of time without the unrelenting destructive emotions affecting them.

He stepped close to the painting she was working on,
slowly removing the cover and shining his light over it. His
breath stopped in his lungs. Something hard blocked his
throat. This was Judith's nightmare. The torture and death
of her beloved brother. Jagged glass, tipped with dark blood,
slashed angry lines through the canvas. Bold angry strokes
with a broad brush, none of the fine little brushstrokes for
this painting that he'd observed in all of her other works.
The only real color was a bright, bold Japanese character.
He knew it was her brother's name painted over the rivers
of blood and the broken, tormented body.

He peered closer and Judith's eyes eerily stared back at
him filled with a mixture of grief and anger. His own eyes
burned and his gut churned. Shame and guilt descended
over him, a heavy blanket weighing him down, nearly
crushing his chest in the vicinity of his heart. Intellectually
he knew he was feeling her emotions, the intensity she felt
each time she gave into the concentrated, unrelenting sorrow and came into this room where she felt it was safe to
allow her emotions free rein, to rework the painting.

She hadn't signed the graphically detailed depiction of
her brother's death, but she'd brought it to life. He could
almost see the figures moving in that room of blood and
pain. The men turning on one another as her brother lay in

agony, gasping for his last breaths. The policeman's lifeless body crumpling over the top of Judith, driving her down into the blood and torn flesh of her brother, while the policemen's blood and fragmented flesh sprayed over her like a fountain.

It was a ghastly scene, even to a man used to violence, mostly because it was viewed through the eyes of a woman who loved the victim—through the eyes of Judith. He knew she wasn't finished with it because she hadn't signed her name. It didn't matter how much he told himself it was Judith's feelings, his heart nearly exploded in pain. Looking at her eyes, the guilt there, the anger and grief, he felt a murderous rage begin to smolder in his belly, growing stronger the longer he stared at the painting. He needed to make this right for her.

A muscle ticked in his jaw as he covered the painting. He'd told her he was her man. He was certainly capable of vengeance. Her brother hadn't been tortured to extract information vital to the safety of a country; it had been done as a lesson. He knew he was justifying his own life, his own terrible sins, but at this point, he couldn't change what the men who had shaped his life had made him into. He could do this for her and if anyone deserved to suffer before he died, it was Jean-Claude La Roux.

In the center of the room a dark cloth covered a large object. The cloth seemed to stir, although there was no way for a breeze to have moved it. The slight ripple of the fabric drew his attention. The room whispered, an insidious buzz in his ears, never quite grew loud enough for him to make out words.

He walked around the object, which nearly came up to his chest. He used the tips of his fingers to remove the cloth. The kaleidoscope was large, almost as big as a telescope to view the night sky, and sat on a tall tripod. Four individual sealed cells were stacked in a black canister and a fifth, which she appeared to working on, was on top. He assumed each cell represented a year gone by without her brother's killer paying adequately for his crime, yet when he picked them up, he couldn't make out the images inside of them.

Puzzled, Stefan examined each cell from every angle, laying them out carefully in order. His mind always remembered the smallest detail, but he was still methodical, always double-checking the small things, taking no chances anyone would feel his passing. No real phantom could afford to overlook the tiniest detail.

He turned the first cell over and over. It was filled with mineral oil and sealed, clearly finished but no matter how much he shined the penlight on it, he couldn't make out the objects that should be floating around inside of it. He frowned, his mind working at the problem. She wouldn't have empty cells, but she'd found some way to protect what was inside them. Just viewing her kaleidoscope studio had taught him that cells were very personal. Each item chosen was selected with meticulous care and meant something important.

Judith told stories with her kaleidoscopes. She brought peace and joy into people's lives all around the world. The scopes were more than art, they were useful for medical issues, bringing down blood pressure and aiding an autistic child or adult to find a healthy escape. Stefan studied the large kaleidoscope again. What was she telling? And how?

The kaleidoscope itself was much larger than he'd seen in her other studio and that had to be significant in some way. The outside was powder-coated over metal rather than a wrap of some kind. The color seemed an unrelenting black, but there was something about it that made him think, just like the cells, she'd hidden something from view.

Again he checked the room with his penlight. He was missing something important. It was difficult to think when the room was so alive around him. Emotions battered at him and every lungful of air was difficult to draw in, seething with bright hot rage. His belly coiled into tight knots and blood thundered in his ears, howling through his mind, thundering for revenge.

A portable ultraviolet light sat on the workbench, near her rolling chair. It looked as if she used it often, and yet it didn't fit with the set up of the room. The handle opened to provide the stand and although it wasn't plugged in, it was close to the cell she was still working on. Stefan plugged it in and flipped the switch.

At once he could see an array of objects in a small bin beside tools. She had created the various items she wanted to use in her cells from materials that would only reveal themselves under the ultraviolet light. Ingenious. Stefan shook his head at her creativity. Not only was she able to hide her work, but the secretive nature of the cells reflected the intensity of the emotions she kept so hidden from the rest of the world. Essentially, she'd locked a part of herself away in those sealed cells.

Stefan choose year one to examine first. Not only was it evident to him that this particular cell was the beginning from being on the bottom of the stack, but when he took it close to the light and swirled the contents, he clearly saw the number one in the midst of the other items. Red drops that looked like blood dripped over the images. Purple swirled through the contents and once more sorrow settled heavily on his shoulders.

Year one was all about grief. Judith imprisoned her anguish at losing her beloved brother in this cell for all time. The heartache cut deep, slashing wounds that refused to close. Through the cell were images of guilt and a faint trail of shame. Twisting sticks of metal, a broken heart and weapons of torture swirled slowly, tumbling over one another, all while the cell wept drops of blood. The same Japanese character in red that was the name of her brother tumbled in the mix. A glittering object proclaimed "I'm sorry" and another was a very telling clock turning back the hands of time.

He found himself nearly weeping and, glancing down, realized his finger stroked the trigger of his gun. Abruptly he pulled his hand away, understanding just how intense her emotions were. He was feeling what she felt. Here, in this room, surrounded by relentless sorrow, she contemplated ending her life to make up for her sins. She knew better, he could read that as well, but the thought was in her mind occasionally. She couldn't bring him back; she couldn't turn back the clock.

In the second cell he studied the objects representing Paris. A broken paintbrush. A slashed canvas. A palette of colors that ran to darker blues and purples. A tiny replica of the Louvre. A torn picture of herself and her brother that nearly broke his heart. Small things that told him her guilt was growing.

Subsequent cells revealed a Japanese Kanji symbol for shame and another that represented guilt. A police badge. The small Greek island where Jean-Claude's men caught up with her brother. Things he believed portrayed her brother's life. As the years progressed, the rage in Judith obviously grew and more items showed the slow, torturous death, slice by slice as they tried to extract information about Judith's whereabouts. In a single cell she had created tiny replicas of torment so detailed he knew her spirit had merged with her brother's as he lay dying and she felt every cut, every burn, just as he had.

A burning flame took fire in his gut. His mind snarled and raged with murderous intent. His body crawled with the need to avenge the murder of Paul Henderson. Murderous rage for Stefan was unfamiliar. He killed coldly. Without emotion. His feelings had long ago been stamped out of him. Until Judith he hadn't realized he had such a well of passion to draw from.

This—this *need* to make La Roux suffer had to come from Judith, not from him. His hands didn't shake, his body didn't coil tight, his brain never roared for the kill. She'd poured those emotions into this room, and then trapped them here and his spirit always absorbed hers. He was soaking those darker sentiments into his body.

Taking a breath, Stefan managed to push the rage down deep as he fit the cell into the large kaleidoscope and added the portable ultraviolet light. The wand fit into the cylinder and illuminated the cell. Placing his eye to the glass he turned the cell. The scenes were duplicated in a starburst pattern through the mirror system so that he saw the torture as if he was looking through a macabre nightmare, probably in the way Judith had to revisit the memory when she closed her eyes at night. He turned the cell.

Instantly a great cosmos burst through all the blood and gore and rage like a wild primordial mix of pure emotions. The pinpoints of exploding stars unwittingly revealed Judith's character no matter how hard she tried to conceal it from herself and the sight was raw beauty and yet terrifying. Chaos reigned, and still there was order. Passionate hatred and love mixed together in a swirl of stark, raw emotion no other human had the right to witness. He was looking into Judith's exposed soul.

He saw the truth of what and who she was. She had spent five long years working up her anger and need for revenge because Jean-Claude La Roux deserved to pay for what he'd done, yet her true essence always prevailed. The light in her, the compassion and natural brightness refused to be dimmed. She trapped those dark emotions in one room and tried to live there, tried to separate herself, become something she wasn't and could never be, but he knew when he viewed each separate cell he would see those bursting rays of light spreading over the dark, hostile buildup of her need to take revenge.

The shame and guilt she felt was not as much over the death of her brother and the policeman—she'd worked through her responsibility over the years, and had obviously come to the conclusion that the circumstances were

beyond her abilities at that time. But shame and guilt had
grown in this room, stayed hidden here, like a terrible
wound she couldn't cauterize. She was incapable of making another human being suffer. She certainly couldn't kill
someone. He had no doubt she would defend herself and
those she loved passionately, but to kill cold-bloodedly was
an impossibility for a woman with her character, and deep
down, she knew it.

Judith wanted to avenge her brother, she even felt she
should, but she was not the kind of woman who would ever
do such a thing and guilt ate at her constantly. She felt as
though she were letting him down all over again. It was no
wonder she didn't sleep.

It had been natural for Judith to call on her older brother
to help her out of a bad situation. He'd raised her after her
parents had died. He'd been the one she'd always counted
on and of course he had rushed to help her. She probably
closed her eyes and saw him looking at her accusingly. In
her painting, Paul's eyes had been wide open, staring at his
sister as the life ran out of him and she saw his indictment
of her guilt. Stefan knew better, knew that was her con-
science talking.

The revelation brought out those protective instincts he
hadn't known existed until Judith, every bit as raw and stark
and passionate as her wild chaotic emotions. He needed to
wrap himself tightly around her and shield her from outside
eyes until she could bring the two halves of her spirit back
together. She had to forgive herself for being gentle and
kind. For being compassionate. Judith didn't seem to realize
the world would be a much better place populated with
people like her instead of people like him.

She feared her own passionate nature so much that she
thought about death, about ways to keep others she loved
safe. She was so afraid that her darker emotions, as natural
as they might be, would contribute to the pain and suffering
of others she loved.

Stefan shook his head. He was not about to let her go. He knew he had the capability to fill every shadowed space inside of her with his own spirit, merge so deeply that she would never feel the burden alone again. His gifts somehow intertwined with hers, allowing him such intimate closeness that he knew he could shield not only Judith, but others around them until she had full understanding and control of her gift.

He had to leave this place of sorrow and revenge before the emotions trapped inside became too overwhelming even for his strength. Unlike Judith, he didn't have that bright spirit prevailing over every dark emotion. He had shields, but the power in the room was overwhelming even to him.

Very carefully he replaced the ultraviolet light and the cells for the kaleidoscope and covered it, ensuring the cloth lay in the exact position he'd found it. Stefan took one last look around the studio to make certain that everything was exactly as he'd found it and there was no evidence that anyone had discovered Judith's secret. The drapes were put back in place and he secured both locks before sitting down on the patio and taking in great gulps of fresh air.

He dropped his head into his hands, oblivious of the rain coming down. It was a gentle shower, very light, and he welcomed the clean, fresh droplets of water on his burning skin. The rain felt like tears on his face when he looked up to watch the water fall from the sky. Judith needed him and he was eternally grateful for that revelation. He had thought she would be his salvation, but it was entirely possible he was bringing something to their union as well.

She needed to accept herself as she was, incapable of harming others. She had to realize everyone had dark thoughts, including her brother, but he would not want his sister to spend her life looking for revenge. If Paul loved her as much as she'd loved him—and that was evident, from everything he'd seen—the last thing he would want would be for Judith to waste her talent by fearing it. She was powerful in her creativity, and equally as passionate in her spirit and that included all emotions, not just the gentler ones.

Stefan stood up slowly, stretching out his muscles, aware just how tense the dark studio had made him. Fighting against the assault every moment had taken its toll. He felt wrung out, exhausted and in need of a safe place to retreat to. Not the hotel where Thomas Vincent was staying—that was out of the question. If Ivanov wasn't hurt as bad as Stefan suspected, then he'd come hunting. Already, there might be a trap in the hotel room and he was too damned tired to deal with it. Tired men made mistakes.

He was trained to keep going no matter the toll on his body, his will simply kicked in to provide the necessary impetuous to keep going until his mission was complete. He was used to working through fatigue, through wounds, through days without food or sleep, but the toll on him from the battering of emotions was the worst he'd ever experienced. He was left too drained from the battle to shield the bombardment of such intense destructive energy.

Stefan began to weave his way through the tall grasses and bushes, edging back toward the side of the house where Judith's bedroom faced. He half hoped she'd gone to bed, but the rain was still too directed and someone was conducting the symphony, each element contributing, but Judith amplifying the power of each. If he was honest with himself, he just wanted to see her once more to make certain she was all right. Now that he'd found her, he was reluctant to be away from her.

Out of the corner of his eye he caught something large coming at him from above his head as he rounded the corner of the two-story structure. Ducking low, he spun to face the creature coming in fast for the attack. The owl dove silently, talons extended, intending to rake his eyes and at the last moment recognized Lev's visual guide and tried to pull up, the great wings beating hard, in an effort to stop the rapid descent. Talons streaked across his face, under his left eye and then bird was gone, taking to the sky, heading for the nearest tree.

Stefan touched his face, a streak of fire burning like a brand. He'd been lucky. The owl could have taken out his eye. He might have to revise his opinion on the birds as guards. This one had come in savagely and without sound. The wing feathers of the owl muffled the swish of the raptor in flight, allowing the night raptor to attack in complete silence. If it hadn't been for his warning system, Stefan doubted if he could have escaped so easily, even with the bird recognizing him as a friend.

The owl settled into the top branches of the pine tree, wings slowly folding in close to its body, round eyes staring down into the trees growing thick on the knoll above Judith's house. Something about the way the bird concentrated on that knoll bothered Stefan. He was exhausted, fighting unfamiliar emotions and trying to ease the tension in his body, putting it all down to his experience in the dark studio. But now that the bird had made him aware, he wasn't so certain his body's warning system wasn't screaming at him in alarm.

Lev, you out here? He sent the question with great caution, not wanting to give his location even to his brother.

The owl had gone for his eyes. Had he pulled up because Lev had warned him off, or had it been Stefan's reflexes? *Something* was up on the knoll that had caught the bird's interest. Owls had keen eyesight, and their acute hearing was amazing. Stefan continued to move around the house until he had Judith's balcony in sight.

She stood outside, her face turned upward toward the light rain, the water molding her tank top to her lush curves, emphasizing her narrow ribcage and flaring hips. Her hair should have looked like a drowned rat's tail, but instead, wet, it glistened like a waterfall cascading around her body. Stefan's breath hissed out, afraid for her. Anyone concealed in that stand of trees on the knoll could easily see Judith and that could be considered a killing offense.

Stefan? Are you all right?

Stefan's heart thundered in his ears. Lev's voice was faint, as if coming over a good distance. The range of their telepathic abilities had never been tested, but Stefan knew it couldn't be too far.

Where are you?

With Rikki. You need me?

I think we have company. On the knoll above Judith's home. Thick stand of pine trees.

Stefan felt Lev's reaction, a kind of jerk of awareness. The entire farm was pulsing with energy as the elements came together and power flowed through Stefan heightening his abilities, yet at the same time, the force was so strong, it was easy to attribute the uneasiness and tension to the building intensity. Lev had to be feeling the power as well and it could be misleading all of them.

The owls would warn me.

Even with the disruption of power, all the energies merging together like they are?

The owl had attacked, although Lev had previously sent Stefan's image to the predators in the area, clearly showing them that Stefan belonged to the farm. Something had confused the bird. If the pulsing power in the air could confuse a raptor belonging to the night, no doubt it could also mislead Stefan's warning system.

I'm on my way. Disgust edged Lev's tone.

Immediately Stefan felt the break in the whips of pulsating power as if one of the threads had snapped. Energy crackled and snapped in the air, thin lines glowing, radiating out from a central point. The bright lights could have been electricity zipping out of control, like a dazzling light show. No doubt when Lev abruptly rushed from the house, his wife had stopped playing her rain symphony, breaking the connection between all five elements.

He glanced up at Judith. She stood in the suddenly driving rain, looking toward Rikki's house in surprise, but she
made no move to take shelter. Stefan's vision blurred for a
moment. His stomach lurched, his mind disoriented. When
it cleared, he was merged with his brother, looking through
the eyes of the owl down into the grove of pines trees. The
shadowy figure of a man crouched there and he was pointing something at Judith.

Judith! Both brothers called the warning at the exact
same moment, their voices thundering in her head. *Drop to
the ground and stay down now.*

Stefan poured sheer steel into his command and wasn't
surprised that Lev did the same. The result was gratifying.
Judith didn't hesitate. Stefan didn't know if it was the shock
of hearing such a decided command or that both men were
near her.

Stefan dropped all pretense of stealth and sprinted for
the grove of trees. Lev was a distance away, but he was on
his way. A branch snapped audibly, the sound carrying in
the stillness of the night. His prey was fleeing, having spotted Stefan.

Send the owl, he instructed his brother. *Block his path
to his vehicle. He has to have one. I can't get to him in time.
Slow him down. Now, Lev, slow him down!*

He ran with his weapon drawn, fear for Judith tripping his heart. Had the man been trying to kill her? Was it
Ivanov? Ivanov wouldn't have anything to gain by killing
Judith. He couldn't possibly know how Stefan felt about her.
Even if Stefan told the exterminator the truth, swore to him
his feelings for Judith ran deep, Ivanov would never believe
him.

He had an abundance of cover as he ran through the gardens, the taller flowers and brush screening him from a
good marksmen. He made certain to weave and duck, not
choosing a straight path, expecting a hail of bullets any
moment.

The owl took flight, joining several others suddenly circling around to the other side of the grove of trees where they disappeared.

Where is he? Stefan demanded.

On the western trail. I can't see his car yet, but he has to have one. If he makes it to his vehicle, I'll be able to cut him off before he gets to the front gate or tries to make it around to the back part of the property. These upper acres are fenced in.

He could go through a fence, Stefan pointed out.

Lev had to be driving partially blind if he was connected to the owls, but his information was vital to Stefan. Knowing his prey was running allowed Stefan to choose the shortest route instead of the most protected. He veered from the garden and cut across a field of wild flowers that took him up the slope of the knoll.

Get inside, Judith, he ordered. *Stay low, and for God's sake, set your security system. If anyone tries to break in, call the sheriff.*

He expected her to pepper him with questions and demand, but she did neither. He felt her quiet acceptance and risked one look over his shoulder to see the doors to the balcony closing firmly.

I will expect to see you both alive and well, she replied softly. *With a good explanation.*

12

I'VE never worked with anyone else, Lev, not like a team. I was trained to work separately, completely alone and cut off from all aid. Often, as a teenager, I'd be sent into hostile environments with another boy from my classes, one I'd trained with, slept in the same barracks, ate with and inevitably, halfway through the mission, when my back was turned and I was totally focused on accomplishing the task, the other boy would try to kill me as part of the assignment.

He wanted his brother to understand why trust came so reluctantly to him.

It was a tactic used often, late in our training, turning the students on one another, keeping them separate and heightening their sense of awareness as well as the belief that no one else could be trusted.

He loved Lev. There was no doubt in his mind that he loved his brother, but the Lev that he loved and was infinitely loyal to was a small boy who, like Stefan, lay beaten and bloody in the snow, horrified as soldiers murdered their parents. He was loyal to the boy who had clung to him, had been ripped from his arms and taken to another part of the country so they couldn't form an alliance against their enemies.

They did the same thing to me.

So he wasn't so alone after all. Lev had shared those experiences, that childhood, and he knew how surreal it felt to run through the night chasing an enemy with someone else closing in on the same man. Ahead as he raced through the trees, he could hear the heavy, almost frantic breathing of the intruder as he sprinted for his car. He must have parked outside the gates, climbed over the fence and hiked through the property to get to Judith's home.

That's worrisome, Lev said. *There are six houses on the property. How the hell did he know which one was hers?*

That was a damned good question, one Stefan wanted the answer to. *Don't kill him,* Stefan cautioned. *We need a few answers.*

He was closer. He could hear the thud of the footsteps and the sound of twigs and small, dead branches snapping in two as the intruder raced through the forest back toward the road.

Funny, I was about to say the same thing to you.

Stefan burst into the open, running at a steady, fast pace, falling in behind the intruder, slowly closing the gap. There was little cover in the meadow and as the man gained the other side, the owls swooped down, seven of them, great wings beating hard, flying straight for the man's face. He screamed and dropped to the ground, covering his head to escape the wicked talons.

We might not be the ones to kill him. Call them off now, I'm on him, Stefan said.

His father had been able to merge with animals, and he vaguely remembered a time when they were all together in a park and squirrels and birds had flocked around them. The squirrels had performed tricks that made him, along with his brothers, laugh. It was a scene far different from this one, where owls flew at a man's face with every intention of taking out his eyes. That had been a different time, back then, when he was a child, one he hadn't revisited until he met Judith. She'd given him back precious memories.

SHE'D given him back precious memories.

Judith sat on the floor shivering uncontrollably just to one side of the windows. Ice-cold, she wrung out her hair, uncaring that water dripped onto her carpet. She didn't really know much about Levi's past, only that he'd been working undercover on a yacht that had gone down and he wanted to stay dead. That brought up the disturbing thought that Thomas Vincent was not the gentle soul she'd thought him to be. It was very obvious Levi and Thomas knew each other—that much was certain—and the two of them were chasing someone who had come onto the property.

She often lost track of time when she was weaving spirit through the other elements and she had no idea how long she'd been on the balcony before she heard the voices commanding her to crawl back inside the safety of her house. She recognized the two men instantly. Energy was so powerful, swirling around her gardens and out into the farm, that both men's psychic talents had naturally been included in the woven circle, amplifying their ability to speak telepathically. Because her spirit was the thread weaving the entire tapestry together, she shared their natural link. She still did.

A part of her wanted to pull back, not know the truth, but she'd been blindsided once and others had paid the price for her poor judgment. She refused to be a coward and hide under her covers. She'd let Thomas Vincent into her life, *wanted* him with every fiber of her being. If he was as corrupt as Jean-Claude had been, she needed to know.

Worse, if Levi had deceived them all and was using Rikki in some way, that would be unforgivable and Judith would have to find a way to tell Rikki.

She didn't have telepathy, not in the true sense of the word. Brain waves generated pure energy and her element boosted energy, it was really that simple. She didn't hear thoughts, but if someone like Thomas—or Levi—was a true telepathic, her spirit would easily amplify and retrieve the conversations so that she was part of them. It was intimate and sexy when she shared telepathy with Thomas, but truly frightening when she was hearing Levi and Thomas. They were obviously familiar with each other—yet not.

She wiped her face with her hand and climbed unsteadily to her feet, making her way to the shower. She'd been more than halfway in love—or lust; it was difficult to tell—with Thomas. She'd felt so right with him and yet she didn't really know him at all. How could she? She'd just rushed into something headlong and impulsively in much the same way she had five years earlier with Jean-Claude.

She let the hot water pour over her, slowly driving the chill from her bones. They had spoken with Russian accents and the assassin sent to kill Levi a few weeks earlier had been Russian. The conclusions she'd drawn from the horrific images of Thomas's past had obviously been erroneous. He had been in some kind of military training camp at a very early age. He'd been sympathetic and understanding—truly understanding of how she felt about her brother's murder because he'd witnessed the murder of his parents.

There was a connection between Thomas and Levi—she'd almost caught it in the sudden emotion rising in Thomas. But the answer was as elusive as what or who Thomas really was. She drew in a deep breath and stepped out of the shower, wrapping a towel around her, determined not to panic. If not for her own sake, then for Rikki's, she had to fight through the need to pull a blanket over her head and retreat from whatever mess she'd gotten into.

She'd given him back precious memories.

In spite of her determination to remain distant from Thomas, Judith couldn't help but hug that small gift to her. She had given him something he obviously treasured. She could hear it in his voice and feel it in his mind. If he was using her, his emotions for her were still very real.

THE intruder lurched to his feet the moment the owls backed off. He cast one wary look toward the sky and took off running again. His shirt was torn in several places, long slashes that had cut into his skin. Bloodstains spread rapidly across the taut material. The man was in good shape, but the birds had rattled him. Suddenly, he veered away from the road and made for the far side of the meadow where the taller grass grew.

The sudden departure from the fastest route warned Stefan this was no peeping Tom who had come to spy on the women who lived on the farm. The fact that he'd chosen Judith's home meant he hadn't done so randomly.

Cut the engine, Lev. He can hear you coming and he's up to something. Do you have a visual?

The man had disappeared into the thick, tall grass and there was no movement to give him away. Stefan halted the chase abruptly and slipped back into the shadow of the trees.

Who is he? Ivanov?

Hell if I know. He doesn't move like Ivanov, but he's up to something. Watch yourself. Stefan studied the grass as he replied to his brother. What the hell was the intruder up to? He had to be crawling through the grass, staying low, making certain there was no ripple to give his position away.

Overhead, the owls circled. One gave a cry, and instantly Stefan's vision blurred. He pulled away from his brother immediately. Judith was still feeding the energy, boosting the power, and he was picking up remnants of his brother's craft. He took a step to his left, looking for a better visual and something spat wood splinters into the side of his face. He dropped to the ground and rolled, then, on his belly, using his elbows and toes to move fast, scuttled across the open ground to the patch of small boulders at the start of the meadow. There was a shallow depression and he fit his body inside it.

You hit?

Don't sound so upset. Stefan knew he sounded irritated, but truthfully he was annoyed with himself. Once he was certain they weren't dealing with Ivanov, he'd minimized the danger in his mind.

Yeah, you're all right.

Stefan felt rather than heard the relief in his brother's voice. It was hard to let yourself care when you hadn't for so long. Emotions were worse than rusty, they'd become so thin and tattered, feelings were hardly recognizable.

Did you just get shot at? Judith's voice reverberated through his mind, shocked, frightened. *Thomas. Levi. I'm calling Jonas.*

No! both men answered simultaneously.

Stefan took a breath. *Who the hell is this Jonas charac-ter to you?*

There was a moment of silence. Stefan cursed inwardly in a mixture of several languages. He'd just displayed a man's worst trait and he'd never known he even had it. Jeal-ousy. Pure, black jealousy at the absent and unsuspecting Jonas.

Lev's laughter spilled into his mind. *He* is *the local sheriff.*

Judith gave a little sniff. *I told you I was making a ka-leidoscope for his wife. Ordinarily when someone starts firing guns, a civilized person calls the sheriff.*

The anxiety in her voice belied her words. And what the hell was she doing still connected to them? He was going to have to do some fast explaining. Another bullet whined through the air like an angry bee and smacked into the tree where he'd last been and this time he located the intruder. He'd made his way into the middle of the field.

Where's he going, Lev? He's got to have an exit plan. We cut off his retreat to his car.

Stefan's heart began to pound. Even as he asked the question, the answer came to him. The intruder was circling back around toward Judith's house with the intention of taking one of the vehicles there, or using her as a hostage. He was a distance away, but there was no doubt now, that was his only real option to a successful retreat.

Judith, you'd better have that fucking security system on. Are you armed? When she remained silent, he probed further. *With a gun?*

Stefan moved to cut the man off, picking a route that would intercept him long before he reached Judith's home. Still . . .

Judith is a terrible shot. Lev put in his two cents.

I am not. The stupid gun is always jumping at the last second, Judith defended indignantly.

I fucking told you to practice, Lev snapped, his voice edged with worry.

You don't need to talk to her like that, Stefan objected, ignoring the fact that he'd just used the same word a couple of moments earlier. *Swing around to the left and send the birds straight at him again. Herd him back toward me. And don't kill him yet, we need answers.*

Don't kill him at all, Judith objected. *He's probably some lost hunter.*

He shot at me, Stefan reminded. *Turn on that security system.*

Again there was a short silence. Stefan worked his through the tall grass, careful now not to give the angle of his pursuit away. *Judith?*

Is he really heading this way? Her voice trembled slightly.

You don't know how to set the security system, do you? Stefan guessed.

Well, I've never actually done it, Judith admitted reluctantly.

Lev gave a snort of disgust. *Damn it, Judith. How many times have I told you it's important to lock up at night?*

Don't swear at her, Stefan snapped. *Just walk her through the damn thing. Don't worry, Judith, he's not going to get near you. It's just a precaution.*

He could hear the brush of a body moving just to the right of him. He was closing in on him. Lev recited the instructions for arming the security system in Judith's home. Even as Stefan angled his body, crawling through the grass, to intercept the intruder, he made a mental note to go over security with Judith until she was comfortable with the idea.

An audible crackle gave away Lev's position and immediately the intruder turned toward the sound and fired. Stefan lunged forward, crouching low, sprinting toward the gunman.

Lev. Answer me.

The intruder fired twice more toward the sound, giving away his position. Stefan took the opportunity to close the distance fast, his heart in his throat as he waited for his brother's response. He could feel Judith holding her breath as well as time seemed suspended for a moment.

Just a bruised ego. I tripped over a damn rock.

The grass parted in front of Stefan and a man's face appeared. Shock spread over the horrified features even as a hand came up, his gun clutched in his fist. Stefan had forward momentum going for him, hitting the body hard, catching the wrist and turning the weapon away from him as it went off, the sound nearly deafening next to his ear. They rolled together, Stefan slamming his knee into the man's groin at the same time he smashed the wrist against a rock jutting out of the ground.

The man tried to scream, but the groin shot had taken

the air from his lungs. The gun fell from his limp fingers, as the wrist broke with an audible crack.

I've got him. Judith, stay in the house.

With that last command, he rapidly built up his shields to push away the energy surrounding him, effectively shutting her out of his mind and cutting her off from any knowledge of what might happen.

He threw the gun a slight distance away and did a quick, but thorough search for any other weapons. The only other thing the man had on him was a camera. Lev crouched down beside him.

"Who is he?"

"No wallet. Must have left it home while he came snooping around," Stefan said. "Tell me your name."

The man spat at him.

Stefan yanked the broken wrist hard in instant retaliation. The scream was explosive, but muffled as Lev clamped his hand over the man's mouth. Stefan stared down into the intruder's eyes.

"You need to know something about me. I know more ways to inflict pain than any other man you will ever meet. We can do this hard or easy, but we're going to do it. I was very gentle with you. Your name."

"Mike," the man mumbled. "Mike Shariton."

Stefan tossed the camera to Lev. "Take a look." He glanced down at the intruder. "See how polite I can be? I'm not giving you the opportunity to lie."

Lev studied the images. "All the pictures are of Judith. The first ones were taken with you and Judith outside the gallery. He didn't get a shot of your face, but they look . . . compromising." He passed the camera to Stefan.

The photograph was taken when he was locking the gallery door, Judith's body imprisoned between his body and the door. He handed the camera back to Lev.

"You work for La Roux." He made it a statement.

Shariton didn't respond, but the truth was in his eyes and his swiftly drawn breath.

"You sent those pictures to someone already, didn't you?"

Shariton was a little slow in responding and Stefan went for his wrist, this time slower, giving the man time to think about how it would feel all over again.

"Yes. Yes. Last night. I sent them last night," Shariton blurted out. "I was hired to take the photographs and send them to a man by the name of Badeaux, a guard at a prison in Paris. I send the pictures to him and he takes them to a prisoner."

"Which prisoner?"

"Jean-Claude La Roux."

Stefan hadn't wanted to hear it, but he'd known the moment he saw the camera. "Maybe you should go on home," Stefan said to his brother. "I'll take it from here."

Lev shook his head. "We have to turn him over to Jonas. I'll have Rikki call him. They'll get him on felony charges and . . ."

"He'll be out of jail before the night's over," Stefan said. *Go home, Lev. I can't let this man threaten Judith.*

If you're serious about her, this is no way to start a new life. We'll let Jonas handle it.

Shariton remained absolutely still as if he knew his life hung in the balance and it probably did. He was a petty criminal, but he'd been around men who were lethal long enough to recognize them.

"If we call the sheriff, you know he's going to make bail."

Lev nodded. "Exactly. And off the property. We can go hunting then."

Stefan understood what Lev was doing immediately. Shariton was listening attentively. Fear had a smell and the man was perspiring profusely. Shariton knew nothing really. They couldn't get much more out of him. He carried a gun, but he wasn't very adept at using it. He was too scared to come back and retaliate against Judith.

"His gun's over there," Stefan indicated with a small nod of his head. "Let's just get comfortable and wait for the law." He nudged Shariton. "You can make bail, can't you?"

Shariton stayed frozen, obviously too scared to move.

"What he's saying to you, Shariton, is," Lev added, looking right into his eyes, "own up to what you did here, and who you're doing it for. Take a plea and you're safe. If it goes any other way, nothing will stop us from hunting you down. Do we understand each other?"

Shariton nodded his head vigorously.

Jonas is a good man, but a hard-ass. He'll come in by the book, red lights, guns, and he'll take us down and check us for weapons. Walk away and stash whatever you need to, but make it far from here, because he'll do a thorough search. We won't have much time, Lev advised.

Stefan nodded. *I was careful because I knew I'd be with Judith. Not much to find.*

He left his brother with Mike Shariton while he slipped away from the area to rid himself of the knife concealed in his boot. The garrote sewn into his jeans wouldn't be detected. He was much more reluctant to part with his favorite gun, but he wasn't about to get caught with it on him and try to find a plausible explanation. Being armed would simply complicate matters.

Sirens in the distance told him it wouldn't be long. He was a shadow, nothing more, a ghost that disappeared as if he'd never been. Staying was more difficult than he'd expected. Lifelong training ingrained in him the need to vanish as if he'd never been. Lev sat waiting, looking back toward his home, as if it was only his woman who kept him in place, a caged tiger waiting for dogs to snap at his heels.

You sure this is the way?

Lev shrugged. *It's my way now. This is my home. I abide by the laws as much as I can. This one is easy enough.*

*Jonas is a fair man. You have to make your choice, Stefan.
If you choose to make your stand here, I'll help you, but if
you're going to walk, do it now before Judith gets hurt.*

Judith. He could easily kill for her. But enduring the indignity of allowing someone to trap him even briefly—that
was a test he hadn't expected.

Two sheriff's cars plowed over the grass, divided, one on
either side of them, hemming them in. The vehicles skidded to a halt, the sirens blaring and lights flashing. Driver
doors popped open and weapons appeared.

"On the ground. I want to see your hands."

Lev immediately complied, kneeling, hands outstretched,
palms facing the officer. "I'm armed, Jonas. Gun's in the
shoulder harness and my knife's in my boot," he called out.

"Put your hands behind your head."

Lev did so, linking his fingers. Stefan hesitated. The officer behind them had remained silent and he didn't have a
good sight on him. He didn't like being so exposed, or vulnerable.

Get down, Stefan, Lev hissed.

Very slowly he knelt, his hands outstretched to show
they were empty. His gut knotted. He *detested* the indignity
of it.

Shariton obviously knew the drill. He rolled to his knees,
struggling to raise his hands.

"I'm going to put you in handcuffs, Levi, for our safety
and yours." The officer—presumably Jonas—held his gun
very steady without moving position.

The officer approached from behind and reached for
Lev's wrist, drawing first one, and then the other behind his
back. It was impossible to see with the glare of the headlights, a deliberate move to blind them, but Lev remained
passive while the deputy removed the gun from Lev's shoulder harness and the knife from his boot before thoroughly
searching him as well.

Stefan hadn't allowed anyone to manhandle him since he was a boy. He could feel the need to survive, the drive to fight building relentlessly. For a moment he couldn't breathe and something lethal unfolded inside of him.

It's just handcuffs, Stefan, Lev's calm voice filled his mind. *You know you could kill either of them if you needed to, even with the cuffs on. In any case, you can get them off in seconds. Just cooperate. It will be over soon.*

Stefan fought back the memories of beatings. Of betrayal. When he was twelve he was dropped into Siberia and told to survive, that someone would return for him only if every single one of the men hunting him were dead. He had no idea of how many men were planning to kill him or even if there were men. The ice rained down and the temperature was so cold his blood felt like ice water flowing through his veins. He had no food and only a knife, with no idea of the size of his enemies or when they would come at him.

He couldn't trust anyone. What was he doing, allowing a man to come up behind him? His breath burned in his lungs. His heart accelerated. He could take the deputy coming up behind him, but the headlights were blinding him and he couldn't see the exact position of the officer behind the door. He hadn't moved, hadn't stepped out of position and the gun had never wavered.

Thomas, talk to me. What's wrong? I can feel something's wrong.

Shockingly, Judith breached the space between them. The surge of energy was powerful, so powerful, electricity snapped and crackled audibly and the hair on their bodies stood up. He wasn't the only one who felt it. Both officers and Lev looked warily around them. Fortunately, he was the only one to hear her.

Thomas, I'm coming out. Are you hurt?

How did he answer that? She showed concern now, but the moment this was over, she would most likely run from him—and he couldn't blame her. Losing her was going to be worse than all the tortures he'd endured, all the survival games he'd been forced to play.

Stay in the house. The sheriff is here.

Why are you so cold?

The officer behind him grabbed his left wrist. It was now or never. He knew exactly every pressure point, every vulnerable target on the man. He took a breath and relaxed his hand, allowing his wrist to be cuffed and pulled behind him.

They're handcuffing me. I'm not good with this kind of thing.

That much was the truth. The last time he'd had his hands tied he'd been beaten senseless and burned in long patterns all over his body—a reminder not to ever let an enemy take control of him. He broke out in a sweat as the officer caught his other wrist.

Thomas, I'm so sorry. I'll come out. Jonas will listen to me.

No! He couldn't bear for her to see him this way. On the ground. Cuffed. Vulnerable. She *couldn't* see him this way. He would never be able to maintain his control.

The deputy was thorough in his search, but he didn't find the garrote, or the small pin he had shoved into his thumb.

Tell me what I can do.

Hearing her voice had tipped the scales, allowing him to try his brother's way. *You've already done it by distracting me. I'm fine now. We'll talk later.* He didn't know if that was a plea, a threat or a command.

When she was gone, all her potent energy dissipating as fast as it had surrounded him, he felt entirely alone. She filled him up with her light, that compassion and spirit that was wholly Judith—the one she tried so desperately to suppress. Every part of him that was insubstantial, no more than a transparent phantom, she brought back to life. Without her, he was back in the cold, in the shadows, where so long ago, Sorbacov had shaped him into the ghost he'd become.

"This one is injured," the deputy said as he helped Shariton to his feet.

"Secure him in the squad car and take his statement. I'll talk to these two."

Jonas Harrington was a man with a few secrets of his own. His energy, hot and bright, reached Stefan well in advance of the officer. Tall with sun-bleached hair and very focused, sea blue eyes, he crossed to them with long, confident strides. He looked a man to be careful around, but more, he *felt* like a man to be cautious around and Stefan always paid attention to his warning system.

Stefan recognized Jonas's deputy immediately, from the papers years ago in their homeland, although they'd never formerly crossed paths. This man had grown up in the state-run home with the youngest Prakenskii. He'd been a formidable police detective in Russia and later, like Ilya, had worked for Interpol.

Aleksandr Volstov had midnight blue eyes and dark wavy hair. Stefan read *lethal* all over him. He glanced at Lev with a raised eyebrow. Lev shook his head, indicating he hadn't met Volstov as of yet, but recognized the man from his pictures in the newspapers in Russia when he'd worked as a detective.

Volstov's gaze sharpened when he saw Lev, his gaze flicking quickly to Jonas. Harrington gave a small shake of his head, but Stefan caught it.

He recognized you, Lev. He's from Russia.

I know. Let it be.

"Sir, I'm going to put you in my car just while I talk to Levi."

Stefan didn't respond. He concentrated on remaining passive. It took discipline to walk to the car and slide into the backseat. He'd been a prisoner more than once, but he'd been young and much more trusting back then. One betrayal had been a man he'd considered his best friend. He would have turned on his trainers before he would have followed the order to outwit and kill his friend, yet Uri, no more than a boy—a teenager—had waited until his back was turned and struck. At the last moment, Stefan had seen the attack coming in the reflection of a window. He had thrown himself to one side and still carried the scar where the knife went in deep.

He stared out the window at his brother and the cop. He could read lips and, with the lights still on, he could see both men easily.

"Tell me what happened, Levi," Jonas instructed Lev.

Lev shrugged casually, his expression completely closed. "Judith invited a stranger over and I watched him." He was unapologetic. "Just to be safe I was armed. I didn't really know much about him so I waited until he went to leave and struck up a conversation. We were walking, talking about his business and we spotted a man hiding up on that small knoll just above Judith's house, hiding in the trees there. He was making a racket, must have gotten spooked by the owls nesting there. He's all torn up."

"The birds living on this property are particularly vicious," Jonas observed dryly. "This isn't the first time someone's had a problem with them."

"He shot at us," Levi continued, ignoring the comment. "I can show you where one of the bullets hit."

"Just once? One shot?" Jonas asked.

Levi shook his head. "Three at Vincent. Two at me. Five all together. His gun's over there."

"I'll need to swab your hands for residue. You know the drill. I've got the GSR kit in the car. Let's get it done and then I'll talk to Vincent."

"Shariton has a camera with a lot of pictures of Judith on it," Lev added.

The expression on Jonas's face changed. He walked with Lev to the car, pulling out his kit. "My partner will swab Shariton's hand and get his story."

While he was talking, he was looking Stefan over. Stefan was very grateful he'd taken after his mother in coloring. While he had his father's height and bulk, a fighter's solid muscular build, his eyes and hair color differed significantly from Lev's. The sheriff's eyes were just a little too sharp.

He seemed satisfied with the results of his test and removed Levi's cuffs. "Wait over there while I talk with your friend here."

He opened the door, allowing Stefan to step outside the vehicle. Pushing down the need to remove the cuffs, Stefan complied, breathing in the night air.

"Your name?"

"Thomas Vincent."

"Tell me what happened here."

"It all happened fast. I was visiting with Judith Henderson and when I went to leave, I ran into Levi Hammond there. He lives on the farm and is married to one of Judith's sisters. We got to talking and he was showing me a little of property, just walking really while we talked, and there was a man in a grove of trees just above Judith's house."

"Who spotted him?"

Stefan frowned and shook his head. "I don't honestly remember. We were talking and then a bird called out loud, and he screamed. Maybe that's what drew our attention. In any case, Levi shouted something, and the guy took off running. We separated, trying to come at him from two positions and he shot at me."

"How many times did he fire his gun?"

"Three times. Well, at me. He shot at Levi a couple more times."

"You've got a few splinters in your face."

"It happened so fast," Thomas reiterated. "I didn't have

time to think. I just reacted. I tackled him when he was shooting at Levi. I thought he was going to kill me."

"Not the smartest thing in the world, tackling a man with a gun," Jonas observed. "You're lucky he didn't kill you. I need to check your hands for gun residue."

Jonas unlocked the handcuffs. Stefan noticed his eyes never shifted away. The sheriff was ready for anything. He dutifully held out his hands for the swab.

Aleksandr Volstov approached, using a small hand gesture to summon his partner for a conference. "His name's Mike Shariton. He lives in Point Arena. I read him his rights. He tested positive for gun residue. He said he gets paid for taking pictures of Judith and has for the last five years. This is only the second time he went over the fence and onto the property. He admits to shooting at both men. In fact, he didn't hold anything back."

Jonas cast a suspicious glance back at Lev. "He confessed to shooting at them?"

"The way he tells it, he was scared and trying to just frighten them enough to back off."

"He's stalking Judith."

"He claims he gets paid to take the photographs for someone else. He was contacted and offered money to do the job and the pay is good and comes immediately when he sends the pictures over the Internet."

Distaste crossed Jonas's face. Stefan could see the idea of anyone stalking a woman and sending her pictures over the Internet bothered the sheriff on a very personal level.

"The pictures are sent to a guard at a prison in France. That guard delivers them to Jean-Claude La Roux." Volstov said the name expectantly.

"That name mean something to you, Aleksandr?" Jonas asked with a small frown.

"He was convicted of running guns some five years ago, but was suspected of everything from espionage to murder.

Anyone in his way disappeared. Twice, Interpol agents investigating him disappeared, but no one could connect him."

Jonas shook his head. "I'll finish up here and talk to Judith. See if she knows this man or if she has any idea why a criminal in France would want her photograph. Take Shariton to the hospital and get him help for that wrist. Book him on felony assault with deadly a weapon and felony negligent discharge of a firearm. We can add anything else we need to later."

It took what seemed like forever to answer all the questions and recover two of the five bullets fired. One was in a tree trunk, the second in the branch of the same tree. The others were impossible to recover, although Jonas made a thorough inspection of the area. He interrogated them again, both separately and together, dropping seemingly inane questions into the conversation designed, Stefan knew, to trip either of them up. He had interrogated more people than he'd ever want to admit to and knew the tactics.

Stefan just wanted everyone gone. He had no problem maintaining his role as American businessman Thomas Vincent, but all the same, he was happy enough that the sharp-eyed Volstov had left before he could inspect Stefan too closely.

Aleksandr Volstov had quite the reputation as a police detective and Interpol agent. What was the man doing in Sea Haven? Had he been friends with Ilya? There would be no talking with Judith tonight, not with the sheriff heading to her house to interview her.

What would she tell him about her relationship with Thomas Vincent? Any way he looked at it, she wasn't going to welcome him with open arms again. He was going to have to crawl back and find a loophole or two to get her to even listen to him.

13

JEAN-CLAUDE *La Roux*.

Judith stood at the door watching Jonas walk back to his squad car, her entire body numb, the color draining from her face. For the longest time her mind refused to work. She just stared out into the night, shocked, guilt-ridden and afraid. She'd put everyone she loved in danger. Jean-Claude was capable of anything.

She had never really been rid of him, not when he haunted her every night, invading dreams to turn them into nightmares. She would never truly be rid of him, but to know he was keeping tabs on her . . . *paying* someone to send him pictures for the last five years was truly frightening.

And Thomas. What about Thomas? She was crazy about him. It had happened too fast. Burned too hot. Of course it wasn't real. And if it was real, if there was a good explanation for everything, she couldn't risk him. She *wouldn't* risk him.

She couldn't risk her sisters either. Jean-Claude had ordered the torture and murder of more men than just her brother and he was certainly capable of striking at Judith through her sisters. What was he planning? What did he want? She would have to leave. What else could she do? Her mind refused to answer questions, just ran everything together until nothing at all made sense to her.

A sob welled up and she pressed her hand to her mouth to keep from crying.

"Judith?"

Blythe's voice effectively shredded any control she might have had. Judith flung herself into Blythe's arms almost before her sister managed to reach the top of the stairs. Blythe caught her, steadied them both and just held her while she sobbed. Judith had no idea how long she cried, but when she looked up, she was surrounded by her sisters—all of them. Her heart expanded, landed in her throat and she cried more.

Blythe smoothed her long hair, murmuring soothing noises. "We'll deal with it, honey. We will. All of us together."

"How did you know?" Judith managed to get ahold of herself long enough to lift her head and looked at them, her eyes still swimming with tears.

"Rikki called us. Levi told her about the pictures and Jean-Claude. Of course we would come," Blythe said. "Airiana is going to make some tea for us and Lexi brought a few things for a late night snack. We're going to need energy to figure this out."

Blythe sounded like, well, Blythe. She was always practical, the mother of all of them, big sister, the boss without being bossy. Blythe always made everyone feel better just by her steady presence alone. Or maybe it was her touch. Judith already felt a little lighter, the waterworks slowing enough to allow her some semblance of control.

Blythe caught Judith's arm and firmly led her back into the house. The others filed in after her, with Lissa deadbolting the door and setting the alarm system.

Judith looked around her at the circle of women. These

were the people she could count on, the ones that always—
always—stood for her. They weren't sisters by blood, but
her heart had chosen them and they were every bit as close
as a blood relative. These women had saved her life, had
supported her when she was at rock bottom with nowhere
to go. They'd made her believe in herself again and now,
once again, when her world was crashing down around her,
here they were, standing with her.

Judith took a deep breath and let it out, watching as Lexi
began taking candles from her bag and placing them around
the room. Following Lexi, Lissa blew on wicks, and flames
sprang to life, dancing merrily, the healing aroma filling
the room.

Water filled the kettle at Rikki's command and Airiana
set the kettle on the stove where Lissa had the flames already burning.

"You're such a show-off," Airiana teased her.

It was a show of power for Judith, the women coming
together bound to the elements, bound together by the love
they shared.

Judith's heart eased, the terrible ache threatening to
crush her lessening. She let Blythe lead her to a chair and
she sank into the soft cushions.

"Jonas put Levi in handcuffs," Rikki announced.

There was a collective gasp.

"Levi *let* him?" Lissa asked.

"Yes." Rikki sounded proud, but there was a hint of
laughter in her voice. She took the chair closest to the door.
She always had to fight her reluctance to sit in a house with
all the doors closed, filled with those she loved.

"How come he isn't here with us?" Judith asked. "He's
usually glued to your side."

"Well . . ." Rikki's mischievous grin lit her eyes. "I told
him no."

That brought another collective gasp, more astonished
this time, and then the women burst into laughter—even

Judith. The thought of Rikki telling Levi no, when he was so protective and *male*, had them all howling.

Judith wiped the last of her tears away. "How did he take that?"

"Not very well actually," Rikki admitted. "He's prowling around your house like a wounded hound dog, but this is women power. He can be all macho and sulk outside."

Another round of laugher restored Judith's natural balance. She sent her sisters a loving smile. "Thanks. I'm better now. At least I can think. I panicked when I heard his name. I barely heard anything Jonas said after he told me where the pictures were going."

"I was afraid, when I first got the message, that maybe this man had installed a camera in your bedroom and you were the latest sensation on the Internet," Airiana said. "It's crazy that anyone can do that kind of thing now."

"No, not the Internet, but I'm the poster girl for the prisoners in France," Judith said, with a small, broken smile.

"Just for the one man, I hope," Blythe said. "I doubt if he's sharing your picture."

Judith swept a hand through her hair, shoving it from her face in a quick, restless gesture. "I don't understand why he's keeping track of me. Five years, Jonas said. I've never heard of Mike Shariton. He evidently lives in Point Arena, and he's made quite a good living sending photographs of me—and my work—to Jean-Claude."

Airiana turned from where she was pouring tea, leaning one hip against the kitchen sink. "Shariton? That's an unusual name. I remember it. He came in and bought one of your scopes. I think it was a sea-scope, the one with the waves and shells and interchangeable cells. He was in about a month ago."

"Great, he can play with it in jail," Judith said.

"At least you made money off of him," Lexi pointed out with a quick grin, settling onto the floor across from Judith's chair. "That's something."

"I suppose I should be happy about it," Judith said. "Seriously, maybe it will help him figure out what he was doing was wrong."

"Airiana, I take milk in my tea," Lexi said.

"I don't," Rikki said hastily.

Airiana rolled her eyes. "You two always say the exact same thing. You've been saying it for five years. I think I've got it by now."

Teacups floated from the sink to the living room, one after the other, a parade of them, making their way into the hands of each of the women.

"Talk about showing off," Lissa said.

"I'm practicing," Airiana defended. "Did you notice I was a little weak holding back the wind in the redwoods while I was attempting to keep a lighter touch over the vegetable garden. I still haven't gotten divisions down very well. I felt so much power tonight when Judith wove us all together and the wind was a little harder to control."

Rikki nodded. "I'm getting used to it. But your strength really increased tonight, Judith, which is a good thing, but when I pulled water from the clouds, the water in the ground wanted to respond as well. I had to work a little harder on control."

"I didn't realize I was boosting everyone so much," Judith said, a touch of alarm in her voice. "I guess I let myself go a little more tonight than usual without realizing it."

"A little more?" Lissa asked. "You're always so contained and under control, but tonight you felt different. Although, yes, it was harder to control the power at first, it was awesome. Does that mean you can amplify our abilities even more?"

Judith felt the weight of all of her sister's stares. The rule was they didn't lie to one another. Sins of omission might be okay, but outright lies were not okay ever between them. She hesitated. Inhaled. Exhaled. "Yes."

"Wow," Airiana said, slipping onto the floor beside Lexi. "Just *wow*, Judith."

"I imagine it must be very difficult for you to control all that power at times, Judith," Blythe said, getting straight to the heart of the matter.

Judith nodded. "Until Levi pointed out that each of us was bound to an element, I didn't even realize there was something useful and good I could use all that power for. I've suppressed it the best I could. By weaving it with yours, I feel good about it for the first time. I've been doing it all along, since we moved here, but not consciously, not using spirit to bind all the elements into one tapestry to work for us improving the farm. Before, when I could feel the water, or the wind, I just tweaked them a little, the same with the soil calling to me."

"It's easier to understand after Levi explained why I needed to have my hands in the soil," Lexi agreed. "And how we were all intertwined. Don't you think it's strange that we all have an element we're bound to, basically a tremendous gift, yet we all suffered some terrible violent, tragedy in our lives? Do you think there's a correlation?"

There was a small silence while they thought it over. As usual it was Blythe who tackled the big questions. "There's a balance in everything, we all know that. Good and bad. Happiness and heartbreak. You never have one without the other. All of you carry a great gift, very powerful, and the balance of that might be difficult. Whatever the reason, this is our here and now. Nothing has changed that. We all agreed we wouldn't live in the what-ifs. We have our lives and we all made a vow we'd live as best we can. Jean-Claude rearing his ugly head hasn't changed that. It will serve to unite us and make us stronger. Not knowing what he wants, but knowing he's looking over Judith's shoulder, gives us the opportunity to explore the talents we have and how we can better use and control them. His presence in our sister's life will only make us stronger."

"He's very dangerous," Judith pointed out. "You know what he did to my brother. And Paul wasn't the only one. It's very possible he'll attempt to strike at me through one of you."

"No one ran away when I brought danger here," Rikki said staunchly. "And no one's going to now. If that man is planning something—anything at all—you're not alone, and he's going to get the surprise of his life."

"My brother was strong," Judith said softly. Her heart clamped down hard, a vise grip of pain at the thought of what he'd gone through because of her.

"That's true," Blythe said. "But this is different, Judith. You're not a young girl anymore. We've all gone through the fire in our own way and its honed us, made us stronger, and we're together now. I believe that together, there is no possible way for this man to harm us. You have to believe that too."

"Levi is helping all of us with security and personal self-defense," Lissa said, "but we can be a little more proactive in that department as well as working on our ability to control our elements. Practicing a craft always perfects it and I know we've just started tapping into our strengths together as a unit."

The women nodded.

"What made you release so much energy tonight, Judith?" Blythe asked.

"Not only was it powerful," Airiana said, "but happy. You felt happy to me."

"Me too," Lissa agreed. "*Real* happiness."

Judith took a sip of tea, allowing its familiar soothing properties to help calm her suddenly pounding heart. "Thomas. Thomas Vincent. That's why."

Her sisters exchanged long, shocked looks.

Again it was Blythe who took the bull by the proverbial horns. "You might elaborate on that just a little, Judith."

Judith put down her teacup, to keep from betraying that her hands were shaking. "I thought a lot about this. When I'm with Thomas, I feel alive, truly alive—my spirit does. It's hard to explain, but I'm not afraid of that power inside of me. I feel as if—" She broke off, took a breath and tried again. "When I'm with him, I feel as if I'm totally free to be me, yet safe at the same time—that everyone around me will be safe as well."

Her eyes met Blythe's. "I know it makes no sense. When I'm not with him I tell myself all the things I'm certain you'll tell me. It's too fast. Physical attraction isn't something to rely on, but all that goes out the window when I'm with him. He just . . . makes me happy—with who I am. I'm not afraid and I don't have to hide from him. Even the worst in me, I think he can handle."

Blythe looked at Rikki. "What does Levi say?"

Rikki shook her head. "Levi hasn't said much because I didn't give him the chance. I knew Judith needed us and that took precedent."

"Besides," Judith pointed out, "Levi doesn't like anyone besides us, so that's hardly fair."

Lissa laughed and covered it with a slight cough. "She has a point, Rikki."

Rikki sighed. "Well, I don't like anyone else either, so it works."

Airiana held up her teacup, toasting Rikki. "You love us, and that's all that counts, baby." She took a sip and looked over the rim at Judith. "What's his aura like?"

"Sort of muddy, like you see in a lot of powerful businessmen. Good and bad. But sometimes I can't even see it." Judith sighed. "I've tried not to see auras. I don't trust my reading of them, and his is sort of difficult. The more I tried to focus on it, the less I could read it."

"Great." Airiana scowled. "I *hate* that."

"Why?" Blythe asked.

Airiana sent an apologetic look toward Judith without meeting her eyes. "Because that kind of aura almost always is a product of concealment."

Blythe frowned and leaned toward Airiana, rubbing her left palm on her thigh, a habit that usually signaled she was becoming upset or unhappy. "On purpose? Someone could conceal their aura on purpose? Wouldn't that mean he had some sort of psychic talent and that he would know to conceal his aura around us?"

"No, I didn't meant that, Blythe," Airiana corrected. "More that the person is hiding something of great importance."

"It doesn't really matter," Judith said. "I can't see him with the threat of Jean-Claude hanging over my head."

"Of course it matters," Lexi disagreed. "I don't think a perfect person comes along all that often. If the opportunity is there and you connect with him, I say, take a chance. Rikki did and look how happy she is." She frowned. "I mean . . . you *are* happy with Levi, aren't you? He is a little intimidating. He never smiles."

"I'm very happy with Levi," Rikki said, rocking slightly. She looked around. "But maybe we could open a window or something. Would you mind, Judith?"

"Levi's out there, probably armed to the teeth," Judith said. "Open the door, hon. I'm fine with it open."

"He'll come in," Rikki said, twisting her fingers together in her lap. "He won't be able to help himself. He'll have to walk through the house and make certain it's properly locked down." She rolled her eyes. "He checks my garden hoses to make certain they're in good working order."

All the women burst out laughing. Rikki blinked and looked around the room. "What?"

"He checks the garden hoses around your house?" Blythe prompted. "Like you do every single morning?"

"*Exactly.* I would notice if there was anything wrong

with the hoses, wouldn't I? The man is just over the top when it comes to safety. And he wants a *dog*."

"Now we're getting to what really bothers you," Judith said gently. "Baby, you know it doesn't upset you in the least that Levi checks the entire farm, your boat and our shops a million times. It's his thing and he takes it seriously. He just wants to keep us all safe. It's the dog."

"He won't drop the subject," Rikki admitted, flapping her fingers back and forth, obviously becoming more agitated.

"We've talked about it before Levi ever came," Blythe pointed out. She laid a calming hand on Rikki's arm, very lightly, careful not to invade her space. "Lexi really could use a companion here on the farm. She's alone a lot and would really love to have a dog. Airiana would like one as well. Levi isn't alone in wanting one."

"But if we get one, it will come in my house and on my boat," Rikki protested.

"Not necessarily," Blythe contradicted. "A lot of people have outdoor dogs."

Airiana's breath hissed out and she opened her mouth to protest, but Blythe shot her quelling look. Everyone knew how she felt about leaving dogs outside.

Rikki shook her head. "Oh no, I couldn't do that, Blythe. If we get a dog, it would *have* to be with us all the time. I would worry about it being alone while we dive. And I wouldn't be able to sleep at night if I made the poor thing sleep outside because I didn't want dog hair in my house."

"There are breeds that don't shed," Airiana said. "And you really like animals, Rikki."

"I know." Rikki rubbed her thumb on the inside of her palm as if it itched. "I just managed to let Levi into my house and now he wants a dog. What's after that? It's too many changes too fast."

Blythe smiled at her. "Rikki, you know you're going to

get a dog. I can hear it in your voice. You want us all to agree with you and talk you out of it."

Rikki sighed. "You know I'll obsess over the darn thing. It's going to be embarrassing. Levi doesn't know what I'm like yet. Not really. Not about how crazy I can get. The dog will be *mine*. Under my protection and care. I take that kind of thing very seriously. I'll be reading dog books and wanting the best of everything for it. I'll probably want organic dog food if there's such a thing." She blew on her fingers in disgust. "Sheesh."

"Levi is not going to leave you because you love a dog," Blythe said. "He's going to be just as bad."

"Besides," Lexi added, "he obsesses over your protection and ours. It will give him something to distract himself."

Airiana laughed. "Are you kidding? Every dog that comes onto this property will be trained in security. That man will make certain of it."

Rikki nodded. "He's going to get big dogs. And he knows Airiana is a trainer, so expects her to work with him and with the dogs to get them to be guard dogs."

"Is that a bad thing?" Blythe prompted gently.

Rikki rocked more. "No. Yes. I don't know." She blew on her fingers again. "It's a big responsibility."

Judith leaned toward her. "Honey, is this about the fires when you were a child? You lost a dog in one of the fires, didn't you?"

Rikki had lost her parents and fiancé, as well as several foster homes in fires. For a long time she'd believed she was in some way setting those fires.

Rikki slowly nodded in response. "I have a difficult time with the idea that something might happen. I know I wasn't responsible . . ."

"And the man who is responsible is behind bars," Blythe reminded, her voice very gentle. "Baby, you can't let him dictate to you any more than Judith can allow Jean-Claude to dictate to her. You have Levi in your life and things are good. Bringing a dog into your life isn't going to put him in danger. And you'll be great at taking care of a dog regardless how it's trained."

Judith sighed. She knew Blythe wasn't just talking to Rikki. She was reminding Judith that they'd all vowed to live life again, not hide from it. She hadn't shared her concerns about Thomas Vincent, that he might be far more than he seemed. Rikki hadn't really indicated that she knew more about him than Judith did, and Levi seemed to share everything with her, yet it seemed that Thomas and Levi were familiar with each other.

Thomas had called Levi, *Lev,* in a perfect Russian accent. The childhood memories Thomas had seemed to be violent and ugly as were Levi's. She knew Levi was Russian, and Thomas's adopted mother was Russian. Was there a connection? Was she running from the relationship because she feared what Jean-Claude might do? Or because she was afraid Thomas would rip out her heart?

It was so much easier hiding behind the gates and staying in her own little protected world than putting her heart on the line and taking the chance that Thomas would break it. No, not just break it, shatter it so completely she might not recover. Thomas wasn't like any other man she'd met. Her spirit had *never* reacted to a man, wrapping sensuously around him, enfolding the two of them into a single skin.

That sounded so dramatic and ridiculous. How could she possibly explain such a thing to even those she loved when she didn't understand it herself? She knew she fit perfectly with Thomas. Everything about him. Everything about her. They belonged. It didn't matter that they barely knew each other and both had secrets. She didn't care that his aura was muddy, or hinted at concealment. Maybe he had a secret or two—but so did she. That wasn't the point.

"I know Airiana and Lexi wouldn't mind dogs on the farm, but Blythe, Judith and Lissa haven't really weighed in one way or the other," Rikki said.

"I'm all for it," Blythe said. "I wouldn't mind having a dog to go running with me and I'd probably feel a little safer."

Judith shrugged. "I'm not certain I'd have a dog—or at least a *big* dog. But I'm not opposed to them on the farm for anyone else."

"Lissa?" Blythe prompted when she remained silent.

Lissa's face seemed paler than normal, her firm body shrinking a little as she made herself smaller. She shrugged and remained silent, drinking the last of her tea.

"You have to weigh in on this issue, Lissa," Blythe prodded. "Everyone should have a say. Are you afraid of dogs?"

Lissa shrugged again. "It sounds to me like everyone wants dogs so, like Rikki, I'll get used to them."

"I suppose getting used to dog hair will be all right," Rikki conceded. "Levi fits into my life without asking much. A dog would be fun for us . . . maybe." She didn't sound terribly sure of herself.

And that was the real problem in life, Judith decided. There was no certainty about anything. Rikki loved Levi with everything she was, her intense loyalty, her all or nothing nature, and still, that wasn't enough. Her ordered world—the one she needed to survive—would be turned upside down in order to accommodate a need for her partner.

Judith pressed her lips together tightly and shook her head. Life had just taken an ugly turn. She looked around the room at the women who had left their beds in the middle of the night to comfort her. They'd successfully distracted her long enough to get over that first rush of shock and horror. She realized the changes in subject had been for her benefit, skillfully directed by Blythe with all of her sisters willingly following to give her time to pull herself together.

"I'm so lucky to have all of you." The intense emotion she had for them welled up and spilled out into the room.

Lissa blew her a kiss. "I think what we've got to do, my sister, is figure out why Jean-Claude has kept tabs on you for the last five years, because it doesn't make sense. If he paid this man here, to take pictures of you all this time, he went to a lot of trouble and expense. He's in France. He had to have someone find Shariton and hire him, bribe the guard, and arrange for payments. That couldn't have been easy from prison."

Judith suppressed the wince at the sound of his name. Jean-Claude belonged in her dark studio surrounded and kept prisoner by hatred and sorrow. Judith pressed her fingertips to her eyes. Maybe she was the one kept prisoner. All along, maybe she'd been the one locked up. Thomas had come along and opened her eyes, although she hadn't wanted it to happen and she felt guiltier than ever. If she let go of those feelings after carefully cultivating them for so long, how could she ever face her brother's memory again?

"Jean-Claude has more money than any of us can conceive of. Money buys a lot of loyalty and he has a large, widespread organization. He has a long reach, longer than I realized."

"But what does he want from you, Judith?" Blythe asked. "He must know you despise him. He can't think you would ever want to get back together with him, it just isn't logical. He had your brother murdered and he knows you're well aware it was him, right?"

Judith nodded, biting down on her lower lip. "I have no idea what he wants."

"Did you testify against him?" Lissa asked.

Judith shook her head. "He was never prosecuted for murder. How could I prove that he'd ordered the torture and murder of my brother? We were in Greece. He was in France. I saw a man being tortured at his house, but I didn't get a look at the man, just the blood everywhere. If the body disappeared, and there's no doubt that it did because I didn't read a thing about a body being found, what could I prove? I was in hiding when he went to trial for gun running and had nothing to do with his conviction."

"So what then, if not getting you back or revenge?" Lissa persisted. "What's left? Why did he send those men after you in the first place? Did he know you saw the man being killed in his house?"

Judith frowned. "I don't think so. I didn't make any noise and I don't see how he could have, unless he had cameras, which is entirely possible."

"But if he knew where she was, why didn't he just have her killed?" Lexi asked.

Blythe nodded. "That's a good question. If he was afraid you could pin a murder on him, he would have had you killed. You knew him better than anyone else, Judith, what do you think? Could he have some twisted idea that you'd take him back?"

Judith tried to separate the last five years of guilt and shame from the years as an art student when she'd first met Jean-Claude and was so swept away by his charm. He'd been sophisticated. Elegant even. She'd been awkward and shy with him, far too innocent to ever imagine what a monster he'd been. She'd had no idea men like Jean-Claude even existed. Wrapped in her world of art, she saw only colors and beauty in the world around her. She'd been in Paris, haunted the museums, ate at the little street cafés, and studied, all the while soaking up the atmosphere of France. She'd loved the entire experience and Jean-Claude had been such a part of that.

He was good-looking, built, so French with his compliments and accent and elegant manners. Who could possibly believe he was a criminal? He knew policemen, politicians, movie stars. Life at his side was glamorous. She had never met anyone in her life like Jean-Claude and she had looked at him with stars in her eyes. He was part of her experience in France, a courtly man with impeccable manners who handed her into cars, bowed low over her hand and took her to places she'd never dreamt of going. He made her feel like a princess.

Could he have faked those looks he gave her, long intense looks, straight into her eyes, as he proclaimed his love. He bought her an amazing ring when they'd known one another only a couple of weeks. She'd refused him, crying in her room at night, but something had told her to be just a little more cautious.

It hadn't mattered at all that she'd turned down his proposal of marriage and that made her feel all the more special—that he would give her time when he could have any woman he wanted. Had it all been real on his part? Was it even possible for a man capable of the horrific things he did to actually feel love for someone?

A thought hit her hard. She looked at Blythe with stricken eyes. "Could I have given him the ability to actually feel real love just by my presence? By the way I loved France? Loved who I believed he was?"

Lissa leaned forward, taking Judith's hands in hers. "You didn't do anything wrong, Judith. What's wrong with falling in love? If Jean-Claude had been the man he pretended to be, your life would have been so different—and quite amazing. *He* was the one who was deceptive by pretending to be something he wasn't. Loving someone is never wrong."

"I must have been projecting and he thought it was real on his part."

Lissa shook her head. "You're so mixed up, babe. Look at Rikki with Levi. When they're together all of us can feel how much they love each other. They radiate love, even when they're in one of their ridiculous arguments. When I love, I intend to love completely. There shouldn't be any other way. You don't know if what he felt for you was real or not. Maybe he was lucky enough that for the first time in his life he connected with someone good and it moved him. You can't be responsible for what he did or didn't feel."

Airiana nodded in agreement. "We can only control ourselves, not others, remember? We all vowed we'd live that way. We're responsible for our own happiness and we make our own choices. You can't allow Jean-Claude to control you or how you choose to live your life, nor are you responsible for whether he's capable of loving or not."

"You always do this, Judith. You're afraid of your talent," Blythe pointed out. "You find ways to blame yourself and because of that, you spend half the time refusing to acknowledge that everyone needs to be whole. No one is all good. No one is all bad. You have to allow yourself to be you."

Judith knew they were all making sense but . . . She swept her hand through her hair. "I feel whole when I'm with Thomas. Not because I need a man to see myself, it isn't that. It's because somehow he can handle intense emotion, good or bad, and the intensity doesn't seem to affect him, at least not adversely. I'm unafraid when I'm with him. Of myself. Of my power."

She pressed her thumb deep into the center of her left palm. "He makes me laugh. And I feel beautiful when I'm with him, even with no makeup and in my jeans and T-shirt. I can't say he's exactly handsome, but he's all man and very compelling. I think he's the hottest man I've ever met."

She made the confession fast, the words tumbling over one another. She hadn't said *soul mate* but she felt that way. She didn't know if she'd ever talk to him again, didn't know how to feel about what had transpired between him and Levi. But that didn't negate the truth of her words.

"Wow." Airiana said it for all of them, a little stunned.

Judith nodded. "*Exactly*. The first time I laid eyes on him, he took my breath away. He was standing in the shadows and I swear the earth moved when our eyes met. I knew. Right then I knew it was him and it was always supposed to be him."

She rubbed her hands together and pushed her thumb harder into her palm, the gesture somehow soothing. "I know it's not supposed to happen like that, but it did. I had no idea in my head of meeting anyone. I was late and I was hurrying and then I looked up and it was like he came inside my mind and filled up every single lonely place inside me. I shouldn't trust it, intellectually I know I shouldn't, but I can't seem to resist him."

"It can happen that way," Blythe said. "And maybe he was meant for you, just like you say, soul mates, but Judith." She leaned close, her gaze intent. "Honey, that doesn't mean you shouldn't be cautious. I know from firsthand experience, that even if every single part of you knows with absolute certainty, that he should be the one, that he *is* the one, it doesn't always work out as it should."

"When I'm with him I'm not afraid of myself and I feel as if he sees me. He can see inside of me and he isn't afraid of my power," Judith blurted, wanting all of them to understand, but especially Blythe. It was important Blythe understood, because, God help her, if she saw Thomas again, she was afraid she would fall right off that cliff all over again. If all of them thought she was crazy and told her so, she would still fall.

Her eyes met Blythe's in a kind of agony of need. She *needed* her to understand. These women in this room with her were the people she loved, her family—all she had left in the world. If she was making a terrible mistake they would love her enough to tell her, but she didn't know if she had the strength to resist him if he came to her again.

"Just go slow, baby," Lissa said. "Let us meet him."

"Blythe met him," Judith defended quickly, and then felt silly. She bit her lip. "Okay, see? See how I am? And even if he's everything he seems to be, the perfect man for me, what about Jean-Claude? I know what Jean-Claude is capable of and is it right for me to put Thomas in danger? Jonas told me that there were pictures of Thomas with me already sent to the prison."

"Then it's too late to worry about that, isn't it?" Lissa said. "Tell your Thomas the truth and let him decide whether he wants to take the chance or not. You can only be responsible for yourself and your decisions, Judith. Thomas has to be responsible for his, and Jean-Claude owns his own sins."

"You make it sound so easy when it really is complicated," Judith said.

"Because you're afraid," Rikki said, shocking Judith.

Rikki shrugged and set her cold teacup down. "I know you are because I was. It's very scary to let another man into your life, but you know you're also bringing him into our lives as well. This is our home. Would he fit in here? Would he contribute and love this place and all of us? Even when the relationship is brand-new, when you know your life is going to be different, complicated and you're going to be the one to complicate everyone else's life as well, it's terrifying."

"So true," Judith admitted. "And I'm a coward. I don't want to get hurt. When I figured out what Jean-Claude was, I realized I loved the illusion, not the man. He was all wrapped up in my love of art, the romantic idea of Paris and I was all caught up in the fantasy. Thomas is real to me and even though I haven't known him long at all, I've been in his mind and I *feel* him inside of me. I've been inside of him and we fit. If he breaks my heart, I'm afraid I won't be able to put myself back together again." Her eyes met Blythe's.

Blythe nodded, her eyes swimming with tears. "I understand, Judith. Take it slow. Be sure he's the man your heart tells you he is."

14

JUDITH'S heart leapt as a hard hand clapped over her mouth. Her eyes snapped open and she stared at the familiar face peering down at her. Her heart settled into an accelerated rhythm and something deep inside melted into a soft liquid welcome before she could control herself.

"You didn't answer my calls."

Thomas didn't lift his hand so she only nodded, drinking him in. His hair spilled onto his forehead, disheveled and so attractive. She wanted to touch it, to push it back for him, to feel the silky texture on her fingertips. She could barely breathe—and it had nothing to do with the fact that his hand lay over her lips.

"It's been four very long days. You don't get to hide in your house, behind the gate and security system and avoid what happened between us."

That was *exactly* what she was doing, but he should be at least considering that she might be avoiding him because she was aware he knew Levi. He obviously was more than just Thomas Vincent, the businessman. Righteous indignation glittered in her eyes as she glared at him.

He removed his hand carefully, as if she might snap at him with her teeth. The idea did occur to her, but she figured biting him would be undignified.

"I had the security system turned on. Apparently it's quite useless." Feeling suddenly very vulnerable, very aware of her body beneath her perfectly adequate and not in the least sexy pajamas, she sat up, pulling the sheet to her chin. "What is the point of a very expensive security system if it doesn't keep everyone out?"

She gave a little indignant sniff. Did he have to be so incredibly compelling with those amazing eyes and his rakish scars and solid muscle *everywhere*? She was angry at him with good reason and worse, afraid of what he could do to her. She had to stop reacting to him. Her heart refused to obey, pounding until she could hear the beat thundering in ears. Her veins coursed with hot hunger, rushing through her like a runaway train. She hated the happiness blossoming in her no matter that she tried to squash it. He had come to her.

"Your security system is adequate, and it's not meant to keep me out."

Judith tasted passion. She knew she was drinking him in with her eyes, devouring him, when she should just push him away, scream, do something to save herself. "Leave, Thomas."

His eyes changed to piercing aquamarine, vivid and brilliant. She saw the darkness rush over him, obliterating every color of his aura until he was nothing but a shadow. Her breath caught in her lungs, fingers digging into the sheet for an anchor.

"My name is Stefan. Stefan Prakenskii. Levi is my brother."

He made the confession in a low tone, his gaze holding hers captive. She couldn't look away from him, mesmerized by the sheer power she saw there. This man was no businessman. The aura surrounding him pulsed with danger. For a moment she thought she hadn't heard him right. She knew Levi's life was shrouded in secrecy and that he was a very dangerous man. Now the glimpses into Thomas's—no, Stefan's memories made more sense. She shook her head, but no sound could escape her closed throat.

"I couldn't tell you the truth and put his life in danger. In any case, Judith, you would have shut down immediately and closed me out. There's a retirement order out on him and an exterminator is in Sea Haven."

He touched the scratch on his jaw that was already healing. "I ran into the assassin the night you showed me the gallery. He's been here awhile. I had to come to Sea Haven and find Levi. I knew he was alive and I wasn't going to let anyone kill him. Once I realized you were the woman I wanted to spend the rest of my life with, that my emotions were very real, I wanted to tell you the truth. But I couldn't risk his life, not until I had talked to him first. I hope you can understand."

Judith pressed her lips together, afraid of saying the wrong thing. She didn't know what to feel. She had fallen off a cliff with this man, built dreams, let go of her tight control on herself and now she had no idea who he really was. Unconsciously she shook her head.

"Don't do that. Don't close down on me, Judith. You would do the same for any one of your sisters and you know it. Levi knows I'm talking to you. You can call him and confirm everything I'm saying. Ivanov hunted him once already and he'll never stop. Never. He'll hope I can lead him to Levi and then he'll kill us both if he gets the chance."

"You have to tell Jonas."

Something lethal flashed in his eyes, a brief flare of emotion that frightened her. "Your solution is always this man Jonas. He's not in Ivanov's league, Judith. Believe me, I know killers. Jonas might be very good at what he does, but he's hampered by rules he has no choice but to follow. He would try to take Ivanov into custody, and Ivanov would kill him."

"I don't know what that means." Judith clutched the sheet tighter to her and drew back, away from him. She was very afraid she knew exactly what that meant. It was one thing to dream of making Jean-Claude suffer and die, but that tightly coiled power so evident now in Stefan told her he was really quite capable of things she couldn't conceive of.

"It means you can tell Harrington that Ivanov is hunting Levi, but you'll likely get him killed. You haven't been to bed for three nights, Judith."

She blinked at him. "Are you *spying* on me?"

"I'm watching over you. There's a difference." He rubbed the bridge of his nose. "Okay. Maybe I was spying on you," he conceded. "I needed to know you were all right."

Her heart contracted in her chest. There was nothing boyish about Stefan Prakenskii. Not in his looks, not in that smooth sensual tone, yet he sounded so astonished and a little self-deprecating, as if he couldn't quite believe his own behavior. He was a man even more disciplined, more controlled than she was, if she was reading him right, and yet, with her, he seemed a little out of his depth and she couldn't help responding to the lost note in his voice.

"I have no experience with emotions, Judith. I'm going to do everything wrong and screw this up. I've never actually been in a real relationship."

Her heart jumped again. "*Never?*"

He shook his head. "In my line of work, relationships are impossible." He sighed and pushed his hand through his hair until the thick strands were wild and disheveled. "If I'm being entirely honest, I didn't think I was capable of feeling anything real for a woman. And then I saw you and it's like I'm no longer in control. You just took me over and I haven't a clue what to do about it, Judith."

He looked so uncomfortable, so completely at a loss, she

couldn't imagine that the things he was saying weren't true. "I know I don't want to mess this up by trying to move on you too fast, but I pretty much already screwed that up, didn't I?"

"I think that was both of us, Stefan." Judith wasn't letting him take all the blame. "I make my own choices, and that was a conscious decision."

He shook his head. "I was in it for the long run and you were hoping we'd burn hot and the need would be gone. Admit it, Judith. One night was all you planned to give me."

She couldn't help but smile at him, self-mockingly. "I planned to give you a tractor ride. That was all." At his somewhat crestfallen look, she couldn't help but give him something. "I find you a little hard to resist."

He let his breath out as if he'd been holding it for a long time. And maybe he had. She felt as if she'd been holding her breath for four long days.

"In Russia, my parents sided against a very powerful man. Unfortunately they underestimated his abilities and he came one night with soldiers and murdered my parents right in front of us. We were separated and taken to different military training facilities. I was raised to be an asset, and I know no other way of life, Judith. I've lived so long in the shadows, a ghost, untraceable, and then I saw you and the world around me changed—became real. It's hard to put into words, but I know what I'm feeling is real."

Stefan was totally uncomfortable, out of his element, exposing his soul to this woman, that one small piece of him he'd hidden from his trainers, kept locked away and safe all these long years. He'd been empty of emotions, a machine designed to carry out orders and in finding Judith, he knew there was no way back. If she rejected him, he had nothing left of himself.

"Every moment I spent with you, no matter how hard I tried to be Thomas Vincent, and I spent years building his cover, the real me kept pushing through and Judith, in all the years I've worked, that's never happened to me. I want to be Thomas Vincent for you, I do, but I need to be honest about who I am. If you're going to do this with me, I want you to know who I am. Good or bad. And most of it is going to be bad."

He was telling the stark, raw truth of who he was, praying she'd give him a chance and knowing she'd be crazy to tie herself to him.

"You're doing a lousy job of selling yourself and, keep in mind, I'm a little upset with you right now."

There was an underlying truth beneath the humor. Stefan shook his head. "I'm trying to be as honest as I can be. I don't want you going into this without knowing all the facts. I'm fairly certain that Sorbacov has retirement orders out on both Levi and me. Even if I manage to get Ivanov, Sorbacov could very well send someone else." He sighed. "The odds are very high that he would."

Judith's gaze moved over his face, studying him for what seemed like an eternity. For the first time her fear subsided completely and serenity surrounded him. He loved the way her spirit was so strong, encompassing everything in its path. Sometimes—like now—it felt as if she enfolded him in a blanket of peace.

Her expression changed and she dropped the sheet abruptly. "Come on. Neither of us is asleep. We may as well have some tea." She scooted out from under the covers, fully expecting him to give way, allowing her to leave the bed.

He couldn't move. Not when she was dressed in a flimsy, nearly nonexistent lacy tee and small boy shorts that hugged her hips, emphasizing her curves. He didn't budge, his much larger frame solidly blocking her way. Because she had scooted forward, her body had slipped practically under his. He leaned forward, his chest pressing against her, forcing her to lean back. Her dark eyes went wide with shock, with helpless hunger, desire spilling into her expression. Her generous mouth beckoned him, lips parted, small tongue lick-ing delicately over her lower lip.

He took her up on the offer, such as it was, half hesitant, half helpless. His mouth took hers with relentless demand. Once he touched her, once his tongue sank into velvet heat, he was lost. He gave himself up to the sheer pleasure of kissing her. One arm curved around her waist and he sim-ply lifted her more closely under his body. For one moment, she kissed him back, pouring herself into him, a liquid fire filling his veins, rushing straight to his groin and pooling there in a heated, urgent need.

Judith pulled away, resting her head against the mattress, her eyes searching his. "If we go any further, you know what will happen, Stefan . . ."

He pressed his hand to her mouth. "You're going to have to call me Thomas for now. If Ivanov ever suspects that I've told you the truth, he'll use you to get to me, and be-lieve me, *moi padshii angel*, it would work."

"Thomas then. See, I don't even know what I'm sup-posed to think of that, not calling you by your given name. No matter what I call you, I have to be certain. I don't trust myself when you're this close to me."

"I'd be a fool to let you slip away, Judith."

"Please let me up. I have to be certain. I can't make an-other mistake. You have to admit this is happening way too fast. Doesn't that bother you?"

Stefan shook his head, his belly knotting tight. She was flight ready. She wanted him, but she didn't trust her-self. She hadn't trusted herself since she'd made a mistake with Jean-Claude La Roux. It seemed to always circle back to that man. He should have broken his neck and been done with it.

He forced his tense body to ease back and give her room, even when everything in him urged him to hold her tight. "When a man has gone his entire life and never felt an overwhelming natural need—a hunger—to be with a woman, believe me, honey, he doesn't care that it's happening too fast. He's just grateful. I thought I was incapable of real physical attraction, let alone real emotion."

Judith gingerly eased into a sitting position as he gave way. Stefan stood with a small sigh and took her hand to tug her to her feet.

"You don't know if it's real, Thomas. Not when you're living a lie."

"My life isn't real, Judith. It hasn't been real since I was taken from my family. Funny, I blocked my childhood out, both good and bad, but since I met you, I can remember the way my mother smiled and my father playing with us inside the house, away from prying eyes. He was . . . magical. I can also remember how all that bright red blood turned pink and muddy in the snow when the soldiers shot my father and turned on my mother. My oldest brother fought them. They beat him until he couldn't move, his body lying over my mother's there in the snow. I could see his eyes, the anger there, but never defeat. Maybe that's why I survived, my brother's strength and resolve."

Stefan pulled back, shock registering on his face, in his brain. He *never* allowed those memories to surface. He hadn't thought about his oldest brother in more than twenty years. It had been easier to let go of all of them. As long as they were vague and shadowy somewhere in his mind, far away where he could believe they were safe and their lives hadn't been as his had been, he remained sane.

He didn't want the compassion he felt surrounding him, or the sympathy in her eyes. He didn't need those things. They made one weak. He turned away from her abruptly and paced across the floor, restless energy building fast. At once he felt that soothing presence surrounding him, pushing at him until there was no choice but to surrender.

He stared out her bedroom window, keeping his back to her, shaken by the memories of his family and by the power of her element, the manipulation of his own feelings. Above him, stars glittered against the night sky. Below him, white star flowers waved gently, rippling in the breeze, giving them the same effect as the stars overhead, so that he felt surrounded by the universe, the constellations all around him. The effect was mesmerizing and soothing. She had created a sanctuary, this woman with her amazing talents.

He turned to face her, automatically sliding to one side of the window, his back to the wall while he studied her. He allowed his gaze to drift over her, drink her in, and absorb her. He could look at her forever. He felt as if he was waking up after a long sleep, a hibernation from actual living. He had never participated, only watched from the shadows. Judith, with her brightness, had drawn him out into the light. Exposed him. He stood before her, vulnerable and effectively naked.

She stood tall, her body firm, curvy, that glittering gold chain catching his eye and drawing attention to her tucked-in waist and alluring belly button. Her shiny hair and dark eyes were exotic and intriguing, and all that soft, exposed skin beckoned him. Physically, she was perfect to him, but far beyond that, there was that spirit surrounding him, drawing hope out of him, drawing out things he'd long forgotten or never known.

"Rejecting me is out of the question, Judith. It just is. Obviously, you have no real comprehension of what you've done, but that doesn't exempt you from the consequences."

A slow smile curved her soft mouth and crept into her eyes. "Rejecting you is out of the question, is it?"

He nodded. Serious. He had nowhere to go after she'd destroyed who and what he'd been for years. There was only . . . Judith. "That's it exactly."

"*I* did this?"

He nodded again, knowing he had no control left, not when she'd taken his pride. He was asking her to save him—save his soul—to save that small part of the real

Stefan Prakenskii he'd protected for so long. She'd opened the floodgates for love—and for pain. He'd blocked pain for all those years, yet now the memories felt raw and all too real. Close. So close he felt almost as if he were losing his mind. She'd left him alone for four endless days and three nights.

"I can be the man you need, Judith—for anything. I can be that man. You can't shut me out because you're afraid of this."

He needed to hold her to him. There was no out for him. He was in far too deep. He felt as if he'd fallen off a cliff and was freefalling through space without an idea of where he might land. This was the type of woman who would stand by his side no matter what happened if she committed to him. She would stand forever with him. There would be no going back for her either. She had allowed herself the fantasy, she'd even made a few advances toward him, but she was still holding herself in check. Controlled. Careful. Afraid of getting to that place he was already in.

Judith had a wildly passionate nature and she feared to lose the control that enabled her to protect those around her from the ups and downs of her intense emotions.

"You don't understand, Thomas." There was pain in her voice. Need. Want.

They both winced when she murmured his false name.

Judith shook her head. "Life isn't quite so black and white. I can't always just do whatever I want. I have family I love. People that matter to me. Those women saved my life and made me believe in myself again. They've given me hope."

"As you've done for me," he stated quietly.

Her gaze jumped to his. She swallowed hard. "Before you came along, I felt frozen. I did, Thomas." This time she said the name firmly. "I felt like there would never be love in my life, not the love of a partner—a man for myself. I had no hope of a family of my own. Children. Laughter. Love every day. And then I saw you and before I could take a breath I was so wrapped up in you I couldn't breathe. I don't let people in. I *can't*. You have no idea how dangerous that can be and I don't want to make a wrong move. I'm protecting you as well as my family and me."

He held out his hand to her. She looked so forlorn, unable to take that step toward him. She looked at his hand and tears swam in her eyes. She shook her head.

"I can't, Thomas. I can't explain, but you're better off without me."

The more agitated she became, the more negative energy filled the room until the walls pulsed with it. At first the heavy emotion battered at him, chipping away his resolve and confidence that they fit perfectly, but as her fears grew, his determination hardened and calmness descended.

"Moi prekrasnyi padshii angel." He covered the distance separating them and took her hand. "Locks don't mean anything to me. I can go wherever I want. It is impossible to shut out a man such as I am. You have no secrets from me. I can't live with them and you don't need to." He kept his gaze locked with her, willing her to understand.

Her eyes widened. Her breath caught in her throat. Dark anger spread through the room. He didn't let go of her hand, not even when she tensed up and tried to jerk away from him. He kept her shackled to him, while anger spread like a cancer and the floor rippled beneath his feet. The power expanded and the windows rattled. He held on to her and stayed calm, the eye of the hurricane, never moving, never looking away from her.

"Just breathe now, Judith," he said, keeping his voice quiet. "I'm every bit as exposed as you and we're still standing. *I'm* still standing with you. Your worst is nothing at all, honey. Everyone gets angry and feels rage and even hatred at times. You're a spirit element so unfortunately, if those darker emotions get away from you, others can feel them as well. But the emotions are normal. They don't make you a terrible person."

Her gaze shifted from his and she looked down, guilt and shame making her shoulders sag. He knew her guilt wasn't over her rage, or her dark wishes. The shame was because she didn't have it in her to avenge her brother.

Stefan stepped close to her, close enough to share his body heat without physically touching her curves. He tipped her chin up, forcing her to meet his gaze. "My shame, Judith, is that I'm wholly capable of doing terrible things to other human beings without mercy, without emotion. If you asked me to make this man suffer for you, or to kill him for you, I would get the job done. You wanted a weapon, and I'm standing right here, willing to do anything for you. Sadly, if you asked that of me, it would be the easiest thing you'll ever ask of me."

He made the confession looking her straight in the eyes, wanting her to hear, feel and see the terrible, ugly truth of his declaration. She had to know him—the real Stefan—not the fantasy of Thomas. Stefan was a man of action and that action wasn't always going to be pretty. His training was ingrained in him. He couldn't be anything with her other than what he truly was. He wanted Judith to see him and fall in love with him, commit to him.

"I don't need a man to rescue me."

"Is that what it feels like to you, Judith? A rescue? I don't mind saying I need you. Can I live without you? Of course. I have for years, but can I sleep at night? Breathe right? Feel happiness? I don't know, I never felt happiness before so now that I know what it's like, maybe I'll have a more difficult time. I want a partnership with you. I want your joy in my life. Your sense of fun. The bright colors you bring to life in me. I think you're the one rescuing me, not the other way around."

She pressed her lips together, standing absolutely still, afraid to move in any direction.

"It's only a matter of time before you learn to control your element. You're more than halfway there already. You bottled up the darker side, but you know you can't keep doing that. For one thing, it's missing from your paintings and you need it. Everyone needs a balance. Once you learn control, why would you need rescuing, Judith? I'm here for myself. Pleading with you to see me, with my soul in my hands, asking you to save me."

Judith felt her heart turn over. Could anyone fake that look? She'd been broken for so long after Jean-Claude. Shattered inside. Her sisters had glued her back together, but the cracks showed. This man was standing in front of her, baring his very soul to her. Exposing his sins, giving his life into her keeping. Whatever he was, whatever he'd done in his life, there was good in him.

On the other hand, he'd broken into her house, into her locked studio and spied on her. Wasn't that stalker mentality? How could breaking into her studio in the least be considered reasonable? He hadn't even shown remorse, nor did she think he felt that particular emotion. She let her breath out slowly in a hiss of need.

She couldn't help herself. He had never had anyone. The glimpses she caught of his life, the small things he'd told her, were heartbreaking. Someone needed to love this man. She didn't pretend to herself it would be easy. She wouldn't be signing up for a fairy tale. He was a dominating man. Levi had the same traits, but Rikki needed her world a certain way and Levi "got" Rikki and loved her enough to give in to her needs and always, always, he was gentle when he pushed her out of her comfort zone.

Stefan—Thomas—wouldn't have that same motivation. He would give orders and ask questions afterward. Was she strong enough to live with that kind of force? A man who would always push to dominate? A man who didn't mind getting past locked doors? He would be a force in her life always. He would also be a strong anchor.

His plea appealed to her compassionate nature. She moistened her lips. "How could there not have been a woman in your life, Thomas? You're a very sensual man."

He brought her hand to his chest, opening her fingers so her palm fit over his heart. "I didn't say there weren't women. I work for a man named Sorbacov. He's a very dangerous man, always behind the scenes in our government, but he wields tremendous power and influence. There are of course layers between Sorbacov and men like me, but when he assigns me to seduce a woman, I've done so."

She heard the distaste in his voice and it helped to ease the stabbing at her heart.

"I was trained to perform on demand, to prolong my performance in order to tie a woman to me through sexual prowess."

He was obviously choosing his words carefully, being painfully honest with her when he would prefer not to discuss the subject.

"Men like me don't have relationships, Judith. We get the information we need, use the woman to help us and then we're gone." He hesitated and his fingers closed around her hand. "If the woman is an agent for another government, sometimes it becomes a matter of who kills the other first."

"That's horrible."

He shrugged. "It's the only life I've ever known so it's normal to me. Women like you are not part of the life I lead."

"And Levi did the same thing?"

"We were trained in different military camps and I'm not certain what work he did. I do know that, like me, he's considered disposable and since Sorbacov can't control him, he's expendable—as I will be."

Her heart jumped in protest. "The world thinks the Russian agent aboard the yacht that sank is dead. Levi isn't known to be that same man. Sorbacov must know you're Thomas Vincent."

"Not necessarily. When I go undercover, I go off the grid for long periods. I spent a great deal of time and effort creating Thomas Vincent with the idea that I might use him when I disappeared. In my business you always have to have a contingency plan. Sorbacov knows I'm in Sea Haven, but not anything else. Ivanov isn't going to bother telling him anything."

"You came here with the idea you'd disappear like Levi did?"

He nodded. "If Ivanov is going after my brother, it's because Sorbacov ordered him to do so. I won't let that happen, which means I'm going directly against Sorbacov. That's what my father did and he had him killed. I came here knowing I'd be next on the hit list if I came."

"But you did." Judith made it a statement. She could see the determination in his eyes. He would have come if there had been a firing squad waiting for him and back home, there just might be. Still . . . he had come.

"He's my brother. Sorbacov killed my parents. That's all the blood he'll get from my family."

Judith shivered. She might be the spirit element, amplifying her own emotions and that of those around her, but she felt his absolute resolve and deadly intent.

"I need a cup of tea, Thomas. Come into the kitchen with me and let's talk in there." If she was being entirely truthful, she didn't trust herself to resist him, not when his loyalty to his brother threatened his life. Or the way he stood before her, revealing things about himself she knew he had never told another human being.

She tangled her fingers with his and gave a little tug, leading him toward the door. Her heart ached for him. She had been raised in Japan by a loving mother and father as a child. When her father had wanted to return to the United States, her mother hadn't hesitated, moving with her father and making the trip fun and adventurous. Her mother had turned their home into a place of love and peace, surrounding them with her serenity and love of gardening. Her older brother had been loving and protective. She'd had a wonderful childhood. Even after her parents had been killed in an accident when she was in her teens, she still had Paul. He had stepped into the role of parent, watching over her and making her life stay as stable as possible.

What had Thomas's life been like as a child? She'd seen her brother tortured and killed, and she'd been a grown woman. What would it be like to be a child and see both parents murdered and your brothers taken from you? Her heart stuttered a little and squeezed down tight, aching for that little boy. Looking at Thomas, she couldn't imagine him as a child. Those violent brutal men "training" him had stamped the boy out quickly.

Stefan followed Judith down the hall into her kitchen. She hadn't turned on the lights, but with all the windows, the stars and moon provided faint light to illuminate the room. Her long hair skimmed the center of her bottom, drawing his eye to the sway of her hips and the length of her slender legs.

He could barely stand the flash of pain in her eyes when he shared some of his memories with her. She was too compassionate, and he wasn't compassionate enough without her. He shouldn't need her so much. It was too much to put on one person, but he knew he could be good at this—at being with her.

"Judith." His voice ached with the need to convince her. "I'm not going to pretend I've ever been a good man. Hell, I can't claim to have been a man. I'm a tool and I'm a damned good one. I don't know any other way of life, but I want to live differently. I know I could be good at being with you. I don't see anyone else. I'd know when you needed something, when you were sad or happy. And I can shield you from other people's emotions, make it easier when you're out in public. More than that, I'm capable of shielding others from your emotions. That alone is sheer freedom for you."

He felt like an attorney trying, at the last hour, to save a man's life.

Judith glanced at him over her shoulder, a completely natural look he found sexy. His body stirred in spite of his rigid control. He wasn't going to bring sex into this. She needed to want him because they fit, not just because their chemistry together was explosive—although . . .

"Don't," she warned him softly, but without much conviction.

He filed that information away to pull out later if he was losing the battle. She was more than susceptible to seduction and that was one thing he was damned good at. He gave her a wan smile. "I'm fighting for us, Judith. You have to give me something."

She filled her teakettle with water and set it on the burner. "Your life has been so different, Thomas. I can't even imagine the places you've been and the situations you've been in. I live quietly here. This is a small town; a village really. We're a strange little collection of people, very tolerant of one another, but quirky. It's peaceful here. Not much in the way of action. We don't even have a police force, just the sheriff if anyone's in trouble. Death here is from old age or the sea. Abalone divers, that sort of thing. How would a man like you find anything interesting here?"

He took his time, instinctively knowing she wanted him to be thoughtful. He didn't need to be. "I've never had a life, not a real life with a family and truthfully, I can't be around people for long periods of time. I've lived outside civilization. I don't know the rules and I'm not polite. I can fit in when I need to, but I'm never *me,* I'm someone else, playing a role, anything to achieve my goal. I need peace, I need a place where I can live out my days in freedom, and Sea Haven seems perfect. Thomas Vincent would love to have an art gallery and a wife who paints and makes amazing kaleidoscopes."

Judith kept her back to him, busying her hands by filling the teapot's little screened container with loose-leaf tea. "What about Stefan Prakenskii? I'm more interested in him and what he wants." She turned then to face him, leaning back against the counter, studying his face, locking her gaze with his. "What does Stefan want?"

"I want you, Judith. I want to live with you and love you. I want to be everything you need."

He cupped the side of her face, unable to keep from touching her, his thumb brushing back and forth over all that smooth, soft skin he couldn't resist. She was so beautiful to him. Her bone structure, her exotic eyes, her mouth, that small, straight nose and her intriguing dimples, yet it was what was inside of her, spilling out, that brought him a kind of joy singing through his veins.

"I can be good at this one thing, *radost' moya,* making you happy. Keeping you safe. Loving you. I can do that."

When she started to speak he shook his head, laying his fingers across her lips.

"But you have to be sure. There's no going back. You have to know what kind of man I've been, what I've done, Judith. You have to realize that you're *nothing* like me. All those dark places inside of you are normal, people are supposed to have them. I *am* those dark shadows, the embodiment of them. Can you live with a man who is scarred inside and out? People like me don't recover. We have certain things ingrained in us, and we can't change. You have to be able to love the real me."

The teakettle began to whistle and Judith spun around to pour the hot water into the teapot. Stefan didn't step back to give her more room, instead, stood close to her, inhaling her fragrance and willing her to understand him. He knew himself, knew he was a hard man, honed in the fires of hell and probably dwelled there most of the time, lost in the ranks of the damned, but he saw the way out. Right here. Now. In spite of Ivanov hunting him. In spite of Sorbacov panicking because a journalist had begun digging for information regarding a rumor that orphans and children of political enemies had been taken to military camps and raised for all kinds of purposes.

Mostly, Stefan knew, the outside world pictured young children being prepared as sleeper cells to be sent to the United States, the United Kingdom and a few other countries. Those few people, living in the open, marrying, having children, would probably never be called into play and how much real damage could they actually do? It was the others, trained to live in the shadows, assassins and seducers, men and women who could kill in seconds and vanish as if they'd never been, that the countries needed to fear. And those were the ones Sorbacov feared would come into the light.

Sorbacov's methods had been brutal and only the toughest children with the strongest wills had managed to survive. If his torture of children came to light, if the true deadly nature of his small army of agents was to reach the light of day, the man and his political ambitions would be destroyed and he knew it. He couldn't afford to allow the information to be made public.

Judith poured two cups of tea and turned to face him, the cups in her hands. "We need milk. In the fridge over there." She nodded toward her refrigerator.

His heart skipped a beat. Getting the milk for the tea was such a domestic thing to do. He forced himself to walk slow, determined to tell her as much of the truth as he could. "If you choose me, Judith, the way won't be smooth. Your sisters are going to try to pull you away from me," he said. "I can't blame them, they'll be doing it out of love for you, afraid you're doing something crazy, tying yourself to me. It will be difficult not to listen to them, Judith, because the things they say will most likely be truth. I'm not a good man and they'll point that out. I've killed people and they'll know. I'm capable of hiding my true aura and they'll know that at some point as well. They'll be afraid for you."

He poured the milk himself into both cups, noting Judith wanted more than he did. She took a sip, regarding him over the rim of her teacup.

"Make a kaleidoscope with me."

He frowned at her. "Judith, I need to know if you're with me or not."

"I don't know yet. Make a kaleidoscope with me. That's what I need. Right now. Tonight. Come to my studio and make the scope."

"Is this some kind of test?"

She nodded slowly. "I can't trust my instincts with you. I can't listen to my sisters. I can't even trust my ability to read auras. I'm left with my own truth. Will you do it? Make the scope? Be certain, Thomas, because you won't be able to hide from me," she warned.

He had never opened up to anyone, but if he made the kaleidoscope himself, she would see inside of him—just as he'd seen inside of her when he'd looked into her dark scope. She was giving him this one chance. For her, he knew he would close his eyes and step off the cliff. He held out his hand to her and nodded.

15

"YOU can sit right there in my work chair and I'll lay out bins with beads, charms, wire, glass and crystals for you to choose from. You'll have to start with a mirror system," Judith explained. "This one is five-point and is a standard star pattern. This is one I like to use and it's a six-point. This one here, is a seven-point system. A seven-point system creates a more complex mandala. A mandala is the image created when looking through the mirror system at the cell."

Her studio was soothing to her, a familiar place where she spent hours of happiness, designing scopes and knowing people in other countries, people she didn't know, would look into the world she created and get comfort or joy through her work.

Judith kept an eye on Stefan as she pulled out bins of charms and glass, spreading them out in a haphazard manner, adding the colorful crystals and wires for him to choose from. Stefan carefully examined each mirror system, looking from every angle, studying them as if committing each to memory—and maybe he was.

Stefan was a very intelligent man, there was no doubt in her mind about that, and he'd spent a lifetime reading people and giving them what they wanted to further his own agenda. He might try to choose things he would think she would approve of, but with so many choices, eventually his true nature would be revealed, he wouldn't be able to help himself.

Her heart pounded and she tasted fear in her mouth. She was baiting a tiger and this could go wrong very fast. Her world would come crumbling down if he chose all the wrong things, but she had no real choice. She wanted this man. She wanted to be that woman he lived for, the one he built his life around. She wanted to belong to him. Her element had chosen him, and then her body, long before she'd ever had a chance to think clearly. She was already free-falling, it was up to him whether or not he caught her.

Stefan studied the mirror systems, intrigued by the idea of constructing his own kaleidoscope. Until he'd looked into the one in Judith's dark studio, he hadn't really considered what a kaleidoscope could actually do. Most people thought of them as a child's toy, and he had inadvertently fallen into that category. Even when she'd told him that kaleidoscopes could lower blood pressure and aid women in childbirth or help an autistic person, he still hadn't realized what the colorful instrument could do. When he'd looked into Judith's scope, there in her dark studio, he knew he was seeing into her soul.

He looked over the long table with charms, beads, wire and crystals everywhere and knew whatever choices he made would give Judith that same glimpse into him. Essentially, if he did this, he would be revealing his true self to her. There were thousands of options laid out before him. Those tiny bits of metal and crystal would give Judith every reason to run from him, but he refused to cheat. Either she could love him as he was, broken and twisted like the metal, or they wouldn't stand a chance.

The seven-pointed system appealed to him. He glanced at her as he handed it to her.

Judith nodded. "You're a complex man and I imagine choosing the seven-pointed system means far more to you than just the complexity of it."

"I'm one of seven brothers. Although they separated us, our lives mirrored one another. Are there choices for the outside of the scope?"

"I have wraps for the outside, or you could powder-coat it."

"I would prefer to powder-coat it," he said immediately. He wasn't a fancy man. In fact he wanted it plain and the powder-coating could look like gunpowder . . . "Or . . ." He spotted a scope already made at the end of her table. "What's that?"

The scope sat on a tower made of what looked like stained glass. The scope itself was powder-coated, yet around the edge was that same stained glass look that appealed to him. The glass seemed to shimmer and change color when he looked at it.

"That's called dichroic glass."

"It's fascinating. It changes color when you look at it from a different angle."

"It's made using various metals in micro-thin layers, vaporized using an electron beam in a vacuum chamber. I don't make them myself, but I love the versatility. Some are clear backed and others have a black back."

Judith sipped her tea while she watched him get lost in the artistry of making his own kaleidoscope. She loved teaching classes on making scopes, because no one could be surrounded by the bright colorful objects and not slip into a dream of creativity. Some clients hummed, others were silent, but all smiled while they worked. She always felt joy surrounding her when she taught a class.

Stefan Prakenskii was a serious man with a tragic past. She doubted he saw it that way. His life simply was what it was. He accepted that his parents had been murdered and his brothers ripped away from him. He accepted that he'd been shaped into a killer through rigid disciplined work and punishment, just as he accepted the strange magnetic pull between them.

He was a man who found moments of joy in beautiful things. He found her beautiful, like the art he so admired. The type of work he did—and she didn't want to think too closely about what that was exactly—had hardened him into a watchful, lethal man. He had to need action after living that life for so long, so did that mean she would be a momentary thing for him?

She sighed and instantly she had his attention.

"What is it?"

Even his voice could stroke her skin. She watched his long, capable fingers turn the dichroic glass over and over as the colors shifted and played, all the while feeling the weight of his eyes. He could have been a pianist with fingers like that. He moved his hands so beautifully over her body. His touch was sure, as if he knew instinctively every way to heighten her pleasure until she was blinded by everything else around her—even sheer common sense.

"I'm trying desperately to believe you could give up what you do and lead a quiet life, here, with me." She tried to talk past the sudden lump in her throat. "Chemistry lasts only so long and then there has to be something else, Stefan." Deliberately she used his name to remind herself he wasn't sweet Thomas. He was a man who killed other human beings. She might wish for Jean-Claude to die horribly, but this man actually could do such a thing.

She couldn't pretend that the temptation to use him for such a dark, destructive purpose hadn't crossed her mind, both alarming her and making her feel ashamed.

"What I do isn't living, Judith. I get no pleasure from my work. I'm good at it, but hiding my own identity, even from myself, is no way to live. I know this is where I want to be, here on this farm, living on the edge of the sea surrounded by a beautiful forest. With you."

He looked from her down the long table filled with color. He gestured around the room. "Your home is made for laughter and love, Judith. For the sound of children. The sounds of a man and a woman loving each other. You understand these things as I never will, but I want to share them with you."

"You want children?" She didn't know why that surprised her, but it did. She definitely wanted children. She always had. She wanted them to know all about her Japanese heritage. She wanted to be like her mother, so serene, moving gracefully through her home, making her children feel as though they were the smartest, most loved children in all the world.

He nodded his head slowly. "I would love to see little girls running around with your hair and smile and little boys with my eyes and your hair."

She touched her hair and couldn't help the smile welling up. "You do like my hair."

His smile crept to his eyes. "I won't waste this chance if I get it. I'm having it all."

"I thought you said even if you get rid of Ivanov, that man Sorbacov would send someone else after you."

He nodded. "I won't lie to you, Sorbacov will definitely send another exterminator, but my brother lives here as well. And we'll be prepared. With two of us here, believe me, honey, we'll be safe enough."

Something in his voice made her shiver. He picked up one of the small pieces of wire, the aqua color attracting him. The metal was soft and without thinking, he began to bend it into softer curves. She watched him work, unable to look away from the intensity on his face. When he focused on her, she got that same rapt attention, yet she knew he was aware of every movement of the house, and especially her presence. She seated herself on the other side of the table and busied herself with the kaleidoscope she was making for Jonas's wife to focus on when she went into labor.

"Look into the cell with the mirror system every now and then," she encouraged, without looking up from where she was working. "And don't give in to temptation and overfill it. The objects have to move freely in the liquid."

She knew every piece he picked up and discarded. She wondered at the collection of wire, charms and crystals he collected in a small area near him. She let him roam the bins and study everything through the mirror system he chose. His facial muscles relaxed and the tension went out of his shoulders. He looked a little less like a caged tiger and more like a contented one stretching the boundaries of his territory.

She tried not to look too often, but it was impossible to resist. He took several inch-lengths of very fine black wire. He wrapped about a dozen or more pieces of the wire at one end and carefully spread the wires out. He seemed very intent on getting the wires exactly the way he wanted them, which meant that particular piece meant something to him.

At first glance the tools he collected from the silver charm bin appeared to be farm tools, but she realized each item had a dual purpose. Like the shifting colors in the dichroic glass, the implements he chose had multiple uses. Each had been used as lethal weapons to defend farmers from warlords in times past as well as for working the land.

Judith disarmed the security system she considered absolutely useless anyway and opened the French doors leading to the gardens to allow the fresh ocean air into the room. She was restless and weary of the entire experiment. She almost didn't want to see what he'd constructed, now that the scope was near completion. The night air was crisp. She could hear the bark of the sea lions as they called to one another. The more she paced around the room, the more she was aware of his stillness—his silence. He lived in silence. He was coiled and ready to strike even as he appeared so focused on his work.

He worked in silence for more than an hour, methodical in his approach to finding just the right objects for his cell. He didn't seem to be worried about pleasing her, never once looking to her for approval—or for help. He seemed determined to show her who he really was and damn the consequences.

She snuck another peek. He appeared to be gluing teardrop beads filled with red liquid onto a white snowflake charm. His actions were sure, precise, no hesitation at all. She didn't have to remind him to view the contents of his dry cell through the mirror system. Each time he added something to his cell, he was careful to look at it through the seven-point system.

Her stomach fluttered and she pressed her hand hard to it to keep the somersaulting down. It was difficult to be in the same room with him and not want to go over to him and kiss his neck as he bent his head close to his work.

He suddenly looked up at her, his eyes meeting hers with dark lust. Her stomach did a fast roll and her body dampened with liquid heat. He smiled at her.

"Me too."

Her mouth went dry. Her palm itched. She was *desperate* for him and it didn't help that they had made wild, intoxicating love right here on her table.

"We're using the bed next time."

He made it a statement of fact, certain there would be a next time. Oh, God, she wanted there to be a next time. *Please* let there be a next time. She felt the brush of his gaze like fingertips stroking her skin. Her nipples hardened beneath her thin tee. She should have put on something else.

"We'll make it, angel," he said. "Have faith."

Funny that he would be the one to tell her to have faith. He smiled at her. "You're my personal angel, fallen from the sky, and I've clipped your wings, honey. I'm keeping them safe, right here. Now tell me how to seal this."

She wasn't certain what he meant by clipping her wings, but she wanted the suspense over and yet she didn't want to actually know if it was going to turn out wrong.

"I like what I have." Again he spoke with absolute finality, which told her a lot about him. Once he made up his mind, he was certain of his decisions and he acted on them.

"Seal the lid on with the acrylic cement," Judith directed. "When you're finished, there's a tiny, predrilled hole in the side of the cell. Pump in the heavy mineral oil with the needle." She indicated where. "Use the tiny set screw there, to close the hole after you've filled the cell with the oil."

Judith watched him work, her heart accelerating. She would have to look at his work soon and she was afraid of what she might see. She crossed to stand in front of the French doors, staring out at her garden. The plants always soothed her. She loved the many colored maples, shaping them into draping, graceful limbs hanging above the narrow ribbon of water running over rocks creating a small waterfall to feed the large koi pond on one end. A narrow bridge crossed the deepest section of water. Her favorite reading spot was located under one of the larger maple trees. Part of her wished she were out there now, in the cool night, sitting beside her koi pond with the wind on her face.

"Come look," he invited.

Her heart leapt. Her eyes met his and she braced herself. Closed her eyes. Took a deep breath. There would be no turning back once she looked into his kaleidoscope. She would know him, know his true nature. And she'd probably be the only person in the world who would.

She took the scope carefully into her hands and turned it around, glancing at him once before lifting it to her eye. Light spilled through the cell, illuminating the images, so that the seven-point system burst into life like a new constellation. Droplets of blood fell against a white snow, the movement flowing and graceful, as if she could see that long ago murder that had begun Stefan's life.

The scene inside the cell was mesmerizing, almost hypnotic and very intense, the dichroic glass shifting colors, dark and light, bloodred and black changing to lighter colors, just as Stefan shifted from skin to new skin, shedding the old and donning a new one to complete each assignment. Darkness settled and color burst through the darkness bringing crystal stars glittering through the various weapons and farm implements.

Through the stream of weapons came unexpected things, long black hair falling like soft silk, tiny seashells tumbling through blue-green waves, an effect created by the dichroic glass the exact color of his eyes, an artist's color palette, two gold rings locked together, a small pewter charm with *joy* on one side and the Japanese glyph on the other. A kimono lying amid a field of white star flowers.

Judith's heart clenched. Darkness streaked through the cell as she slowly turned it, shadows playing on the edges of the stars while blood drops on the snow fell like rain. This was Stefan's world of hope, of pain and artistry. He was both a killer and a lover. He was a man of principle, with a hard code and tremendous discipline. Everything in his cell was about duality. He had two sides and the fall of silky hair, the shells, the farm tools, the double rings, even the Japanese symbols were his looking toward a future.

This man was capable of love, of changing the direction of his life. And his need centered on one woman—the only woman. Her initials were in that scope. J.H. She saw them there along with the S.P. It was significant to her that he hadn't put a T. V. for Thomas Vincent. For her—with her—he was giving his true self. He hadn't tried to hide from her. He'd given her his past, his present and his hope for a future.

Tears blurred her eyes. Everything about the scope appealed to her. It was entirely masculine and without show or embellishment, much like Stefan. It was a quiet declaration, a statement of intent and like his quiet decisions, she felt like she already knew him, knew that he would never turn back from his resolution. For him, it was written in stone, just as it was written here, in this tremendous gift he had given her.

It must have been difficult for him to choose to be so vulnerable. He had to know that she would see his implacable nature. The warrior in him that was so deeply ingrained that it was impossible to ever stamp out. That edge of hardness she would come up against at times. The silky flow of midnight black hair against that terrible fall of snow and blood sent a spiral of heat curling through her. It was soft and sensuous and very unexpected—a statement of healing love. Her Stefan was every bit the artist as he was the assassin.

And then the last tumble brought a black pitchfork with the set of golden wings covering it. His fallen angel with clipped wings. *His.* He'd claimed her for his own, and she saw clearly he meant it. She was his salvation, his joy, his reason. The devil had claimed his angel.

Outside she could hear the soft wind fluttering through the leaves of her Japanese garden and inside, she could hear her own heart beating. She moistened her lips, carefully making certain that she had turned the cell enough times that she had managed to see everything. Every scene would always be different, but each one would always be a glimpse into Stefan's soul. She could barely find the strength to lower the scope when she found it so enthralling. Her hands were shaking, her body trembling. He was claiming her with every turn of the kaleidoscope and God help her, everything in her responded to his call.

She moistened her lips. Without thinking she clutched the scope to her heart, her gaze meeting his. "This is an incredible gift. Thank you."

"Give yourself to me."

Her heart did that funny little flippy thing inside her chest as her stomach did a slow roll. His voice was low, so quiet it was merely a thread of sound, but there was no denying he was making a statement. A demand. She'd challenged him and he'd more than accepted it. Stefan hadn't tried to soften his true nature, it was there in the cell he'd made, the weapons, including a small garrote he'd twisted from metal.

"I just gave myself to you, Judith. I handed over whatever was left of Stefan Prakenskii. Give yourself to me."

She drank him in. He was a big man, all muscle, no soft edges, but she could drown in his blue-green eyes, get caught up in his reluctant smile and burn hot under his touch. He would be hers completely; she had seen that in his single-minded purpose. "If you left me I'd be shattered," she admitted. "You have to know whether or not you're capable of staying."

"When I make a commitment, Judith, it's forever. And I expect the same of my woman." It was as much a warning as a promise. "She has to trust me, have faith in me, as I will in her. I don't know how to do things by halves. Be certain it's me you really want, angel."

"I'm taking a lot of things on faith, Stefan."

"I know I'm asking a lot of you. I've never been a good man. I've lived by a code and tried never to allow an innocent in harm's way, but I've killed, Judith. Many times. And I've used what I know to get information from other agents. The things I've done I'm not proud of, nor am I ashamed. That's been my life. I'd like to say that part of my life is over, but until Ivanov is dead and Sorbacov realizes we won't be a threat to him unless he pursues us, I can't promise that."

Judith nodded. "I still think we should talk to Jonas."

"I have no idea how to be in a relationship, and I'm bound to make mistakes. I'm not a social man. Hanging out with people is not something I'll ever be comfortable with."

"I noticed that." She couldn't help the beginnings of a smile. "Don't worry, I'll protect you. I'm very good at socializing."

He walked purposefully over to the French doors and closed them, securing the locks and once more setting the alarm.

Judith rolled her eyes. "Don't you think that silly alarm is rather useless?"

"It will keep everyone else out." He turned to face her, his brilliant gaze drifting over her, hunger growing in the depths of his eyes. "Take off your clothes. I prefer you wearing only that gold chain and all that soft skin."

She felt heat rush through her and settle low. Her nipples reacted, growing into hard pebbles. Color crept up her neck. She felt almost weak with wanting him. There was something so sexy about the way he took command. She loved that he belonged to her. And he did. She had known it the moment her spirit had merged with his. It was comforting to know she could let go with a violent storm of emotions and he could handle it.

"Judith."

The soft impatience in the way he said her name sent another surge of heat coursing through her veins. Electricity sparked in the room. She caught the edge of her shirt almost without thinking and pulled the material over her head. His swift inhale sent a shiver down her spine.

He stepped close to her, close enough that his masculine scent enveloped her. "Sometimes when I look at you, I have to remind myself you're real. You're so beautiful to me, everything about you," he confessed and caught her up as if she weighed no more than a feather.

Judith, still holding the racer-back tank top, circled his neck with her arms and held on as he carried her from the room. He didn't stop to use the light switch or close the door, but she felt a surge of power and the two things happened almost simultaneously. She sucked her breath at the realization that Stefan wasn't simply telepathic, or a shield for her emotions, he was capable of telekinesis. Locks opened for him and he could move objects, a rare talent.

"Your spirit amplifies my abilities," he said as he took her up the stairs. "I felt it the first time we shared an erotic fantasy. I didn't know if I initiated it or you did, but the power was incredible. You must have felt it."

She couldn't wait for the bedroom. She kissed his chin, the corners of his mouth, and then settled her lips quite firmly over his. Liquid gold poured into her veins and moved through her body in a slow, delicious thick molasses in the summertime heat. The feeling was exquisite, and she couldn't stop kissing him. She loved his taste, all that masculinity, the spicy, sexy demand in his mouth when he kissed her back again and again.

She seemed to float, and somehow was in the bedroom, Stefan going down to the bed with her, kneeling over her as he kissed her, his hands sure on her shorts, stripping them from her hips without pause. His mouth trailed fire from her throat to her breasts, robbing her of breath and sanity. Her body trembled with hunger for him, her hips and legs moving restlessly beneath him in an agony of need.

Often she felt so completely and utterly alone and empty. No one had ever made her feel the way he did—so filled by him. He poured into her mind, just as she poured into his. They filled each other, so that there were no empty spaces, no shadows, only a complete merging of spirits.

His tongue flicked her nipple, his teeth bit down and she arched into him, offering him her full breasts, aching now, needing his attention. Her arms circled his head, holding him to her while he feasted. Whips of flame connected her breasts to her weeping feminine channel. Fire sizzled through her so that she cried out, nearly sobbing with her need to feel him inside her.

"Take your clothes off. This time, I want to see all of you," she gasped.

He lifted his head, his ever-changing eyes dark with tur-
bulence, with lust. "Are you certain you're ready for that,
Judith? My body's a little banged up."

She touched his face—that beloved face, so perfectly
sculpted. It was a man's face, no sign of the boy long gone
from his spirit. She traced the scars with shaking fingertips.
"Let me love you, Stefan," she whispered. "These things
that have happened to you shaped you into the man I want.
Let me have you completely."

Stefan wordlessly knelt above her, his eyes growing even
more brilliantly blue-green. His hands dropped to the buttons of his shirt and he slowly opened the edges and
shrugged the material off. She bit down hard on her lower
lip. His chest was crisscrossed with scars and old wounds.
There were slashes across his belly and around his hip, disappearing into his jeans.

Judith ran her finger along the edge of one long scar that
led into his waistband before opening the jeans herself. She
tugged them down to his knees, her eyes widening as his
heavy erection jutted into her face. Scars marred his thighs
and one edged across the hair above of penis. There was no
doubt he'd been through battles.

Stefan slid one leg off the bed, shed the jeans and followed suit with the other, holding his position above her,
turning just slightly so he could follow the angle of her
body, straddling her, allowing her to take a good look at the
roadmap of scars. Judith twisted her body slightly, giving
herself a better angle to examine every scar, her fingers
whispering over them reverently. She leaned up to press a
series of kisses over every line.

Stefan closed his eyes and just allowed his body to feel.
She was a miracle, bringing him to life. He had always
commanded his body when he seduced a woman. He'd
never given himself to her, never allowed her to touch him,
to claim him as Judith was doing so if he loved her a little
more than other men loved their woman, he felt not only

was it acceptable, but it was entirely understandable and he forgave himself for his loss of discipline and control.

Her touch felt like the very first time. He knew he would never forget this moment. The slide of her hair over his thighs was so damned sensuous his cock swelled to a painful aching. He brought his hand to the thick length, circling it lightly to ease the terrible craving while she took her time imprinting on his body with her fingers.

His heart jumped when he felt the brush of her tongue along his thigh. Her hands slipped around the column of his leg, holding her torso up while she lapped her way up the inside of his leg. His heart stood still a moment, then began to pound as her tongue found his scrotum. There was no hesitation on her part, only an eagerness to bring him pleasure and claim him with the same determined efficiency as he'd claimed her.

He had always been the seducer, always making certain his chosen target succumbed fast to his expertise. And he'd never expected—or allowed—a woman to give him the same pleasure, not like this. Not a complete takeover of every one of his senses. After his training he had been unable to function without his brain working, judging his mark and reading always, always what was best for her pleasure in order to carry out his mission. His mind actually hazed over, enhanced by her spirit element, seduced by this woman he had fallen fast and hard for.

Her hands moved up to his buttocks, massaging, gripping as she kissed her way up his cock, her tongue dancing over the thick veins and around the dark head. His breath left his lungs in a rush when her mouth slipped over him, as tight as any fist, hot and moist and velvety soft. His heart nearly exploded. He caught her shoulders and lowered her onto the bed, her head slightly over the edge while he knelt above her. The angle allowed him to slide his cock more deeply into that amazing haven. His hands found her breasts, rolling and tugging on her nipples as she suckled, the pull strong, then gentle. Her tongue danced over him, flat and hard, then licking like a little kitten.

He fought for air, fought for a little control. Sex was just that—sex, another tool, a weapon. But she turned it into something far different, something so far removed from what he'd ever known that he didn't have a chance against her. Emotion burst over her along with pure sensation, turning his brain to mush and his body to fire.

She made a sound, a plea, the vibration running through his body until he trembled with the need to thrust into her. *Please.*

Oh God. That small plea. So generous. So Judith. His woman. She wanted to give this to him, to allow him to surrender to the sheer carnal desire of using her body for his exclusive pleasure. She was asking nothing in return and God help him, he couldn't help but feel love rising with the lust, intertwining until the two were no longer separate, but tightly woven together, bound for all time.

She'd found a way inside him to break through that solid steel door his trainers had so brutally erected to block all emotion and close him off. She'd crept in with her soft serenity, with her exotic, generous, compassionate nature and she'd found a way to lead him to another world, one he'd never imagined he could enter. His eyes burned along with his chest as he fought for air, fought for balance. It was far too late; she swept him into her heart on a tidal wave of sheer desire.

Her mouth tightened, sliding along his shaft, unable to take the full length of him, but she didn't use her hand to stop him, trusting him, willing to give him her best. She wasn't tutored like the women he'd been with, but her joy and completely giving nature wrapped in such a feeling of love transported him close to euphoria. If there was a subspace where every sensation came together, merged into ultimate pleasure wrapped in emotion—he was there.

His hands gripped her hair, holding her head still. He

started as gently as possible with his body screaming at him, getting her used to his control. She didn't fight him, not when he slipped another inch into her, feeling her throat close, squeezing down on him. He threw his head back and held her still, his head back, letting the amazing sensation wash through him. She took a breath when he pulled her head back and he began a rougher rhythm, sliding deep and holding there for a moment, experiencing paradise.

Her hands gripped over his thighs and cupped his tight balls, massaging gently and then as he slipped deeper, gripped again. He could feel his body growing hotter and hotter, until the boiling heat made his thrusts harder to control. The seduction of her mouth wasn't helping. In fact, she encouraged him with her hands and mouth.

"Moya angel, ya tebya lyublu," he said between his teeth, the words torn from somewhere deep inside of him. Love was such an insipid word for the emotion welling up inside of him like a volcano. He had to stop before it was too late, and never once in his life had that ever happened to him.

Very reluctantly he loosened his hands in her hair and, closing his eyes, pulled away from the paradise of her hot mouth. "I want to worship your body tonight, Judith."

"I thought I was worshiping yours," she said. "If nothing else, Stefan, I sent you a love letter. I'm hoping you understand I'm giving my heart to you."

He kissed his way over her chin and down her throat to her neck. "I understood perfectly, and I hope you understand what I'm saying to you."

Judith could barely breathe with his mouth pulling at her breasts and his teeth and tongue teasing and flicking her nipples into tight peaks of aching desire. He took her up so fast and she was already half crazy with need and hunger. She loved driving him over the edge, knowing she was the only woman who had ever done such a thing. It was a heady experience, craving the taste and texture of him, loving the way she could make him feel nearly as helpless with desire as he made her. Touching him, using her mouth on him had fed her own deep hunger.

His tongue traced her ribs and found her belly button. She had no idea she could be so sensitive. Were those sounds coming from her throat? Desperate. Pleading. She was on fire, and couldn't still her hips from bucking almost desperately. She wanted to weep with need. How could the chemistry between them be so out of control, a firestorm that burned so hot she didn't think she could stand it?

I've got you, baby, he assured her. His tongue dipped again into her navel and blazed a trail to the junction of her legs.

The brush of his voice inside her head only served to heighten her pleasure even more. There was something so intimate about communicating with him on such a level. She could feel the intensity of his hunger for her, the driving need to possess her, to claim her for his own. He wanted life with her—forever with her—and he envisioned years here on the farm, in her home. He planned on making love to her in every single room and out on the balconies as well. The erotic images in his head enhanced her own fantasies.

And then he dipped his head, his tongue lapping at the liquid heat spilling along her thighs in welcome and every sane thought disappeared. She thought she might have screamed, but it came out a pleading sob. His tongue made a slow circle and then pushed deep, still deliberately slow, driving the breath from her lungs.

"I'm ready. I am. You don't have to do that," she pleaded, because she was too close to flying apart.

I want to do this. I love the taste of you. I may just eat you up.

His voice was a velvet growl, his hard hands pinning her hips still when she would have thrashed beneath him. Judith couldn't still the little gasps and keening wails escaping her throat as he devoured her like a man possessed.

Music. I love the music you make.

He was killing her with pleasure. With his mouth. With his fingers. Even with his voice. If he'd stuck to one rhythm she might have been able to keep a clear thought, but he continually changed, licking and sucking and flicking until she felt wild and a little crazed. Deep inside the tension coiled tighter and tighter until she was gasping for air and begging him to fill her.

His face struck her as he knelt above, his hands sure on her hips, dragging her to him, lifting her body so easily. She was an artist, and if she was going to paint him, she would try to capture that sculpted, carved-from-stone look of sheer sensuality stamped on his face. The dark desire in his eyes, the hunger in the stamp of his mouth. He was beautiful and so sexy a lump welled up in her throat, blocking all sound as she stilled, feeling the broad head of his heavy erection pressed to her needy entrance.

She heard her heartbeat thundering in her ears as his shaft slowly invaded her body, one stunning inch at a time. He filled her so full, sending streaks of fire—of lightning—rushing over her skin, enflaming every nerve ending to a point almost beyond endurance. His rock-hard flesh pushed deeper and deeper into her body, searing her body with scorching heat.

She wanted him with every cell in her body, wanted him to belong solely to her. She tightened her muscles around him, gripping hard, desperate for him. His hiss of agony shocked her, his eyes going turbulent and stormy with lust. He actually groaned, a tortured, strangled sound that sent her heart pounding and her body writhing beneath his.

"Angel, I'm going to lose control if you keep that up. I swear, baby, you're so damn hot and tight I'm going to lose my mind."

She wanted him to lose his mind, to lose all that perfect control—for her, with her. "Lose it then, Stefan. With me. Lose your mind with me," she whispered, not fully under-

standing what she was asking, but knowing with him she'd
go anywhere.

He pulled back, pistoned forward in a harsh, nearly brutal stroke, driving through velvet folds, deep, so deep and
she rose to meet him, her muscles throbbing around his
pulsing flesh. Deep inside, every movement he made filled
her, caressed her, sent those streaks of fire arcing over her
until she was nearly mindless with the sensations tearing
through her.

His hands gripped her tighter and she felt the difference
in him as if he'd coiled tighter himself, as if that long held
control was at an end. The ride turned wild, he drove hard
and fast, deep and full, a jackhammer intent on finding her
womb and lodging himself there. She heard her own keening cry as he plunged into her over and over, the rhythmic
thrusting setting her blood on fire and nearly driving her
right off the bed. It was only the tight grip of his hands pinning her in place.

Tension grew, coiled tighter and tighter until she was
tossing her head, digging her heels into the mattress, desperately trying to get away, to push herself harder into him,
impale herself on that steel spike that never stopped thrusting into her. He was tormenting her, driving her insane with
such a frantic need that seemed never ending. Her breath
came in gasping sobs, as the firestorm rushed over her.

Her mouth opened wide, a soundless scream, as his
shaft pressed hard on her sensitized bud. Her body clamped
down on his, claimed his, gripping like a vise of silk and
steel. Wave after wave shook her, swept both of them up in
the torrent of sensation. His hoarse cry was harsh, a startled
yell of triumph somewhere caught between love and laughter that he could burn with her, feel with her.

Stefan, with his remaining strength, dragged her completely onto the bed, collapsing on top of her, while they
both fought for breath. Her hair was damp, and a fine sheen
dampened both their bodies. Their hearts beat like crazy,

an accelerated rhythm that made them both laugh. Stefan wrapped his arms around her and rolled until she sprawled on top of him. He held her in his arms for a long time, breathing deeply, before he lifted his head to trail kisses over her face, one hand smoothing back her hair. His gaze drifted slowly over her, his eyes—those deep blue-green eyes smiling, his face relaxed.

"We're not finished by a long shot, *moya angel*. We're just getting started."

She looked down over his body, not yet soft, not even close. "That's not possible."

He smiled at her. "You have no idea what I can do."

16

"I'M never moving again. Two days and nights in bed has just about killed me." Judith tilted her chair back, set her feet up on the balcony railing overlooking her garden and stared up at the stars.

She was exhausted, completely and utterly exhausted. Her body was boneless and every muscle felt limp and useless. She was sore in places she hadn't known existed, but it was a delicious soreness.

Stefan's arm curled around her neck from behind and she looked up at his face looming over hers. He always looked so intent, so much the hunter. There was no way for him to hide what he was. She found herself smiling, joy bursting through her.

"If you've come to assault me, crazy man, I'm not moving."

His mouth quirked. "A challenge then. I do not like to lose."

"No! No way. It's not a challenge. I made that mistake an hour ago and I had to crawl out here. I can't even stand up." Laughing, she held her hands up in surrender.

"In that case, I've come bearing gifts." He bent his head and took her mouth.

She loved the confidence in him that bordered on arrogance. He knew he had wrapped her around his little finger. She wouldn't say no to kisses—or sex—with him. Ever. It didn't take much persuasion on his part and her body belonged to him. She lost herself there in his kiss, in the heat of his mouth, the taste of passion and love. She had to come up for breath before she simply drowned in him.

"Hot chocolate," he announced. "I would have made tea, but you need to sleep if you're going to work tomorrow."

She took the hot mug and licked at the dollop of whipped cream on top. "You're my savior. I was just thinking chocolate would revive me, but I didn't have the strength to go get it."

"I read your mind," he admitted, toeing another chair around to sit beside her. "You don't have to work tomorrow. We can take another day."

"I wouldn't survive another day," Judith admitted, laughing. Happiness danced in the air around, small threads of silver and gold that sparkled with the stars. "And Airiana definitely would do me in if you didn't—in a completely different way, of course. She's covered for me at the shop, but she can't keep it up."

"I suppose I have to share you with the world," he said. "I'll go with you to Sea Haven tomorrow and go over the books at the gallery."

"You're really thinking of buying it?"

He shrugged. "I've got plenty of money, but I wouldn't enjoy doing nothing. I spend a lot of my time going to galleries all over the world and maybe in the back of my head I always considered what I'd do with one."

"This is a small town, Stefan."

"Thomas. Stefan Prakenskii doesn't exist. There's no photograph of him and no fingerprints. I doubt if a birth certificate exists. I'm a ghost, Judith. Sorbacov has never heard of Thomas Vincent, the American businessman. All of us develop numerous covers we can disappear into when needed and Vincent's cover is solid. He's going to settle here with you, make kaleidoscopes, own an art gallery and make babies."

She laughed, taking a cautious sip of the hot chocolate. She should have known it would be the perfect temperature. Stefan saw to little details, she was learning that about him. He always saw to her comfort, running a bath, carrying her to it after they'd made crazy, wild love, wrapping her in blankets or handing her a sweater almost before she knew she was cold. He would never have served her chocolate that would scorch her mouth.

"You're obsessed with babies."

He grinned at her. "With *making* babies," he corrected. "I'm practicing until I get it right."

"If you get any better at it, Stefan . . . Thomas, I'll be dead. I'm getting schizophrenic just thinking about this. So you'll be Thomas Vincent."

"And you'll be Mrs. Thomas Vincent."

"Is that even legal?"

"I have all the credentials to prove it. It's more legal than Prakenskii. In any case, when it's all done, we'll have someone we trust do the ceremony in my native language using the name my father gave me." His eyes met hers. "It's important to me that you carry my given name even if we can't use it."

Love flooded her. She pressed trembling fingers to her mouth to keep from making a big deal out of his declaration. He couldn't hide sincerity from her, there was no way. He wanted to marry her using his father's name and it meant the world to her that he would try to find a way even if they lived under another name.

When she looked at him, sometimes she couldn't breathe with the intensity of her emotions. "You surprised me with the way you pay such close attention to what matters to me." It was more than paying close attention, he focused so completely on her, observing everything, her smallest expressions, every nuance. She would never be able to hide anything from Stefan.

He reached out to take strands of her long hair between his fingers. She noticed he did that quite often, at the oddest times.

"I'll always pay attention to what matters to you," he said, his voice that low, almost velvet tone she'd come to love. "When a man has nothing in his life worth anything and he finds a treasure, he guards her with everything he is. I'm a man of many talents, angel, and keeping you happy will be my first priority."

She regarded him over the chocolate. His face was back in the shadows. She realized he often sat in the shadows and probably always would. There was something in what he said that made her shiver, a cold chill sliding down her spine, but she wasn't certain she could put her finger on just what it was.

"Sometimes you're a little scary, Thomas." She tested the name. Now that she knew him as Stefan, Thomas didn't quite suit him, but she'd learn to live with it, just as he would.

"I don't mind you being a little afraid sometimes, Judith. You're a woman who could twist a man around your little finger."

She burst out laughing. "I swear I just was thinking you had me around your little finger."

He tugged on her hair until she yelped. He brought the strands to his mouth. "I'm very fortunate you enjoy sex. Whenever I see I might have an argument on my hands, I kiss you senseless."

There was a little too much truth in his quiet statement to be entirely comfortable. He could kiss her senseless. She forgot her own name when he was kissing her. "I'll have to watch out for that."

He smiled then and her heart leapt. He didn't smile often, not a genuine smile that crept into his eyes like now. "You have nothing to worry about, angel. You're the only woman in the world who is capable of making me lose all control. I think we both have a good shot at distracting each other."

"Well, you do make the best hot chocolate I've ever had. What did you put in this?"

"It's a secret Russian recipe for falling asleep. You've had a hot bath, hot chocolate and my promise to let you sleep until morning."

"What time would you consider morning?" Judith asked mischievously.

He flashed a small grin at her. "Well, I haven't quite decided that yet. You aren't getting enough sleep and I have to quit being so selfish."

Judith took another long swallow of the chocolate and studied the stars overhead. "Actually, I believe it was me waking you this last time. You were sleeping all sexy and I just couldn't resist temptation, so technically, I suppose it really is your fault after all."

His eyebrow shot up. "Your logic completely eludes me. When I'm asleep I can't be responsible for looking sexy."

Judith laughed again, that low, melodious sound Stefan listened for, like soft, perfectly tuned chimes in the wind. He could listen to that sound forever. Sitting on her balcony with the stars sparkling overhead and her sea of white star flowers below, he found he was perfectly content. He knew Judith worried he would find their life together boring, but for the first time since he was a small boy, he felt he had a home. There was no way to express in words what having a real home meant. Sitting on a balcony with the wind touching his face and mist beginning to creep in from the ocean, he felt absolute freedom.

"When I was boy, we were snuggled in our apartment, the fire going and my father stretched out on this couch, his head in my mother's lap, two babies on his chest. I remember he looked at my mother with such love on his face and he took her hand and said, 'This is a golden moment, my love.' At the time I didn't know what that meant, but it stuck in my head because of the way he looked at her, with so much happiness. Now I know what he meant." Once again he brought the fistful of her hair to his mouth.

He loved the feel of all that silk. He thought it looked like a shining waterfall, dark and mysterious on a dusky night. When Judith lay on a pillow, with her hair spilling all around her, he'd never seen a more beautiful or seductive sight. He rubbed her hair over his jaw, wanting this moment to last forever. He glanced at her, was immediately caught in the spell of her. Tears swam in her eyes, diamond droplets caught in her eyelashes.

Without conscious thought, he leaned over and kissed her tears away, sipping them from her soft skin. "Don't ever feel sad for me, Judith. My life brought me to you and that's enough for me. That's everything."

Judith shook her head and finished off her chocolate, too choked up to answer him. Sometimes, when those small memories came back to him, Stefan broke her heart. She wanted to hold him forever. He thought he saved him. She could tell in the way he looked at her, in the things he said to her, but it was the other way around. She had become lost in her need to avenge her brother's death. In her belief that she didn't measure up because she couldn't find a way to make Jean-Claude suffer.

She sighed. The chocolate was definitely doing the trick, making her sleepy. She let herself drift, thinking of the man beside her. He was an anchor in the storms of emotion that washed over her so intensely. Sometimes she couldn't contain all the force of her passionate nature, so concentrated by her element, but when she was with Stefan, she didn't need to keep constant vigil. She found she could relax and just feel what she was supposed to feel. She'd felt half alive, desperate to control the growing power within her, yet the moment she'd met Stefan her spirit had recognized him as some sort of protective shield. It made no sense—yet it made perfect sense.

"You make me happy," she said, half closing her eyes, allowing herself to drift further toward a dreamy place. It was more than that. She'd felt empty and he'd filled her. She'd felt afraid of herself and he gave her confidence. There wasn't any rhyme or reason to it, but strangely, they fit, two misfits completing one another.

She turned her head to look at him, struggling to keep her eyes open. Her lids felt heavy and her body deliciously exhausted. "I was happy here, and I knew I'd have a decent life. I didn't know I was empty until you came along. And I didn't have any idea what real happiness was until I laid eyes on you. Isn't that crazy?"

He shook his head. "No. I didn't consider another way of living. Even when I prepared for it, I never really thought I'd disappear into the real world. Men like me live our lives apart and we die that way. No one knows we exist and no one mourns our death, because we're ghosts. I didn't consider myself unhappy. My life was just what it was."

He allowed the soft strands of her hair to slip through his fingers, watching it slide back around her, a cloak of silk framing her face and falling with grace below her waist. "Until I saw you. The world just seemed to hold its breath, waiting for you to notice me."

Judith felt as if he had given her the world. He didn't think he knew the right words to say, but nevertheless he found them, at least for her. He made her feel as if she were the only woman in the world.

"Tomorrow your sisters are going to talk to you, angel. You know they'll come at you from a million different ways."

She could hear the concern in his voice, the worry that once away from him, she would be persuaded she'd made a terrible mistake. "I worry that once you're away from me, you'll change your mind, Stefan," she admitted.

"Thomas. Think Thomas all the time. You can't think of me as Stefan. And you have nothing to worry about, Judith. I said forever and I meant it. I'm a fairly single-minded man."

"I meant it too. My sisters will eventually accept you. They have Levi. He kind of grows on you." She paused, and then gave a little sigh. "When he's not forcing us all to learn self-defense."

"You know I'll side with him on that issue," Stefan said, unrepentant. "I'll probably be far worse than he is. And we're getting a couple of dogs. Big ones."

"I'm a little concerned about the dog issue. Rikki brought it up the other night and we discussed it. Everyone seemed to be okay with it with the exception of Lissa. She's sort of a warrior woman and I would expect her to totally want dogs on the property, but she was very silent on the subject. She didn't advocate for them. Airiana did, but Lissa stayed quiet. I asked her if she was okay with getting dogs, but she didn't exactly answer me."

"Would the others balk if she did?"

"We tend to do everything around here together. It's worked in the past. Blythe is the leader and the most diplomatic. She reads people very well," Judith explained.

"I doubt if she reads them as well as you do. You're empathic."

She yawned and hastily covered it with her hand. "I thought I hid that very well."

"Not from me." He stood up, taking the mug from her hand and putting it on the small tray table beside his chair. "Come on, angel, you're exhausted. I'm putting you to bed."

"We get into trouble when we're in bed. I thought I'd just sleep right here."

Stefan shook his head and leaned down to pick her up, cradling her close to his chest. "I don't think so, baby. You'd hurt your neck. I can restrain myself when it's necessary."

She wrapped her arms around his neck and leaned into him. "I wasn't worried about you restraining yourself. It turns out I don't have any discipline. At all. Not when it comes to you."

Stefan took her through the open French doors to her bedroom, bending his head to reach her tempting mouth. She tasted of chocolate and passion, an inviting combination. He acknowledged to himself it might have been a mistake to kiss her. Once he started, he always found it difficult to stop. Kissing her was fast becoming a favorite pastime and it definitely led to other, erotic and pleasurable things, but she really was exhausted and he had work to do.

With a small sigh, he lifted his head and took her on through to the master bath. "Brush your teeth and I'll rinse out your chocolate mug."

"You don't have to do that."

"You never go to bed with dirty dishes in the sink."

She shrugged. "I don't like to wake up to them."

He sent her a small, smug smile over his shoulder as he went to collect the mug. "I know." He had made it his mission to know everything about her in the short time they were together. He retained information, small details, easily and he filed everything about her away, her likes and dislikes, the things that annoyed her and the things that intrigued her.

Essentially, Judith was a happy person. She enjoyed life, loved her sisters and her work. She saw in color and to her, everything and everyone was a blank canvas she painted in her head. She took great joy in making kaleidoscopes for people all over the world, choosing each thing that went into them with tremendous care. The scope she had completed for Hannah Drake Harrington, the sheriff's wife, was a perfect example. Hannah intended to use the kaleidoscope to focus on during her labor, and Judith had made it as easy to see the images as it was to turn the cell during difficult labor.

Maybe that was her secret: the caring of individuals. He

didn't have that, and maybe he never would, but he could feel the intensity of her spirit and it made him proud of her. He "got" her. He saw her. Even her sisters couldn't see her the way he did—well, maybe Blythe could. Blythe was different. Not an element, but she had tremendous gifts.

"Are you coming to bed?"

Judith sounded drowsy, sexy, and her voice played his body the way her fingers did. He found himself smiling, aroused and happy for no other reason than that she could do that to him. His little miracle. "I'm on my way."

She was already in bed, not a stitch on, just the way he liked it, her long hair in a braid, as if it was really going to stay that way. He shucked his jeans and stretched out beside her, gathering her close, curving his body around hers protectively. His hard cock snuggled perfectly between the soft firm globes of her ass. His hands stripped off the tie at the end of the braid to release the thick mass. He smiled at her resigned sigh, cupped the soft weight of her breast in one palm and held her close.

"Go to sleep, angel. Sweet dreams." He kissed her bare shoulder and lay quietly, waiting for her even breathing.

It didn't take long before she succumbed to her exhaustion. Stefan took another half hour for himself, just enjoying being able to lie so close to her before carefully slipping from the bed as he had each night they'd been together. He was surprised how reluctant he was each time to put on his "shadow skin," but there was no safe place for them until Ivanov was out of their lives. Sorbacov had no idea of Thomas Vincent, but Ivanov did. He'd tried to draw him out and so had Lev, but either Ivanov was really hurt and lying low, or he was too cunning to be tricked. Stefan suspected the latter.

He looked down at Judith, her face relaxed, long lashes two thick crescents on her face. He loved that she slept naked for him and never protested when he took the braid from her hair. No matter how often he reached for her, she always met him eagerly. No matter how often he stripped off her clothes, she laughed and complied no matter where they were in the house and once, out on the grounds. Even now, he was tempted to reach between her legs and caress her, knowing she'd be damp and ready for his possession.

He reached down and took strands of her silky hair between his fingers, his heart in his throat. She took his breath away every time he looked at her. He could hold her forever. It seemed a miracle to him to be able to curl his body around hers, the soft weight of her breast resting in his palm, breathing in the scent of her, of them, combined. Most of the time he lay awake and exulted in his ability to feel such intense emotion.

He didn't have pretty words for her, but he had his body to show her just how much she meant to him. He could do all those little things that counted, watching and noting all the things that were important to her, all the habits she had. He wanted to be her everything.

Stefan looked around the room. The space was feline cream, serene and calm, with splashes of silken color that would always be Judith, that bright well of deep joy and compassion. She might try to feed the passion of her anger and need for revenge, but her true nature would always rise to the surface, her empathy for others always there, forcing her to see their side. The artist in her ran too deep.

With a sigh, he pulled on his clothes and weapons. He was a little late meeting his brother, and it was becoming difficult to deceive Judith. He didn't like it at all. If they were going to be together, and he wasn't going to have it any other way, then there had to be honesty between them. His first reaction was always her protection and the less she knew about Petr Ivanov the better. And the less Ivanov knew about her, the better. But damn it all—he reached down and brushed back her hair—leaving her out of what he was doing felt wrong.

Resolutely he turned and left, careful to set the alarm before jogging down the road to meet Lev. His brother waited for him beside a small Jeep. He flashed a quick grin and slid behind the wheel, waiting for Stefan to jog around to the passenger's side.

"You look like hell, brother," Lev greeted.

"I feel like I'm lying to her," Stefan admitted.

Lev had driven down the road, but he slammed on the brakes, giving Stefan a disgusted look. "Are you telling me you're lying to her about what you're doing?"

"I don't tell her anything. She's asleep."

"What are going to say if she wakes up?"

"She won't wake up. I made certain of that."

"You rotten bastard. Get the hell out of my car. You *drug* her? You *drug* Judith?"

"I already feel like a bastard," Stefan admitted. "Don't fuckin' lecture me." He dragged both hands through his hair. "You think I like doing it? I don't know what else to do. I've never been in a relationship with a woman. What do you tell your wife?"

"I tell her the truth. Everything. I told her we were hunting Ivanov and we'd kill him if we found the bastard, that there would be no other choice. If he gets to her or one of her sisters, they're dead. Rikki's autistic, she isn't stupid. She understands a life or death matter. And damn you, Stefan, so would Judith. What the hell point is there in being with someone if you don't trust them with the truth?"

Stefan considered hitting his brother for voicing what he'd been thinking. "I don't know, Lev. Judith is big on Jonas Harrington. She thinks the man can solve anything."

Lev shook his head. "That's not it and you know it. You think it was easy for me to let Rikki see what I am? You're holding that back, afraid she won't accept you if she really sees you. Telling someone about our work and asking them to live with it when we're hunting are two different things. You're afraid, Stefan."

"Maybe."

"There is no maybe. Man up. You can't be with her if

she doesn't accept you, and you're not even giving her the chance."

"And if she doesn't? What then, Lev? And don't tell me you could walk away from your Rikki, because if you could, you don't feel for her like I do for Judith."

"Rikki grounds me. She's the center of my world. No, there'd be no walking away from her, but we talk things out. If you're going to do this with Judith, you have to trust her with who you really are." Lev glanced at him. "I think you already know that."

"I'll think about it." The idea of Judith rejecting him was impossible to think about. He'd been tortured, shot, knifed and faced threats to his life every day. Nothing he'd ever done scared him as much as just the thought that Judith would look at him with loathing.

Lev took the road leading into Sea Haven along the ocean, a roundabout way in, that allowed them to park out a distance from one of the small places Stefan had rented as a bolt hole. He needed to check his computer and didn't want anyone tracing it back to Judith's farm. He'd pick up his hunting supplies, a field kit and glasses.

As they approached the backstreets, Stefan put his hand on his brother's arm. "He's here. Close by. I can feel him."

Lev didn't argue with him. He pulled his baseball cap a little lower. He wore a beard and dressed as a local might, much more casual, his shirt open, his jeans faded and worn. "He won't recognize me."

"Don't count on it. Never underestimate Ivanov," Stefan said grimly.

"I'm not associated with this vehicle at all. I've completely remodeled it, and added a few additions in a barn on the farm. Rikki and I avoid towns as a rule. We do shop in Inez's store, but we use her truck. Most of the people here in town will swear they've known Levi Hammond for years."

The Jeep had no doors, but it had plenty of power and

the ability to go through the forest where there was no road. Stefan kept his hands inside, close to his weapons, where he could use them fast. "Take a left up here. There's a small house. Use the alley. You can go right into the garage."

"He's got to be holed up near here," Lev said. "I wouldn't be surprised if he's next door to this place. Good escape routes from either direction and the rooftops are close enough to use. You've got the sea to cover noise, and no children that I can tell in any of the houses."

"These small houses are old. Mostly seniors who've lived here forever and mind their own business. They're friendly enough, but they don't pry."

Lev pulled up to the garage, Stefan was out and opened the door fast, allowing Lev inside. There was a vehicle already parked inside, a fast Audi, compact, and built for hugging the curves.

"I see you're prepared," Lev observed.

"Is there any other way to live?" Stefan asked. He checked the door. "Stay back just in case Ivanov's been here. I don't think so, and nothing appears to have been tampered with, but I'd rather you stay out here while I take a look around."

"You don't need to protect me, Stefan."

Stefan shot his younger brother his shut-up-and-back-off look. Lev shrugged and stepped behind the Jeep while Stefan went into the house. Every sense on high alert, Stefan moved through the small house. Only seven hundred square feet, it wasn't difficult to check every room for signs Ivanov had found his bolt hole. He examined the windows and even the kitchen sink and small refrigerator before he waved Lev inside.

"I put the weapons behind the wall by the bed over there. Get what we need and I'll check my laptop. When I'm working under deep cover I only check a couple of times a week, but I'm expecting the news that La Roux's been taken by our agents."

He powered up his laptop and waited a few heartbeats before typing in his code. At once a single message came across the screen:

Entire team killed. La Roux escaped us. Recover micro-chip and terminate immediately.

Stefan sat very still, staring at the screen. Sorbacov had sent a team to break La Roux out of prison and yet the criminal had somehow gotten the drop on them? Sorbacov was going to have to provide more information, especially with Ivanov lurking around. The entire thing stank. He wished he hadn't found Lev.

He sent his demand, insisting on a full explanation.

La Roux agitated and anxious to break out several days ago. His men were waiting and they massacred our agents. La Roux in the wind. Find him. Get the micro-chip and terminate.

Several days ago. What had changed? La Roux had seemed ambivalent about trying to escape. He had his organization running strong, a cushy sentence that would be over with good behavior in two more years. He was hooked up with corrupt guards. Stefan could understand why the man might hesitate. He'd been interested when he looked at the photographs of Judith, but if nothing else, La Roux had patience. He seemed willing to wait.

"Something changed," Stefan murmured aloud. He turned the screen to show his brother.

Lev whistled. "You believe it?"

"Yes. More than anything, Sorbacov wants that micro-chip. There's too much damning evidence on it. He'll come at the two of us later, but I don't think he'll be able to pull his dog off. Ivanov is locked on us and I wounded him.

That'll hurt his pride. He won't acknowledge any of Sorbacov's transmissions and he'll keep coming at us."

"You know him well."

"I learned a lot about him when we were in training together. I let him think he was better than I was. I've never had a big ego, so for a while he didn't catch on. Whatever it took to get the job done was all that mattered to me. Sliding from one skin to another was easy enough, but through the years, I couldn't stay under the radar. Ivanov noticed when I kept defeating the enemy. He's going to keep coming."

Lev rubbed the bridge of his nose. "You two have a run-in before this?"

Stefan shrugged. What could he say? Everyone had run-ins with Petr Ivanov growing up. Ivanov had held him underwater, thinking he would kill him that way. As a teen, he'd been sick and sadistic, torturing animals and graduating to his classmates. He would often loop a rope around a sleeping child and drag him or her to the window, throwing them out, and watching them dance on the end of the rope. Most of the time, other children overpowered Ivanov and rescued the victim, but sometimes, they didn't get the child up in time.

"Time and again the instructors had warned Sorbacov about him, but Sorbacov cultivated him, giving him freer and freer rein until one of the instructors who had angered Ivanov turned up dead, cut into small pieces and arranged in a hallway, sightless eyes staring in horror at the children as they came out of the dormitories for classes. After that, Sorbacov kept Ivanov away from the rest of us as much as possible. He wasn't in the dorms, but we all knew he had his own quarters and ate better meals. The thing none of them understood was, while he led the good life, protected by Sorbacov, we were still fighting for our lives. We were honed into fighting machines and he grew soft. No less mean, he's sick enough to need to kill, but he doesn't have the endurance and the sheer will to survive like the rest of us do."

Lev sketched a question mark in Stefan's mind.

"When he's hurt, he runs. I would have kept going unless the bastard knocked me out. He might have been able to kill me when I was on the ground, but he couldn't take the pain. He's soft, Lev, and he won't kill unless it's a sure thing."

"So basically, he's a perverted sadist bent on killing us."

Stefan nodded. "But he's not gone rogue. He may be ignoring Sorbacov now, but make no mistake, Sorbacov ordered him here in the first place. If he managed to kill us, he'd go home with some tale of how he didn't get the new orders and Sorbacov would swallow it because he'd have no choice. He's got a monster on a leash, but he doesn't want that monster to turn on him."

"You have to tell Judith."

Stefan pushed down the illogical fear swamping him. "Keeping her alive is more important. I think La Roux took the escape offered him, suspicious the offer could be a trap and got word through one of his guards to his own men. They killed our agents and La Roux most likely came here. He had to have seen that picture of Judith with me that Mike Shariton took of us together at the door of the gallery. That's what prompted him to agree to get out of prison. He's no one's fool, La Roux."

Lev pressed his lips together as if to keep from saying anything more and followed Stefan out into the night. They separated the moment they were on the street, each taking an opposite side. Stefan took the sidewalk closest to the ocean. It had the least cover, a short fence and wild plants shooting up all over the bluff, but not high enough at the fence line to provide any shadows to disappear into. He didn't try, but sauntered along as though out for a late night walk.

It makes better sense for me to be over there. He wouldn't recognize me.

Stefan scowled, but didn't bother with an answer. He'd come to Sea Haven to warn and protect his younger brother from an assassin. Nothing had changed his intentions, not even meeting Judith. It was bad enough that Lev insisted on coming along, but he wasn't going to allow him to take the dangerous position.

The wind had risen, slapping at the sea, pushing the waves into higher and higher crests so that they broke in towering peaks over the rocks and sprayed white foam high into the air. The sea was an angry power, showing no mercy to anything in its way, dark and turbulent. He felt the power, inhaled it and drew it deep into his lungs. Waves of energy rode on the power of the wind and sea. Violent energy. He had no doubt Ivanov was up to something sadistic—and he was close.

He's here—close, Lev. He's hurting something or some-one. Stefan tried to narrow the direction down. *Stay in the shadows. Don't come near me.*

Whatever Ivanov was doing had to be close, the energy was too strong. He took a chance and crossed the street, angling ahead of his brother. The moment he neared a cross street, he felt pain, suffering, intense fear. The victim was still alive, but he could feel lifeblood ebbing away. He turned down that street and broke into a run. He was a big man and running lightly down an uneven street, expecting a bullet any moment wasn't the smartest thing, but if there was a chance to prevent an innocent dying, he had to take it.

The scent of blood was strong, but with the wind coming in off the sea and shifting continually, he had to guess at a direction. A dog began to bark one street up so he continued running up the road, hoping he was choosing the correct direction.

One street over, parallel with the one he was on, the lid of a garbage can crashed to the ground. Immediately, Lev broke out of the shrubbery and headed in that direction just as the dog abruptly quit barking.

Warning radar went off, screaming at Stefan, tension coiling in his gut. He didn't like that his brother was out of his sight and possibly rushing toward a sadist. He slowed with the thought of turning back when the scent of blood hit him again. The dog had ceased barking, but he'd marked the general area and rounded the corner and skidded to a halt. The house was dark, but the dog lay just inside the fence, his belly cut open.

Stefan swore under his breath, took a careful look around and slipped over the fence to kneel beside the dog. It was still alive, the eyes looking at him as if he could somehow save the day. "Fucking psycho," Stefan whispered. He put his hand gently on the dog's head. "I'm sorry, boy." There was nothing to be done for the animal, Ivanov had seen to that, ensuring that even if the owners found him immediately, he was too damaged for a veterinarian to save.

Stefan took the time to stroke the animal's head one last time and then quickly and mercifully broke the dog's neck. He slipped back over the fence and headed for the street Lev had turned down. Ivanov was out tonight and he was doing damage. Stefan had always known, from the time they were boys, that Petr Ivanov couldn't go very long without making a kill. Animal, man, woman or child, it didn't matter. Watching others suffer and die gave him a rush of godlike power.

Lev, be careful. He's killed a dog.

He killed more than a dog. I found a pool of blood in a backyard here. He's been busy. I followed a blood trail but it disappeared abruptly.

Get out of there now. I mean it Lev, he's too close and we've got to pull back and reassess. You're walking into a hornet's nest.

Stefan's heart accelerated when Lev didn't answer him. Swearing in Russian, he raced down the street, deliberately making noise, hoping to draw Ivanov's fire.

17

LEV! Damn it, answer me.

Stefan was experiencing waves of fear, but they were feminine in origin, not masculine, which meant his brother was connected to his wife and she knew her husband was injured. Before he could caution Lev to break the connection, something slammed into his arm hard enough to spin him around. Almost simultaneously, a sound like a firecracker reverberated down the street. He dropped to the asphalt and rolled toward the nearest yard and cover.

Fucking bastard, Lev snapped. *You hit?*

Stefan made it to the overgrown shrubs and belly-crawled forward. A spray of bullets cut through the leaves all around him. He found a depression in the ground and rolled into it, making himself as small as possible. Up and down the streets, dogs began to bark.

A nick. You? Blood dripped steadily down his arm and his shoulder felt like it had been hit with a two-by-four, but he could still use his arm, and that was what counted.

Could use a little help. I ran into a trap and can't move. Lev pictured a steel trap, chained to a thick tree, modified with serrated teeth and a punishing hydraulic system. Stefan had seen those traps before. Every movement would send the teeth sawing deeper into Lev's ankle.

I tried shoving my knife down into it to get myself loose, but there's no way that's going to work. The damn thing almost took my leg off.

Stefan swore between his clenched teeth. *I'm working my way around toward you. Don't shoot me. And don't move. The more you move, the worse it will get.*

I've got that part, Lev said, his tone dripping with sarcasm.

Several porch lights went on along the street. Stefan needed to keep Ivanov focused on him and away from his brother and any innocents. It didn't help that any minute some civilian would unknowingly enter into the killer's path. He counted to three, pushed himself up and sprinted for the count of fifteen and dropped, rolled and scooted forward on his belly, using elbows and toes to propel his body behind a screen of rocks and fern.

Bullets spat dirt into his face and ricocheted off the rocks closest to him. He was grateful Ivanov had always been a close range killer and rarely used a gun for the actual kill. He preferred blades, in close, where he could see his victim suffer. That said, an automatic machine gun definitely was up to the job if Stefan allowed himself to grow careless.

What the hell are you doing, Stefan?

Keeping him away from you. What the hell do you think I'm doing? Stefan snapped.

He was running out of garden cover on his side of the street. Few cars were parked and his only choices were to go up, onto the rooftops, or risk crossing the street. Neither was a great idea, but he had to keep Ivanov focused on him. Reluctantly he pulled his gun from the harness, the butt familiar in his palm. He didn't want to risk stray bullets going into a house, but damn it all, he had to get the upper hand here soon with Ivanov.

I don't hear return fire, Lev said.

I don't fire unless I can hit what I'm aiming at and I don't have the bastard in my sights. I'll get him, Stefan said, pouring confidence into his voice. *Right now, I want to work into a position where he'll keep his focus on me, and yet not have a clear shot while I get that trap off your ankle.*

Calf, Lev corrected. *It's locked on my calf. The son of a bitch probably knew we'd be wearing boots. We interrupted his kill. Someone's bound to call the sheriff. This time of night, Jonas and Aleksandr will answer the call. Aleksandr is going to recognize a killing ground. And my wife is on the warpath. She won't stay put, Stefan. She's going to come running.*

Stefan didn't like the note of pain creeping into Lev's voice. Men like his brother never showed pain unless it was bad. He was hurt. Really hurt. If Stefan could feel his brother's pain, no doubt his wife could as well. He didn't know her yet, but any woman who was a match for his brother had to be strong. She was a sea urchin diver, captaining a boat out on the sea. She had to be fearless.

I'll get to you. Hold still and give me a couple of minutes. Lev sighed. *Easier said than done.*

Stefan listened intently. Ivanov wasn't making a sound, careful not to reveal his location, but the shots had been angled from his left. Lev was in that direction as well, somewhere behind Ivanov. Stefan didn't want to give Ivanov the chance to circle back toward Lev and catch him while he was trapped. He had no doubt Lev could put up a fight, but the more he moved, the more the trap would saw at his leg.

Describe the trap in detail. Stefan couldn't be wrong. It was possible he could open the device from a distance, but he'd need some breathing room. The thought of Lev's wife rushing to Sea Haven was disconcerting with Ivanov on the loose and in a killing mood.

It looks like an old bear trap only taller with giant claws. It's around my calf and I can't open it. I'm a strong man, but he's done something to it and it's sawing at my leg every time I move or try to open it. There are chains buried along the ground radiating in several different directions. At least five of them.

Lev's description confirmed to Stefan that he'd studied this particular type of trap in detail. *Clever bastard. I've seen those traps. He killed a boy with one before. You watch for him, Lev. I'll need a minute. Once I free you, be very careful. Those chains means he'll have at least five more hidden close so that if you step out of one, you can get caught by the next. He called it his little minefield of hell.*

And Sorbacov encouraged and protected this sadist?

As long as Lev was talking to him, Stefan knew he was alive. He leapt up, deliberately giving Ivanov a target, determined the killer wouldn't have time to slip away and go after Lev. Stefan needed time to remember every detail of Ivanov's steel trap. He'd modified the device long ago, and, of course, Stefan studied its workings carefully once he'd run across it. He'd studied everything about Ivanov, knowing as a teenager that Petr Ivanov was his most dangerous enemy.

Sorbacov will always protect him. That's how I knew his order to terminate was a ploy to keep him here and draw you out. He believes Ivanov can take us both.

It mattered little if a team of adults hunted him with automatic weapons in the coldest place on earth, or that he was dropped into a desert with nothing but a knife, while the adults hunting him had every convenience—it was Ivanov that Stefan had feared as a child. Even as a teen, Ivanov had been insatiable, needing the pain and suffering of others the way others needed air to breathe.

I think this thing is sawing my leg in half.

Stop fucking moving. Just stay still. I'll get it off you. And for God's sake, when I do, don't take a step without testing for more traps.

I'm shoving as many things as I can down inside it, hoping it eats through the sticks and my knife before it does my leg.

Stefan wasn't about to allow Lev fall into Ivanov's hands. The exterminator was royally pissed that Stefan had managed to spot him, chase him and actually wound him. The blow to his ego would be enormous. Stefan raced across the bare street and dove over a fence into the middle of a trumpet tree split trunk. He scrambled through the thick limbs into heavier foliage. A bullet hit the heel of his boot, knocking it off, and another plucked at his sleeve, far too close for comfort. But Ivanov was still focused on him, hating him with a cold fury, determined to kill him.

Ivanov had no idea he had trapped Lev or the exterminator would have abandoned Stefan to kill his brother. Stefan used his elbows and toes to make his way through the yard, crushing flowers as he went, all the while turning his mind to the trap on his brother's ankle. It would be difficult to open the jaws from a distance and for the first time he wished he had Judith's power to tap into.

You drugged her, you idiot, Lev pointed out helpfully.

Shut up, that's not helping, Stefan growled.

Dividing his mind, keeping part of it on survival and the other tuning his energy to opening the serrated teeth digging into his brother's calf was actually painful and he didn't need his brother's pointing out he'd be facing a firing squad when he confessed.

The wind rushed inland from the ocean, bringing in a heavy veil of mist fast. Overhead clouds built fast and furious, a tower of angry, dark cauldrons, heralding an ugly storm.

That's my woman, majorly pissed and coming for her man, Lev announced.

That's the last thing we need, bringing a woman into this mess. He's a wily old wolverine, Lev, more dangerous than anyone you've ever faced. You don't want him to have a way to get to you and he'll use a woman without compunction.

She's going to come, Stefan, and she won't be alone.

Stefan cursed under his breath. He had to flush out Ivanov fast, before Lev's wife came, thinking she was going to rescue him. As if Lev needed rescuing. Even with his leg caught in a trap, his brother was a dangerous man.

Stefan began to work his way slowly through the garden to try to get a better angle on Ivanov. The man had to reveal his location soon and all Stefan needed was a single moment to take him out, because unlike Ivanov, Stefan didn't waste bullets—and he didn't miss.

THROUGH layers of sleep, Judith heard frantic voices and footsteps pounding through her house to her bedroom. It had to be a dream—or a nightmare. She'd just gone to sleep.

"Stupid security system is a total waste," she muttered and put the pillow over her head. She couldn't clear her brain enough to think properly let alone sort out the feminine voices calling to her.

"Judith! Get up! Wake up!"

Okay, that was definitely Rikki and she sounded scared and imperious at the same time. Because it was Rikki, Judith forced her leaden body to move. Nothing worked. Her arms and legs felt numb right along with her brain and she landed with a thud on the floor. Struggling into a sitting position, the sheet falling in a puddle around her, she gasped, realizing she was completely naked. There were marks of possession on her body she couldn't possibly hide, so she yanked up the sheet as Rikki raced into her room. Judith could hear the others rushing down the hall. Swearing under her breath, she managed to yank the sheet up to wrap herself in. She blinked rapidly, trying to clear her hazy vision. There was no sign of Stefan anywhere.

"Get up!" Rikki demanded. "Hurry."

Judith started to frown, took one look at Rikki's enormous eyes, black as midnight and very frightened and swallowed her protest. She nodded. The haze was beginning to clear, and she could recognize that something was really wrong.

"Give me a second, hon, I have to get dressed."

Her mind felt unusually fuzzy. As a rule she woke up sharp, but it was hard to think and even more difficult to get her body functioning. Rikki stepped out of her room, stopping the others in the hall and Judith hurried to her bathroom. "Do I need a robe, or clothes?" she called.

"Clothes!" five voices answered.

"Who's in trouble?" Judith fumbled around for the sink and splashed cold water on her face. "Tell me what's going on."

"Levi's in trouble. Hurry, Judith. He's hurt. I can feel it," Rikki said anxiously.

Stefan wasn't in bed with her. Her brain was so fried it took her this long to wonder where he'd mysteriously disappeared to. Where Levi was, Stefan was.

She hurried to her dresser, shimmied into a bra and underwear, tank and jeans and raced out of her bedroom, uncaring what she looked like. "Where are they? Is Thomas with him?"

She was proud that in her very befuddled state she'd managed to remember it was Thomas, not Stefan.

"I think so." Tension rang in Rikki's voice. "Hurry, Judith. I need you."

"You have to talk to us, Rikki," Blythe, always the voice of reason insisted. "We've answered your call, but we don't know what's wrong. Judith, help out here."

Judith had no idea how she was going to be of any assistance. She felt like she was moving through a fog, desperately trying to force one foot in front of the other. "Rikki, did Levi call to you for help?"

"I felt an explosion of pain. Here." She grabbed her calf. "It was horrible, like something was sawing through my leg. He cut it off abruptly, but I knew it was him. When it first happened, he was unguarded. He must have been in agony, but when I reached out for him, he said they were handling it. *Please*. I don't want to talk anymore. Let's just go."

"We can discuss it in the car then," Blythe decided. "Let's go."

Her sisters were already rushing down the stairs. Judith followed them, stumbling a little, trying to find her legs. "Where are they?"

"Sea Haven. I know they're in trouble. We've got to help them." There was a sob in Rikki's voice. She twisted her fingers together tightly.

The night air hit Judith, mist so thick it was nearly impossible to see her hand in front of her face. She could hear the water running out of her hoses and she glanced around her gardens. Rikki was very agitated for water to be answering her call with such ferocity. Her fears were catching, moving from woman to woman, until all of them were agitated. Judith, always careful to stay in control, yet had a difficult time with all of her sisters surrounding her, clearly upset.

It was impossible to control her natural empathy, not when her mind was so fuzzy and she could barely figure out what everyone was saying to her. Overhead, storm clouds boiled across the sky. The wind rose, howling through the trees, blowing leaves and debris into the air. In the dark, ominous clouds, whips of lightning lit the edges of the clouds, glowing red-hot.

Judith did her best to stay in control, but already, even before they all were in the close confines of the car, she could feel the other women's emotions rising in direct proportion to her own. And hers were swinging out of control because Rikki was so frightened for Levi.

"Would either of you like to explain what's going on?" Blythe asked calmly as they piled into the farm's suburban waiting. Blythe seemed the only one remaining grounded as she put the SUV in gear and raced down the driveway toward the ornate gate.

"Thomas is Levi's brother," Judith admitted. "He came here to warn Levi that the awful man who came here from Russia never bought the story that he was dead and came here to find Levi and kill him."

Stefan. Where are you? She reached for him, needing to know he was all right.

For a moment she thought she'd reached him. She actually felt his solid presence, but her brain was still hazy and the connection slipped away.

Lissa's breath hissed out. "I remember Inez talking about that man. His name was Petr Ivanov. He asked all sorts of questions around the village, in Fort Bragg, at Noyo Harbor and Albion. He even went to Jonas and said he represented the Russian government and was looking into the death of one of their citizens."

"He came into Judith's shop," Airiana added. "His aura was truly frightening. I'd never seen anything like it."

Judith remembered the sick feeling she'd gotten when Ivanov had come into her kaleidoscope shop asking questions. She'd barely been able to stay in the same room with him. She'd had the same sick feeling when Stefan had confessed he'd come to Sea Haven to warn his brother about the killer.

"Ivanov came to my house," Rikki said, dragging her weighted blanket around her for comfort. "Jonas brought him out. I thought I'd convinced him I'd never seen Levi."

"You must have done a good job," Judith consoled, "because he had no idea where Levi was, he came back looking for clues. Had he thought Levi was with you, he would have been spying on the farm."

"Why didn't Levi and Thomas just call Jonas?" Airiana asked. "He's the sheriff."

Judith's heart felt as if a vise was gripping it hard. She tasted fear in her mouth. Nothing could happen to Stefan, not now that she found him. She exchanged a long knowing look with Rikki. At least Rikki understood how frightened she really was.

"This man, this Ivanov, is a very scary killer. They worried that he would kill Jonas. They know Ivanov's reputation and felt that Jonas would be hampered by the law."

Blythe inhaled sharply as she fishtailed around the curve in the road leading to Highway 1. The sky had darkened ominously and now the clouds were boiling, rolling across the sky so thick and black that only the lightning lacing them provided any light in the unrelenting darkness.

"So they're taking the law into their own hands?" Blythe shot Judith a look of sheer reprimand.

"They didn't know where he was," Rikki defended. "They've been trying to flush him out every night."

Judith inhaled sharply, the edges of anger beginning to form as realization tried to penetrate. She turned her head slowly to look at Rikki. "*Every* night? What do you mean every night? Thomas was with me."

"Yes, but then Levi and Thomas went out around two and came back around four-thirty," Rikki explained, huddling deeper beneath the heavy blanket. "Levi says Thomas would go on his own, but Ivanov is here because of him and he feels he has no choice. They both are protecting Jonas." She chewed at her thumbnail betraying her agitation. "Levi is adamant that Ivanov would kill Jonas. I can tell he believes it."

"*Every* night?" Judith repeated. She could hear her heart roaring in her ears. Thunder boomed in the sky overhead and a fork of lightning streaked in a jagged fork from earth to sky and back. The crack was loud enough to shake the car.

"Calm down," Blythe said firmly. "Everyone needs to calm down."

Judith narrowed her eyes and pushed a shaky hand through her hair in agitation. There was no calming down, not now when suspicion was slipping into her mind. Not suspicion—knowledge. "I'm a light sleeper. How could I not know he was leaving the bed—the house?" She pressed her lips together, afraid she knew the answer. What had he said? "Russian recipe for sleeping"? He'd told her the truth and she hadn't understood.

The earth rolled and a small crack developed along a berm on the side of the highway.

"Maybe what the two of you were doing exhausted you," Lissa tried helpfully.

Stefan, where are you? She had to know he was alive and well before she decided to boil him in oil.

Her fear for him fed the other women's jumbled emotions in the close confines of the car as it streaked along the highway. Rushing parallel to them just over the cliffs was the sea, angry and turbulent now, reflecting the intensifying emotions of all the women in the car. The ocean rose up toward Rikki, huge swells crashing onto the bluffs, booming a warning, reaching toward the village of Sea Haven as if it might devour it.

"Rikki," Blythe said in a very low, firm voice, "calm down before you create a rogue wave that comes over the highway and takes us out to sea. Take a breath. *All* of you take a breath. We'll find him." She glanced over her shoulder at Judith. "Both of them."

"And then I'm *killing* Thomas," Judith hissed between clenched teeth. "With my bare hands. He has no idea what he's messing around with. Damn that man." Because she *always* woke up, no matter how soft the sound in the middle of the night. "Secret recipe, my ass," she muttered. "Who

do they think they are? Sea Haven is *our* home. Some psycho comes here and threatens us, our men, or Jonas, we're
not little sissy girls cowering in our houses. *Damn* that
man."

With each condemning word, the interior of the car
pulsed with her mounting fury and terrible fear. Glass shattered on the passenger's side.

"Hey!" Blythe raised her voice, taking the turn into Sea
Haven on two tires. "Breathe or something. Don't destroy
the car."

"I'm sorry," Judith hissed, "I'm just so . . . so upset.
Angry. Afraid. I have no idea what's happening to them.
Do you, Rikki?"

Rikki rocked back and forth beneath the weighted blanket. She shook her head. "He's telepathic, not me. I don't
know how to keep the connection if he isn't reaching for me,
not over such a distance. But I know he's really hurt."

Out on the ocean, a tower of water rose, spinning, racing
toward the bluffs. A second and then a third joined it. The
inside of the car bulged outward. Judith gulped air, desperate to control her anger and terror. Rikki fed her and she
fed the others and amplified Rikki's fear. It was a vicious
circle and she tried to concentrate on Blythe's voice.

"We need a plan."

"That plan is going to include calling Jonas," Blythe
stated, "the moment we know for certain what is going on."

"Agreed," Lissa and Airiana said aloud.

Lexi nodded her head. Rikki just rocked and stared
straight ahead.

Judith pressed her lips together. She had shared glimpses
of Stefan and Levi's childhood memories and she feared
that Jonas would be out of his depth with a man as perverted and sick as Petr Ivanov.

"We can park the car and go on foot; we'll have more
control that way," Judith decided. "Rikki and I can locate

the men and assess the situation. Call Jonas when we know
if the danger is real and we'll do our best to help them.
We've got enough power between us, if we can keep it under
control."

She'd never tried to weave all five elements together
when she was upset and angry. She felt every bit as angry as
the sea crashing against the bluffs. The street seemed completely deserted as Blythe pulled the car over on the main
street of town and hastily parked.

"Get out, all of you. And for God's sake, Judith, try to
tone it down. You're all over the place. You're boosting the
other elements until they're completely out of control."

The howling wind caught the cars doors and slammed
them closed, rocking the vehicle and rushing down the
empty street in a fury. A shelf cloud, ripples of various colors spread across the sky as the black, boiling clouds merged
together and burst open. Torrents of water poured down,
drenching the streets, pounding them in an uncompromis-
ing fury.

Judith knew Blythe was right, but now they were all
feeding one another, trading intense emotions that Judith
couldn't rein in. Rikki's storm gripped all of them, and the
sheer force of it was shocking.

Where are you? Judith demanded, searching for Stefan.

She reached out, pushing her spirit further than she'd
ever consciously tried before. Power swept through Sea
Haven, rattling windows and shaking buildings. The ground
buckled.

Judith?

She could feel Stefan's instant rejection, the impression
of great danger, pain cut off, and fear for her. She knew at
once that he was wounded. For a moment the world around
her disappeared and there was only Stefan. She caught
glimpses of blood, thick and congealed on his shoulder and
running down his arm. Her heart stuttered in her chest and

for a moment the edges of consciousness blackened. The earth buckled and a narrow crack raced down the shoulder of the street closest to the ocean.

Oh, God, you're hurt. Nothing else mattered. No one else mattered in that moment. She saw him and she saw her brother, fallen, bloody, lifeless.

Thunder crashed and lightning struck the street, exploding a small shrub, setting flames dancing and blackening the earth around it. The flames should have gone out with the drenching rain, but instead, they took on a life of their own, growing and spreading until they were a long train, rushing down the middle of the street as if the water was jet fuel.

Get out of here now. Ivanov is at his most dangerous when he's cornered.

A volley of shots rang out and Judith's heart skipped a beat. *Stefan!*

Levi!

Rikki's voice burst through Judith's head, anguished, terrified for him.

I'm all right, baby. Calm down a little, I'm drowning. That was definitely Levi, finding a little amusement in his wife's storm.

Judith realized she was connecting all of them, all five elements, Levi and Stefan. She even felt Blythe's presence.

Judith, since you're here, stay where you are. Keep out of sight. I'm going to use the boost of power to try to free Levi's leg. Stefan was the calm in the middle of the turbulent storm. *Levi, whatever you do, resist the impulse to move around. You know he set more traps.*

Then I'll have to find them and spring them before some innocent kid stumbles on them.

Judith couldn't fail to hear the pain in Levi's voice. He was every bit as calm as Stefan, but he was hurting.

Thomas. Even in the middle of a crisis, she noted Levi kept to Stefan's cover. *Don't take any chances. He's all over you.*

Stefan didn't reply and two more shots rang out. Lightning slammed to earth a street over and flames raced up and over the houses following the lightning. Fortunately Rikki's violent thunderstorm seemed to be able to keep the glowing blaze from setting the wood on fire.

"Lissa!" Blythe hissed her name. "Reel it in. I'm telling all of you, get control before something terrible happens."

"If we could see this Ivanov," Rikki said, "we could keep him away from both Stefan and Levi. Maybe even drive him out of the village."

Judith didn't bother to point out that Ivanov would surely return, he'd already come and gone once before, but Rikki did have a good idea.

"We came to keep him off our men," Judith affirmed, "so let's do it."

Blythe sighed. "You know not only are those men going to wring your necks, but so is Jonas. And I've got my cell phone out to dial. The storm's interfering with the signal so back it off, Judith."

Judith didn't care if Jonas was called, all she cared about was making certain Stefan and Levi weren't in immediate danger. She sprinted to the narrow space between two storefronts that connected the street to the one behind it where some of the residents had homes. Her sisters followed her. The moment they were close to the street, still hidden from view, she halted and peered cautiously around the corner.

She was disappointed when she couldn't locate any of the three men, but she knew she was much closer to the actual battle zone. The street pulsed with violent energy. A bullet splintered wood on the back gate of the neighboring house. The shot came from across the street, but she couldn't see anyone, nor could she see Stefan, but he had to be in that yard somewhere.

You hit? Levi asked.

No, he's fishing. But I've got to get that trap off you before he circles around.

"Why isn't he shooting back? They have enough weapons for a small army," Rikki said.

Judith shrugged, trying to pinpoint Stefan's exact location. She felt his concentration, an intense energy focused directly on an object a great distance from him. She caught the picture in her mind and nearly cried out. The surge of fear added to Rikki's mounting terror. Both caught a glimpse of the medieval, vicious-looking device—a modified bear trap with serrated teeth honed to a razor's edge.

Judith's breath caught in her throat. A collective gasp came from her sisters and Rikki gave a shattered cry.

Is that thing on your ankle, Levi?

Rikki's wail of horror was loud in Judith's mind, amplifying her own near panic.

Raindrops turned icy cold, pummeled the street in the form of small icy golf balls. The wind bit at the fences.

More like my calf, honey, but Stefan will get it open. Stay put and trust us to handle this. I need you out of harm's way.

The love in his voice only added to the mix of emotions the women were sharing. Clouds swirled and the wind blew sheets of rain down the street. In the center of the dark overhead mass, lightning danced and on the street, driven by the wind; a tower of flames rose high in spite of the rain—or maybe because of it. The flames fed by Lissa's fiery element.

Another volley of shots sprayed the dancing fire tower, but the sheer force of the wind caught the bullets midflight and held them hovering in the air.

"Airiana," Blythe hissed. "Stop playing with ammunition."

"Sorry," Airiana said. "I didn't mean to do it."

"At least those bullets won't go into someone's house," Judith pointed out.

Through it all, Stefan's concentration didn't waver. He seemed to be the eye of the storm. Everything around him was chaos, the hail pounding cars and rooftops, the wind swirling in a vicious twister rushing down the street to sweep up everything in its path. Stefan blocked it all out. Judith could feel his absolute composure.

Two shots rang out again in quick succession, and Judith winced, as they hit just past the fence into the thick shrubbery where she feared Stefan had taken cover. Stefan never flinched, keeping his mind focused on what he was doing, slowly separating the wick jaws clenched around Lev's ankle.

She actually felt the draw on her power and she gave him everything she could, reaching for that deep well inside of her to boost his abilities. Instantly, the lock on the gate close to her popped open with a rusty creak. Up and down the streets, gates flew open and doors unlatched.

"Whoops," Judith said. "Didn't mean for that to happen."

"Take control, Judith," Blythe urged. "I've called Jonas, but you can weave all the elements and push that man far away from Thomas and Levi. You weave them all together at the farm, you can do it here."

"Everyone's all over the place," Judith said, shaking her head.

Because you are, Stefan said. *You have the power and control, angel, you can handle anything. You just have to believe in yourself.*

Thomas.

Levi's voice was absolutely calm. He didn't say anything else, but Rikki moaned and Judith felt the tension in Stefan coil tighter. Not just tension. Resolve. Something in him changed, grew cold and she knew immediately what he was going to do.

Levi had spotted Ivanov coming back toward him.

"Rikki." Judith's voice rang with authority. "Locate Levi. Show him to me. Everything around him. Do it now. Take a deep breath, connect with him and let me see where he is."

Judith knew every street and yard in Sea Haven. She'd owned her shop for five years and she'd walked every street over those years, up and down, unable to contain her restless energy.

Levi? Rikki reached for her husband with every bit of strength she possessed, amplified a hundred fold by Judith's spirit element.

For one moment Judith was disoriented, her mind so divided she felt sick and knew she was feeling Levi's emotions, but she caught glimpses of an old water tower and a broken fence, a wooden cart partially sunk into the ground and filled with flowers. Triumph burst through her. She knew *exactly* where Levi was.

She could feel Stefan's absolute confidence in her. *I've seen you at work, angel.*

Judith took a breath, glanced over her shoulder at her sisters and raised her hands. At once the symphony began. Fire danced into the sky and rained embers, the wind pushing the wall of flames over the street, impossible to see through. Rain fell in sheets in front of the flames and behind it, building a tower that seemed impenetrable.

Stefan broke out of his cover, running behind the dancing wall of flames, across the street to the yard she was certain Ivanov had deserted. The fire and rain pushed forward, straight toward the yard behind where she was certain Levi was. In the distance, the sound of sirens penetrated the edge of her consciousness. Jonas was on the way.

Levi and I have illegal weapons on us. If you're going to trap Ivanov and keep him from hurting anyone, do it now. We have to be gone when your friend gets here.

Judith hurried across the street, behind Stefan, keeping Lissa's advancing wall of fire moving forward fast, pushed by Airiana's wind.

Levi, leaning heavily on a large branch, hobbled toward the far end of the yard where the wooden wagon with flowers lay. Blood ran heavily down the leg dragging along the uneven ground as he made his way toward the fence to get out of the assassin's minefield. Ivanov burst around the corner of a building, weapon out, aiming for Levi. Simultaneously, Stefan rushed from the other side, firing, the first bullet catching Ivanov and spinning him around.

Hoses reared up like angry snakes, water shooting out of the gaping mouths, whipping at the exterminator, driving him away from the two men, making it impossible to fire a shot. One hose lashed at him repeatedly, wrapped around his wrist and wrenched the gun from him. Ivanov dropped to the ground and crawled behind the shed. Stefan kept running across the yard, tackled Levi, taking him down and dragging him toward cover.

The shed exploded, wood flying outward as a heavy car burst through the front of the structure, aimed straight at Stefan and Levi. Even as Stefan wrapped his arms around his brother and rolled to try to get out of the path, the pounding water curved, formed a tunnel and engulfed the car. A second tunnel merged with the first, a violent wind that caught the car and spun it, pushing it away from the men, into the street and down toward the ocean.

Levi caught Stefan's arm and pressed his mouth to his brother's ear in order to be heard above the shrieking wind. "Get out of here now. Take the weapons, and get to the Jeep. Go back to the farm. Let me handle Jonas. If you're caught with all these guns, you'll go to jail. Jonas will take me to the hospital and Rikki and Blythe will stay with me. Judith, get him out of here now."

The sound of brakes screaming told them all that Ivanov was frantically trying to control his car. Judith kept the pressure on, pushing the vehicle almost into the sheriff's path before she eased up on the wind. Ivanov responded by shoving a machine gun out the driver side window and letting loose a barrage of bullets at the sheriff, spinning his car around and heading out of town. The sheriff's car followed, lights whirling, sirens blaring.

Judith directed the slashing rain over Ivanov's car, hoping to not only slow him down, but make it impossible for him to see Jonas or Aleksandr through the sheets of water pouring from the turbulent skies. More shots rang out and she dropped a twister of wind and water right over the car. Drawn to the sea, the wild cyclone swept the car closer and closer to the edge of the bluffs. It crashed through the wooden fence and tumbled onto the grass-covered bluff.

Judith nearly screamed in frustration, desperately trying to control the terrible force of five elements interwoven and feeding each other power and fear.

Lexi pushed dirt upward in an effort to stop the forward momentum of the vehicle. The twister whirled, the rain poured down and the car slid closer to the edge of the bluff. Judith tried to shut down the fury of the weave, easing back on the wind and rain. Lissa's flames had long since gone out. The car seemed to hesitate and then it went straight over the edge.

The storm collapsed in on itself. Judith slumped against the side of the building. "I tried to stop it," she whispered. "I wasn't trying to push him over the edge."

"You didn't," Stefan said. "Ivanov sent the car over. It went in a straight line."

"You've got to go," Levi reiterated as Rikki and Lexi reached his side. "Now, Thomas. And none of you can say he was here." He looked around at the women. "You don't have to lie, just leave him out of it. Ivanov was hunting *me*."

He wasn't satisfied until all of them nodded in agreement—even Blythe.

18

"YOU *drugged* me, you cretin," Judith accused the moment they were inside her house, whirling around to glare at Stefan, hands on hips. "In the chocolate—your old Russian recipe. You drugged me. And don't you dare tell me you didn't."

Stefan nodded his head. "I can see that was probably a mistake."

"*Probably*? It was *probably* a mistake?"

Judith looked around for something to throw at his head. All that she could find was a kaleidoscope sitting on the end table. She launched it at him, instantly regretting it, *not* because it might dent his thick skull but because she loved that kaleidoscope. It was one she'd created for all of her sisters, a mandala for each of them, and one for herself. Each of them had one in their homes.

The ornate cylinder stopped in midair, inches from him. Stefan reached out and carefully wrapped his fingers around the kaleidoscope and set it gently back on the end table, wincing a little as his bloodied arm protested.

"*Definitely* a mistake. I clearly should have said

definitely," he stated. "Do you have a first-aid kit? I think I need a couple of stitches." As a bid for sympathy, he thought a little reminder that he was wounded might be just the right touch.

Judith's scowl deepened. "Do you have to play hero all the time? You made me crazy with the way you were just *inviting* him to shoot you. You have a gun. Lots of guns. I didn't see you shooting back at him."

"I shot him," he defended, allowing his gaze to drift over her body.

Judith was drenched. Completely, utterly drenched and dripping water on the carpet. Her long hair hung in thick black tails and droplets of water beaded on her skin reminding him of dew on rose petals. Her clothes were nearly transparent and she was shivering continually, her teeth actually chattering, although she was so upset she didn't appear to notice. She was shivering and it wasn't all due to the cold. She believed herself responsible for a man's death and that sort of thing could take its toll on a civilian. She was bordering on shock.

Stefan frowned and took a step toward her. She stepped back and swift impatience crossed his hard features.

"Judith, you're soaked. We can do this after you've gotten in a warm bath."

When he saw her head shake, he turned his back on her and walked down the hall to her bedroom, stripping as he went. He wasn't about to argue with her. If she didn't follow him, he was going to do more than act a cretin, he was going to throw her over his shoulder and dump her shivering little ass in the bath.

His shoulder stung like hell and he had to limp with the heel of his boot missing. God, he was tired and worried about his brother. The last he'd seen of Levi, he'd been taken away in an ambulance. Stefan would never believe Ivanov was dead, not until he saw the body.

He piled his wet clothes in the sink, started Judith a bath

and wrapped a towel around himself, more for warmth than modesty. He was every bit as soaked as she was. He waited there in the bathroom, studying his arm. It was the second time he'd gotten nailed and he had a fresh chunk of muscle missing. His shoulders were just too broad for cat-and-mouse games with killers.

He heard her padding down the hall on her bare feet. The moment she stepped through the door he reached for the buttons on her jeans, yanking the waistband open and jerking the denim down to her thighs. "Off," he commanded. "Just take the damn things off and get in the bath." Even as he let go of her jeans, he caught her tank top and dragged the soaked material over her head, tossing it on top of his wet clothes before she could protest.

Judith steadied herself by placing a hand on his chest as she kicked off the wet jeans. "I'll look at your shoulder first."

"You'll get into the bath. You're shaking like a leaf. This is nothing I haven't had happen before. Hurts like hell, but won't kill me." He took her arm and urged to her toward the bathtub. "Get in. I'll take a shower and wrap it."

"You're so bossy," Judith complained, making a face at him as she stepped into the steaming water.

"Your teeth are chattering and if you shake any more you're going to break something." She was understandably upset, although he still wasn't entirely convinced of Levi's "truth under any circumstances policy," but if she wanted him to, he'd give it a try—as long as she wasn't in any danger. Of course, she'd handled herself very well and she'd probably use that as an argument. It wouldn't fly with him, but he'd listen.

"What did you mean when you said Ivanov drove his car off the cliff?"

"I doubt he was in it." There. That was the truth. Her face went white and he cursed his brother under his breath. "Go under the water and get your hair wet with hot water.

You're still cold, Judith. And don't worry about Ivanov. If he's still alive"—and he had no doubt in his mind Ivanov was alive and nursing his wounds somewhere—"we'll find him."

She narrowed her eyes at him. "By drugging me and going out every night to search for him?"

He caught up a towel and stood behind her until she did as he'd asked and dunked her long hair under the hot water. He waited until she wrung it out, and threw the thick mass over her shoulder with a careless gesture and a smoldering glare. He towel-dried the long, silky strands, rubbing and massaging her scalp to get her warm.

"I admitted that was a mistake, Judith," he said quietly. "I've never been in a relationship before, and my first instincts are always to protect you. I thought I was doing that. Apparently I was wrong."

She started to turn her head but he held her firmly, preventing her from moving while he dried her hair thoroughly. He realized he was vaguely angry. He wasn't used to acknowledging emotions and at first thought he was sharing her anger, but he had to admit, this time, the anger was all his.

"Is there still a doubt in your mind, because you don't sound sure?"

"Of course I have doubts. You could have been killed tonight. A million things could have gone wrong, Judith. I won't take chances with your life."

He didn't try to prevent the edge to his voice. His belly was in tight knots and he had a sick feeling in the pit of his stomach. Since the moment he had realized she was there in Sea Haven and there was nothing he could do about it, he'd felt anger at his lack of ability to control the situation. He *needed* her safe and she wasn't. He obviously wasn't like his brother who could watch his wife dive under the sea and put herself into harm's way. He had spent an entire lifetime alone and now that he'd found Judith, he found he couldn't handle her in danger.

His hand bunched in her hair in his hand and yanked her head back, taking her mouth before she could protest. The moment his mouth settled on hers, the moment his tongue swept inside that soft, hot haven, his world righted itself. He'd been off-kilter, but even anger tasted a lot like passion when he was kissing Judith.

"I know you're cold, angel. And you're angry with me, but I need you. Right now. Right here." He murmured the words against her soft lips and kissed her words away. He didn't know if she protested or acquiesced, nothing mattered but the feel and taste of her, the knowledge that she was alive and kissing him back.

He slipped one arm around her bare, wet back and lifted her, wincing a little when his arm protested. He didn't care that blood was still leaking from the wound and running down his arm, or that she was soaking wet. He *needed* her.

She turned in his arms, leaning over the back of the bathtub to reach him, feet still in the water, sliding her arms around his neck as she pressed her wet body against his. "I'm really angry with you," she whispered into his mouth, even as her lips moved over his, kissing him over and over.

He felt that edge of anger in her kiss, the sizzling passion rising with a needy demand. "That's okay, Judith," he whispered into the heat of her mouth. "Be angry with me later."

His mouth blazed a trail over her face, down her chin to her throat. He lifted her right out of the bathtub, uncaring of the water dripping onto the floor.

Judith's breath caught in her throat. "I'm no little pixie like Lexi or Airiana, Thomas. I'm tall, so I'm not a lightweight. You'll hurt yourself."

He kissed his way around to her neck, his teeth nipping, and his tongue dancing over her all that soft, enticing skin. "I want to eat you up, Judith."

"Your arm," she hissed, pulling back.

"Fuck my arm. Who gives a damn about my arm? Right now, I need one thing." He caught her leg and wrapped it around him. "I need to be inside you right now. Put your legs around my waist."

His voice had gone hoarse, the urgency in him catching him unawares. He didn't *need*. Not like this. Not as if his very life depended on it, yet he couldn't stop his hands from gripping her thighs, fingers digging deep as he raised her up. She hooked her ankles around his back. If he felt his arm protesting, it seriously didn't register. The only thing that mattered was this woman, being inside her body, joining them, skin to skin, heart to heart. He needed her melting into him, surrounding him with her scorching heat.

Whatever soul he had left was hers. His heart pounded in his ears. Blood roared, the thunder loud in his mind. *Save me, angel. Give yourself to me.*

He couldn't stand that he'd put her in danger, that he'd been the one she followed into hell, opening the way for a man like Ivanov to get to her. And there would be another and another after that. What right did he have to bring her into his world of shadows and death?

I'm so in love with you, Thomas. It doesn't matter. None of that matters. Just this. Just us. Love me. Show me you love me.

Judith placed both hands on his shoulders, rising over him, pressing her center down until the head of his heavy erection was tasting the hot slick honey pouring from her body in welcome.

Her soft voice filled his mind, slipping inside every shadow, erasing every doubt, driving him beyond sanity. He didn't wait. Didn't give her any time for adjustment. Lifting her in strong arms and slamming her over him, driving upward as he drove her down to seat her fully on him. Her body was tight and hot, all those silken folds strangling him with exquisite pleasure, giving way for his fierce invasion.

She cried out and threw her head back, twining her fingers together behind his neck for support. Her breasts swayed, her stomach muscles bunching and rippling as she began a furious ride under the demand of his hands. Heat blazed through him, seared him, righted him. The terrible fear tearing at him began to ease with every jackhammer surge. He drove into her hard and fast, needing the flames rushing through his bloodstream. Needing the fire engulfing his body, coming up from his toes to consume him— both of them—to weld them together, binding heart and soul even as flesh melted together.

Her breathless, mewling cries were sweet music he was coming to love. The sobbing, gasping pleas as she chanted his name shook him to his very core. He tightened his hold on her, uncaring of the passage of time, just losing himself in the scorching heat of her body, in the silk of her tight sheath and the pleasure rippling through him.

He couldn't believe she was his. Angry or not, she welcomed him, rode him hot and hard, a wild, crazy ride without inhibition, giving herself completely into his care. Her gasping cries grew more frantic and her nails dug into his neck. The tiny pinpoints of pain only made him hotter, more possessed in his frenzied need.

"Mine," he stated. "Say it to me. Now. Right now, Judith. Who do you belong to?"

Her eyes opened and she looked directly into his eyes. For a moment his heart stopped as he felt himself falling. Drowning.

"Stefan Prakenskii. I belong to him and I always will." Her words came out in soft little gasps of conviction because he hadn't stopped driving into her like a jacked up piston. "And he belongs to me." She threw back her head again, her breasts jutting up, jiggling madly, an erotic image he would hold in his mind for all time.

"Who do you love?"

"You, you bonehead." Her muscles clamped down

around him possessively, hot and tight and oh so perfect. "Always you."

The last vestiges of fear and anger melted away with her declaration. His fingers gripped her buttocks tighter and he lifted her, pulled her down while lighting streaked through his body and a song sang in his blood. Everything he'd ever been, ever done, had brought him to this place, to this woman. She was everything he'd ever been looking for. There was no one before her and there would be no one after her.

He didn't bother denying what he felt was love. It ran deep and strong and burned like fire. The emotion was so intense it was primal, shaking him to the very core of his existence. He wanted to wake up every morning to her. Go to sleep with his body wrapped tightly around hers. He wanted her to have his child—his children. He knew he wanted to live out the rest of his life with her by his side and when he died, he wanted to die in her arms.

Sensuous fire burned him from the inside out, taking him higher than he'd ever gone, pushing her limits until she could only cling to him, gasping, pleading, her soft cries growing more frantic. His body exploded like a fiery volcano, a rocket bursting through him, a total assault on his senses.

Her body clamped down on his, her muscles wrapped tight around his cock, strangling and fiery hot, dragging every last drop of his essence from his body while lightning streaked through his veins and rushed through his blood. This was what love felt like. All encompassing. A frenzied, insatiable need that left one completely wrung out, yet strangely at peace.

Judith dropped her head on his shoulder as her body continued to ripple with aftershocks, her breath coming in sobbing gasps, her eyes closed as if savoring him. He held her tight, wanting the closeness, the skin to skin contact while he stayed buried deep inside her, feeling absolute tenderness, an emotion he'd been unfamiliar with and now overwhelmed him.

"I could stay like this forever, buried deep inside you. You're a safe haven, Judith, a place I can be real," he whispered, trailing kissed down the side of her face to her neck.

"You are real," she answered, her mouth against his shoulder. "At least I think you are. You're really hurt, Thomas. You shouldn't be holding me like this."

"This is *exactly* what I should be doing. Russians are tough, angel." He kissed the top of her head as he allowed himself to slip out of her. And he did allow it. He might not want to, but he'd been rough with her and she needed the soothing heat of her bath water.

He lowered her back into the bathtub. "Do you need me to add hot water?"

Judith tilted her head back, looking up at him with her exotic eyes, more mysterious than ever with her sleek, gleaming hair, and sensual bone structure. "I need to know what's wrong, Thomas. If we're going to do this . . ."

He bunched her hair in his fist. "There is no *if*. We've both made that commitment, Judith, so don't try to put your foot out the door because you didn't like something I did. That will happen a lot before I figure out this relationship stuff."

Her dimple appeared, as if she was trying to suppress a smile. She couldn't suppress the sudden surge of happiness spreading through the room. "Relationship stuff?" she repeated. "I can see I'm going to have a tremendous amount of romantic apologies. Take your shower, Thomas, and we'll get your arm fixed. Suffice it to say, if you *ever* try drugging me again, I'll hit you over the head with a frying pan."

"You probably would."

"Don't doubt it for a minute."

Stefan found himself laughing. "You're so damn beautiful."

"Get in the shower, Thomas," Judith said in her firmest you'd-better-do-what-I-say voice.

He found he liked it when she bossed him around. There was something very sexy when a woman got all proprietary and dangerous with her man—and he liked being her man. He grinned at her and stepped under the rain shower head.

The hot water pushed exhaustion from his bones. He took his time, enjoying the pleasure of watching her take a bath while he showered. He'd been right about that bathtub, he could stand next to it and it would be just the right height for her to lean her head back against the high side, open her very sexy mouth and lavish attention on his suddenly aching cock. His hand dropped down, loosely circling his rapidly hardening flesh. The spray of water on the sensitive flesh only added to erotic fantasy.

"Stop it," she said, without turning her head.

"I haven't done anything—yet."

"You're going to fix that shoulder of yours."

"After." His voice was unconsciously commanding.

She turned her head and looked at him, eyes slumberous, a siren's tempting look on her face as her gaze drifted over him. She crooked her finger at him. "Come here. I think you're insatiable."

The purr in her voice hardened his cock even more. He shut off the water and walked toward her, holding her gaze with his. Judith's eyes smoldered with heat. She tilted her head back as she reached for him, her hands lovingly cupping his heavy sac, urging him closer. Stefan closed his eyes as her hot mouth closed over his throbbing, jerking flesh. She turned him into a steel spike immediately. All that hot silk closing around him as tight as any fist, but it was the look in her eyes that took his breath and added to the scorching heat coursing through his body.

He groaned with sheer pleasure as she sucked hard, drawing him deeper, her tongue working his shaft. Her mouth was nearly as much heaven as her body. She took her time, teasing, lavishing attention on him, tongue and fist, teasing the head of his cock and lapping at the shaft before she got serious, her mouth working him tightly.

He closed his eyes, ecstasy washing over him, the heat sliding up from his toes to his groin, rushing from his head to the his heavy erection. He couldn't stop himself from tracing her beloved face with gentle fingers while he watched himself disappear into the hot depths of her mouth. Her eyes, the high cheekbones, her soft inviting skin. His hand slid down her jaw, caressed her throat as he stepped a little closer, forcing her back so that he had a better angle to slip deeper.

He remained as passive as possible for as long as he was able before the sensations began to overcome his control. Stefan knew that a good part of his enjoyment was Judith's enjoyment, the way she offered herself to him. He took a little more control as the flames began burning hot in his veins, licking over his skin. He sank his cock an inch deeper and held her there for just a moment, allowing her to get used to the sensation before he pulled back.

She stroked the underside of the broad, sensitive head with her tongue, as if memorizing every line, rapt concentration on her face. His hands gripped her hair and held her still as he took over completely, sinking deeper than he'd ever gone and holding himself still.

"Swallow, angel." He bit out the instruction between his teeth.

The gripping tightness forced a groan from his throat. He eased back and found her tongue dragging deliberately against his pulsing vein. He began to set a rhythm, trying to find a balance she could keep up with, that wonderful swallowing sensation and her need for air. Bliss. Total bliss, her mouth and throat and tongue. He felt the boiling rise and gripped her hair tighter, the coiling tension in his body.

"Look at me. Keep looking at me." He could barely get the words out as the explosion started somewhere around his toes and burned through his thighs, jetting hard and fast while his blood thundered in his ears and his heart pounded with love.

Her eyes met his unflinchingly as she took him in, mouth working hungrily, and that love in her eyes as steady as a rock. For him. She'd seen the worst and best in him and she stuck with him, still gave him her love and loyalty. The last vestige of his anger slid away, as he realized she accepted his inability to understand relationships even more than he did. Judith would stand with him. The terrible roiling in his gut subsided and he found himself smiling down at the woman he loved, wrapped in the blanket of her natural serenity.

WALKING down the main street of Sea Haven in full view of the townspeople, while holding hands with Judith, felt strange and yet exhilarating. Across the street, the ocean acted up, waves pounding at the cliffs and bluffs. White spray rose high into the air, crashing over rocks, the sound a loud boom the wind caught and carried inland. Fingers of fog streamed toward the buildings and streets, brought in by the breeze coming in off the ocean.

"Most people here are bothered more by the wind than by the fog," Judith said, "but I love the wind and the storms here. I always feel like no one can quite tame this place."

Stefan liked that idea. He wasn't the type of man to stroll down the street, boldly holding a woman's hand. His gaze moved restlessly over rooftops and delved into alleyways, although a part of him enjoyed every moment of the new experience. He seemed to be having all his firsts with Judith. He was a man used to the roles he played and he was comfortable in society when he was undercover. If he meant to become Thomas Vincent and settle in Sea Haven, he would have to grow completely comfortable in the art world with Judith. She traveled and went to galleries and conventions. She taught classes. Where Judith went, Stefan would be going, but he would always have the wildness of this place to make him feel comfortable in his own skin.

A trickle of unease slipped into his mind. He took a quick look around. The fog was heavy and massing fast, veiling the buildings in a gray mist.

Judith turned her face up to the gathering mist and smiled. "I love our sea here. It's so wild, the mood changing every hour. It was so beautiful this morning at the farm and yet we drive a couple of miles and fog is pouring into town so fast and thick you can barely see your hand in front of your face."

Stefan knew his "honeymoon" with Judith was about to be over. He could feel the building tension in him as surely as he could recognize the building storm of an impending tornado. He always knew when trouble was close, and as they approached the art gallery, the hair on the back of his neck stood up and every cell in his body went on alert. Without conscious thought, he dropped Judith's hand, and crossed behind her, to put his body between hers and the buildings, rather than the street. Instincts were everything and he didn't question himself, he simply reacted.

"Let me go in first," he ordered as they neared the small lane between the buildings where Old Bill made his home. "Stay behind me until I clear the gallery."

Judith frowned at his grim face and taut, very domineering tone, but she didn't argue with him. As they passed Bill, she paused. The veteran was lying under his blanket, covering his head with one hand, shivering a little in the thick fog.

"Bill, do you need another blanket? What happened to your sleeping bag?"

The world was gray and somber, the sea crashing angrily against the bluff where Ivanov's car had gone over to the rocks below. Stefan took a long look around while Judith talked to the homeless man, aware, even as he studied roof-

tops and towers, that Bill made an attempt to sit up, coughed
and lay back down.

"Do you need a doctor?" Judith asked.

Bill shook his head and waved her away, clearly as inde-
pendent as ever.

Judith frowned at him. "If you aren't better tomorrow,
I'm bringing Lexi, Bill, and you know what that means.
She'll be making some horrible-tasting potion for you to
drink and you'll do it because no one can resist her, not
even you."

Bill made a muffled sound that could have been a snort
of laughter or agreement. Stefan urged Judith forward toward the gallery by taking her upper arm and tugging with
commanding strength. She shot him a scowl, her concern
for Bill overriding her good sense.

His radar screamed at him, his muscles coiling, ready to
spring into action. The weight of his gun was reassuring.
He had a knife strapped to his calf, one in his boot, another
up his sleeve and a small throwing knife taped between his
shoulder blades where he could reach and throw in less
than a second should there be need. With all that, he didn't
like Judith out in the open.

Now, Judith. Something's wrong. I can feel it. He hissed
the warning into her mind.

Judith flashed Bill a smile and lifted a hand toward the
older man, clearly still torn that she should insist on getting
him medical attention. *He hates doctors,* she explained, but
she began to stride toward the art gallery.

They'd gone no more than five feet, when two shadowy
figures stood up on the enclosed porch where they'd been
sitting in chairs. Stefan's heart sank. He recognized the
couple immediately. Inez Nelson and Frank Warner waited,
both looking distressed. Inez clearly wrung her hands,
twisting her fingers together in agitation.

"What is it, Inez?" Judith stepped forward, compassion

in her voice, on her face and in the hand she put out to touch the older woman's arm.

Stefan's natural inclination was to shield Judith from the couple. His warning system was so loud he could hear it booming through the blood thundering in his ears. He crowded close to Judith, his body sheltering hers protectively as he reached around her to shake Frank's hand. "Is something wrong?"

"I went into the gallery this morning to open up before you came," Inez explained, "and . . ." She trailed off. "You'll have to see. I've called Jonas."

Stefan swore softly to himself. The last thing he needed was a meddling sheriff around. He followed Inez and Frank into the gallery, keeping Judith in front of him, so that anyone on the street with a gun didn't have a chance to shoot her. Once inside, Stefan saw the damage immediately. Someone had dragged paintings off the wall and thrown them carelessly on the floor after taking canvases out of the frames and removing them from the stretcher bars.

"Who would do this?" Judith asked. "We don't get this kind of vandalism here. If those canvases aren't stretched soon, it will ruin the paintings. Most of those are oil, but a couple are acrylic and those will be more of a problem." She pressed her fingertips to her eyes. "All that work destroyed."

Stefan stepped closer to the paintings strewn around. Each of them was a painting Judith had done. He went still. This was deliberate. Ivanov sending a message? He took a quick look around at the banks of windows. He suddenly felt as if Judith was very exposed. He took her arm and pulled her away from the paintings, back into the shadowy interior where it would be more difficult for a sniper to get a clear shot.

"Inez, they look like they're my work," Judith said, one hand going to her throat defensively. "Are they all my paintings?"

Stefan thought she looked very vulnerable, and his heart turned over. He curled his arm around her waist and pulled her tight against him. *We'll get to the bottom of this, angel.*

"They didn't destroy the artwork," Inez pointed out hastily. "They removed the canvas from the stretcher bars. You can fix them, can't you, Judith? After Jonas sees them, take them back to your studio and fix them before they're ruined."

"He'll want to keep them for evidence," Judith pointed out.

"Well, he can't. He can photograph them and if that's not good enough, too bad. We'll let it go, because the gallery can't afford to take that kind of loss," Inez said heatedly. "And we're not losing all of your work."

"Could the vandals have been looking for something," Stefan said, watching Judith closely.

"What could they possibly be looking for beneath the canvas?" Judith asked. "I stretch the canvases myself. They're just wrapped around the stretcher bar and stapled with oversized stainless steel staples to keep the canvas taut."

"Where do you get your stretcher bars?" Frank asked. He cleared his throat, glanced at Stefan and then at Inez. "Remember, Judith, the trouble I got into a few years back."

The Russian mob had gotten their hooks into Frank and had run stolen treasures through his art gallery. He'd gone to prison for his part in the smuggling operation.

Judith shook her head. "The stretcher bars can be picked up anywhere—at any art supply store. There isn't anything special about them."

"The canvases?" Inez asked.

Judith frowned. "Like most artists, I stretch my own canvas so I purchase rolls of canvas from an art supply store. Sometimes I reuse canvases, but again, there's nothing special about them."

Stefan could feel her mind working, puzzling, trying to

figure out why her work was chosen to vandalize while all the other artwork remained intact. On high alert, he felt the twinge of power that seemed to precede Jonas Harrington as he entered the gallery. Keeping his arm around Judith, he observed the sheriff who immediately put his arm around Inez to comfort her, but his sharp gaze went to Stefan and the way he was holding Judith so protectively.

"Have you heard anything on Levi?" Jonas greeted Judith. "I meant to check on him yesterday, but time got away from me."

"He's back home," Judith said. "Limping around, but he's fine."

Jonas kept his gaze steadily on Judith. "That storm the other night, Hannah said it wasn't natural. The surge of power was outrageous and the combination of wind, water and even earthquakes didn't make sense. Some people reported seeing a tower of flames."

Stefan tightened his arm around Judith. *Be very careful, angel, he's fishing.*

He felt the hesitation in her. She didn't like to lie. She pressed her lips together and then sighed. "You know Rikki has an affinity for water. Levi was in danger. I think emotions were running high and for a good reason. That man had been here before hunting Levi."

"We found a mess inside the small house Ivanov had rented," Jonas said. "Blood everywhere. Too much blood and it was human. Someone died in there and it wasn't pretty. There were shreds of material from a down jacket, very old jeans and a sleeping bag."

"Oh no," Inez said in horror. "Has anyone been reported missing?"

Jonas shook his head. "Not so far. And Danny and Trudy Granite's dog was killed as well the same night. Their son, Davy, was devastated." His piercing gaze jumped to Stefan. "You wouldn't know anything about that, would you?"

"How would I know?" Stefan countered a little belligerently. He was Thomas Vincent, an American businessman about to buy an art gallery that had been vandalized.

"Just being thorough," Jonas said.

"I'm about to make an offer on this gallery," Stefan said. "I think it's fairly common knowledge in this town that I'm here for that purpose. Quite a lot of property is involved. This art gallery and building, but Frank also is thinking of selling the entire next block with those buildings as well. Maybe someone here doesn't want an outsider to make that purchase."

Inez gasped and clutched Frank who leaned into her, his arm circling her waist.

"I can't imagine anyone would want to sabotage the deal," Frank said firmly, more for Inez's benefit than from conviction.

"Something like this wouldn't scare me off," Stefan assured. "Judith can stretch the canvases again and the paintings will be fine. I intend to make an offer as soon as I'm finished going through the inventory and books."

Judith glanced at the two acrylic landscapes. "I need to work on this artwork fast. Jonas, I'll have to take all the damaged paintings back to my studio with me."

"I'll get to work photographing everything," Jonas said immediately. "Why don't you go get some coffee, Inez? This shouldn't take too long."

Stefan had to hand it to the sheriff. Inez was not a young woman and she was truly distressed. He guessed that financially, she and Frank needed the gallery to sell and they were both afraid, in spite of his assurances, he'd back out of the deal.

"Come on," Judith said, taking charge. "Let's all go down to the coffee shop. We can visit while Jonas is working on this. Frank, I can fix the paintings, so no worries."

She flashed a smile at the couple, but Stefan could feel anxiety. As always, in public, Judith hid her emotions, refusing to allow them to spill out and affect others around her.

She kept that control very carefully. He ran his hand lovingly down her spine just to remind her he was there and knew how concerned and distressed she was that someone would do such a thing to her work.

He doubted Ivanov had vandalized the paintings. It wasn't the exterminator's style. He'd never even think about such a thing unless it was bait to draw everyone into a building to blow it up around them. And that meant only one thing. Jean-Claude La Roux had made his way to Sea Haven. He hadn't wasted any time. If he was searching Judith's paintings, removing the canvases from the stretcher bars, that meant he'd hidden the microchip in between the canvas and the stretcher bar. Judith must have taken the painting with her when she left.

Why? Why, if she was running for her life, would she take a painting with her? That made no sense to him. If she'd known about the microchip, and had deliberately taken it with her, why hadn't she tried to sell it on the black market? His life was about to become very complicated. Judith had to be questioned and she wouldn't like that he had misled her, failing to admit he was working for the Russian government to recover the microchip.

The four of them left Jonas to his work, stepping outside onto the covered porch. The fog had come in even thicker, turning the world into a thick gray mist. The outline of trees and buildings were shadowed and vague. The knots in Stefan's stomach hadn't let up and the tension in him coiled tighter than ever, knowing he was going to have to get Judith home and find the microchip. Aside from the threat of Ivanov, La Roux was lurking around. He was certain of it.

Judith drew her sweater closer around her. "It's definitely cold today."

"And a little dreary," Inez added. "I don't mind the fog as a rule, but when it's like this, you can't see anything, it can get depressing."

Frank wrapped his arm around her shoulder and smiled

down at her. "Not if we're home watching an old movie and eating popcorn."

Inez brightened immediately. "That's true. And on a stormy day, we can find the old-fashioned scary films, like Hitchcock's. I love those." She turned a smile on Stefan. "Do you enjoy old movies?"

Entertainment films weren't shown to the boys and girls training in the camps he'd grown up in and his job didn't exactly send him to the theaters often. He gave a casual shrug. "The movies I've managed to see, I've really enjoyed. Watching old films when it's foggy or stormy out sounds good to me. I'm ready to settle down and enjoy life a bit."

It was surprising to him when he said the words, how much he meant them. He was more than ready to trade a life in the shadows for a life with Judith. A real life. The home, the kids, the farm, traveling to kaleidoscope conventions, he wanted the entire package.

"Do you work a lot?" Inez asked as they started down the sidewalk in the direction of the small local coffee shop.

"I travel a lot for work," Stefan admitted. "It can get old. It's time I settled down."

His radar refused to fade away. The fog was a definite problem when he needed to see an enemy coming toward him. He didn't like the closed in feeling the blanket of heavy mist gave him. Every step he took added to that coiling tension. He was missing something important and his warning system was screaming at him to heed it. Judith and Inez chattered away, and he tuned them out, listening for telltale sounds, running footsteps, anything at all that might tell him there was danger close.

Ivanov had been wounded, there was no doubt in his mind that Stefan's bullet had taken him down, but there was no way he'd gone over the cliff with that car the way the cops thought he had. Stefan didn't believe it for a moment. He'd escaped and slipped away to another lair, shedding his skin and growing a new one in the way he'd been taught.

His mind began a rapid assessment, fitting pieces together, all the while his warning system shrieked at him. *Where's your sleeping bag, Bill?* Judith's voice. Shed his skin, grow a new one. A soft sound penetrated the thick layer of fog. Muffled. Stealthy. *Found material that could have been a sleeping bag.* Jonas's voice.

Instincts shouting to be heard, Stefan shoved Judith and Inez backward hard enough for them to fall to the sidewalk in a heap, even as he flung his body into the small opening between the two buildings. The sound of a gunshot was loud, reverberating through the narrow passageway. Far away, he heard yelling, a high-pitched scream, even as something smashed into his chest, driving him backward. He refused to go down, refused to black out, refused to let panic take him when he couldn't breathe. He dug his heels in, and dove forward, tackling Old Bill.

19

STEFAN and Ivanov crashed together, the sound of their bodies like a clap of thunder there in the tiny alley. Stefan's chest burned like hell. It felt as though he'd been hit with a train, but the only thing that mattered, the one thing he focused on, was keeping Ivanov's gun from firing toward Judith. He managed to catch Ivanov's gun hand and apply pressure backward against his wrist. Even as he did, the assassin whipped up his left hand, the razor-sharp knife rushing toward Stefan's neck.

Judith scrambled to her feet, yelling frantically for Jonas, rushing toward the two struggling men. The only weapon she had was her oversized purse and she smashed Ivanov over the head as the two men grappled for the weapons.

Stefan clamped down like a vise on Ivanov's left hand, driving him backward and away from Judith. The two men crashed into the side of the building so hard the building shook. Both grunted, Stefan bringing up his knee to take the exterminator down to the ground. Ivanov's breath left his body in a whoosh of air, and he went down, but his grip on both weapons remained vise-like.

"Out of the way, out of the way," Jonas commanded.

"Judith, get out of there." He reached out and physically removed her by yanking her away from the two men struggling in the close confines of the two buildings.

Out of the corner of his eye, Stefan could see the sheriff, gun drawn, trying to get a shot at Ivanov. Deliberately, he tightened his grip on the killer.

"Get off me. Are you crazy?" Playing the part of the innocent American businessman struggling for his life required a little drama.

He smashed Ivanov's gun hand into the ground while retaining an unshakable grip on the knife hand. He used a burst of strength, turning the knife toward Ivanov's chest even as he writhed as if Ivanov was getting the better of him, forcing the killer to roll over and sprawl on top of him, giving the sheriff a target. Using the thick fog for cover, he grunted a lot, repeated his plea for Ivanov to get off of him and forced the gun hand to turn slowly, relentlessly in the direction of his own head.

"Drop your weapon," Jonas said. "I'm a sheriff and I'm giving you an order."

Ivanov broke out in a sweat, making him slippery, breathing his vengeful hatred into Stefan's face. Stefan had him in a death grip, fingers digging into tendons and pressure points, fully controlling Ivanov's actions.

"Drop the gun," Jonas commanded, stepping closer. "Drop it now."

Stefan renewed his grip on the knife, forcing it closer to Ivanov's chest under cover of the struggling killer's body and the thick mist. They stared into each other's eyes, Ivanov recognizing Stefan's superior physical strength. His eyes widened in horror, in the recognition that he was about to die. He could try to surrender to the sheriff, but the grip on his gun hand, turning the weapon on Stefan would preclude any talk.

"Damn it, drop the weapon," Jonas said, resolve already creeping into his voice.

Deliberately Stefan turned his head to look at the gun slowly turning toward him, forcing a look of fear onto his face. He shoved the knife upward into Ivanov's heart simultaneously as the sheriff's shot rang out. Blood and brain splattered across his head and shoulders. Ivanov's body slumped heavily over him.

Stefan shoved Ivanov to one side and lay there, breathing hard. Judith ran to him in spite of Jonas's restraining hand and biting command. Wedged between her, the building and the killer, Stefan used the cover of her body and the fog to transfer his knives and gun into her oversized bag, one careful move at a time, all the while making a good show of gasping for breath and seeming to pat himself down for wounds. Judith ignored his actions, although he saw her glance once to his hand sliding into her bag. She was too busy examining him for injuries.

He shot you. I know he did. I saw him.

Her anxiety spilled over, the emotion spreading to the gathering crowd.

I'm wearing a vest, honey. I knew Ivanov was still alive and I figured he'd come at me. I had too much to lose not to take a few precautions. Let's just keep that to ourselves.

Jonas had already stepped forward and kicked Ivanov's gun away from the dead man's outstretched hand. Following every precaution, the sheriff quickly cuffed Ivanov's hands behind his back.

"I think he's dead, Jonas," Judith said, her voice gentle, filled with compassion.

"I've seen men still alive after taking six or seven bullets. You never know." He reached to check for a pulse, but with half of the back of Ivanov's head gone, it was a moot point.

He spoke into his radio, answered a couple of questions and turned his attention to Stefan. "You all right?"

"I don't know yet," Stefan said, managing to look very shaken. "Give me a minute. And thanks. You saved my life."

"You hit?" Jonas persisted.

"No. Yes. I was wearing a vest because I didn't have my bodyguards with me."

Jonas's gaze sharpened. "You wear a vest often?"

Stefan nodded. "More than I'd like." He appeared to work hard to control his breathing.

"Judith, go sit on the steps of the art gallery," Jonas ordered. "Inez, if you'd sit on the porch there, I'd appreciate it. And Frank, please go sit in the patrol car until the others get here. I just shot and killed his man, there'll be an investigation and we want it by the book."

Inez raised her chin. "I'll sit in the patrol car," she stated firmly, reminding Jonas silently that Frank had already suffered that indignity and didn't need to do so again. "Judith, honey, you take the porch and get out of this wet fog."

The sheriff waited until the other witnesses had done as he asked. "I've got my recorder on," Jonas advised Stefan. "Can you tell me what happened?"

"It all happened so fast, I honestly don't exactly know," Stefan continued, making a show of allowing the sheriff to help him into a sitting position. "Maybe Frank or Inez can tell you. I just saw the old man come up out of his blanket with a gun. He was muttering a lot to himself when we stopped earlier. Judith spoke to him, but he really didn't answer her. He must have been ill and thinking he was in the war or something." Stefan ran a shaky hand through his hair, pulled it away covered in blood and visibly winced.

Jonas pulled open Stefan's bloody shirt and whistled. "Good thing you were wearing this. That bullet would have killed you. We'll have the EMTs take a look at you."

"Just hurts like a son of a bitch. Man, I'm sorry you had to shoot him, but if you hadn't, I don't know how much longer I could keep him from turning that gun on me. I could see it inching around and there wasn't a damn thing I could do about it."

"Can you get to your feet?"

"Yeah. I'm just a little shaken." Stefan stood up. He

managed a wan grin, flicking a quick look toward Judith on the enclosed porch of the gallery. She had her tote bag next to her. "I haven't done this sort of thing since I left the service and that was far longer ago than I want to admit to."

"I've got to pat you down for weapons. You have any on you?"

Stefan made a quick assessment, but he was certain he'd gotten all them transferred to Judith's tote bag. He submitted to Jonas's quick, but thorough weapons' sweep. In the distance, sirens could be heard.

Stepping back away from Jonas he shook his head, looking down at the dead body. "Thanks again, man, you definitely saved my life. I only spoke to the old man a couple of times. Gave him coffee once and a few bills I had in my wallet. I don't know what any of us did to provoke this. Judith noticed he was acting sick and talked to him about going to a doctor. Maybe that's what set him off." He let the words tumble out fast, as if he couldn't stop talking.

Jonas crouched beside Ivanov. "This isn't Old Bill. Have you ever seen him before?"

Stefan took a good look at Ivanov's face. He frowned and shook his head, shrugging. "If I have, I don't remember. I travel a lot and I make a lot of enemies."

"You thought he was trying to kill you?"

Stefan shook his head again. "I just saw the gun and don't remember too much after that." He touched his chest. "He got off the one shot. I remember feeling like I got hit by a truck. To be honest, I don't even remember hearing it. I just felt something slam into my chest very hard."

"We'll need your clothes and the vest." Jonas waited a moment, his eyes never leaving Stefan's face. "The knife is yours?"

Stefan frowned and looked closer at Ivanov, as if for the first time noticing that a knife had gone deep into the chest of the deceased. He shook his head. "No. When I grabbed his gun hand, the knife came at me fast from the other side.

I never touched it. Just his wrist. All I did was hang on. All I really remember was hanging on and thinking he was damn strong for such an old man. He must have fallen on it when you shot him. I can't even tell you where that hand was, I was more worried about his gun."

Officers showed up, taking over, removing Jonas immediately, taking his gun, and separating him from Stefan. Stefan had to repeat his story to another officer, reiterating that the sheriff had saved his life. Someone taped off the area while another led him into the gallery to change from his clothes to a paper zip-up jumpsuit. His clothes and vest disappeared into evidence bags. He could see officers talking to Judith and others to Frank and Inez, all separately.

Where is the bag?

Judith's head went up and she looked at him across the crowd of officers. *In the gallery. I put it behind the counter. I can just see the corner of it sticking out a little.* She was still inside the large enclosed porch and looking through the windows inside the art gallery. *I put it inside when I saw Jonas searching you.*

Keep looking at it.

Like the lock, he just needed the picture in his mind, but still, utilizing his greatest gift while police officers surrounded him required tremendous focus. Stefan took a breath and "pushed" the large tote back far back behind the counter out of sight.

Judith's eyes widened. *When you stopped the kaleidoscope in midair when I threw it at you I knew you were capable of telekinesis. I have to say, that's a rather sexy talent.*

He flashed her a wan smile. *Keep that in mind when you try to run out the door on me.*

I don't plan on doing that any time soon, she assured.

Stefan wasn't so certain of that. He was going to have to talk to her about Jean-Claude La Roux. She'd thought he'd made a full disclosure to her admitting he was Lev's

brother. She'd agreed to keep his real identity a secret and
live with him as Thomas Vincent, but he couldn't imagine
she would be so accepting of his part in her past.

He shook his head when an EMT insisted on examining
him, but allowed an officer to photograph the huge purple
bruise blossoming across his chest over his heart. The man
raised an eyebrow at the myriad of scars, but nodded his
head when Stefan murmured something about serving in
the military.

The body of Ivanov was put in a special body bag and
tagged with a blue coroner's seal before it was taken away.
All the while, he kept his eye on everyone inside the art
gallery. Even with the bag safe behind the counter, he still
felt vulnerable. So far no one had gone near it, no one really
paying attention to the gallery with the dead body outside.

A crowd had gathered around outside the gallery, walking around the crime tape and talking all at once. He was
grateful for the heavy fog that seemed to have worsened
instead of lifted. Inez waved Blythe through the crowd and
indicated to the guard at the door that she could come in
now that the police were finished questioning the witnesses.

Stefan could see that Inez and Frank looked exhausted.
He motioned to Judith and indicated the couple as Blythe
hugged them both.

Judith responded immediately. "We've all given are
statements. Can you clear out the gallery and let us recoup
a little?" she asked the officer at the door.

He nodded and waved everyone else out, stepped out
onto the enclosed porch and closed the door, effectively
sealing out the chaos and noise in the street.

"Mr. Vincent," Inez said, turning to him. "Thank you. If
it wasn't for you, we'd probably all be dead. I still can't
believe you reacted so quickly."

He shrugged it off and caught her arm gently. "You're
hurt, Inez. You should have the EMTs look at this."

"I'm old," she said, with a wan smile. "I don't bounce so good. It's a bruise, nothing more."

Blythe handed Stefan a package. "Hannah, Jonas's wife called me and told me what happened. She suggested I bring you clothes. They took Jonas's uniform and everything else from him and he's at the hospital. They always take blood in an officer involved homicide . . ."

"*Homicide?*" Inez protested. "Jonas had no choice. That man was trying to kill Mr. Vincent. He would have killed all of us. Jonas wasn't given a choice."

Blythe hugged her. "Jonas will be fine. Any time someone is killed like that, whether by an officer or someone else, it's considered a homicide. They'll investigate, they have your statements and Jonas will be fine. Don't worry about him, Inez. Hannah's worried enough for all of us. You might want to drop by and see her later, just to check on her."

"Yes. Yes, that's a good idea," Inez agreed. Her shoulders sagged and she sank into a chair. "This has been such a terrible day. First someone vandalized the gallery and then that horrible man tried to kill us." She looked around the room, a look of worry on her face. "If he had Bill's sleeping place and his things, where's Bill?"

There was a small silence. Blythe sighed. "I'm so sorry, Inez. I know you went to high school with Bill."

"He really was a good man. He lost his way in the war, that's all," Inez said. "He belonged to the village. We all took care of him. I don't understand any of them. Why would that man want to hurt Bill and then take his place?"

"We may never know the answer," Blythe said.

Stefan took the clothes Blythe brought him into the back and changed. He would never consider himself modest, but a paper jumpsuit didn't give him a lot of confidence in its ability to stay together. His only consolation was the thought that Jonas Harrington had to suffer the indignity of wearing one as well.

Judith had stayed across the room from him most of the time, but he could see her need to be held and comforted even if she didn't know it. He couldn't go to her with another man's blood all over him and he was very grateful for the small shower stall someone had installed some years earlier. It didn't work the best, with low water pressure and the water scalding hot one moment and then icy cold the next, but with a little time he learned the trick of it.

He looked in the mirror. Damn. He was tired and it showed in his face. For the first time he allowed elation to sweep through him. Petr Ivanov was dead. He could never be a threat to Lev again. Or to Stefan and his relationship with Judith. He only had one more complication to get rid of and his life was his own. He had to find the microchip and get it home to Russia where it belonged.

But first, before anything else, he had to hold his woman close and see for himself that she was all right. Barefoot, he walked out of the back room and right up to her, uncaring what any of them thought. He pulled her close to him, fitting her snugly against his body, his fingers gripping her hips to guide her into him. His arms slid around her back, his body protective, hard and very much in control.

Judith melted into him, sagging against him as if in relief. She turned her face up to his, dark gaze moving over him. He bent his head and took her mouth, his lips moving over hers, shaping hers, teeth tugging at her lower lip. His tongue swept inside, and he kissed her as if his very survival depended on her—and for him, it did.

He pulled back enough to rest his forehead against hers, his hand bunched at the nape of her hair. "I might have to wrap you in cotton and put you in a safe," he whispered.

"I was thinking the same thing about you," she said, her hands sliding to the back of his neck while she lifted her face for another kiss.

Stefan took his time, before he turned to the others,

sliding his arm around Judith to keep her close. "Frank, I'm definitely interested in purchasing the gallery. Give me a little time to look at the books to make you a decent offer."

Inez beamed at him. She shot a quick, pleased look at Frank. "Judith knows the inventory better than anyone else and what the real value is, but we're both happy to help you in any way possible."

"You're planning on settling here permanently then," Blythe said.

Stefan couldn't tell whether she was pleased or not. Blythe was very reserved around him. "Very permanently," he announced firmly. "I've asked Judith to marry me and she's said yes."

Judith's hand tried to slip from his, but he held it tight. "You didn't exactly ask me."

"Do you need me to go down on my knees? Because, for you, I could manage it."

Judith blushed. He'd been down on his knees in her kaleidoscope studio and there was no way to forget it. "No." Her eyes went wide. "Thomas, I have to get back to my painting studio immediately. Otherwise all this artwork will be ruined."

"The paintings are insured," Inez said soothingly. "It's such a terrible desecration of your work, Judith, but if you're worried about Frank and me, that's the one thing we made certain of—that we kept up the insurance."

"I don't understand," Blythe said. "What happened?"

"Someone broke in and vandalized the gallery," Frank explained. "They took all of Judith's artwork out of the frames and off the stretcher bars."

"I have to put them back on or the paint will be ruined," Judith said.

"Are you really going to marry Mr. Vincent? Because if you are, I'm calling him Thomas," Inez said.

"She's going to marry me," Stefan said. "She's just being difficult because I haven't found the perfect ring yet." He carried Judith's left hand to his mouth, his thumb pressing into the center over his mark on her.

"I don't care about the ring," Judith said. "It's just that you've swept me off my feet so fast I haven't had time to think."

"Always the best way with a woman, right Frank?" Stefan looked for help.

Frank reached over and took Inez's hand. "I'll have to agree with that. It took me quite a few years to reach the point where I realized if I was going to get my chance with this woman, I was going to have to just take it."

Inez blushed. "Silly man." But she sounded pleased.

"I'll get Judith home so she can work on these paintings," Stefan said. His hand slid down her spine to rest on the curve of her hip a bit possessively.

"I don't know how you're going to get to your car without everyone mobbing you," Blythe said. "Give me your car keys and I'll bring it around for you."

When he'd stripped off his clothes, he'd tossed his wallet and car keys on the desk. He kissed Judith's hand and moved around the counter to the other side of the desk. His wallet was in plain sight, but the keys had fallen between a stack of papers and a book. He reached for them, his gaze running a quick scan of the desk. It didn't seem right to him. He'd looked at the books with Judith a few nights earlier, but when they'd left, everything had been stacked neatly. None of the officers had come around behind the counter.

"Frank, did you or Inez touch anything on this desk today?"

Frank shook his head. "When we came in and saw the paintings, we checked all the inventory after we called Jonas, and the safe, but we didn't have money here and there isn't anything of value in the desk. I just glanced at it."

"Someone's gone through the papers since I was here the other night."

"Are you certain?" Judith asked, coming up behind him. She wrapped an arm around his waist and peered over his shoulder.

"Yes." He pushed her hand away when she reached for a paper. "Let me. After what happened earlier, I'm not taking any chances with you."

Using the end of a pencil, he pushed the papers around, separating each one. In the middle of the pile of invoices was a single photograph. Judith and Stefan were locking the door of the art gallery, Stefan's body only inches from Judith's, looking every inch possessive.

Across the picture was a single line written with a black fine-point marker. *Who is he, Judith?*

Stefan felt her shock. Her body stiffened, fingers curling hard into his shoulder, nails biting deep.

Oh God, Thomas, it's him. I know it's him.

Her voice trembled and stark images of her brother's death pushed into his mind. At once the room filled with overwhelming sadness and sheer terror. Judith had gone pale, but Frank and Inez actually staggered, reaching out for chairs.

Easy angel. Take a breath. Focusing and breathing through that sudden violent storm of emotion was difficult.

He palmed the photograph and casually turned, pulling her into his arms and sliding the picture into his pocket with practiced smoothness.

Jean-Claude's in France. In prison. Who could have done this? He can't be here—can he? Judith pressed her face tighter against his shoulder. *It's him. I know it is. I can feel him.*

"What is it?" Frank asked, pressing a trembling hand over his heart.

Angel, I'm here. This man is nothing. He can't hurt you

or anyone else you love, not with me standing in his way.
Stefan had to find a way to calm her down before the art
gallery filled with such dark horror that the elderly couple
had heart attacks.

"I don't think it's anything, Frank," he assured as he
tightened his hold on Judith, his arms a steel cage, his body
fiercely protective. "The vandal most likely leafed through
things on the desk looking for something of value. He didn't
know artwork or he would have taken your most valuable
pieces."

He could feel Judith desperately trying to regain control.
Jean-Claude was a monster from her past and he'd grown
into such a demon over the last five years he wasn't certain
Judith could get a realistic perspective on him.

"Judith." Blythe's voice was pitched very calm, cutting
through the thick sorrow and horror. "There's nothing we
can't face together. We're stronger than our pasts. All of us.
Thomas is here with you and so is Levi. Whatever you're
afraid of, you aren't alone this time."

Stefan felt his warning radar rise. Blythe. The mystery
woman. She was far more than she appeared. It took control
and power to push through the surge of emotional energy
Judith was throwing off. Her emotion had amplified even
more as Frank and Inez reacted. He felt power coming at him
in waves, battering him, like the sea, continually and without
mercy pounding away at his emotions. He managed to stay
above it all and at the same time, work to shield the others in
the room, but Blythe, although clearly feeling Judith's influence, remained unscathed by the surges of power.

"Maybe it was a kid," Inez ventured, her hands shaking,
obviously trying to appease Judith. "I know most of them
and I can't think of any who would want to hurt Frank or
me, but maybe I've had to talk sternly to one or two when
they've come into the grocery store during their lunch
break. They don't try to steal, I've never had that problem,
but they are smoking pot and they reek."

"Whoever it was," Stefan said firmly, "he or she didn't take anything of value and if I get Judith home, she can stretch these paintings before they're ruined." He held out the car keys to Blythe. "I would greatly appreciate it if you would bring Judith's car around and then reassure her sisters that she's fine, but needs to work."

Blythe's eyes met his over Judith's shoulder. She slowly reached for the keys, as if she hadn't quite made up her mind about him. "Thank you for saving Judith, Inez and Frank," she said quietly as she took the keys. "All of them said if it wasn't for you, that killer would have probably shot them all."

"I don't know about that, Blythe," Stefan replied in the same calming, quiet voice. Already Judith was managing to pull her emotions back from the others. "But I can tell you nothing will harm Judith while I'm around."

Blythe nodded. "That's good to know. She's very loved by all of us."

"I can see that." He wrapped his arms more firmly around Judith, the knots in his belly tightening.

There was no way he wanted to have a talk with her about Jean-Claude La Roux. It would be so difficult to explain that he'd not come to Sea Haven with the sole reason of warning his brother. The sin of omission was beginning to loom large and there was nothing left to him but the truth. He dropped his head over hers, his mind racing. He'd been cornered a million times in his career, life and death, kill or be killed. It was his way of life. But this . . . this was entirely different.

Losing Judith was unacceptable to him and he had a feeling this was one of those very important things about relationships he was only beginning to understand. She trusted him. She believed in him and she'd given him every chance for disclosure.

We'll be fine, moi padshii angel. I clipped your wings and put them in my kaleidoscope. I'm not going anywhere because you're mine. He knew his murmur of reassurance was more for himself than for her.

Judith lifted her head and blinked up at him. His heart nearly shattered at that love in her eyes. The absolute trust. *I believe you, Thomas. Jean-Claude isn't going to take any more of my life from me.*

He nearly groaned in despair. He wanted that kind of trust, but now he knew he had to confess. How understanding would he be if the roles were reversed? He had a suspicious nature, never trusting anyone. How many times had it crossed his mind that she was involved in the theft of the microchip and that it had driven La Roux's obsession with her? He'd even considered briefly that her guilt and shame for her brother's death stemmed from the fact that she'd taken the microchip and La Roux had sent his men after her to get it back.

Stefan waited until Judith was safely buckled into the passenger seat and he was behind the wheel of her car. She'd given him a little frown when he'd handed her inside, putting the tote bag with his weapons within easy reach, but she hadn't protested when he'd taken the driver's side.

She pressed her lips together as they drove out of Sea Haven. The fog was still heavy and darkness was creeping in as well. "Thomas, if you want out, I'll understand. My shady life seems to be catching up with me."

He reached for her hand, tucked it close to his heart and shook his head. "Don't be silly, Judith. I have no intentions of going anywhere."

"He's got to be out of prison. Or he sent someone to do his dirty work, but this *feels* like him. That 'Who is he, Judith?' is so like him. He always looked at me as if I was the beginning and end of the world for him." She looked down at her hands and sighed. "Which is probably why I fell so hard for him. There's such a lure in that you know . . ." She trailed off, her breath catching in her throat, her gaze jumping to his face.

He was so connected to her in his mind, he could follow her sudden reasoning and he nearly groaned aloud. He needed her like that, so close he could feel her breathe, his world, the entire world was this woman beside him. Without her, there was no reality. Stefan Prakenskii would remain forever a shadow, slide in and out of danger, taking lives like death itself and eventually he would cross a line he could never go back from.

"Like me. Like me, Judith. Just say it." A touch of anger edged his voice because her sudden insight wasn't going to make his confession any easier. If she could reason that out, she would know a man like him studied a mark and figured out how best to insert himself into his or her life to get what he wanted.

Judith nodded slowly. "You do make me feel that way, Thomas."

"Because I feel as if you are my world. There will never be anyone else for me, Judith. I love you. I don't know how it happened. Hell, I didn't even know it could happen." He turned down the road leading to the farm. "There's more to this Jean-Claude mess than you know. I came here as Thomas Vincent for a reason." He glanced at her, judging her reaction.

She frowned at him, her long lashes fanning her cheek. "I'm well aware of that."

He waited while the gates opened automatically and drove on through, pausing just long enough to assure himself the gates had closed properly behind him. In his life, there had been so many times when he felt on the brink of a precipice, but nothing like this. His heart was actually pounding, and he knew he could feel sweat beading on his forehead.

He parked the car and helped her out, carrying the tote bag for her up the stairs into her house. "You know, Judith, about my coming here to warn my brother, but I was working for my government at the time. I had another assignment."

Judith turned slowly to face him, there in the middle of her living room, surrounded by the serene beauty he'd come to associate with Judith. Very carefully she set the canvases down on the low-slung, black-lacquered table. "I don't understand. You said you came to Sea Haven to warn Levi that Petr Ivanov was still hunting him."

He ran a hand through his hair, rubbed the bridge of his nose and nodded. "And that was the truth, but not the entire truth." He set the alarm on the house, more to give himself breathing space than anything else.

"Just say it, Thomas."

"A little over five years ago, a very important man working on a new defense system for our government was attacked. His wife had been compromised and she helped by providing extremely sensitive information to the man who was behind the theft. One of my brothers, Gavriil, was one of his bodyguards. Gavriil is about eighteen months older than me and we were closer than a lot of young kids when our parents were massacred. He was severely injured. In our business, that's a death warrant. We don't get nice retirement checks. Men like Gavriil and me live without real identities. Sorbacov, the man who came up with the idea of taking the children of his country and training them . . ."

"Using brutal force to turn them into killers and spies," Judith corrected.

He nodded. "He has too much to lose if any one of us starts talking. We're ghosts and he can't afford for any of us to surface. The moment I knew Gavriil's wounds were serious, I made my way to him and helped him escape the hospital. I took him to a doctor I knew was safe. He disappeared after that, although we have a way to get in touch with one another to indicate we're alive and well."

He watched her face closely, knowing he was starting the story with his injured brother because it would appeal to her compassionate nature. He couldn't stop being who he was. His training had given him the ability to read every expression, to adjust quickly if he was losing a battle. So far, she was looking at him with soft eyes, not really understanding where he was going with it all, but willing to understand.

"The information stolen was on a microchip, a tiny little speck really. It had been sewn into a coat and the thieves had known exactly where to find it. They cut it out of the coat and disappeared. That chip is extremely important and I was sent to track it down."

He studied Judith's face. She'd gone very still and there was a very small frown forming on her face, as if she was puzzling something out in her mind.

"I found the wife and her lover and they led me straight to Jean-Claude La Roux."

Her head went up, her gaze jumping to his. The breath left her lungs in a rush, as if he'd sucker-punched her—and he probably had. He took a step toward her. Judith backed away, shaking her head, raising one hand palm out to ward him off.

"I don't understand."

"Before I could get to him, La Roux was brought up on charges in France and was sent to prison. The chip was never offered on the black market and we knew he hadn't had time to sell it. We tried diplomatic means to get him transferred to Russia, but France refused to cooperate. In the end, as a last resort, I was sent to the prison to assess the situation. We needed to know if he still had the chip and how were we going to get it back."

Judith pressed a hand to her stomach. "You didn't come here to retire as Thomas Vincent. You came here because you think Jean-Claude gave me the chip." Her dark eyes went stormy. "Did you think I let him murder my brother rather than give it back to him?"

"Judith." He took another step toward her, but she backed away again, this time putting the counter between them. "That's not true. I shared his cell. The walls were covered in photographs of you. I believe he's obsessed with you, but wasn't certain why. I spent two months in that cell with nothing to do but look at those pictures of you."

"Oh, God. You want me to believe you fell madly in love with me because of some pictures in a prison cell? Do you really think I'm that stupid?" She looked around her as if desperate for a way to escape. "What do you want, Thomas? Or is it Stefan I'm talking to now? Just tell me, and then go."

"I don't know when I fell in love with you, Judith. I wish I could tell you, but I realized that first day I met you, when you came toward me that my life was going to change."

She shook her head, rejecting his admission. "Tell me about you and Jean-Claude and why you're here. The *real* reason."

"I knew, after meeting him, the only way to get the information we needed was to get him out of prison and take him to a place where we could interrogate him ourselves. That was the plan, and then Sorbacov stepped in. He ordered other agents to aid La Roux's escape and sent me here. I knew it was a setup. I'm too valuable to babysit an ex-girlfriend on the off chance that La Roux would somehow manage to escape our agents. He had to be planning to use me as bait to bring Lev out into the open." It was a measure of his distress that he called his brother by his given name.

"So you were really sent here to babysit me? And your government helped Jean-Claude escape? Wow, you found the perfect way to keep an eye on me. All those times you admitted you'd been trained in the art of seduction, you weren't kidding, were you? And I was so easy. All you had to do was study my personality and I was easy pickings. You're damned good at your job, Stefan."

"You're making it sound far worse than it was. I had no intention of babysitting you—or seducing you. I'm telling you, Judith, I'm in love with you. The rest of it wasn't supposed to happen. La Roux had his men waiting. They killed the agents and he's in the wind now."

"How handy that you're right here, in the exact place that he's bound to come."

"Judith," Stefan began.

She shook her head and gathered up her paintings. "I don't want to hear any more. I'm going to work. You can leave."

"You know I'm not going to leave. We'll work this out."

She looked him up and down, a long, slow perusal of distaste. "There isn't enough time in the world to work this out." Abruptly she turned her back on him and went downstairs.

20

JUDITH refused to cry in front of Stefan. She just wouldn't let him destroy her hard won poise. How could she have let him into her life—into her heart—so fast? She was so *stupid*. Tears blurred her vision as she hurried down the stairs carrying the paintings with her. It was growing dark and she flicked on the lights to better illuminate the canvases to see how much actual damage there was to the artwork while she stretched them. Unlike the happy chaos of her kaleidoscope studio, this room was where she earned money as a conservator of old paintings and she kept it immaculate.

Closing the door firmly she contemplated whether to bother locking it. A man like Stefan Prakenskii could get through a security system, he certainly would have no problem getting through a locked door. She stood there, in the middle of the room, wanting to throw a childish tantrum, to hurl the canvases around the room and scream out her anguish.

Instead, she stayed in perfect control, tears running down her face, as she placed each of the paintings on the table. She breathed in and out, pushing pain away. For a moment she covered her face with her hands. She was so shaken, all the way to the very foundation of her existence. Her hard-won faith in herself, built inch by inch, piece by piece over the last five years, was gone—shattered. She pushed back an anguished cry.

She *wouldn't* go back to darkness. Stefan might have been a fraud, but he had shown her the way out of the dark. She could do this—survive without him. There were millions of women who fell in love with the wrong men and they lived happy, productive lives. She just had to make up her mind that she would be one of them. Her track record was perhaps going to go down as one of the worst in history, but she wasn't going to let a Russian agent destroy her.

The temptation to call her sisters and cry on their shoulders was huge, but she resisted. She didn't want to face Rikki right now, and Rikki would be hurt if she wasn't included in the circle of support. But damn it all, Levi had betrayed her. He had to have known what his brother was really up to. They'd counted on her compassion, her loyalty, so ingrained in her that she would never consider betraying either of them to anyone. They'd played her so perfectly—and did that mean Levi was playing Rikki?

She brushed a hand over her face. She could barely breathe in her beloved studio. She turned on the music system to flood the silence with soft music, needing distraction. She just had to work and she had plenty of it, enough to keep her up half the night. And if that wasn't enough, she could always invent more—after all, she was a pro at finding things to do in the middle of the night.

She glanced out the double French doors into the night. There were no stars tonight, only a heavy, fog, turning her gardens to vague wet shadows. She wandered across the room, drawn by the misty gray veil. It was one of the things she loved most about living on the coast. When she saw the fog creep in over the surrounding forest, the atmosphere always reminded her of a gothic novel.

"Get to work," she admonished aloud and shut off the alarm so she could open her French doors.

Technically, she didn't need the fresh air—she wasn't painting—but her lungs felt tight and the lump in her throat refused to dissolve. She wouldn't acknowledge that she wanted to scream and throw things, to weep until there were no tears left in the world. She loved him. *Loved* him with everything she was. How could she have been so deceived?

She stood in the doorway, staring into her garden, the mist on her face, in her eyes, dripping silver tears into her heart until she was so weighed down with sorrow she had to turn back to her work or succumb to the numbing cold— and she *wouldn't* go back there. Not ever again. Not for a man.

She'd been so stupid falling for a man like Jean-Claude. All the signs were there, she just had been too naive to read them. So many people deferred to him, stepped out of his way, or froze when he came into a room. She'd thought him so commanding of respect, she hadn't paused to consider it had been fear everyone felt. She found him attractive and engaging, although very intimidating with his supreme confidence, so of course everyone around her had to have felt the same.

Resolutely she squared her shoulders and walked back inside to look over the artwork. Most of the paintings were seascapes. It was impossible for an artist to live in Sea Haven and not want to capture the beauty of the ocean in her most tempestuous moods. There were a few pictures of old buildings and one of the bluffs with a long broken fence, worn with age and weather, which was a personal favorite.

She looked at the paintings with a prejudiced eye. The wild sea always frustrated her a little bit. She never felt she actually captured the mood of it in the way she wanted. Grays and blues and swirling purples never quite gave the full effect of an angry sea, moody and temperamental. There was one with the mist veiling the trees so that the forest looked like a great army, shrouded in mystery, hidden in the vague, shadowy interior.

Pressing her lips together tightly, she forced herself to pull out the first of the stretcher bars, to stretch the canvas, hoping the paint itself wasn't already damaged on the two acrylics. She focused completely on the work, taking care to keep all four corners perfect as she wrapped the canvas around the bar. Using the stainless steel staples was much more difficult when there was paint on the canvas. One acrylic was definitely damaged and she would have to repair it, if she was going to save it. Had it been another artist's work, she wouldn't have hesitated, but there in the privacy of her studio, she could acknowledge she would always associate these paintings with Stefan's betrayal.

He'd broken her heart as no one else could ever do. He'd told her half-truths over and over while she'd bared her soul to him. Damn him for that. And damn her for being so stupid to fall into his arms because he looked at her with his soul in his eyes. She tossed the canvas down and shoved back the chair, too upset and restless to contain the bitter, sorrowful emotions welling up and swirling around like a dark whirlpool.

The cool night air whispered to her and she stepped outside onto the back patio where her flowers and shrubs could surround her with their bright colors and soothing beauty. Her vision blurred, tears swimming in her eyes, brimming over and trickling down her cheeks. She pressed the heel of her hand to her burning eyes.

A hard hand clamped tight over her mouth as a large body shoved hers against the wall. The scent of expensive male cologne washed over her, throwing her back into another time. Her heart slammed hard in her chest, fear a slick taste in her mouth.

Jean-Claude kept her against the wall with one hand, while he thrust his finger under her nose. "You ripped out my heart," he accused in a low hiss, his dark eyes boring into hers. Both hands gripped her shirtfront and dragged her to him, his mouth descending hard on hers. His mouth mashed against hers hard, a display of ownership. His tongue forcing its way into her mouth was a violation.

She tasted murder. Blood. Her brother's terror and her own hate. Bile rose and when he broke away from her, she coughed it down, rubbing at her stinging lips with the back of her hand, her gaze never leaving his. She pressed herself against the side of her house, facing the man who had ordered the torture and murder of her brother.

"Did you think I could just forget you, Judith?" Jean-Claude demanded. He took a long, slow look around. "I know you haven't forgotten me. I waited all these years and you never came. You never wrote to me. Why, *ma belle,* did you desert me when I needed you most?"

"How can you ask me that?" She couldn't help the sudden flash of temper. There was no way to suppress the surge of anger. "You had my brother tortured. Murdered. Did you think I would love you for that?"

He shook his head, those dark eyes still boring into hers. "That was his decision alone. My men had orders to let him go the moment he told them where you were. That was all he had to do to gain his freedom and his life. Such a small thing I asked and he refused. I will not have you put his death on me. That was entirely his choice."

She opened her mouth, but nothing came out. She could see he had no understanding of why she didn't see his point of view. He considered himself reasonable. Judith shook her head. "You're not even denying that you had your men torture him."

He pointed his finger at her again. "You ran from me. No note, no explanation. You just took off. What did you expect, *mon amour*, that I would just take something like that lying down?" He stepped closer to her, his breath hot in her face. "You are mine. *Mine.* You don't end us. Not ever. That's not allowed, Judith. I won't have it."

"You were in that room, Jean-Claude. I saw you telling your men to hurt that poor man. He was pleading for mercy . . ."

"He *stole* from me. You shouldn't have seen that. That was not for your eyes. And you should have come to me and told me . . ."

"I was afraid."

"Of me? How could you be afraid of me?" He looked genuinely shocked. "I showed you nothing but love. I was careful with you, always careful. You were so young and I understood that." He caught her arm and urged her back inside. "I have to remind myself that an innocent like you would have been overwhelmed by what you saw. But you should have come to me."

"It isn't okay to torture and murder someone because they cross you, Jean-Claude."

His face darkened with impatience. "You're coming with me, and this time, *mon amour*, you will do as you're told. I'll have you watched every moment of the day until you realize where your place is."

Judith stumbled as he shoved her into the studio. She caught herself on a table's edge, turning slowly to face him.

"You're so predictable," Jean-Claude said, looking around her studio. "My industrious little Judith, always doing the responsible thing. I knew you'd want to protect those paintings and you'd rush to your little studio to put them all right again." He shoved one of the canvases. "And of course you did. You never paint without opening the doors and letting in the fresh air. All I had to do was wait. See how well I know you?"

She winced at the triumph in his voice. She'd certainly done exactly as he predicted. Temper fluttered in her stomach and she pressed a hand there as if somehow that would ward off the flaring rage beginning to bubble like a hot pool of magma. "What did you come here for, Jean-Claude?"

"What did I come here for?" he repeated, biting out each

word through clenched teeth, his smoldering anger beginning to catch fire.

Judith knew she was the one fanning the flames. Her own
anger was rising and feeding right into his, but she didn't
care. She was damned tired of being pushed around emotionally because she had to protect everyone.

"That's what I asked you," she snapped back.

"I came for you. You're *mine*. Did you think prison was
going to keep us apart? Did you think it was safe for you to
find someone else?"

She shoved her hair out of her face, glaring at him. "Your
little spy was a bit premature with his report to you. And it's
not your business if I see anyone. You *killed* my brother and
I'll never forgive you for that. Get out of my house."

He stepped forward, catching her upper arms to give her
a little shake. All the strength she'd mistaken for suave confidence was really something evil lurking beneath the surface. He was a man who felt little emotion. Because her
feelings were so strong, hers spilled over to those around
her—including him. He wanted those feelings back and felt
she was withholding his emotions from him, by not allowing herself to love him. Judith understood now. Jean-Claude
was cold and lacked the ability to connect with others.

As a young woman with no experience, she had admired
and loved the man she thought he was—a fantasy she'd conjured up in her head. He had basked in that love and admiration, feeling her projection so strongly, but once she was
away from him, he'd gone back to that cold, emotionless
man who had no moral compass whatsoever.

"I'm not going to argue with you, Judith, not when
you're being unreasonable. Where's our painting?"

The question caught her off guard. That was so like
Jean-Claude. She had never realized all the times he'd
abruptly ended a conversation and made her feel young and
stupid, just how often he manipulated her to get his way.

"Painting?"

"You took our painting. The one of our meeting. I loved that painting and so did you. It was the only thing you took. Even your clothes were left behind."

For a moment that horrible realization came back, that moment of truth. She was in love with a killer. She had taken the painting because she was young and silly and so in love with such a wealthy, sophisticated Frenchman. The tragic end to her love affair would always be remembered when she looked at the painting—and then he'd had her brother murdered. That painting had become her nemesis. She poured her hatred and anger and sorrow onto that canvas over the last five years.

"I painted over it. I couldn't stand to look at it."

"You heartless bitch. That painting meant something to me." He slapped her hard, sending her sprawling on the floor.

The attack was so fast and so unexpected Judith almost didn't understand what happened, and then her cheek seemed to explode, a blossoming pain that wrenched her teeth and eye, and she realized he'd hit her. Fury burst through her, shaking her to her very core. She kicked at him as he bent over her. Her foot connected with his shin and he spat out curses. Judith rolled, trying to get under the protection of the table, but he swung his booted foot at her, slamming into her ribs and driving the breath from her body. Before she could recover, he gripped the back of her hair in his hands and yanked her up.

"Stop it, Judith," he hissed. "Do you understand me? You stop or I'll beat you senseless, and then tear this house apart until I find that painting. Regardless, conscious or unconscious, I'm taking you with me anyway. You can choose."

She nodded, fighting for air. Judith forced her body under control. "Tell me what's so important about that painting, Jean-Claude."

"I put something there and I need it back. Something very important. Where the hell is the painting?"

Judith closed her eyes briefly. She knew exactly what he was talking about. Even when Stefan had mentioned a microchip, it hadn't clicked, but now she knew. Her brother had been the one to stretch that canvas for her. He'd been the first person to ever show her how and she'd taken the canvas with her when she went to Paris intending to give him her very first painting as a tribute.

She'd met Jean-Claude, had fallen hard for the handsome Frenchman and had painted their portraits, one of the few she'd ever done. She'd put all a young girl's love of the fantasy handsome prince, into that painting. Jean-Claude had hung it on the wall of his bedroom. She'd grabbed the painting and at the first opportunity, Paul had helped her ship what little she had home so they could make their way across Europe, hoping to stay under Jean-Claude's radar until they could get to Greece where a friend of Paul's was waiting to take them back to the United States on his ship.

"I told you, I painted over it, but it's in my other studio. You'll have to let me get it. Going in there is dangerous."

She honestly didn't know how dangerous, but Jean-Claude had already shown he was very susceptible to her emotions and anything violent would be extremely strong. The buildup of five years of pent-up rage lay in that room, just waiting to find a way out.

"I'm not letting you out of my sight," Jean-Claude declared, grabbing a handful of hair and yanking her toward the door. "Do you think I'm stupid?"

She kept her feet under her somehow, as he dragged her down the hall.

"Where is it?" he demanded, turning around and around, looking at the various doors.

"It's that one. It's locked." Should she lie and say the key was upstairs? Stefan might not have left. Did she want Stefan brought into this?

Her heart fluttered and then went still as realization dawned. Stefan was the perfect killing machine. He'd been raised to be a killer. Jean-Claude was a criminal and cold-blooded, but if she called Stefan back, she had no doubt that Stefan could do *exactly* the things she'd thought about—and had planned for the last five long years. He could be the instrument she used to destroy Jean-Claude. He was more than capable of killing the Frenchman.

Her right hand crept toward her left hand, to that mark itching in the center of her left palm. Elation swept through her. She could finally punish Jean-Claude, exact revenge. See him tortured and killed, just as he'd done to Paul. All she had to do was call Stefan back and she knew she could call him. He would come for the microchip and she knew where the microchip was. Jean-Claude wouldn't find it, but she could use it to get Stefan to do what she wanted.

She took a deep breath, her thumb pausing over the center of her palm. She just needed to press down hard and call to him telepathically. If he had already left and was too far away to hear her, he might still feel her.

"Damn it, Judith," Jean-Claude thrust the bedroom door open. "I'm getting impatient." He yanked at her to drag her farther down the hall. "Where the hell is the painting?"

She was filled with so much hatred for this man she hadn't been able to see straight. She was tired of living that way, with so much anger and rage. She'd been happy with Stefan—genuinely happy—and she had pushed the memories of Jean-Claude's sickness away from her, refusing to allow it to taint her life. She'd be damned if she allowed it to taint her love for Stefan. And she did love Stefan whether he returned the emotion or not. Her feelings for him were very real and she would *not* give in to the temptation of using him for revenge.

Instead of pressing down on that mark already faded until it was just below her skin, she brushed her fingertip lovingly, even protectively over it.

"That painting is in the studio right there," she said quietly. "I keep it locked. The key's on a chain around my neck." She pulled out the thin chain so he could see she was telling the truth.

Jean-Claude let go of her hair and took the key from her with a quick smile. "I knew you'd come to your senses, *ma belle*."

He bent his head to kiss her. She turned her face away and his kiss landed on her sore cheek. He laughed and patted the blossoming bruise before turning to insert the key into the lock.

STEFAN stood in the middle of the living room almost frozen. Judith had completely, utterly shut off, closing him out so effectively he couldn't reach her. For one moment there had been a flare of anguish and pain. The emotions had burst through him like a rocket, settling into a jagged knife through his heart and then . . . nothing. The feeling of dread had been building for some time, settling around him like a heavy cloak. He'd felt doom in the air the moment he'd gotten out of the car.

He felt as if he was drowning. She believed everything he'd said to her, everything he'd done with her—including making love to her—had been nothing but a pack of lies. He'd been waiting for her, holding his breath for her, all of his life. He just hadn't known it until he found her and now, just like that, he'd lost her. He was alone again. In the dark and shadows with pieces of his heart scattered all around him. He had no idea how to put it all back together. Relationships were something he had no clue about, no experience to fall back on.

She'd looked so shattered. So utterly devastated. He knew what she thought of him. He'd been playing games, seducing her to get close to her in order to find the microchip. His life suddenly seemed so wrong, everything he'd done to get his work accomplished. She lived such a different life. She'd gotten touched by evil, brushed shoulders with it, but she hadn't immersed herself in it, she wasn't covered in it.

He swore in Russian and stood there, feeling helpless, something a man like him couldn't stand. He was a man of action. What was worse, waiting it out, let her have a little space to realize he'd stood there with his heart in his hand telling her the stark ugly truth of his life, admitting he loved her, or going to her and demanding she see the truth.

His brother's advice to tell the truth quite frankly sucked. Evidently drugging her wasn't as bad as omitting certain facts. She'd forgiven him that mistake, but not this one. Not when he was standing there trying to do the right thing. He was at a loss, a state he'd never thought he'd ever find himself in.

He closed his eyes. He wanted to marry her. To have her as his wife, and not as Thomas Vincent. They could live with that name, but he wanted to know she was his, a part of him. How could he show her he meant every word he said to her? Every touch? Every caress? He couldn't imagine going through the rest of his life without her. Without her laughter and her light. Without her kisses or the flash of her dark eyes.

He knew one thing. He wasn't going to give up. He loved Judith Henderson with every fiber of his being. He might make a million mistakes, but the bottom line was he loved her and he knew he could make her happy. With Jean-Claude in the vicinity, Judith was in danger. The man was a ruthless criminal. So if he couldn't fix his relationship with Judith, then he needed to do what he did best. His job. That was the one way he could keep her safe. He might not be good with women, but he was damned good at his job.

The microchip had to come into play somewhere. Stefan had carefully followed the trail the killers had left and the chip had ended up in Jean-Claude's greedy hands. He'd been arrested before Stefan could get to him and retrieve the chip. There was no way he had time to hand the stolen microchip off and he clearly hadn't done so from his prison cell. Stefan would have heard it was for sale if that had been the case. It had to here. A painting? Was that the reason the art gallery had been vandalized?

Was it a message to Judith? No, Judith would have told him had she known about the microchip. She'd been so hurt and angry, she would have flung the information in his face. So she didn't know. Could La Roux have hidden the microchip in a particular painting? Over the last five years, Judith's paintings had been sold in galleries all over the world. She'd earned a certain reputation and particularly in Japan, her name was growing.

La Roux could easily have slipped the microchip in between the stretcher bar and canvas of a painting. But why would Judith take a painting with her when she left him if she hadn't known about the microchip? And if she had known, wouldn't it have been easier to just take the chip? No, she hadn't known about the chip. So if it was behind a canvas, what painting had it been and why had La Roux been so certain she'd keep it?

A ribbon of unease slipped into his mind and he glanced at the security system. The green light was off. Damn it all. The woman really hated that system. He should have known if she went down to her studio she'd open the doors—but she wasn't painting. She was stretching the canvases over the bars and she sure as hell could keep the door closed. He actually took a couple of steps toward the hall leading to the stairs but stopped himself.

This was Judith's house and her pain. She had the right to deal with it in any way she saw fit. Uneasiness was growing in leaps and bounds, tying his belly into knots but she had him so damned messed up he couldn't think straight. Was his radar going off because Judith was making up her mind to reject him for good? Or was Jean-Claude prowling around?

They needed dogs. That was all there was to it. He went to the door and stepped outside, intending to circle the house, just do a slow search to assure himself the Frenchman hadn't found his way to her home. He looked up at the night sky. The stars and moon were completely obliterated by the gray veil drawn so thick around them. The trees were vague outlines and all sound was muffled by the dense mist.

He was reluctant to leave, even for a moment. His left palm itched. Pulsed. He felt love brush across it—a soft caress he couldn't mistake.

JEAN-CLAUDE turned the key in the lock and pulled the door open. Judith held her breath as savage power rushed out, pulsing through the hallway in search of a target. The energy was so strong when it hit the Frenchman, he felt the impact like a physical blow, although she could tell by the look on his face that he had no idea what happened. He pressed his hand to his heart and stepped back, waving her inside.

"This room is dangerous, Jean-Claude," she warned again, knowing he wouldn't listen, but feeling as though she needed to at least give him that much.

He pushed her inside and stepped in after her. The inside of the studio was nearly pitch black, making it impossible to see anything. The light in the hallway was too dim to illuminate the interior of the room.

"Where's the light switch?" he demanded, turning toward Judith.

Already she could feel the ominous pulsing of power surrounding them. She cleared her throat. "I don't use light in here. Just candles."

"Well light them. Open the curtains," he snapped impatiently.

The door swung closed of its own accord, a hard, final sound that boomed like the thud of drums at a funeral. The room was instantly plunged into absolute darkness.

Judith felt the swirling emotions gathering strength and

she hastily stepped forward, intending to light the candle closest to her. It was black, with a red center, and she knew the approximate position. The room groaned and creaked, and soft footsteps padded across the floor toward them.

Jean-Claude jerked her in front of him, fumbling for his gun. "What the hell? Judith, light the damn candle."

Before she could do so, another surge of power ricocheted off the walls. Candles sprang to purple life all over the room, macabre pinpoints of light there in the sea of darkness. Smoke rose, blossoming out to slowly spread across the ceiling. The dancing light followed, slowly illuminating the twisted, gnarled branches and the weeping sorrowful splashes of purple on the walls and overhead. Crystalline tears dripped from the branches and ran down the walls.

The walls creaked and something dark moved in the shadows. A sound much like a branch cracking had both of them spinning toward the far side of the room where she'd painted a large dark trunk of a tree, twisted and misshapen, a grotesque apparition of a living, breathing tree. Even while they watched, the trunk seemed to split open and weep thick, black venom.

"What the hell is this?" Jean-Claude demanded.

"I told you this room is dangerous," Judith answered. Her heart accelerated and she tasted real fear in her mouth.

She had no idea how dangerous the studio really was until that moment. Jean-Claude's presence had awakened the darkest of spirit weave. Here, where her every ugly thought, every dark emotion, had been about him. Revenge. Rage. Sorrow. Everything she had ever considered doing to him in the name of revenge had been conceived in this room. Spirit had bound those dark emotions together and now, Jean-Claude was present, a living key to unlock that very lethal, dark power.

He showed her the gun. "Don't think I won't use this if this is some kind of trick. Where's the painting?"

She pointed to the middle of the room where she'd draped a cloth over the easel. "Under there." There was little point in reiterating her warning. He wasn't about to listen.

Judith looked around her warily. Dark bloodred wax bubbled from the centers of the candles and cascaded down in streams. She took a breath and the room pulsed, the walls breathing in and out.

Jean-Claude's fingers closed over her upper arm in a vise-like grip, taking her with him to the center of the room. He reached out to grab the cloth. Vines stirred overhead like great snakes lifting their heads to watch. The air in the room seemed denser, harder to breathe. The Frenchman jerked the cloth from the painting and dropped it onto the floor. His hand slid across one of the jagged pieces of glass embedded in the canvas and came away bloody.

He swore and glared at her, lifting the side of his hand to his mouth. Drops of blood splashed onto the painting, and hit the floor. Beneath their feet shadows moved, stretching across the dark tiles reaching toward the liquid, greedily absorbing the fluid. Shapeless silhouettes emerged from the twisted trunks, amid creaks and groans. Power pulsed like a heartbeat.

Judith caught Jean-Claude's arm. "We have to go. Let's go now."

"Not without the microchip. It's behind the canvas." Shaking her off, he reached for the painting before she could stop him.

He dragged the canvas from the easel, turning the shifting symbols and her brother's name away from him, but she caught a glimpse of those dark shadows rising like wraiths from the layered painting of jagged, painful emotions. The rocking branches overhead picked up the pulsing drumbeat as if a heart had come to life, born there in those swirling darker spirits.

Judith pressed her fingers into her palm, her own heart following that ominous ghastly rhythm. Silhouettes began to take shape, rearing back as the candles leapt toward the center of the room—toward Jean-Claude. The man with no emotions was empty, and energy sought to fill that vacuum. She could see his skin change subtly under the play of purple light, turning his perfect color to a mottled ash.

She tried to project happiness, but fear radiated through the room and the apparitions expanded, coming out of the running black venomous sap and growing as her fear swelled. He didn't notice the shadows running up his arms, his blackened fingers, or the subtle changes in his skin. Every time he turned the painting, trying to rip it from the stretcher bar, the jagged pieces of glass embedded in his skin. Blood fed the phantoms so that they took on monstrous shapes. She grabbed at the canvas, trying to get it out of his hands.

Jean-Claude growled, ripping the painting from her, nearly tossing her to the floor, cursing as he stumbled himself. Blood dripped steadily.

"It isn't there," Judith whispered. "Jean-Claude, please let's go. It isn't there. We have to go, right now."

Jean-Claude tossed the painting against the wall. The crash reverberated through the room, his anger growing in direct proportion to the building violence of swirling emotions. The energy spun madly, like a terrible twister forming from the ceiling to the floor, shooting through the room seeking a target—seeking Jean-Claude.

He backhanded her, sent her flying, her body sprawling across the shadowed floor. Droplets of blood showered down around her. She tried to crawl toward the door, hoping he'd follow, hoping to lead him out. How could he be so oblivious? How could he not feel the swelling demons reaching for him as the purple lights of the candles stretched toward him? Everything in the room, above and below, the cracking branches, the venomous tree trunks, the crystalline tears, all of it extended toward him with greedy delight.

He kicked at her several times, following her just as she

wanted. His face, in the purple light, revealed a vicious, building anger slowly boiling until rage erupted and he caught her legs just as she reached the door, dragging her back to the center of the room.

"Where is it?" he hissed, his lips drawing back in an ugly snarl. His teeth looked sharper, his lips thinner. The outer shell of the man, always handsome, seemed to be dissolving right before her eyes, and the inner man, dark and ugly emerged, as if those dark spirits were giving birth. "You treacherous bitch. You sold it!"

She shook her head. "I didn't. I found it and Paul had worked for a computer company. I thought he'd put it there when he stretched the canvas for me. I had no idea there was anything on it. I thought it was his good luck symbol for me. I put it in a cell for my kaleidoscope."

His head whipped around, a hound on a dark scent. He stepped in the middle of the canvas, right on Paul's name, those weeping Japanese letters, the only beautiful thing on the work of hatred and destruction. Glass crunched beneath his boot and the crimson letters layered over with blackened soot as if the burning candles had spread a filmy layer on the floor and it had collected on the sole of his boot.

Jean-Claude waded through the spinning energy as if he didn't see it. The room hissed in triumph as he stepped up to the large kaleidoscope and jerked off the cover.

Judith used her heels to try to push herself to the wall, making herself as small as possible. "Don't," she whispered.

"How does this work?" he snapped, frustrated when the cell remained dark. He looked around the room, and then glared back at her, raising his gun menacingly.

Judith shook her head but pointed to the portable ultra-violet light sitting on the table just within his reach. He snatched up the light, shoved it into the space built into the cylinder and switched on the light. At once images burst toward him, dark and hungry and filled with powerful energy. He saw himself there, as he was inside, and he couldn't look away, held by the whirling emotions, so tightly woven, so alive and strong, they gave birth to the true image, matching the outside shell to the inside substance.

Judith covered her face as the walls streamed black venom and overhead the weeping tears dripped blood. The door splintered. She hadn't realized the shadows had locked it. Stefan shouted her name and his shoulder slammed into the door a second time. Then his boot. The door cracked and he reached inside and thrust it open, rushing into the room, taking in everything.

He bent over her, looking like the very devil—or an avenging angel. He scooped her up and she closed her arms around his neck, burying her face in his neck. "I've got you, Judith," he murmured, raining kisses over her face as he raced out of the room. "*Ya tebyA lyublyU.* In case you didn't understand me, I love you. I love you with all my heart."

"I can't believe you came for me."

"Always, Judith. I wasn't lying when I told you that you're everything to me. I meant every word." He turned his head to look into the dark room with the strange flickering purple lights, a little diminished now. "I have to get him out of there."

She clutched his arm. "Don't go back in there, Stefan. It's too dangerous."

"We can't leave him in there. I'll bring him out. My defenses are strong. I'll get him, angel, and nothing will prevent me coming back to you."

Judith reluctantly allowed him to step away from her. She slid down the wall, pressing trembling fingers to her mouth. She believed him. There was nothing evil inside of Stefan for those dark emotions to devour. His life had been shaped by the circumstances of his childhood, but he had not been born, nor had he developed, twisted.

He came running out of the room, carrying Jean-Claude over his shoulder. He deposited him gently on the floor beside Judith, removing his gun with that sleight of hand so familiar to her. Jean-Claude's hair was streaked white, his eyes sunken and his skin wrinkled and mottled with dark spots. His eyes appeared vacant, staring straight ahead, pupils dilated in a kind of horror. Judith passed her hand in front of Jean-Claude's face. He didn't blink.

Stefan squeezed her hand and raced back into the studio to rip down the curtains and throw open the French doors.

"Don't! What if . . ."

He shook his head. "The emotions have nearly completely spun themselves out. I'm going to air out the room. There's nothing we can do for him right now. He'll need a doctor and I'm not certain that will do much good."

"The microchip is in the first cell I did for the kaleidoscope. Don't look in there, just grab that first cell and we can open it. I thought my brother had put it there. It's been floating in heavy mineral oil this entire time. I doubt you'll be able to get much off of it after five years in oil." She frowned. "But I suppose it might be possible, although not the best odds."

She knelt up beside Jean-Claude and wiped at the saliva dribbling down his chin.

"I don't have to get the information off it, just return it to Russia," Stefan said. He pocketed the cell after he'd opened up the room. "As long as no other country can steal the information, I don't care whether it's destroyed or not." He helped her all the way to her feet.

Judith sagged against him, rubbing her face over his steadily beating heart. "Thanks for coming back for me even when I was angry with you and told you to go."

He wrapped his arm around her and dropped a kiss on her upturned face. "Next time, angel, there's no breathing room for you when we have an argument. We're making a rule right now that you stay in my sight at all times until it's resolved."

Very gently he picked up Jean-Claude as if he weighed no more than a child. "We'll have to call an ambulance.

We'll have to say we found him wandering in the yard. He's unrecognizable so if you say you don't know who he is, it will make sense. They'll identify him through his fingerprints and take him to a hospital."

"Stefan." Judith held her breath until he looked down at her.

She drank him in, a tall Russian, with blue-green eyes and scars. He was so gentle with Jean-Claude it turned her heart over. Hers. She gave him a shaky smile. "I love you."

His smile reached his eyes. "I know that better than you do."

21

"YOU'RE certain you want to do this?" Judith whispered to Stefan. She tightened her fingers around his and glanced over her shoulders at her sisters and Lev. "You don't have to do this for me. The civil ceremony we had together is enough. I don't mind being Mrs. Thomas Vincent. I'll keep my name Henderson for my work, because my name's established, but seriously, you don't have to take such a chance just to prove something to me."

Stefan settled his arm around her shoulders. "I have always wanted to give you my name and this is a way for us to be married as Stefan Prakenskii and Judith Henderson. It is legal in the eyes of both our countries, although as I don't exist I suppose our civil marriage is more binding. This man is a friend of mine and he'll make certain this is done properly. Lev wants to marry Rikki the same way and we have arranged for it to be done."

San Francisco in the dead of night was not nearly as busy as during the day, and the cars had easily maneuvered up and down the steep hills. The small church was set deep in the middle of the Russian community. When they had parked their cars, it seemed as if they were the only ones there, but as they approached the steps, the door creaked open and a man in robes stood waiting.

"He is a holy man, a priest, and he's traveled a great distance to come here to America to marry us," Stefan whispered. "We did not use the local priest because if the paperwork is discovered, we don't want it traced back to him and this man is a ghost, such as Lev and me."

She understood what he was saying. The priest had been raised like his brothers, a political orphan ripped from his home and sent to those schools to shape them into killers. Like Lev and Stefan, he'd found a way to escape—different, but still, he'd found a way out.

"We're not putting him in any danger?" She needed reassurance after what happened to Jean-Claude. The man was still incoherent, locked in a mental hospital.

"He wouldn't have come if he'd thought he'd be discovered," Stefan said. "And if I thought he was followed, we wouldn't be here. I wouldn't risk you or my brother."

He glanced back at her sisters, following in a tight knot. Lev brought up the rear. Both men were armed to the teeth, and this time, he'd followed his brother's example, taking care to openly prepare for a small war should there be trouble, right in front of Judith. She had watched him in silence, sliding knives and guns into various hidden compartments in his clothing, but she hadn't protested.

"For your wedding present, *moi padshii angel*, I will get you a protection dog. Each one of your sisters should have one. Lev and I have agreed upon this."

"Don't think you're going to get all bossy on me," Judith warned. "It isn't happening. We have rules on the farm. *All* of us have a say."

He laughed softly. "Two Russians versus the six of you Americans? You are beautiful, my wife, but you don't know how hardheaded we can be."

"Is that some kind of warning? You should have told me that *before* the civil ceremony."

He laughed as they approached the priest. Only a single light burned low in the church and it didn't give off enough light to illuminate the priest's face. Stefan greeted him in Russian, but didn't introduce Judith to him. Rather, she noticed, he kept his body between hers and the holy man at all times. She wasn't certain who he was protecting—her or the priest.

Stefan stepped aside to allow the women to follow the priest inside while he and Lev took another slow look around before following.

Blythe walked beside Judith. "I've been here before," she whispered, her voice uneasy. "And I'm certain that's the same priest who performed the ceremony."

"What ceremony?" Judith asked.

Blythe frowned and shook her head, twisting her fingers together tightly, pressing her thumb deep into her palm. "Are you certain you want to do this, Judith? Rikki, I know is so deeply in love with Levi she would do just about anything he asked her to, but you still have time to get out of this. Now's the time to back out if you have any doubts."

"I have doubts about myself, Blythe," Judith admitted, "but not about him. I can be myself with him. He gets me. I don't have to hide and I need that in my life. He gives that to me, that freedom, and I feel loved by him. He wants children right away, and so do I. I've never thought I'd have that chance and he's giving me so much." She looked at her oldest sister. "I need to know that you can accept him in our lives. He swears it's the life he wants. He's buying the art gallery from Frank and Inez and he'll go with me to the art shows. But mostly, he wants us to live on the farm with all of you and lead a quiet life."

"Quiet?" Blythe said with a small smile. "With how many kids did you say he wanted?"

Judith laughed, the tension draining out of her. "I have no idea what he'll do after the first one is born. We'll see."

Stefan took her hand and leaned down to brush her mouth with his. "It's time, angel. The ceremony will be entirely in Russian."

"And you're certain it's legal?" Blythe asked with a small frown.

"Of course. This will make our marriage undeniably legal." He pulled Judith close. "She won't be able to officially use my Russian name, but she'll have it." He glanced at his brother. "As will Rikki. I have to say, my brother looks very happy."

"So do you," Blythe admitted, stepping back.

Judith listened to the priest as he spoke in low, firm tones, the language magical to her. Her entire wedding seemed surreal, her sisters close, Rikki and Lev standing beside her and Stefan, Stefan's hand tight in hers. She murmured the appropriate responses when the priest prodded her and listened to Rikki doing the same. At no time did she fully see the holy man's face.

Stefan slipped a ring on her finger and she turned into his arms so he could fasten his mouth to hers. Her heart leapt, happiness blossoming through her as she wound her arms around his neck and kissed her husband thoroughly.